C0-GIH-936

THE ONCE AND FUTURE SPY

Books by Robert Littell

Fiction

The Defection of A.J.Lewinter

Sweet Reason

The October Circle

Mother Russia

The Debriefing

The Amateur

The Sisters

The Once and Future Spy

An Agent in Place

The Visiting Professor

Walking Back the Cat

The Revolutionist

The Company

Legends

Vicious Circle

The Stalin Epigram

Young Philby

A Nasty Piece of Work

The Mayakovsky Tapes

Comrade Koba

A Plague on Both Your Houses

Bronshtein in the Bronx

Nonfiction

For the Future of Israel (with co-author Shimon Peres)

THE ONCE AND FUTURE SPY

ROBERT LITTELL

SOHO CRIME

This edition first published in 2025 by
Soho Press, Inc.
227 W 17th Street
New York, NY 10011
www.sohopress.com

Copyright © 1990 by Robert Littell
All rights reserved.

Library of Congress Cataloging-in-Publication Data

Names: Littell, Robert, 1935– author.
Title: The once and future spy / Robert Littell.
Description: New York, NY : Soho Crime, 2025.
Identifiers: LCCN 2024042044

ISBN 978-1-64129-714-1
eISBN 978-1-64129-715-8

Subjects: LCGFT: Spy fiction. | Thrillers (Fiction) | Novels.
Classification: LCC PS3562.I7827 O53 2025 | DDC 813/.54—dc23/
eng/20240906
LC record available at https://lccn.loc.gov/2024042044

Interior design by Janine Agro, Soho Press, Inc.

Printed in the United States of America

10 9 8 7 6 5 4 3 2 1

EU Responsible Person (for authorities only)
eucomply OÜ
Pärnu mnt 139b-14
11317 Tallinn, Estonia
hello@eucompliancepartner.com
www.eucompliancepartner.com

For Ed Victor

. . . not a single absolute truth
but a welter of contradictory
truths (truths embodied in
imaginary selves called
characters) . . .

—Milan Kundera

THE ONCE AND FUTURE SPY:
An Appreciation

It comes without warning, five chapters in, initially confusing and then enchanting the reader: *For starters, I'll do my man Nate.*

Never mind that we have no idea who *I* or *Nate* might be; we've just swerved from one distinct narrative to another, from 1990s DC to Revolutionary War–era New York, from a third-person omniscient view of multiple characters moving tightly through an enigmatic espionage plot to the witnessed horror of a military execution by hanging.

With that decision, Robert Littell forged a surprising dual timeline in *The Once and Future Spy*: half spy intrigue, half historical fiction. His usual readers—accustomed to Littell's previous Cold War espionage sagas, peopled with burnt-out cynics battling on behalf of causes they no longer believe in—would find their trust in his experiment justified. Thirty-five years after its 1990 publication, it is the novel's exploration of the human cost of idealism that most engages and absorbs the reader.

Littell is no stranger to historical fiction or the weight of tortured souls; his masterworks *The Company* and *Legends* demonstrate as much. But throughout his early novels, a focus on espionage plotting dominates. *The Once and Future Spy*, with its nod to Camelot's Arthur in the title, reaches for more. On the one hand, we're offered a rotating cast of security-community stalwarts: gray men working in the shadows to destabilize Iran, in ways that may or may not be treasonous. On the other, we're plunged into the mind and soul of twenty-one-year-old Nathan Hale, Yale graduate and colonial spy against the British, who struggles in the autumn of 1776 with what it means to risk his life for an idea.

Uniting the two is Silas Sibley, Hale's lateral descendant and present-day CIA intelligence analyst, charged with the tedious task of sifting communication intercepts for relevance. In another life, Sibley would have pursued an academic career and spent his days researching the Revolutionary War; in this one, he stumbles on a covert operation whose implications turn him from trusted colleague to enemy within. Questions of trust, betrayal, competing loyalties, and clashing ideologies teem through each narrative, and come to a shuddering conclusion in the book's final pages.

Why did Littell plunge himself and us into suspect terrain for his tenth book? For the simple reason, perhaps, that after two decades of trudging the known paths of Cold War fiction, they had nothing more to reveal to him. But I suspect the turmoil of 1989, the year in which Littell finished writing *The Once and Future Spy*, had much to do with it.

The fall of the Berlin Wall and the sudden collapse of the Soviet Eastern Bloc in November of that year were cataclysmic throughout Europe and the West; in a matter of days, those two events redefined security structures and power balances that had been fixed since the end of World War II. The Cold War's end also called into question the relevance of intelligence organizations, intelligence gathering and analysis, and espionage as a career—not to mention espionage writers. If the Soviet threat was gone and the West had won, government pundits argued, then there would be no need of spies or of funding their risky operations. Certainly no need for fictional sagas about them.

The naivete of this judgment still astounds. That same autumn, walking past the statue of Nathan Hale that stands at the agency entrance, I embarked on my Career Trainee year as an analyst with the CIA. Existential angst drifted through the corridors of Langley like a brown-coal fog. Some suggested that the Soviet Union's void would be filled with rogue threats, offering enough future chaos to guarantee espionage for eternity. Others urged the immediate shutdown of the Intelligence Community. Even the breakup of Yugoslavia and the Iraqi invasion of Kuwait failed to dissuade government cost cutters. Downsizing became a catch phrase in the Clinton administration, as seasoned security personnel closed up shop and fled the covert world.

It is unsurprising therefore that the later work of Cold War novelists, from John le Carré to Charles McCarry to Robert Littell, display innovation and greater depth. What *is* surprising is their continued relevance, even decades after publication. Yes, the technology, tradecraft, and gender politics of *The Once and Future Spy* are dated, but its quest for meaning feels more urgent than ever. Reviewing the book for the *New York Times* on its publication, Newgate Callendar wrote that Littell "takes a searing look at the amorality of those who think that the end is more important than the means. It would be terrifying if we really did have such monsters in our Government."

Again, the naivete stuns.

—Francine Mathews, 2024

PART ONE

Walking Back the Cat

INSTRUCTIONS for the inliſting of MEN
. . . let our manners diſtinguiſh us from
our enemies, as much as the cauſe we
are engaged in.

IN PROVINCIAL CONGRESS
at New York June 20th 1775

1

Rank has its privileges. One of them is to keep underlings waiting. Wanamaker was savvy enough to understand that this was the natural order of things; to not take it personally. He peered at the roman numerals glowing on his wristwatch, shrugged a shoulder stoically, tried the car radio again. Again all he got was static.

Sometimes it seemed as if all he ever got was static. Static about budgets being chiseled in stone from the upwardly mobile asshole who ran the Special Interagency Antiterrorist Working Group. Static from his subordinates on Operations Subgroup Charlie, who didn't appreciate the relation between rank and privilege. Static from his contact in the superstructure about deadlines, as if Wanamaker didn't know a deadline when he saw one; as if bellyaching about the occasional delay would make things run more smoothly.

Too much static could give a man ulcers, Wanamaker suspected. He could see himself filling in the Company form, in triplicate, requesting sick leave; under "Description of Malady" he would write "A terminal case of static."

From the bowels of the underground garage came the sudden whine of a motor starting up. At last! Wanamaker stubbed out his Schimmelpenninck (he had given up giving up smoking the instant the love letter, anonymous, ominous, landed in his in-basket) and glanced at the elevator doors. Above them tiny lights began blinking like fireflies as the elevator started down. It stopped on the minus-four level. The silver doors parted. Two young men wearing loose-fitting sport jackets to conceal their shoulder holsters swept out and proceeded to secure the area. They checked the handful of government cars parked on the minus-four level. They checked the alcoves. They checked the emergency staircase. Then they checked Wanamaker. One of them beckoned with a forefinger. Wanamaker opened the door and spilled himself out of the car. The young man frisked him so thoroughly Wanamaker squirmed in embarrassment. Flashing a sliver of a smile, the young man nodded toward the elevator. Wanamaker started toward it.

Sucking on the gnawed end of a dead pipe, studying some notes scribbled in longhand on the back of an envelope, a thickset man dressed in a tuxedo slouched against one wall of the elevator. He noticed Wanamaker and reached into a pocket to turn up his hearing aid. More than one journalist had attributed his success in the superstructure to a convenient deafness; he had the knack of hearing what it suited him to hear, it was suggested, and not a syllable more.

"I assume this is important," the man in the elevator told Wanamaker. No small talk, not a word about being an hour and a quarter late. "I have an after-dinner speech to deliver. The President is one of the guests."

"We've got trouble," Wanamaker announced. "Someone's ticked to Stufftingle."

The thickset man waited for him to go on so patiently that Wanamaker wasn't sure he had been heard. He raised his voice. "I got a love letter in the interoffice packet today."

"You don't need to shout. It mentioned Stufftingle? It used the word?"

"It mentioned rods. It mentioned hair triggers. It mentioned wedges."

"Only that? Nothing more?"

Wanamaker shrugged a shoulder in exasperation. "Rods, hair triggers, wedges are Stufftingle."

"What do you make of it?"

"What I make of it is we have got to get to the bottom of this real quick or call the whole thing off."

"Someone's playing games with you," the thickset man decided. "That kind of thing goes on around your shop, I'm told."

"It happens," Wanamaker conceded. "Somebody you rub the wrong way wants to get back at you. So he tries to make it seem as if you have a leak. On the other hand, it's me that's sitting out there on the limb and I'm not excited about taking the fall."

The thickset man produced a gold and silver cigarette lighter and angled the flame into the bowl of his pipe. He sucked it into life, filling the elevator with a haze of vile-smelling smoke. "Let's try to identify the author of your love letter before we jump to conclusions," he remarked.

Wanamaker made no effort to hide his lack of enthusiasm.

The thickset man realized Wanamaker needed stroking. "Before he died," he said in a low voice, "the Director told me you were one of the handful of people at the Company who could be counted on. He told me you were one of us."

"I am. You can."

"He told me you were an artist at operations. He said you didn't so much plan them as choreograph them. He said you could keep more balls in the air than a juggler."

"I do what I'm paid to do. The difference between me and the next guy is I do it better."

"Stufftingle is not just another operation. A great deal is riding on it."

"It is. I know. Trouble is, we're in no position to ask the Company to walk back the cat for us."

"Walk back the cat?"

"Take the operation apart piece by piece. Find out where the leak comes from. Plug it."

"Call in a freelancer," the thickset man suggested. "Some retired talent who could use the action, not to mention the cash, and knows how to keep his mouth shut."

Wanamaker thought about this. "There's an admiral down in Guantánamo who's done that kind of thing. I used to work for him. Ex-Naval Intelligence. Ex-Company Counterintelligence. Eccentric as a hatter, but brilliant. He was brought in a couple of years ago to walk back the cat on that Soviet defector who skipped home to Moscow first chance he got. It was the Admiral who fitted the pieces together—who figured out the defector had been a double agent all along."

"You won't need to explain Stufftingle. You won't need to mention me." The sentences weren't put as questions.

Wanamaker shook his head in vigorous agreement. Several flakes of dandruff drifted down toward his shoulders. "He'll assume it's a Company operation. Where is it written I have to straighten him out?"

"Keep me posted," snapped the thickset man.

Wanamaker cranked an ingratiating smile onto his normally immobile features. Few people at his level dealt directly with someone who was not only in the superstructure, but a member of the President's inner circle. If Stufftingle succeeded, Wanamaker's star would soar. "Definitely. Count on it," he replied.

"I do." The thickset man reached into his jacket pocket and turned down the hearing aid. It was apparent from his expression that deafness had fallen like a curtain between him and Wanamaker.

"Well," Wanamaker said to no one in particular. He shrugged a shoulder and backed out of the elevator. The two young men backed in. The silver doors slid closed. The motor started up. Over the elevator doors the fireflies began blinking again.

2

The shuttle from Guantánamo taxied to the bitter end of a remote runway at the Bethesda Naval Air Station. Portable steps were rolled up to the fuselage. A petty officer with a handlebar mustache cracked the door, then stepped aside deferentially. Hunched over like a parenthesis, Rear Admiral J. Pepper Toothacher (retired) appeared in the doorway. Listed on the plane's manifest as a Navy dentist deadheading into DC for a symposium on wisdom teeth, he was in his late fifties, but his chalk-colored hair made him seem a dozen years older. His first wife (as he called her, though never to her face) had been after him for years to dye it, but the Admiral flatly refused; every white hair, he liked to say, represented a secret that would go to the grave with him.

Wearing spit-shined oxfords, aviator glasses with trifocal lenses and civilian sport clothes that might have fit him before he went on a macrobiotic binge, the Admiral had the lean, hungry look that comes from pecking cocktail peanuts at one happy hour too many; retirement was slowly boring him to death. With his sloping shoulders, his sunken cheeks, his mournful face, his pasty complexion, his bulging eyes that seemed to take in absolutely everything, he could have passed for a perfect Polonius spying from behind a silver arras; the archetypal *fin de race* nobleman who knew not only where the various bodies were buried, but what they had died of—and who had profited from their deaths and could be accused of murder if the need arose.

The Admiral sucked air into his lungs until his rib cage ached, then plunged down the steps and danced a little one-legged jig on the tarmac to celebrate his safe arrival back on earth. The celebration was cut short when he caught sight of the hulking figure of Chief Petty Officer M. Huxstep (also retired) leaning insolently against the door of a car pool Chevrolet. The Admiral organized the various limbs of his lanky body so that they would function more or less harmoniously and ambled over to Huxstep.

"Of all people," the Admiral remarked.

"Small world," Huxstep agreed.

The Admiral cocked his head. "What is the cube of one twenty-one?" he demanded.

Huxstep yawned. "Too easy," he said.

"You're playing for time," the Admiral said.

"Don't need time. One twenty-one cubed is one seven seven one five six one."

"How about the cube root of 12,812,904?"

Huxstep, who always looked bored, managed to look more bored than usual. "The third power of twenty-three point four."

The Admiral pouted in bewilderment. "How do you do it?"

"How does the Admiral tie his shoelaces?" Huxstep retorted. He indicated with an imperious toss of his head that the seaman deuce struggling with the Admiral's two Vuitton suitcases was to deposit them in the trunk compartment. Toothacher favored the automobile with a baleful stare. "Don't pretend this was the very best you could do," he admonished Huxstep.

"I was instructed not to draw attention to the Admiral's presence in Washington," Huxstep said.

"You might have at least washed the beast." The Admiral dusted the passenger seat with a handkerchief and settled uneasily into it, but pointedly left the door on his side of the car open. Huxstep, whose short cropped hair and eyes were the color of pewter, snorted loudly enough for the Admiral to hear him as he strode around to the passenger side and kicked it closed. He climbed in behind the wheel and gunned the motor. The Chevrolet lunged toward the gate in the chain link fence.

The Admiral nodded vaguely at the Marines in full battle dress guarding the gate, sniffed delicately at the interior of the car, checked the ashtray for butts, wrinkled up an incredibly Roman nose when he found one. He investigated the glove compartment and discovered Huxstep's handgun hidden under the road maps. It was a Smith & Wesson .357 Magnum, a weapon that punched a hole the size of a fist in anything it hit. "I see you are armed," Admiral Toothacher noted.

"Couldn't you have selected something slightly more"—he racked his brain for the appropriate word—"*discreet*?"

"A derringer, for instance? Or a walking stick that opens into a sword?"

Toothacher sighed in frustration. "Another thing—you might have had the decency to give the sailor back there a hand with my bags."

That was too much for Huxstep. "I would like to respectfully point out that the Admiral has been on the ground five fucking minutes and he has so far managed to complain about the car I am driving and the handgun I am carrying and the bags I did not help some sailor with the lowest fucking rank in the entire United States of America Navy put into the trunk."

"If I really wanted to be picky," the Admiral said sweetly, "I would comment on your sentence structure."

Huxstep snorted again and tucked the stray hairs that appeared back up into his nostrils with delicate clockwise thrusts of his thick pinky.

The Admiral closed his eyes in pain. "Tidying up?" he baited Huxstep.

The driver glanced sideways at his passenger. "Fuck the Admiral."

"Tch, tch," cooed Toothacher. He caught Huxstep's eye and batted both of his lids in a conspiratorial double wink.

Huxstep melted, cleared his throat, tried to swallow the emotion that welled up, failed. "I *am* glad to see the Admiral after all these years," he mumbled awkwardly. "The truth is, when I heard the Admiral was coming, I volunteered to meet him."

Toothacher nodded emphatically. "If I had known you were available I would have insisted on you as a condition of my coming." He muttered under his breath, "What a fool I was not to specify the make of the automobile."

Huxstep produced what, coming from him, passed for a laugh. "Just like old times," he said. "The Admiral was always preoccupied with the perks."

"Since when is it a crime for a man to know what he's worth?" Toothacher asked defiantly.

"Since when," Huxstep agreed affably.

Heading toward downtown Washington, Huxstep broke a silence. "So the Admiral is walking back another cat."

"And who in heaven's name planted that idea in your head?"

"I just assumed, the Admiral being here and all. And them laying on a car and driver."

"Where are you taking me?"

"To meet the man I work for, Mister R for Roger Wanamaker."

"Roger Wanamaker," Toothacher repeated, narrowing his eyes to stir an almost photographic memory. He nodded carefully as it came to him. "He was my man Friday when I ran Naval Intelligence. Mid-thirties. The kind of face that normally comes equipped with a lisp. Weak chin. A nose with a knob on it. Broke it at Yale, if I recall, playing intramural squash. Disheveled hair full of static electricity and dandruff. Always overweight, always dieting; he used to eat low-calorie cottage cheese at his desk. I could tell which dossiers he'd seen because they had cottage cheese on them. He was the sloppiest individual I ever had the displeasure to work with. But the sloppiness masked an intellectual rigor. He collected details the way other men collected lint in their trouser cuffs, had a nose for the oddball operation, which is why I took him with me when I was kicked upstairs to Counterintelligence."

Huxstep laughed under his breath. "I remember the Admiral saying something about misery loving company."

"How'd you wind up in Wanamaker's shop?" Toothacher asked.

"The Navy gave me the boot because of a dumb manslaughter conviction. I was at loose ends. I heard on the grapevine that Mister Wanamaker was recruiting for a hush-hush antiterrorist operation. You don't mind I gave your name as a reference when I applied?"

The Admiral was following his own thoughts. "I recall another thing about friend Wanamaker," he said. "Everyone called him Friday. You called him Bright Eyes. You spread it around that he bathed every day but never changed the water. He didn't appreciate your sense of humor."

Huxstep elevated his chin a notch. "The ones who don't know how to laugh at themselves I ignore."

"Error," the Admiral observed wryly. "In our business they are the ones you must pay attention to."

3

"Welcome aboard," Wanamaker said, steering Admiral Toothacher through an outer office wasteland, past a receptionist in a plaid miniskirt filing a broken nail, past a middle-aged female assistant wearing a 1930s scalp-hugging feathered hat with a black veil that fell like a mask over half her face, into an inner sanctum that looked as if it had been furnished with hand-me-downs from a congressional subcommittee examining explosive issues such as evaporation levels in Amazon rain forests. "Sorry about the creature comforts," Wanamaker apologized as he waved Toothacher into a lopsided armchair with stained imitation leather upholstery. "We are the innocent victims of a government conspiracy to spend less money. Coffee? Tea? Something with a kick to it?"

"Tea," the Admiral said without enthusiasm. He eyed the surroundings with a distaste he usually reserved for chain hotels and tried to console himself with the silver lining—the $250 per diem, the nights that would presumably be free, the candles that he would gleefully burn at both ends.

Wanamaker hovered over the armchair like a rain cloud. "With or without?"

"Either or."

Wanamaker scurried across the room and crawled into a squeaking wooden swivel chair behind an embarrassingly small desk whose glass top was nearly opaque with cottage cheese stains. He depressed a lever on the squawk box. "Two teas. Pronto."

A burst of static filtered back through the box. It seemed to say, "With or without?"

"More static," Wanamaker muttered. He punched a lever and yelled into the squawk box, "With. Without. Either or."

The Admiral, sniffing, caught a whiff of staleness, of mildew, of stubbed-out cigars, of synthetic carpet heavy with dust. He glanced at the windows, which were covered with grime. They probably hadn't been opened, the room probably hadn't been aired, in years. Decades even. What had he gotten himself into? He peered at Wanamaker squirming nervously in his squeaking chair. His shapeless clothes looked sweat-stained, his hair matted. When he moved his head suddenly, crystals of dandruff could be seen drifting down through the sunlight onto his shoulders, which bore the unmistakable traces of previous flurries. The Admiral understood what Huxstep had been getting at when he said Wanamaker bathed every day but never changed the water.

Wanamaker twisted a paper clip, fingered a tin of Schimmelpennincks as he attempted to break the ice with his old boss, his icon, his mentor, his father figure. "You will have noticed that in deference to you I have not lighted a cigar," he commented.

"You might have emptied the ashtrays," the Admiral said absently.

Wanamaker's pudgy lips hinted at a pudgy smile. "You will be wondering why I invited you."

The Admiral didn't say anything. He was concentrating on trying not to breathe.

Observing Toothacher, Wanamaker recalled with visceral pleasure his seven-year tour as the Admiral's man Friday. There had been many in the intelligence community who had written Toothacher off as a professional devil's advocate—someone who had no illusions about winning the cold war but simply relished fighting it. Only the chosen few, Wanamaker among them, suspected that the river ran deeper; that the Admiral was a true believer. He detested the Bolsheviks with a passion. And he would go to any lengths to irritate them. Back in his salad days, when everyone was wildly dropping agents behind the Iron Curtain, the Admiral had come up with the idea of dropping shortwave radios and parachutes and letting the Russians fall over one another looking for nonexistent agents. Later, when everyone in the West was desperately trying to penetrate the Soviet High Command, he had run Naval Intelligence as if it *had* penetrated the Soviet High Command. When the Russians picked up the clues that the Admiral had left scattered around, they launched a mole hunt that all but crippled the High Command for years. Pushing for bigger budgets, Toothacher had made enemies on the Senate Armed Services Committee and had been shunted over to the CIA, where he wound up working for James Jesus Angleton's Praetorian Guard, the counterintelligence elite, the born-again pessimists to whom the worst case was always the most likely, the most interesting, the most stimulating; above all, the most congenial. Somewhere along the way there had been a whiff of scandal; as part of a surveillance training exercise, a young recruit at the CIA's Farm had tailed the Admiral and filed a report on the company he kept. Toothacher had been hauled on the carpet and subjected to the indignity of a lie detector test, which he had failed. At which point the Director of Central Intelligence, never one to wash dirty linen in public, had pensioned Toothacher off to early retirement at the American Naval base in Guantánamo, Cuba.

The secretary with the repaired fingernail and the plaid miniskirt barged in with a tray and set it down on Wanamaker's desk. She caught sight of the Admiral sharpening the crease on his trousers with his fingers and discreetly averted her eyes as she left. Wanamaker skidded a mug across the desk top toward the Admiral and offered him a saucer filled with tiny paper envelopes. Toothacher poked at an envelope, read its label. "*Powdered milk!*" He let his eyes take another turn around the room. (Was he looking for a way out?) He noticed the impossibly tacky color photograph of the President hanging on the wall above the bricked-over chimney. He noticed the wilting plants in plastic flower pots on a dusty battleship-gray combination safe. He noticed the conference table overflowing with empty cans of classic Coke and diet cola and low-fat cottage cheese containers and paper plates with crusts of sandwiches on them. "My God, Wanamaker," the Admiral said in a fierce whisper, "what are we here?"

Wanamaker hit the lever on his squawk box. "No calls. No visitors. No nothing," he barked. He swiveled three hundred and sixty degrees in his chair, as if he were winding himself up, then settled back to stare at the Admiral. A muscle over Wanamaker's right eye twitched. "What we are here," he said with quiet urgency, "is an operations subgroup of SIAWG, which stands for Special Interagency Antiterrorist Working Group."

"Is this a United States government agency?"

Wanamaker managed a nervous giggle. Clearly retirement had not dulled the Admiral's appetite for irony. "Very quick," Wanamaker said. "Very clever." He squirmed impatiently in his chair, then leaned forward and lowered his voice to indicate that the conversation had crossed a threshold. "SIAWG was set up after the humiliating failure to rescue American hostages in Iran in 1980. Our particular subgroup—we are Operations Subgroup Charlie—is staffed by Middle East experts. We save string on a dozen terrorist organizations so secret the people in them aren't always sure what cell they belong to."

Watching his former protege's performance, the Admiral was reminded that Wanamaker had the narrowest range of emotions he had ever come across in a *homo politicus*. He seemed to have winnowed his repertoire of facial expressions down to a derisive smirk, often, though not invariably, accompanied by a giggle, and another expression that was expressionless. It was the expressionless expression that was being deployed now, a tired army taking up position on a worn rampart. "I don't quite see what your problem is," the Admiral ventured.

Wanamaker began deforming another paper clip. "Our product is tightly held—it is BIGOT listed, stamped NODIS, NOFORM, ORCON, stamped anything we can get our paws on. Despite this, we seem to have sprung a leak. Somebody outside our subgroup, somebody outside our distribution list even, appears to have access to our product. To the product of our single most sensitive operation, to be exact. Which is why you're here. I am hoping you can walk back the cat and quietly plug the leak so we can get on with our work."

When it came to methodology the Admiral never leapt; he crawled in what he took to be the general direction of conclusions. "What makes you think there has been a leak?" he inquired now.

A derisive smirk replaced the expression that was expressionless on Wanamaker's face. He produced a cardboard portfolio from a desk drawer. On the cover, in large block letters, was stamped BIGOT LIST and NODIS and NOFORM and ORCON. Inside the portfolio was a page of computer printout paper protected by a transparent folder. Wanamaker handed the folder across the desk to the Admiral.

Peering through the lower part of his trifocals, Toothacher studied the printout. "Rods," he read out loud. Then, "Hair triggers." Then, "Wedges."

Wanamaker felt better than he had in days. He was glad he had sent for his mentor. He was sure the Admiral wouldn't disappoint him. Like Mao Tse Tung, the Admiral understood that a journey of a thousand miles began with a single step.

Reading the four words on the printout in the transparent folder had been that first step.

4

The Weeder, as usual, kept most of himself up his sleeve. "A bit of this, a bit of that," he replied. His face corkscrewed into a sheepish grin; having to be coy about what he did for a living made him uncomfortable. He discovered sediment at the bottom of his wineglass and shook his head in annoyance. He had no respect for wines that voyaged badly; also for people. The thought crossed his mind that he was voyaging badly, but what could he say? That he prospected in currents of conversation for nuggets of treason? His physicist friend would laugh if he didn't believe him and leave if he did.

"You haven't changed," the physicist, whose name was Ethan Early, said. "Remember that American History professor who gave you an A because you knew more than you said, and me a C because I said more than I knew?" The physicist snickered pleasantly. "Why don't you try telling the truth for once, Silas. The whole truth, nothing but."

"Whose truth?" the Weeder asked. "Which truth?"

Nodding appreciatively, Early plunged on. "The word out

on you is you don't work for the State Department at all. A lot of your former classmates, me included, think you're some sort of spook." He leaned over the table; the southernmost handpainted sunflower on his silk tie slipped into his bowl of fettucini, but the Weeder didn't say anything. "Own up, Silas. Do you carry cyanide pills and false passports?" Early asked eagerly. "Do you dot your i's with microdots and post your letters in dead drops? Are you armed?"

"I *am* armed," the Weeder said, "with a sense of humor. Which is what protects me from friends like you." More coyness; another sheepish grin.

At the next booth an elderly man raised his voice in frustration. "Admit it," he whined. "Admit you slept with him."

The elderly woman sitting across from him pleaded, "Oh, God, you're not going to dredge up something that happened forty-two years ago."

"Did you, yes or no, sleep with him?"

"That was spilled milk, which you're not supposed to cry over," the woman complained. She was silent for a moment. Then she blurted out, "Sometimes I wish you'd die!"

"I'm trying," the old man retorted. And he emitted a high-pitched whistle that reminded the Weeder, sitting with his back to the two old people in the next booth, of steam seeping from a grudgingly open valve in his SoHo loft.

The physicist leaned toward the Weeder. "What is your position on spilled milk?" he whispered.

"If a historian isn't interested in spilled milk, who is?" the Weeder said. "It's the amniotic fluid of history."

"But do you cry over it, Silas, that's the question?"

"It is an article of faith with me that spilled milk is definitely something to cry over," the Weeder assured his friend. He thought: If I didn't believe that, I wouldn't be walking back the cat on Nate.

"There is hope for you yet," Early remarked.

They were contemplating layered Italian desserts when the Weeder finally got around to steering the conversation onto physics. "And what frontiers are you pushing back these days?" he casually asked Early.

"I am, believe it or not, counting hydrogen atoms," the physicist replied.

The waiter, passing, called, "So, everything all right?"

"Your food is eatable," the Weeder called back. "Your wine needs work. Your prices too." To the physicist he said, "Why are you counting hydrogen atoms?"

"If there are more than three to every cubic yard of space, the universe will eventually fall back on itself. When things get dense enough, there will be another big bang and history will start all over again. If there are less than three, the universe will expand forever. Distant galaxies will flicker out like spent candles. If some poor son of a bitch is still here to observe all this, he will be adrift on this life raft of a planet, alone in a dead universe."

The Weeder said with emotion, "Some people are already adrift on this life raft of a planet. But that's another story."

The physicist spotted the traces of fettucini sauce on his sunflower. He moistened the tip of his napkin in a glass of water and dabbed at the stain. "When you phoned," he said, "you mentioned something about wanting to pick my brain."

"I almost forgot," the Weeder said. He fished some three-by-five index cards from the breast pocket of his sport jacket and offered them to Early. "I came across a batch of notes that don't make much sense to me. I thought they might to you."

The physicist glanced at the first card, then shuffled it to the back of the pack and read the next one. "Well, U-239 is definitely not a German U-boat, if that's any help." Early looked up. The Weeder, so casual a moment ago, was hanging on his words. "It's uranium, and the other 239 is plutonium. The chemical notations mean that U-239 loses two electrons and converts two neutrons into protons to become Pu-239. Given the context, 'rods' obviously refers to uranium rods. They are sealed in aluminum cylinders and inserted in graphite. You slow down a chain reaction by removing rods. You speed it up by adding rods."

"What about 'hair triggers'?"

"The thing that makes uranium and plutonium stand out in Mendeleyev's crowd is that, atomically speaking, they have hair triggers—they can be made to explode relatively easily. How can I explain it? Look, Silas, say you are operating an atomic pile, either with uranium or with plutonium. You are removing or adding rods to slow down or speed up the chain reaction, right? The size of the rods and their spacing are very delicate—get one wrong and you wind up with an uncontrolled chain reaction, otherwise known as an atomic explosion."

The physicist shuffled the top card to the back of the pack and read the next one. "'Wedges' refers to the way early uranium or plutonium bombs were constructed. Wedges of uranium in the case of the Hiroshima bomb, wedges of plutonium in the Nagasaki bomb, were arranged in circles—maybe we should call them vicious circles—and imploded by a ring of conventional dynamite placed around the perimeter. The implosion packed the wedges into a critical mass which, in turn, resulted in a chain reaction and an atomic explosion. The thing to remember when configuring wedges of uranium or plutonium into bombs is this: for any given shape there is a critical weight, and the stuff explodes instantly when it reaches that weight. So you'd better have your calculations down pat before you start to configure."

Early handed the index cards back to the Weeder. "The documents you came across are obviously old hat. Whoever wrote this was worrying about the various ways that someone going through the motions of constructing a primitive atomic device might bring on an accidental atomic explosion." Early smiled across the table. "Has what I said helped you any?"

The Weeder had a faraway look in his eyes as he murmured, "I'm not sure."

5

For starters, I'll do my man Nate:

In my mind's eye I see him dancing leaf in the rebellion's gusts. His hair, cut short because of lice during the siege of Boston, would have grown long enough for him to wear it again in a knot at the nape of his neck, which was the style he preferred. He would have been paler than usual, and weaker; he had "taken the smallpox" (as the inoculation was called) three weeks before when he was home on leave and was only just getting back on his feet. One day in mid-August, when the sky over New York had the dull sheen of pewter, Nate and his friend from New London, S. Hempstead, were sent in from Haarlem to see if they could requisition bayonets, which the eighty or so men in Nate's Company (part of Colonel Webb's Nineteenth Connecticut Volunteers) desperately needed. Rumor had it that a Dutch ship carrying bullets and bayonets had run the blockade and docked on the North River.

Nate wouldn't have been in a particularly good mood that

day. The girl with whom he had had "polite intercourse" (Nate's phrase, not mine) while he was teaching at Haddam's Landing—she had been one of the handful of girls in his early morning Latin class—had written to say that she had gotten engaged to a constable from Hartford. When the cat's away, mice will play, is what Nate must have thought. (It's what I would have thought if I had been in his shoes, but that may tell more about me than Nate; it certainly says something about how I reconstruct history.) The sweltering heat was probably accumulating in drifts, and Nate and his friend would have stopped at Cape's Tavern on the Broad Way for a tankard of cool ale. Later they would have scrambled over the barricades that had been thrown up on the streets sloping down to the river and asked some of Colonel Glover's Marbleheaders, in their tarred fisherman's trousers, where they could find the Dutch ship. The Marblehead men would have shrugged; as far as they knew there was no Dutch ship, and no bayonets.

It would have been like Nate to suggest that they take a gander at the enemy before heading back up the Broad Way to Haarlem; he was by nature and instinct an adventurous soul who had the fears any sane man had but constantly tested himself against them. He and his friend would have climbed onto one of the parapets at Old Fort Amsterdam to gaze at the forest of masts off Staten Island. One of General Knox's gunners, sunning himself next to his cannon, might have noticed Nate was an officer and decided to bait him.

"Count the masts if you got the nerve."

Nate would have made a stab at it (there was never a

challenge he wouldn't rise to), but soon given up. There were too many.

I can hear the gunner drawling, "How 'bout you, Sergeant?"

I can see Nate smiling that broad ear-to-ear grin of his and saying, "Go ahead, Stephen."

Stephen surely shook his head. "A man could lose his taste for rebellion counting the enemy."

The gunner would have laughed pleasantly. "We been countin' them out with long glasses. Ten ships of the line, twenty frigates, seventy-three warships all told, another hundred fifty or so transports. Heard General Knox say as how this was the goldurnest force the lobsters ever sent 'gainst anyone."

If I know my Nate, he would have remarked on the note of pride in the gunner's voice. And he would have thought: He's an optimist because he doesn't know enough.

It was about then that Nate and his friend Stephen heard the slow mournful beating of the kettledrum. The sound seemed to come from the bowling green, Nate's old stamping ground; he had kicked around a football on the green when his company had been billeted there.

"What's that about?" Stephen asked.

The gunner, a burly cordwainer from the Maine Territories, bit off a plug of tobacco and spit some juice onto the parapet. "Ain't you heard? There's gonna be a hangin'. Go ahead and watch if you got the stomach for it. There ain't no charge."

Nate and Stephen surely exchanged looks here. Stephen, who at twenty-two was a year older than Nate and never let him forget it, said "I'm all for heading back."

Nate shook his head stubbornly. He had never seen a man executed, but he figured it was something he ought to know about. All the rebel officers fought with halters around their necks. Nate had torn out from the New York *Weekly Post Boy* the article describing the sentence imposed by a British judge on an Irish rebel. "You are to be hanged by the neck," the judge had informed the condemned man, "but *not* until you are dead; for while you are still living your body is to be cut down, your bowels torn out and burned before your face, your head cut off, and your body divided into four quarters, your head and quarters to be at the King's disposal; and may the Almighty God have mercy on your soul."

It was on the bowling green that Nate first spotted the Commander-in-Chief. He was chatting with his portly Commander of Artillery, General Knox. Nate had never set eyes on the Commander-in-Chief before, but he recognized him instantly. He was a heavy man, easily a head taller than anyone around him, with thick thighs and meaty hips and high cheekbones and a prominent nose. A black cockade jutted from the brim of his hat, indicating he was a general officer. He wore his hair powdered and tied back at the neck with a red ribbon, indicating he was a gentleman. He sat his horse as if he had been born on one.

The Commander-in-Chief was not someone Nate was predisposed to. He had heard too many unpleasant stories about him: how he had been a land speculator back in Virginia; how he had married a rich widow for her money; how he had advertised in newspapers to recapture a runaway slave but had kept his name off the advertisement; how he had turned up, conspicuous in his officer's uniform, when Congress was deciding on a Commander-in-Chief even though he hadn't drilled a militia unit in fifteen years. It was whispered about that the tall Virginian wanted to be an American king, and Nate half believed it. On top of everything, he was clearly an amateur when it came to military matters; faced with an enemy expeditionary force that was said to number thirty-two thousand regulars (if you counted the mercenaries), the Virginian had committed the blunder of dividing his army, which numbered about twenty thousand and included a high percentage of inexperienced militiamen. It didn't take a genius to understand that the military situation was desperate. But the Virginian, whose only experience came from some skirmishing in the forests of the Ohio during the Seven Years' War, seemed oblivious to reality.

Now I'll do the execution:

A nervous clearing of a dry throat here; the author squirms at executions, even when they take place in the imagination.)

A company of black-shirted Pennsylvania riflemen, and another of "shirtmen"—Virginia frontiersmen wearing fringed buckskin shirts and armed with long rifles so accurate it was said they could hit a target that a New England boy had to squint at to see—were drawn up on the green. Those who had hats wore them against the sun. A crude gibbet had been constructed not far from the statue of Farmer George (he normally had a Roman numeral III after his name) on a prancing horse. A thick rope neatly tied into a noose dangled from the gibbet. The muffled beat of the kettledrum faltered as an open-sided dray appeared on the Broad Way end of the green. The drummer boy, staring at the dray, had forgotten what he was there for. An officer kicked him in the ass. The drumbeat started up again.

The dray was pulled onto the green by two beady-eyed oxen that kept their heads down in their yokes and drooled onto the cobblestones. Half a dozen armed shirtmen walked on either side of the dray. Nate noticed their rifles were fitted with bayonets and wondered where they had gotten them. Standing on the dray, his arms tied behind his back at the wrists, was Sergeant T. Hickey, until recently a member of the Commander-in-Chief's personal bodyguard. He had been convicted, a woman whispered to Nate, of plotting with a group of local Tories to poison the man he was supposed to be guarding. There was talk that some peas the Virginian had by chance not eaten had killed the chickens they were thrown to.

Maybe it was true, Nate reflected. But whose truth? Which truth?

The condemned man, wearing homespun breeches and a dirty white collarless linen shirt open at the neck, struggled to keep his balance on the dray as it was pulled past Nate and Stephen and several hundred civilians who had come to witness the hanging. Next to Nate a man wearing a cooper's canvas apron hoisted a small boy onto his shoulders so he could get a better view. Nate, in the front rank, studied the condemned man's face. His cheek muscles twitched, his eyes darted from side to side, spittle dribbled from a quivering lower lip. Nate noticed a stain spreading around the man's crotch, and I think, I imagine Nate thought: If it ever comes to that, I swear to God I will not lose control of myself.

Nate repeated "I swear" out loud, almost as if he were taking an oath.

The dray drew abreast of the Commander-in-Chief sitting impassively on his white mare, which was pawing playfully at the ground with her right front hoof. A general from central casting on a horse from central casting. (I know a historian is supposed to be above this kind of comment, but history desperately needs a giggle now and then. Humor me while I humor history.) The condemned man's darting eyes caught a glimpse of a pine box. It dawned on him that he was looking at a coffin—at *his* coffin—and he spun around toward the Virginian on the white mare and cried out in a brittle voice, "Excellency, Excellency, have mercy on a poor sinner who is not eager to meet his Maker," or words to that effect.

Nate saw the Virginian's patrician eyes narrow into slits and being not far away, he heard him comment to General Knox, "My tenderness has been often abused. Matters are too far advanced to sacrifice anything to punctilios."

(Punctilio/pxnk'tiliav: n. [pl. punctilios] a delicate point of ceremony; etiquette of such point; petty formality. The Virginian had a curious sense of punctilios!)

The dray reached the gibbet. Hickey became aware of the dangling noose and sagged to his knees. Tears streamed down his cheeks and he started breathlessly hiccuping the way a child does when he cries too hard. Two shirtmen, tough cookies who looked as if they had seen their share of scalped corpses during the Indian Wars, climbed onto the dray. They grabbed Hickey under his armpits and hauled him, still hiccuping, to his feet. One of the shirtmen fitted the noose over the condemned man's head and tightened it around his neck.

Stephen tugged at Nate's sleeve. "Come away," he whispered, but Nate didn't move.

The crowd grew deathly quiet. The Virginian's central casting horse snorted. General Knox, his maimed hand concealed in a silk scarf, nodded. An officer elbowed the drummer boy. The beat of the kettledrum quickened. The two shirtmen jumped down from the dray. Another shirtman whipped the flank of one of the oxen with a long white birch branch. The beast blew air through his lips and stood his ground. The shirtman cocked the branch. Hickey, watching from the dray, the noose tight around his neck, managed to scream "Mother!" between his hiccups. The branch swatted down across the oxen's flank. The animal started forward, dragging the other oxen with him. Hickey tiptoed along the floorboards of the dray to keep his footing. Then he ran out of dray and dangled from the noose. A muted sigh, an exhaling of many breaths, came from the crowd. The hanging man developed an enormous bulge in his crotch, the result of an involuntary erection. The women present averted their eyes.

The child on his father's shoulders laughed nervously; he wasn't at all sure what he was seeing.

Nate felt an icy hand caress his spine. He raised his eyes to the pewter sky, to the pewter God, then obliged himself to look back at the hanged man. Still hiccuping, he was jerking at the end of the rope, which was slowly strangling him. The Virginian on his white mare made an impatient gesture with his hand. General Knox signaled to the shirtmen with a crisp nod of his head. One of them strolled over to Hickey. He wrapped his arms around the jerking knees of the executed man and pulled himself up until his weight was hanging from Hickey's body.

The hiccuping stopped. Then the jerking.

Nate saw the shadows of birds racing across the ground and looked up, but there were no birds, there was just Hickey dangling from the bitter end of the rope, and the shirtman dangling from him in an erotic embrace.

Nate and Stephen caught their horses, which were grazing in a fenced-in field behind Cape's Tavern, and saddled them and started them walking up the Broad Way in the direction of the old Dutch village of Haarlem. They passed a fat woman rooting in garbage. They passed a company of John Haslet's Delaware Continentals, whom everyone called the Blue Hen Chickens, heading on foot for Kipp's farmhouse and the cove under it; some carried muskets, some carried pitchforks. The Chickens were handing around a transparent green jug and taking healthy swigs from it as they marched. Nate and Stephen passed a deserted farmhouse that had gotten a

"Hillsborough treat"—thinking Tories lived in the house, rebels had smeared it with excrement.

The day grew heavier. A pall of dust kicked up by horses ahead of them on the Broad Way hung in the air, obliging Nate and Stephen to mask their noses and mouths with bandannas. For a long time neither man said anything. The silence turned awkward. Eventually Stephen broke it. "That was a god-awful thing we saw today."

Nate fingered the hair mole on his neck. When he was a boy his friends had teased him about it, telling him it meant he would one day be hanged. "A long life has a lingering death," Nate replied through his bandanna, quoting the English version of a Latin maxim he had memorized at Yale.

As near as I can figure, all this took place three weeks before Nate got involved in whipping the cat.

6

The first working session had gotten off to a relatively sluggish start. "The desk clerk offered me a room with a queen-size bed," the Admiral was explaining. "I naturally inquired about the view. 'If you are into brick the view is terrific,' he told me. I am not inventing. 'Into brick' were his precise words. I let him know I was into park. He consulted one of those television screens attached to a typewriter. 'I can give you park,' he said, 'but no queen-size bed.' 'What is it with you and queen-size beds?' I asked him. He gave me as thorough a once-over as I have ever had. 'Just playing a hunch,' he said."

"Into brick," repeated the middle-aged woman whose face was masked by a veil. She clucked her tongue appreciatively.

"I am afraid park will cost you slightly more a day than brick," Toothacher informed Wanamaker. "I trust you will feel the additional money was well spent."

"Brick, park, it's all the same to me," Wanamaker said impatiently. He noticed that the Admiral's eyes were rimmed with red. He's been off carousing with Huxstep, he thought, but what he does with his free time is his business as long as he plugs my leak. Wanamaker pushed a batch of dossiers across the felt to the Admiral. "For starters, here are the service records of the twelve staffers assigned to Operations Subgroup Charlie. Mildred here is *my* man Friday. She was raised in Tehran, speaks Persian, Pashto, Avestan and Kurdish fluently, can pronounce the Ayatollah's name without an accent. Only ask her. She will get you whatever else you feel you need."

Mildred reached up and lifted her veil. "I am a navy brat," she announced breathlessly. "I was weaned on stories about you. Admiral Toothacher this. Admiral Toothacher that. For me, Eisenhower, Kennedy were minor figures in the Toothacher era. Frankly, it is a thrill just to be in the same room with you."

When it came to matters of seduction, the Admiral followed an old formula that in his experience seldom failed; he flattered the beautiful people for their brains, the intelligent ones for their looks. "The pleasure is entirely mine," he solemnly informed Mildred. "I seldom get to work with someone who is as easy on the eyes as you."

Mildred, flustered, let the veil drift back across the upper half of her face. "You are not at all what I expected," she admitted.

"Dear lady," the Admiral said, "dare I open that Pandora's box and ask what you expected?"

Under her veil Mildred blushed. "I was anticipating pie." She lowered her eyes, her voice. "But you are all meringue."

Toothacher, absently shuffling service records, turned back

to Wanamaker. "I will need to see the paper trail on the sensitive operation you referred to."

Once again a muscle over Wanamaker's right eye twitched. He started torturing a paper clip. "The paper trail is thin."

"Thin? How can that be?"

"As far as the sensitive operation is concerned, nothing in writing was ever circulated. The few scraps of paper dealing with the operation never left this office."

The Admiral studied his former man Friday through the middle lenses of his trifocals. "I will naturally need to know what you are up to."

Wanamaker's face was utterly immobile. "That's out of the realm of possibility."

"I must be missing something," the Admiral said sarcastically. "You obviously trust me or you wouldn't have asked me to walk back the cat for you."

"I would trust you with my life," Wanamaker said with such fervor only a fool would have doubted him. "But our sensitive operation is another story."

"It will make my task infinitely more difficult," the Admiral noted.

Wanamaker shrugged a shoulder. Toothacher saw there was no point in insisting. "What about deadlines?" he asked. "I should know if there is a clock ticking."

"I suppose it won't compromise the *what* if I tell you the *when*," Wanamaker said. "For reasons I will not explain to you, we must execute the operation by mid-March or call it off."

"How very poetic—I mean to have the Ides of March as a deadline. That doesn't leave me much time."

"One day short of four weeks," said Mildred.

The Admiral favored her with an ironic smile. "Thank you." He turned back to Wanamaker. "Of the twelve people in your subgroup, how many are in on your little sensitive operation?" he asked.

Wanamaker ticked them off on his fingers. "There's me. There's Mildred here. There's Parker. There's Webb. That makes four."

"The others don't have an inkling of what's going on?"

Wanamaker shook his head. "The others keep track of terrorist groups."

Toothacher was a breath away from abandoning the whole thing. How could he be expected to plug a leak on an operation he didn't know anything about? Let Bright Eyes get another sucker to walk back his cat. Suddenly the idea of returning to Guantánamo, to his wife of twenty-nine years who wheezed in her sleep, to the endless boredom of pinochle and happy hours, was too much for him. He batted both eyes in Wanamaker's direction. "Shouldn't I at least know what code name your operation goes by?"

Wanamaker hesitated. He studied a hole a Schimmelpenninck had burned in the felt. He advanced an empty low-fat cottage cheese container across an imaginary chess board, then took back the move. He shrugged a shoulder. He arched an eyebrow and lowered it. He was obviously having a conversation with himself. Finally he said, "Do I have your word you won't repeat it to a living soul?"

The Admiral, who loved secrets the way other men loved women or money or fast cars, shivered in anticipation. "It is another white hair that will go to the grave with me," he promised.

"We call it Operation Stufftingle."

"Stufftingle?"

"Stufftingle.

7

The Weeder's humorless deputy dog, Marvin Wesker, finished cleaning the IBM mainframe with the feather duster. "Would you be annoyed if I vacuumed tomorrow?" he called across the loft to Silas Sibley, who was weeding through the night's crop of printouts at his worktable. "I'm already behind with my programs."

"Vacuum tomorrow if you like," the Weeder replied, "but get yesterday's stuff shredded and down the chute before you attack the new pile."

"My dream in life," Wesker muttered as he ran the reams of computer printout paper through the shredder, "is to work at an operation with a classification so ordinary you can have a cleaning lady." He replaced the empty burn baskets and settled into the chair in front of his terminal, across the enormous worktable from the Weeder. "I don't mind weeding," he explained. "I just don't see myself vacuuming. I have a PhD. I speak four languages fluently. I have a working knowledge of three others. I'm overqualified."

Wesker fitted wire spectacles over his large ears. The

eyeglasses magnified his eyes and made him look as if he were leering. Grunting when he came across anything interesting, laughing out loud at times, he began reading through the pile of printouts that had accumulated overnight. "Here's a nugget," he said at one point. "Senator Woodbridge talks baby talk when he makes love."

"We knew that," the Weeder said.

"Well, lookee here. The wife of the cultural attache, I. Krasnov, is having an affair with the wife of I. Kurchik, the electronics technician."

"That's new. Add it to the pouch."

The Weeder punched an instruction into the keyboard and brought a menu up onto the screen of his terminal. The computer was listing new material under the heading CHINESE BIN—intercepts from a pay telephone on the wall of a downtown Washington Chinese restaurant. The telephone was next to a booth where Savinkov and some of his colleagues regularly ate dinner. The Weeder typed in some call-up codes and waited. There was a whirring of tapes in the mainframe behind the partition in a corner of the loft. Dialogue appeared on the screen. The Weeder copied off a Russian word he didn't know, thumbed through a Russian-English dictionary until he found it. "Ah, I see," he said.

"What do you see?" Wesker asked.

"Remember Savinkov?"

"The Savinkov who is KGB? The one who talks Latin to his wife to throw off the microphones?"

"He's arranging for one of his cipher clerks to sell us the

February key to the embassy's class seven messages. They're obviously going to put out something they want us to read." The Weeder penned a note to himself on a yellow index card. "We'll dress that one up so it looks as if it came from a conventional intercept source. Our people will have to pay through the nose for the key so as not to tip off the Russians that we know about the operation."

"Then we'll have to act on the information the Russians plant or they'll suspect us of suspecting them of having planted it," Wesker said brightly.

The Weeder shook his head. "You've put it on backwards. We'll have to be careful *not* to act on the information so the Russians won't suspect us of reading their class seven codes."

"I don't get it," Wesker said. "They'll know we're reading their class seven codes because they're selling us the key to them."

"But they don't know that we know that they know we have the key."

Wesker groaned. "I think I prefer vacuuming. I'm starting to program the chauffeur's home phone this morning. Any suggestions?"

"Look for the usual," the Weeder advised. "Odd words that could be codes for operations. Conversations in which nobody names. Any reference to Savinkov. Noun-rich sentence structure."

Wesker groaned again. "Noun-rich sentence structure! What if they talk in verb-rich sentences to throw us off the scent?" He lowered his voice to a whisper and stared in mock alarm at the telephone on the table between them. "What if they're listening to us listen to them?"

"That's why we're working out of a loft in SoHo," the Weeder said. "Even if they had the capability to do what we're doing, it'd never occur to them to target this number. We're just another mail-order house in another loft, as far as anyone knows."

"A mail-order house with an IBM mainframe, a two-hundred-and-fifty-phone trunk line, a reinforced steel shield welded on the inside of the door, an alarm system that goes off in some precinct house if anyone blinks after hours, and one of those new State Department cipher safes that needs a combination *and* a key to open it." Shaking his head, Wesker went back to his printouts.

The Weeder consulted the menu again, noticed new material under the heading of Farmer's Almanac, which was the code he had assigned to Wanamaker's Operations Subgroup Charlie. He punched in the appropriate call-up codes. Snatches of conversation began appearing on the screen. Two people were probably talking on the other side of the room from the telephone, which accounted for the computer getting only bits and pieces.

". . . feel bad about the American nationals who are there. Isn't there some way . . ."

". . . out of the question, Parker. The last thing we want to do is open the door to speculation . . ."

". . . thinking out loud. I guess you're . . ."

". . . I know I'm . . ."

Wesker, across the table, swallowed a yawn. The only items that seemed to interest him were the ones with sexual overtones. He loved tuning in on people making love; he claimed that reading what they said to each other during the act was more arousing than watching. Right now all he had were people playing bridge. Two diamonds. Pass. Two hearts. Pass. Two no-trump. Pass. Three no-trump. Noun-rich sentences could be boring as hell. He saw the Weeder peering intently at his screen. "Anything sexy?" he asked hopefully.

The Weeder said, "Savinkov is jerking off the assistant cultural attache. All I'm getting is moan-rich sentences."

"You're being ironic, right?" Wesker asked.

"Right."

Another snatch of conversation flashed onto the Weeder's screen.

"Admiral Toothacher this. Admiral Toothacher that . . . it is a thrill just to be in the same room with you."

The Weeder read the line again to be sure he had gotten it right. What was Wanamaker's old boss, Admiral Toothacher, doing for Operations Subgroup Charlie? Could Wanamaker have brought him in to walk back the cat on the leak? It wasn't a pleasant thought. Toothacher was a formidable adversary. And he had an old score to settle with the Weeder. If the Admiral ever traced the leak back to its source, he would skin Sibley alive and nail his hide to the Company wall.

". . . paper trail."

". . . paper trail . . . thin . . . never left this office."

"... naturally need to know ..."

"... out of the realm ..."

"... if there is a clock ticking."

"... by mid-March or call it off."

"How very poetic ... to have the Ides of March as a dead ..."

"... at least know what code name your operation ..."

"... tingle."

"... tingle."

"... Stufftingle."

The Weeder stared at the screen. He felt himself being sucked into the heart of a mystery. What had started out as a prank had become a puzzle. The snatches of conversation raised more questions than they answered. What was the connection between rods and hair triggers and wedges, and someone named Parker worrying about American nationals? And then there was the code word *Stufftingle*. Chances were that Wanamaker had picked it out of the Company's book of random code words. Still, it might be worth checking into. When selecting a code word for an operation, people sometimes used one that had significance because it was easier to remember.

The Weeder keyed his computer to print out what he had seen on the screen and erase the original from the tape. Then he programmed it to scan Wanamaker's future conversations for the word *Stufftingle*.

Wesker, at his terminal, caught sight of the Weeder staring off into space. "You look as if you lost your best friend."

All he got for an answer was the frustrated grin of someone who knew less than he said.

8

The Weeder rang up his physicist friend from a pay phone that night. “Am I interrupting anything?” he demanded.

“If I said yes, would you hang up?” Early asked.

“I’d talk faster.”

“Talk fast, then.”

“Does the word *Stufftingle* ring any bells?”

Early laughed into the phone. “You’ve been robbing graves again.”

The Weeder force-fed some quarters into the slot and pressed his ear to the receiver.

“You could count the people who recognize that word today on the fingers of one hand,” Early was saying. “Back in the early 1940s we had a gaseous diffusion plant at Oak Ridge, Tennessee, that produced the enriched uranium which went into the wedges of the first atomic bombs. One of the physicists working on the project circulated a spoof describing the finished product produced at Oak Ridge as *ousten-stufftingle*, and the people who produced it as *shizzlefrinks*. It got quite a laugh at the time. Hello? Are you still on the line, Silas?"

"I'm here."

"Ha! The moral of the story is that you aren't the only one to go around armed with a sense of humor."

9

Wesker had finished shredding the chaff and was pouching the wheat for the courier, who was due in fifteen minutes. "Funny about Savinkov having hemorrhoids and complaining about it in Latin," he was saying. "Somehow you'd think a KGB station chief would be above that kind of thing."

"Hemorrhoids or Latin?"

"Hemorrhoids, obviously."

"Hemorrhoids are not a character flaw," the Weeder pointed out.

"You're being ironic again, right?"

"Right. Why don't you pack it in for the day," the Weeder added. "I'll zip up the pouch."

Wesker began slipping into a vast belted overcoat before the Weeder finished the sentence. He hooked enormous yellowish designer sunglasses over his floppy ears, pulled on a fore-aft Russian astrakhan and lowered the ear flaps so that they dangled over his jaw like medieval armor. He leered at his reflection in the mirror above the sink and, apparently satisfied with what he saw, lowered his head and charged the armor-plated door. He punched with his fist at the button that sent electricity flowing to the lock. The door sprang open and Wesker disappeared.

The Weeder, who thought of himself as an *artiste manque*, switched to a graphics program on his computer and began toying with the stylus. He drew a mushroom-shaped cloud coming out of the mouth of someone with a broken nose that had more than a passing resemblance to Wanamaker's. Inside the cloud he wrote, in an elegant gothic script, the words *Stufftingle* and *Ides of March*.

He glanced at the wall clock; the courier would be there any moment. The Weeder depressed a key. In an instant the high-speed laser printer had spit out the hooked nose and the mushroom cloud. The Weeder put on his fleece-lined gloves, tore off the printout and folded it into a plain white envelope. With a red grease pencil he printed in a child's handwriting:

R. WANAMAKER

OPERATIONS SUBGROUP CHARLIE

SPECIAL INTERAGENCY ANTITERRORIST WORKING GROUP (SIAWG)

A mischievous grin installed itself on the Weeder's lips as he slipped the letter into a second envelope, which he sealed and addressed to "Company Mail Room—Classified Material for Eyes Only Distribution." That meant the letter would be put into Wanamaker's hot hands. He would go straight up the wall when he opened it. He'd swallow the soggy

Schimmelpenninck that bobbed on his lower lip. He'd have a coughing fit, turn blue, experience chest pains, have difficulty breathing. An ambulance would be summoned. A mask would be fitted over his mouth and broken nose. Oxygen would be supplied. With any luck, last rites would be administered.

Images of disaster multiplied in the Weeder's head. It occurred to him that waiting all those years was what made it so sweet. Revenge was a meal that tasted best cold.

10

Wanamaker took Webb aside and lectured him about rank having its privileges. Webb swallowed his pride and moved out of his office, doubling up with Parker so that the Admiral would have a place to hang his hat. Toothacher personally presided over the purification of Webb's cubbyhole of an office. "Kindly vacuum under the desk," he instructed the black maintenance man who turned up in response to his urgent requests. "It might not be a bad idea to shake the rug out the window. Better still, take it with you when you leave. The ashtrays, the books on the shelves, the magazines on the coffee table can also go. The coffee table too. I don't drink coffee. And kindly don't forget to wash the windows and sterilize the desk top."

"Wouldn't it be simpler if I removed the desk with the coffee table?" the maintenance man inquired with a straight face.

"If you can replace it with a new one I would leap at the offer," Toothacher cooed. "If not, moisten a cloth with some sort of detergent and scrub it squeaky clean."

The Admiral eventually settled warily into the only chair left in the room, scraped it up to the sterilized desk and started sorting through his notes. When Wanamaker had described the paper trail as "thin" he had been exaggerating. In fact it was almost nonexistent. The handful of written references to "rods," "hair triggers," "wedges," "Stufftingle" and "Ides" had never traveled beyond the four incredibly soiled walls of Wanamaker's inner sanctum, or so Wanamaker would have him believe. Wanamaker, Mildred, Parker and Webb at various times had access to the paper trail; each scrap of paper in Wanamaker's battleship-gray safe bore the initials of anyone who read it. That seemed as good a place to start as any.

The Admiral pulled a single sheet of typing paper from the middle of the pile in a drawer (never having been touched by human hands, it would be relatively germ free) and began to compose a chart. Down the left-hand side of the paper he entered the names of the four people involved in Stufftingle. Across the top he listed the dates at which various elements of the operation (rods, hair triggers, wedges, Stufftingle, Ides) had fallen into place. Across the bottom he put the dates the love letters had been delivered into Wanamaker's clammy hands. Then he attempted to cross-check to see who had known what when. The result was disappointing. Parker, a specialist on getting people and things across Mideast borders undetected, had joined the Stufftingle team eighteen months before; he had known, according to the paper trail, about rods and hair triggers and wedges, but had never been let in on Ides. Mildred had been on sick leave ("female problems," according to Wanamaker) when wedges, whatever they were, became operational. Webb, who had worked in the field with the anti-Khomeini Iranians before being posted back to Washington, had slipped a disc and been out of action when the element known as hair triggers was introduced.

Wanamaker, on the other hand, had his initials on every scrap of paper, which meant that he was familiar with all the pieces. Which was to be expected since he was, after all, in charge of the operation. Was it possible that Wanamaker was writing the love letters to himself? The Admiral had seen odder things in his day.

Toothacher set aside his chart and placed the first of the four thick dossiers in his in-basket on the desk. Perhaps the key to who had leaked Stufftingle was to be found not in the paper trail but in the biographies of the four principal players. One of them might be jealous of Wanamaker or hold a grudge against him for a slight, real or imagined. The Admiral would pore over the dossiers to see which of the four had crossed paths before. He would pry loose rocks and search for worms of treachery—the tiny discrepancy, the microscopic incongruity that would help him unravel the mystery. Insofar as there was only one truth, and it was knowable, he was determined to discover it.

11

Mildred looked up from a thick pile of Mideast intelligence summaries and watched as Huxstep ran the magnetic head back and forth over the felt that covered the conference table. His shirtsleeves were rolled up to his biceps, revealing part of a patriotic tattoo on each arm—BEGUN TO FIGHT on his right arm, GIVE ME LIBERTY OR on his left arm. Huxstep's gestures were systematic. Mildred liked men who were systematic, who didn't leave anything to chance. Out of the blue she asked him, "Is it true you can do funny things with numbers?"

Huxstep kept his eyes glued to the needle on the meter. "Test me out?"

Mildred pulled a pocket calculator from a purse that resembled a carpetbag and punched in some numbers. "Multiply 123456789 by 987654321," she said.

"That's a piece of cake," Huxstep said. "The answer's 121932631112635269."

Mildred glanced at her calculator. The window only accepted nine digits. She saw he had gotten the first nine numbers right. "What's your trick?" she asked.

"I don't got a trick," Huxstep insisted. "I seen right off if you multiply 987,654,321 by 81 you get 80,000,000,001, then multiply 123,456,789 by 80,000,000,001, which is child's play, and divide the answer by 81." Huxstep started to laugh under his breath, but stopped abruptly when he spotted the needle vibrating. "I got a bite!" he called.

The Admiral and Wanamaker, working at Wanamaker's desk, glanced across the room.

Huxstep pinpointed the spot with sweeps of the magnetic head, then gingerly lifted the cloth and felt around with his fingertips. "Fuck," he muttered. He held up a deformed paper clip.

"Keep at it," the Admiral ordered. He turned back to Wanamaker. "I traced the letter to the Company mail room, which is pretty much like tracing it to the Washington, DC, central post office."

Wanamaker grunted; he had hoped for more. "That's a dead end, then."

"Not quite a dead end," Toothacher said. Wanamaker perked up, a smirk of anticipation pasted on his pudgy lips.

At the conference table, Mildred was still trying to strike up a conversation with Huxstep. "You are obviously a jack-of-all-trades."

"I am a jackass-of-all-trades," Huxstep corrected her, his eyes on the meter.

"How so?" Mildred asked.

"Well, I drive the Admiral around, don't I? I take in, I take out, sandwiches, messages, burn bags. I organize things so the

Admiral isn't bored nights. Between chores I debug offices. But I don't really enjoy my work. I do everything badly."

Mildred lifted her veil suggestively. Her voice seemed to lap against the conference table as if it were a shore. "If something is worth doing, it may be worth doing badly. What do you enjoy? What do you do well?"

Huxstep surveyed the upper half of her face. Little lines fanned out from the corners of her eyes. Invisible eyebrows, plucked down to the bone, arched in curiosity. "Before I joined the Navy," he said, "I worked in another circus—a real one. I did arithmetic tricks. People would shout out problems and I'd solve them in my head. Wednesdays I filled in for the firebreather—I'd swig kerosene and light a match and singe the eyebrows off the ones who looked at me the wrong way."

Mildred, impressed, gushed, "You can breathe fire?"

Huxstep's face screwed up into a crooked smile. "Aside from numbers, what I like, what I do well, is violence."

Mildred's tongue flickered at her upper lip. She snapped the veil back over her eyes. "*Chacun à sa faiblesse*," she said in a tone husky with sensuality.

"I don't speak nothing but English," Huxstep muttered. "Even that the Admiral don't think I speak good."

Across the room the Admiral was telling Wanamaker, "Whoever composed these love letters works for the Company. How else could he—or she—have gotten access to the interoffice pouching system?"

Wanamaker shook his head in bewilderment. "Who? Who? Who? Who? Who?"

"Let's come at the problem from another direction," the Admiral suggested. "Let's concentrate on motive. Why? Why? Why? Why? Why?"

"You have an idea?"

"It could be you who is sending these love letters."

This took Wanamaker by surprise. His expression that was expressionless evaporated. "Me? Why would I do it?"

"You might be trying to create an excuse to cancel an operation that you have no confidence in, or stomach for, in a way that wouldn't indicate to your handlers in the Company hierarchy any lack of nerve."

"If I wanted to cancel, I'd cancel. Period. My reputation isn't riding on this."

"Or it could be any of your people—Mildred over there, or Parker, or Webb. One of them may have qualms, moral or operational in origin, and be trying to head off Stufftingle without looking like a left-leaning card-carrying fellow-traveling wimp."

Wanamaker thought about this for a moment. Presently he said, "All three consider me a closet middle-of-the-roader. They are rabid. What we are doing doesn't go far enough for them. So that's not the answer."

The Admiral tried another tack. "Whoever is sending you these love letters could just as well be sending them to the Company Director, or the White House, or *The Washington Post*, with little arrows pointing to Operations Subgroup Charlie, SIAWG. But he's not doing that. He's sending them to you."

"Which means?"

"Which could mean he's not at all sure what rods and hair triggers and wedges really mean and is just doing it to annoy you. Or he has an inkling and is trying to head you off without bringing the roof down on the Company." The Admiral turned to stare at what sky he could see through the grime of the windows. "Or all of the above," he said more to himself than to Wanamaker. "Or none of the above. Or any combination thereof."

At the conference table Huxstep started packing the magnetic head and the meter into a black Plexiglas case. "If there's a bug in this room," he called across to Toothacher, "I'll eat it."

Parker, a sour-faced, sour-breathed man in his early forties, pranced into Wanamaker's inner sanctum carrying the leather interoffice mail pouch. He pulled an envelope from it and dropped it onto the desk between Wanamaker and the Admiral. Printed on the outside of the envelope, in a child's unsteady scrawl, was:

R. WANAMAKER
OPERATIONS SUBGROUP CHARLIE
SPECIAL INTERAGENCY ANTITERRORIST WORKING GROUP (SIAWG)

Mildred, who had come up behind Parker, stared down at the letter in horror. Wanamaker, expressionless, slit it open with a finger and, using a soiled handkerchief, extracted a sheet of computer printout paper. He flattened it on the desk. Inside a mushroom-shaped cloud, coming out of the mouth of someone with a broken nose, were the words *Stufftingle* and *Ides of March.*

"He knows the code name of our operation," Wanamaker moaned.

"He knows the date too," Parker noted.

"And there are no bugs, no microphones in the room," Mildred said in total bafflement.

"None," Huxstep called across from the conference table. "Not one."

"This is getting curiouser and curiouser," the Admiral admitted.

"Curiouser and curiouser," Huxstep muttered, loud enough for Toothacher to overhear. "And the Admiral accuses me of not speaking the King's English!"

12

Wanamaker nodded to the two young men in loose-fitting sport jackets who stood guard on either side of the door to the men's room. Then he lifted his arms over his head. One of the young men began to pat him down.

Wanamaker rolled his eyes and rocked his head in mock boredom. "I am not armed," he said.

"We are not looking for weapons," the second young man told Wanamaker. "We are looking for tape recorders. We are looking for microphones."

"I am not wired either," Wanamaker said.

"There is no such thing as being too careful," observed the young man who was frisking Wanamaker. He stood up and snapped his head in the direction of the door. Wanamaker pushed through it. A haze of vile-smelling tobacco smoke filled the white-tiled room. The thickset man was wringing his hands dry under a hot air nozzle. The rush of air ceased abruptly. Spotting Wanamaker, the thickset man reached into his pocket and turned up the hearing aid. "In a nutshell, what has the Admiral come up with?" he asked.

"In a nutshell, nothing. Zero. Zilch."

"He must have an inkling, an intuition, the beginnings of a theory," he insisted.

"He thinks maybe I'm sending the love letters to myself because I don't have the stomach to go through with it."

"Are you?"

Wanamaker sneered.

"I've been quietly nosing around," the thickset man announced. "The oversight people don't appear to be on to anything out of the ordinary. As far as I can determine, the congressional pulse is normal."

"That's a comfort," Wanamaker said sarcastically. "Because my pulse isn't normal. I got a new love letter in the mail yesterday."

Again the thickset man waited with seemingly infinite patience for Wanamaker to continue.

Wanamaker hated dealing with people who had perfect control of their emotions. He couldn't resist asking, "Don't you want to know what it said?"

"Am I wrong in assuming you intend to tell me?"

Wanamaker shrugged a shoulder. "It said *Stufftingle*; it said *Ides of March*. Whoever sent the love letter knows the code name of the operation and the date."

The thickset man sucked on his pipe and exhaled into Wanamaker's face. The aroma of tobacco overpowered the odor coming from the camphor tablets in the urinals. "I see," the thickset man finally said.

"What is it you see?" Wanamaker asked.

"I see that you are dealing with an isolated person who, for some reason as yet unbeknownst to us, has decided to bait you and you alone. If he had gone to *The Washington Post*, we would be reading about Stufftingle in the newspaper. If he had gone to the Director or the oversight people, you would have been called on the carpet by now. No. No. The thing is not to lose your nerve. There's still three weeks before the deadline—plenty of time for the Admiral to get to the bottom of it."

"That's easy for you to say. It's my head that's on the platter."

"We always foresaw the possibility of something going wrong—of the operation being traced back to you. You would of course deny everything, and as there is no paper trail, who could prove you wrong?"

"Who?" Wanamaker agreed eagerly. He liked to think he knew the answer.

"If worse came to worst you were prepared to fall on your sword."

"Not eager. But prepared," Wanamaker confirmed.

"The late Director often spoke about you. If I told you what he said, your ears would burn."

Wanamaker understood he was being buttered up, but he found the experience pleasant anyhow. "I liked him a lot too," he said.

The thickset man turned reverential. He might have been pledging allegiance. "We owe it to him," he said. "We owe it to his memory."

Wanamaker nodded in grudging agreement.

13

It was the one weekend in two when the Weeder didn't have visitation rights with Martin. So he spent the morning drowning his aching emptiness in history. He wandered around an outdoor flea market lusting after a pre-Revolutionary powder horn and a Pennsylvania rifle engraved with the initials of the German-immigrant gunsmith who made it and a narrow truckle bed and a collection of Continental coins and a worn leather portmanteau with the date 1776 embossed on it. He almost bought a copy of Frederick's *Instructions to His Generals* but abandoned the idea when he discovered the asking price. Reluctantly. Washington, the Weeder remembered, had kept a copy of Frederick's *Instructions* on his desk during the battles of Long Island and, later, Harlem Heights. The Weeder wondered if Nate had noticed the book when he was summoned to the Commander-in-Chief's headquarters. Knowing Nate, knowing his love for books, he thought it more than likely. The Weeder made a mental note to check if the Beinecke Rare Book and Manuscript Library had a copy of Frederick's *Instructions* next time he got up to Yale.

At mid-morning the Weeder headed south toward SoHo and the loft. Even though it was Sunday he couldn't resist seeing if his computer had come up with anything interesting on Farmer's Almanac. Wanamaker often worked Saturdays and sometimes late into Saturday night; he was one of those people who had to be pried away from his desk. Operation Stufftingle consumed most of his working hours, most of his thoughts; all (if you read between the computer's neatly typed lines) of his passion. But what was he up to? Operations Subgroup Charlie, the Weeder knew, was keeping track of a handful of terrorist cells in the Middle East; almost all the chitchat that the Weeder had picked up when he first programmed his computer to eavesdrop on Wanamaker dealt with details of various terrorist groups: where they got their money or their arms or their marching orders. But when Wanamaker and Parker and Webb and a woman called Mildred were alone, the conversations had taken another turn. In the beginning there had been a lot of airy right-wing rhetoric. "America," one of the early Wanamaker intercepts had said, "occupies some hypothetical middle ground in international disputes, feebly supporting the side we want to win, feebly opposing the side we want to lose." "What we have to do," another person had chimed in, "is commit ourselves to the hilt even if it means taking risks." "Bite the bullet," someone had agreed, "set matters right." "Why become a world power if we are afraid to wield that power so that the world functions in a way that is congenial to us?" someone else had asked.

Eventually the theoretical discussions had given way to

something more concrete. The Weeder had picked it up the very day he had gotten the bright idea of programming the computer to register noun-rich sentences. The words *rods* and *hair triggers* and *wedges* had leapt off the printout page. For days Wanamaker could talk about little else. The Weeder had assumed that rods and hair triggers had to do with guns, that wedges were some sort of plastic explosive. It seemed as if Wanamaker's Operations Subgroup had stumbled across a terrorist assassination plot. And the Weeder had stumbled across Wanamaker stumbling across it.

The idea of targeting his computer on Wanamaker had come to the Weeder after he had run into him at a Yale reunion the previous spring. The Weeder had been staring out at the sea of faces in the lecture hall when he spotted Wanamaker in a back row. To hide his confusion he had looked down at his three-by-five index cards spread out on the lectern. Sentences were splashed across them as if they had spilled from tubes of pigment. Phrases trickled down the margins. There was a secret code of asterisks and arrows and underlined words to remind him that some detail was particularly juicy, that it went to what he thought of as the heart of a matter. When the Weeder was still an undergraduate at Yale, a professor of Colonial military history had caught a glimpse of his raw notes and had concluded he would never amount to much as a historian; too unfocused to be scholarly, he said, too willing to fill historical gaps with figments of his imagination. If only the professor, long buried, could have seen him lecturing to this gathering of alumni at a class reunion.

"Which brings me to what we don't know," the Weeder had heard himself saying. "We have a fairly complete picture of what happened to the subject of my study before September fifteenth. We certainly know what happened to him on the twenty-second. But the week between the two is missing—it's a blank, a black hole in history. Where did he go during the missing week? Whom did he contact? What, if anything, did he accomplish? I have discovered a hint buried in an old orderly book that codes were involved, which would suggest that a message might have been sent back. I've also come across reminiscences written many years after the events in question by one of the subject's brothers, Enoch. In it he refers to someone in Brooklyn whom Nate was supposed to get in touch with, a patriot who would provide him with a cover story—Nate would pretend to be an itinerant artisan boarding with families while he repaired shoes. Enoch appeared to know exactly what had happened to his brother during the missing week and claimed to have gotten the information from A. Hamilton in a letter that has unfortunately been lost. I am hot on the trail of the A. Hamilton letter, as well as any record that may have been kept by the patriot in Brooklyn. With their help I hope to solve one of the great mysteries of American history—to tell the world what happened to the subject of my study during the missing week."

There had been applause. Nothing to register on the Richter scale, but polite. The professor who had invited the Weeder to give the lecture had lunged forward to shake his hand.

Collecting his index cards on the lectern, the Weeder had glanced at his former roommate, Wanamaker, in the last row.

He was stifling a yawn.

Once again the Weeder had been struck by the tendency of people who haven't seen each other for long periods to pick up, emotionally speaking, precisely where they had left off.

He and Wanamaker had roomed together in Branford College until the incident; the accident; the murder. Wanamaker, afterward, had put out his hand and said he hoped there would be no hard feelings. Trying the capsules had been her idea, he explained. He merely told her where she could find some. If he hadn't helped her, somebody else would have. As for what happened to her, well, nobody could have foreseen that; nobody could have taken precautions.

If the Weeder had been hoping to avoid Wanamaker at the reunion, he ran out of luck after the alumni luncheon under the blue-and-white striped awning. By coincidence they bumped into each other near the statue of Nate outside Connecticut Hall, the one with his feet tied at the ankles, his wrists tied behind his back, his fists clenched—in fear? in anger? in exhilaration (the Weeder's pet theory, unproven) at the prospect of putting one over on the enemy?

"That was an interesting talk you gave this morning," Wanamaker remarked.

"I didn't think you heard a word I said," the Weeder retorted.

"Actually, I didn't. I was just being polite." Wanamaker hadn't been able to cap the giggle that bubbled to the surface.

"Well," the Weeder said, "everyone steps out of character now and then." He eyed Wanamaker suspiciously. He knew that Wanamaker worked for the Company. As new recruits, their paths had crossed during basic training at the Farm; they had even found themselves in the same classroom when the famous Admiral Toothacher turned up for three days of guest lectures on the fundamentals of intelligence methodology. "So what governments are you stabbing in the back these days?" the Weeder asked Wanamaker as they stood in front of the statue of Nate.

Wanamaker, suddenly expressionless, was all business. "What's your clearance?"

"High enough so I can know if the President can know." The Weeder noticed Wanamaker's clothes. He had dressed his squat American body in a rumpled Italian suit. As far as the Weeder could see, neither did anything for the other.

"Sorry," Wanamaker shot back. And he flashed his smug mail-order smile that never failed to set the Weeder's teeth on edge.

"Maybe I'll ask around," the Weeder said. He would have given anything to wipe the smile off Wanamaker's face.

"Maybe you won't ask around," Wanamaker snapped in annoyance.

"What'll happen if I do? What'll happen if I find out? Will the world come to an end? Or even better, your career?"

"If you were to find out"—other members of the class of 1973 were approaching so Wanamaker lowered his voice—"I suppose I'd have to get you murdered."

It was a challenge if the Weeder ever heard one. Like Nate, there was never one he wouldn't rise to. It had taken the Weeder two months to discover that Wanamaker had been farmed out to an interagency working group; another month to learn about the existence of Operations Subgroup Charlie; several more weeks to get hold of the subgroup's telephone number (the Weeder finally wormed it out of a secretary in Disbursing who believed the story about Yale wanting to offer Wanamaker an honorary degree).

At which point the Weeder had slipped Wanamaker's phone number onto the list that his IBM mainframe was monitoring.

14

The streets of lower Manhattan were teeming with New Yorkers who had seeped out of their apartments at the first hint of sunshine. Most of them, the Weeder noticed, were going around in twos; he couldn't help thinking that, from a historical point of view, it was curious that the basic social unit of Western civilization had become the couple. In older, more heroic times, men had been able to validate their maleness in ways that had nothing to do with women: hunting, fighting, voyages of exploration, or in Nate's case, confronting death with courage. Nowadays it appeared as if most men validated their maleness by seducing women. Which meant that no matter how the deed was dressed up, seduction was essentially a self-serving activity. The women the Weeder had been intimate with in his life—his ex-wife for one, the half dozen or so who had come before and after her also—seemed to have sensed this; seemed to have held part of themselves back, as if the principal sentiment they had for the men in their lives was resentment.

It was an odd trend of thought for a sunny Sunday

morning. Were the Weeder's anonymous love letters to Wanamaker his way of getting back at him, seventeen years after the fact? Or was there more to it than met the eye? Was the Weeder—laboring away in his SoHo cubbyhole on a project far from the mainstreams of history, and notably unsuccessful in establishing long-lasting relationships with the women in his life—was he validating his maleness by jousting in the modern manner with an old foe? Was he taking out his frustrations on someone who was doing roughly the same thing he was doing, and for the same employer? Or as Admiral Toothacher used to say when he outlined alternative scenarios in his course on the fundamentals of intelligence methodology: All of the above, or none of the above, or any combination thereof.

In short: Whose truth? Which truth?

The Weeder was still mining this vein of thought as he keyed his computer and brought the menu up onto his screen. It had been a slow night. There was an interesting item in the Chinese Bin; Savinkov had discovered that the FBI had staked out a dead letter drop of his behind the radiator in the men's room at the Isabella Stewart Gardner Museum in Boston. The Weeder weighed the information for a moment, decided not to disseminate it. The last thing in the world he wanted was for the FBI to call off the stakeout. Savinkov might notice the stakeout had been canceled and conclude that the FBI knew that he knew the dead drop had been compromised, at which point Savinkov, an old pro, would suspect his conversations were being overheard.

The Weeder punched another code into his computer, calling up the new material in Farmer's Almanac. There were pinpoints of light on the screen. Letters appeared. Words began to coalesce into phrases, sentences.

"Who? Who? Who? . . . Who?"

"Why? Why? . . . Why? Why?"

"Me? Why would I do it?"

". . . any of your people . . . qualms, moral or operational."

". . . not the answer."

"Or all of the above. Or none . . . Or any combination . . ."

The Weeder smiled. That would be Admiral Toothacher speaking.

"He knows the code name . . ."

"He knows the date . . ."

". . . curiouser and curiouser."

There was a pause as the computer scanned. The Weeder was hardly aware of the whirring of the tapes coming from behind the partition. More words began to appear on the screen.

". . . target . . ."

". . . center at Kabir . . . an American five-megawatt . . ."

". . . ninety-three percent enriched uranium . . . enough for a . . ."

"Laser enrichment tech . . ."

". . . separate weapon-grade uranium from ordinary . . ."

". . . or move to plutonium two thirty-nine . . ."

". . . Nagasaki-type bomb . . ."

". . . Nagasaki-type explosion . . ."

15

A Puerto Rican handyman wearing a spotless white knee-length surgical smock was putting up the last lithograph in the office of the new Deputy Director for Intelligence as the Weeder was ushered in.

"Higher," ordered the DDI, whose name was Rudd. He peered at the Weeder over granny glasses that had slipped down along his nose and waved him toward one of the two chairs drawn up facing his desk. "That may be a shade too high," he told his handyman. "What's your opinion, Mr. Sibley?"

"I'd move it more to the left so it's off center. I hate things that are centered."

"I'm not sure I agree," the DDI said. He flashed a lopsided smile that had more pain than pleasure in it. "Things that are centered are very . . . satisfying." He turned to the handyman. "Lower it, Henry, if you will, about two inches. Right there. That's fine."

The handyman marked the spot and tapped in a nail and hung the frame from it. Stepping back, he studied the placement of the lithograph. "I think I agree with your friend here," he said.

"If I decide to change things," the DDI said crisply, "I'll give you a buzz."

"Say the word," the handyman said. He gathered up his tools in a rectangular metal basket and left, closing the door behind him.

The DDI nodded toward the lithograph. "It's a Maillol, in case you're interested. Number twenty-three of fifty. In those days they kept the print run small in order to keep the value up." The DDI, who was in his shirt sleeves, toyed with one of his gold cuff links as he studied his guest over the granny glasses. "Trip down all right?"

"I caught a noon shuttle from LaGuardia. I sat next to a lady stockbroker who wore too much perfume. Other than that there was no problem."

"Now that they've banned cigarettes I suppose the next thing they ought to do is ban perfume."

The Weeder nodded. "They ought to put a warning on the flasks. 'The Surgeon General has determined that perfume can be hazardous to your health.'"

"You found the car without any trouble?" the DDI asked.

"It was nice of you to lay it on."

"I'm told you're known as the Weeder. Where does the name come from?"

"It's English, I think. Our friends at MI5 and MI6 call the academic types who sort through old dossiers weeders. I was trained as a historian, which is another way of saying I like browsing through files and I'm not allergic to dust. When I came on board I was put to work in the archives. When someone filed a request for a dossier under the Freedom of Information Act, I had to weed through the files to see what could be safely given out, and what had to be plowed under. My boss, Mr. Linkletter, had done a tour in the London bureau—he took to calling me the Weeder. The name stuck. It was sort of an in-house joke."

"You must have come across a lot of dirty laundry in your day," the DDI mused. He smiled another of his lopsided smiles that seemed to invite a reply.

The Weeder smiled back noncommittally. If the new DDI had an appetite for dirty laundry, he ought to feed him Operations Subgroup Charlie and Stufftingle. A terrorist group was going to try and explode a primitive atomic device at some place called Kabir on the Ides of March. But Wanamaker didn't seem to be doing anything, as far as the Weeder could make out, to stop it. Even American nationals in the target zone, wherever that was, would not be warned. If that wasn't dirty laundry, what was?

"My predecessor," Rudd was saying, "tells me you run a highly sensitive No Distribution operation. He says you report directly to the DDI. No chain of command. No cutouts. You want to put me in the picture?"

The Weeder said, "My pleasure." He glanced again at the Maillol lithograph; he still thought it would look better off center. "About ten years ago, in the late seventies, our technical people discovered that an ordinary telephone picked up conversation even when it was on its cradle. The telephone transmitted tiny impulses that could be isolated and converted into recognizable speech. The hurdle was that the equipment used to pick up these impulses was bulky and had to operate in the immediate vicinity of the telephone being targeted. The tech boys worked on the problem. What they came up with was equipment that was more sensitive and could operate at almost any distance from the target telephone. The impulses were still incredibly weak when they arrived at the monitoring station, but with the help of a computer programmed to read the impulses, we were able to get recognizable speech. The bottom line is that we are able to transform a cradled telephone into a bug."

The DDI's eyebrows actually danced. "Are you telling me that you can sit in your loft in SoHo and dial any number in America and eavesdrop on conversations near the phone?"

"That's about it," the Weeder said. "The way I figure, if you steal documents you can never know for sure whether what you find out you were meant to find out. You can never know if you are stealing the right documents. But when you steal conversations you're getting a look into someone's head—you're getting a glimpse of the thought process. And that's worth its weight in gold."

Rudd glanced uneasily at the phone on his desk. "Could the opposition be doing the same thing to us?"

"Not likely—we monitor their computer capability carefully. They don't have the know-how. Yet."

"How did you come to run this operation?"

The Weeder shrugged. "I picked up a working knowledge of Russian at college, and the Russians were obviously going to be our principal target. I knew how to program computers. I was bored stiff working in Mr. Linkletter's archives. I hated Washington. When they offered me the opportunity to run an operation of my own in New York, I jumped at the chance."

"How long have you been at it?"

"Eight months now."

"How are you funded?"

"Our budget is buried in computer procurement. We're a cheap date. Two salaries. One rent. One IBM mainframe. And since we never actually phone up anyone, we don't even have a phone bill outside the basic trunk line fee."

"How many phones are you listening in on?"

"We're a pilot program, Mr. Rudd. We have one computer and two hundred and fifty trunk lines. At any given moment we target roughly two hundred forty numbers. My computer converts the impulses into recognizable speech. Since it would be impossible to read through everything—during any twenty-four-hour period we collect a mountain of intercepted conversations—I program the computer to scan for key words or phrases. My colleague and I monitor the juicy parts of the conversations."

The DDI's face screwed up so intently it looked as if his skin had been under water too long. "What you're doing is illegal—the Company has no charter to operate in America."

"As I understand it, that's why we're run on a No Distribution basis and I report directly to you."

"That doesn't get us off the hook."

"If it helps any, most of our targets are Russians or East Europeans working out of the United Nations or the various Washington embassies."

The DDI treated himself to a deep breath. "What kind of stuff have you come up with so far?"

"Nuggets. For instance, we learned two days ago that Savinkov is getting one of his cipher clerks to sell us the February key to the embassy's class seven messages."

"How do you disseminate?"

"The nuggets I write up so they look as if they come from conventional intercepts. The rest I burn. My problem is to refine the computer program so that I get more wheat and less chaff. Your predecessor said that when we got the wrinkles out he would push for funds to increase our computer capacity so we could listen in on two thousand five hundred phones at a time. If things went well we eventually hoped to target twenty-five thousand."

The DDI scratched absently at a very red lobe of a very large ear. The Weeder wondered whether Rudd was a closet drinker; if the secrets were too heavy it might be the only way to cope with the workload. "You mentioned," the DDI said, "that *most* of your targets were Russians or East Europeans. I'd like to hear about the exceptions."

A sheepish grin crept onto the Weeder's face. "Your predecessor was hauled over the coals once by Senator Woodbridge."

"I remember that," the DDI chuckled. "I was his sword

carrier when he went up to the Hill to face the music. Woodbridge must have been having his period that day—he was as bitchy as a dog in heat."

"I was instructed to add Senator Woodbridge to my list," the Weeder said. "When I came down to Langley, which was usually once every month or six weeks, I gave your predecessor the transcripts."

"Did he get anything on Woodbridge?"

"Nothing he could use."

"Any other targets who aren't Russians or East Europeans?"

"I have a couple of journalists from *The Washington Post* who were getting too close to some of our Latin American operations—your predecessor wanted to know their sources. I have a couple of assistants to the congressmen who control the Company's purse strings. I have three businessmen who do a lot of import-export business with the Saudis. I have two, maybe three, antinuclear types—one's a well-known movie star. I think the late Director himself asked your predecessor to see what we could come up with on her."

"That's it?" Again, a lopsided smile that invited the confession of sins appeared on the DDI's face.

The Weeder was on the verge of mentioning Wanamaker. But what could he say? That he had targeted his Yale roommate because he once fed LSD to the Weeder's girlfriend, who then jumped to her death from a fifth-floor window? The DDI, who had fingers in a lot of pies, might know that Admiral Toothacher was walking back a cat for Wanamaker;

might put two and two together and realize the love letters came from the Weeder. And he would be out on his ear, job-hunting in academia.

The Weeder shook his head. "That's it."

"Okay. Here's what I want you to do. I want you to scrub all targets that are non-Russian, non-East European. I want you to destroy every trace of these intercepts. If our friends at Oversight ever get wind of what you're up to, they might sit still for it if the targets are Russians and East Europeans. But they'll go straight through the roof—we'll have a major scandal on our hands—if they find out we're bugging journalists and one of their own."

The Weeder nodded. "Only foreign nationals from here on out."

The DDI glanced at his watch, which was gold and curved so that it hugged his wrist. "Why do you stay with the Company, Mr. Sibley? With your skills you could command a lot of money in the marketplace."

"To use a very old-fashioned word," the Weeder replied, "I consider myself a patriot. I want to be useful."

"Do you have a feeling you are being useful?"

"I see myself as a small cog in a large machine that is America's first line of defense," the Weeder said, and he meant every word.

"You believe in this Company of ours?"

"I believe in this country of ours. To the extent that the Company protects the country, I believe in the Company."

The DDI stood up and offered his hand across the desk.

The Weeder stood on his side and accepted it. "I am told you are a descendant of . . ." the DDI started to say.

The Weeder cut him off. "Not of him. Of his brother. My great-grandfather's great-grandfather was his brother."

"Good bloodline," the DDI commented. "When will you be coming down to Washington again?"

"I have three weeks leave on the books," the Weeder said. "I was planning to take them now if you see no objection."

"What do you do with yourself for R and R? Are you an angler? A skier? A mountain climber?"

The Weeder grinned sheepishly. "I am a bookworm, Mr. Rudd. For play, I bury myself in the corners of libraries and read."

16

The head archivist, E. Everard Linkletter, was tickled to see the Weeder. He polished his eyeglasses with the tip of his tie and fitted them back over his eyes. "Always a pleasure to see one of my old boys," he chirped. Linkletter, who had the delicate bone structure of a bird and eyes that watered at the hint of an emotion, lifted a mountain of dossiers off his desk and set them down on the floor. "Pull over a chair. I'll get us some Darjeeling. Things haven't been the same since we lost you. You had a way with computers, didn't you? Oh, dear, which of these buttons do you think connects me with the woman who claims to be my secretary?" He tried them one after the other, shouting, "Anybody home?" at each stop until he found signs of life. "Tea for two, two for tea," he called. He looked at the Weeder and rolled his head from side to side in satisfaction. "You haven't decayed as much as you might have," he said.

"You never change," the Weeder said, but Linkletter swatted away the compliment as if it were an insect. "I'm feeling very short and very fat today," he said morosely. He pouted as if the words themselves had a bad taste. "And very old—too old, too old. You know what they say about old age? Old age, they say, is not for sissies. Well, I'm not sure where that leaves me. My sight's going. My hearing's going. My lower back, my knees have long since gone. My digestion is reasonable if I don't drink too much. But who wants to go through what's left of life not drinking too much? Tell me what you are up to these days, Silas?"

The Weeder offered up one of his sheepish grins. "This is not the kind of shop where you want to ask that sort of question."

Linkletter sighed. "Don't I know it. The only thing that keeps me chained to my desk is my appetite for the pension I get in two years, three months and twelve days."

He pulled a fresh pack of menthol cigarettes from a desk drawer, slid the cellophane wrapper off it and placed it on the blotter halfway between himself and his guest. "I don't remember if you smoke," he remarked.

The Weeder said he didn't and never had.

"Neither do I anymore," Linkletter said with sudden enthusiasm. "But my victory over the weed is meaningless if there is no temptation. In order to feel superior to cigarettes you have to lust after them." Linkletter swiveled impatiently toward his intercom and stabbed at a button. "Where, where, where in God's name is my tea?" he cried plaintively.

"Tea," an aggravated voice replied, "requires boiling water. Boiling water requires the application of heat. The application of heat requires time."

Turning back to the Weeder, Linkletter spread his hands in embarrassment. "You would think they were bringing it all the way from India," he said. "Well, now, to what whim of wind do I owe the pleasure of your calling at my port?"

"I was passing through," the Weeder said. "I thought I'd stop by and say hello."

"Old time's sake, that sort of thing?"

"Old time's sake," the Weeder agreed.

"There's nothing you're looking for? No tidbit of information you want to get your hands on without going through channels?"

"Now that you mention it—"

Linkletter sighed again; it came across as a long drawn-out comment on the human condition. "I have not been a Company archivist for twenty-two years, eighteen months and eighteen days—and head archivist for the last eighteen years, seven months and no days—for nothing, my young friend."

The Weeder leaned toward Linkletter. "Have you ever come across a reference to something called Kabir?"

"Are you thinking of applying there for a teaching position?" Linkletter asked with a small guttural laugh that sounded like a hiccup. "I'm not sure you speak the language."

"What language would that be?" the Weeder wanted to know.

"Persian, some Kurdish, some Arabic, various strains of Turkic. You are talking about Amir Kabir College, formerly the Polytechnic College of Tehran University. As a matter of fact, the Company has been keeping rather close tabs on this particular institute of quote unquote higher learning for some time now. The dossier would take you a week to speed-read through."

"What's so special about Amir Kabir College?"

"Why, it's a nuclear research center—the only one in Iran. That's what's special. It houses a five-megawatt research reactor," Linkletter added. "If my memory serves me, and I will be the first to concede that it almost always does, the reactor has a fuel load of five kilograms of enriched uranium, which is enough to construct a nuclear weapon if the ayatollahs can get the technology right. Which so far, thanks to God, they have shown no signs of doing." Linkletter lowered his head as if he intended to butt it against something. "Amir Kabir College is cross-filed under the heading 'Islamic bomb.' You see what I am driving at?"

In the Weeder's experience there was a magical moment when you were working out any puzzle—it came when a single piece fitted in that suddenly allowed you to see the entire picture. This was such a moment. He saw what Linkletter was driving at, all right, and more. He saw what Wanamaker was up to. He saw what Stufftingle was all about. He saw why American nationals wouldn't be warned. In his mind's eye he saw the Nagasaki-type bomb and the Nagasaki-type explosion, and the mushroom cloud spiraling up into the sky over Amir Kabir College in Tehran.

"I'll bet," the Weeder told Linkletter, "the ayatollahs have lasers to separate weapons-grade uranium from ordinary uranium."

"As a matter of fact," Linkletter said, "there is a school of Company thought which holds that the four lasers supposedly stolen from France in 1978 wound up in Tehran."

"At Amir Kabir College?"

"It would be the logical home for them."

Linkletter, pouting, depressed the button on his intercom again. "Tea," he cried in desperation, "should not be beyond the capacity of the Company to produce in a period of time that has some relation to when the request was made."

"Feel free," the secretary retorted, "to dispense with my services when you judge they are no longer useful. Get someone else to run your errands. If you can."

Smiling blandly, the archivist nodded to himself as if he had confirmed something he already knew. "The secretarial instinct," he informed the Weeder, "is being bred out of the species. What, I put it to you, is this world coming to?" He eyed the Weeder with something akin to physical desire. "Why did you ask me about Kabir? What do you know that we don't?"

"I know," the Weeder said quietly, "that the world is not centered."

The archivist nodded grimly. "If you ask me, it may even be upside down."

17

Waiting to have his pass and thumbprint verified in the lobby, the Weeder considered the options. It was crystal clear what Wanamaker was up to. (How could he have failed to see it before?) Rods. Hair triggers. Wedges. It wasn't terrorists who were going to explode a primitive atomic device; it was Wanamaker and his people at Operations Subgroup Charlie. They had smuggled enough uranium into Tehran—probably onto the campus of Tehran University itself—to go critical and set off an uncontrolled chain reaction, otherwise (here the Weeder mimicked in his head the voice of his physicist friend) known as an atomic explosion. Why become a world power if we are afraid to wield that power so that the world functions in a way that is congenial to us? one of Wanamaker's people had asked. Why indeed? They were going to blow up Tehran University and Tehran, along with the Ayatollah and his army of anti-American fanatics, and make that part of the world congenial. The explosion would be primitive enough so that everyone would assume the Iranians had been trying to put together an Islamic bomb at the Kabir College reactor, which had gone off accidentally. Play with fire, the editorials would say, and you get burned.

My side, the Weeder thought, is going to commit an atrocity. But what could he do to stop it? He couldn't waltz up to the DDI, or the Director himself, and blow the whistle. Wanamaker was a Company employee, which made Stufftingle a Company operation. He couldn't take his evidence to *The Washington Post* or the Intelligence Oversight Committee without ruining the Company and depriving America of its first line of defense; there were many in the press or in Congress who would relish the opportunity to castrate the Company on the basis of Stufftingle. The Weeder wouldn't—he couldn't!—give them the chance. He had meant what he said about being a patriot.

Which left Wanamaker. He would send him a last love letter announcing that Stufftingle had been exposed—that if a primitive atomic device devastated Kabir College, the world would learn that Wanamaker was responsible for the explosion. Under these circumstances there would be no question of going ahead with the plot. The Weeder, meanwhile, would pull Stufftingle and Wanamaker from his computer hit list, would hide the printouts that had accumulated and take off for New England to let the dust settle. It wasn't a perfect plan. But then, as Admiral Toothacher used to say in his guest lectures at the Farm, the perfect was the enemy of the good.

The Weeder's eyes wandered to the inscription on one wall of the lobby. He had read it a hundred times without giving it a second thought, without weighing the implications of such a phrase being in such a building. AND YE SHALL KNOW THE TRUTH, the inscription read, AND THE TRUTH SHALL MAKE YOU FREE.

Whose truth? Which truth?

18

I'm up to the part where my man Nate takes two steps forward:

I see it in my mind's eye: a morning fog saturated with sunlight would have dampened the sound of reveille. Nate would probably not have heard it in any case. Sitting Indian-style on a deer skin inside his tent, he was deeply engrossed in M. de Ramsay's *Travels of Cyrus, Prince of Persia* (given to him, on his graduation from Yale, by his younger brother Richard, who was the great-grandfather of my great-grandfather). Nate loved reading about the heroes of antiquity. He often daydreamed about them, imagining what life had been like back in the time of the *Iliad*; imagining, too, how he would have conducted himself had he lived then. He liked to think he had the makings of a hero. But he wasn't absolutely sure.

It was Lieutenant Colonel T. Knowlton's sixteen-year-old son, Frederick, who roused Nate from his reading and summoned him to the meeting. The Colonel, his father, wanted his four captains (Nate among them), his lieutenants, his ensigns to muster in a field outside the camp immediately. Nate's tentmate, W. Hull, rolled over in his blanket and opened an eye and asked what time it was. "Time to move your ass," I can hear Nate replying in a voice full of playfulness. "Time to beat the lobsters and win the war and get on with the business of constructing a country."

Hull might have snorted in derision. "Spare me," he said, or words to that effect.

Laughing, Nate would have marked his page in *Travels of Cyrus* with a slip of paper—I don't see him turning back the corners of pages the way some who have less respect for books do—and headed for the muster field.

The fog would have burned off early that September day, revealing the officers of Knowlton's Rangers drawn up in a casual line on a field in Westchester. Two or three wore breeches and braces but no shirts. One still had the traces of shaving lather on his chin. Hull arrived at muster barefoot. A homemade pennant with a coiled snake and the words DON'T TREAD ON ME hung limply from a pole planted in the middle of the field. Knowlton, impeccably dressed, paced impatiently in front of his officers. Nate noticed a pistol with a silver hilt and an ivory grip jutting from the colonel's waistband. In the early days of the rebellion Knowlton had held the stone-and-rail fence at the base of Breed's Hill (during what became known as the Battle of Bunker Hill, even though it took place on Breed's Hill) against General Howe's flanking movement. The colonel was a soldier's soldier. His Rangers, all volunteers, all handpicked, idolized him. Certainly Nate did, judging from the letters he wrote to his father. In one of them he swore he would walk through fire for Knowlton. The sun, rising above a distant treeline, angled over the colonel's shoulder into Nate's eyes. Squinting, he heard the colonel's booming voice coming from the silhouette in front of the sun. "Men," Knowlton was saying, "Long Island has been lost. Howe went and ferried fifteen thousand lobsters to Graves End Bay and quick-marched them through the unguarded Jamaica Pass to fall on us from the flank. Our boys, them that could, retreated onto the Brookland Heights and escaped, thanks to the Marbleheaders and their longboats, across the East River to Manhattan Island. The Commander-in-Chief has gone and ordered me to send someone to reconnoiter behind the lobster lines in Brookland. He has got to know where the next blow will fall."

Here Knowlton stopped pacing and, facing his officers, placed his hands on his hips. When he spoke again he didn't beat around the bush. "What I want," he said, "what I need, is a volunteer for a dirty, dangerous mission."

What he wants, Nate thought to himself, is someone who is willing to walk through fire.

Nate was suddenly aware of the total lack of movement around him; his comrades seemed to have turned into statues. The colonel, observing this, grimaced in embarrassment. "Must I return to the Commander-in-Chief and report that none of his officers, not a one, had the courage to take a few steps forward? Surely the rebellion is destined to go down to defeat if this represents the general attitude."

I have imagined the scene a thousand times; imagined Knowlton furiously challenging his officers with his feverish eyes; imagined them avoiding his gaze; imagined what must have been going through Nate's head. He would have been remembering Hickey tiptoeing along the floorboards of the dray until there was no more dray to tiptoe along. He would have been picturing the executed man dancing at the end of the rope until a tough cookie of a shirtman extinguished his hiccuping and his life. He would have felt his heart sinking under the weight of pure fear—spies, when caught, were hanged by the neck until they were stone dead. If I know my man Nate, he would have tested himself against that fear.

Do you see it? I do. On that muggy September morning, with a faint breeze from Long Island Sound stirring the crabgrass and the sun lolling lazily over Knowlton's shoulder, Nate found himself taking two steps forward.

Back in their tent, Hull and Stephen Hempstead both tried to talk Nate out of his decision. "It's one thing to stand up to the lobsters in battle," Hull—who happened to be a Yale classmate of Nate's—declared. "It's another to be asked to undertake something that is unmanly, even dishonorable. Who in his right mind respects the character of a spy?"

"No one," Hempstead offered.

"As soldiers," Hull continued ardently, "we are bound to do our duty in the field. But we are not obliged to stain our honor by the sacrifice of integrity."

"For God's sake, listen to him," Hempstead begged. "Don't play the hero."

"People who want to be heroes are raving mad," Hull said.

"People who want to be spies," Hempstead agreed, "are raving mad."

But Nate, once fixed on a course of action, was not easily dissuaded. "You talk of dishonor," he told his two friends. "I wish to be useful, and every kind of service to the cause becomes honorable by being useful."

Stephen Hempstead tried another approach. "You are making a big mistake if you think spying is useful. In the end it might even hurt the cause."

"Explain yourself," Nate ordered.

Hempstead looked at Hull, who nodded encouragement. "The way I figure it," Hempstead said, "a spy can never know for sure whether what he finds out he was meant to find out. Not knowing, it's just as likely he will pass on what the enemy wants passed on, as opposed to useful information."

Nate shook his head. "A spy ought to be able to discover the enemy's capabilities," he insisted, "and then divine his intentions from his capabilities."

"Just because the enemy has a capability don't mean he's going to use it," Hull argued.

"Why would he go to the trouble and expense of having a capability if he's not going to make use of it?" Nate asked. He thought he had his friends there.

Hull shrugged. "You will wind up having your neck stretched on a gibbet."

Nate only said, "*Dulce et decorum est pro patria mori.*"

"It is sweeter to *live* for your country," Hull shot back.

Nate didn't appear convinced.

Here's Nate reporting to the Commander-in-Chief's headquarters that same afternoon:

From the portico of the Roger Morris house on the lip of Coogan's Bluff, Nate stared out at the small Dutch settlement of Haarlem visible on the flats next to the Haarlem River. Wiping sweat from his brow, the Commander-in-Chief came around from behind the house accompanied by a twenty-year-old major named A. Burr, who was an aide-de-camp to Old Put. Along with a handful of other staff officers, they had been exercising in the garden behind the house, seeing who could throw a heavy iron bar the farthest; as usual the Virginian had won the contest. (Behind his back it was whispered that he seemed to be able to win everything except the war.)

The Commander-in-Chief's features, Nate noticed immediately, looked more drawn than the last time he had seen him. It turned out that Congress had just sent word refusing permission to burn New York City to the ground. Burr had been dispatched by Old Put to headquarters to see if the Virginian considered that the final word on the subject. "What if we made out we never got the order?" Burr asked. "What if we burned New York to the ground by accident?"

The Virginian crankily swatted a fly that had landed on his breeches, then flicked the dead insect to the ground with a fingernail. "Rightly or wrongly, Congress rules and we are its servants," he told Burr. "If we reverse these roles we will have lost even if we win."

Nate heard Burr say something about how the army might have a chance of defending the city. "Which army?" the Virginian, clearly in a black mood, sneered. "Sometimes I am not sure whether ours is one army or thirteen."

A. Hamilton, one of the Virginian's bright young aides, offered the Commander-in-Chief his wig but was waved away. "I told Mr. Henry in Philadelphia, and I repeat it to you, Major Burr," the Virginian said, "I date the ruin of my reputation from the day I took command of the American Armies." The Commander-in-Chief glanced curiously at Nate, who was standing outside the front door. Hamilton whispered something in the general's ear. "Just the man I've been waiting on," the Virginian said. Gesturing for Nate to follow, he set off down the hallway, his riding boots pounding on Mr. Morris's imported teak floorboards.

The Virginian sank dejectedly onto a straight-backed chair behind a desk in the middle of the octagonal drawing room. Hamilton came in behind Nate and pulled the sliding doors closed. Nate looked out through the mullioned windows—some of the general's aides were still tossing the iron bar behind the house and he could hear their cries as they egged one another on. He glanced at the Virginian and noticed him picking with a fingernail at a tooth brown with decay; several of the Virginian's teeth seemed to be false and made of wood. Nate spotted two books on the desk and angled his head to read their titles. One was a worn copy of Frederick's

Instructions to His Generals, with tongues of paper jutting where someone had marked off pages. The other book was a leather-bound edition of Addison's tragedy, *Cato*, easily the most popular English play of the day because of its talk of liberty.

"State your name," the general instructed Nate.

Nate replied in a firm voice.

"The mission is dangerous. Why are you volunteering?"

"To use a very old-fashioned word, I consider myself a patriot. I want to be useful."

"You think risking your neck behind enemy lines will be useful?"

"Excellency, I see myself as a small cog in a large machine that is America's first line of defense."

"You believe in this army of ours?"

"I believe in this country of ours, Excellency. To the extent that the army protects the country, I believe in the army."

"Well answered, in effect," the Virginian said. He had caught Nate eyeing his copy of *Cato*, and asked, "Have you by chance read the Addison play?"

"Several times, Excellency. I own a copy but left it with my other books at my father's house in Connecticut."

"So you are a Connecticut man," the Virginian said dryly. "I regret to tell you that that is not much of a recommendation these days. Hamilton here has been counting noses since the debacle on Long Island. It appears that six of the eight thousand men in the thirteen Connecticut militia regiments have vanished."

"Gone home to Connecticut, no doubt," Hamilton said. "Did the same thing before the battle of Breed's Hill. Their enlistments were up and nothing any of us said could convince them to stay."

"I will tell you frankly," the Virginian burst out, "there is such a dearth of public spirit, such a want of virtue, such stockjobbing to obtain advantages . . ."

(Stockjobbing: *colloq v.* buying and selling, usually stocks, but in the Virginian's sense, anything, to profit from price fluctuations. A curious accusation, coming as it did from the man who introduced the mule into America and was trying to get Congress to purchase, at a handsome price, some of his mules for use as army pack animals.)

"—such a mercenary spirit pervading the whole army that I should not be surprised at any disaster that may happen."

Nate glanced at Colonel Hamilton, but he was sucking on the inside of a cheek and studying his boots. The Virginian reached into his mouth again with two fingers, gripped one of his wooden teeth and gingerly worked it back and forth in his gums. "Damn glue's come loose," he muttered under his breath. "You would think a world that could come up with Watt's steam engine and Arkwright's spinning frame could invent a glue that can hold a tooth in place for more than a week."

The Commander-in-Chief treated himself to a deep breath; the storm seemed to have blown itself out. He fetched a rolled-up map of Manhattan Island from a spruce document box and spread it on the desk, weighing down the ends with two large cut glass cellars, an inkwell and his silver pocket watch. "I take it you are no stranger to Manhattan," the Virginian said. "But are you familiar with Long Island?"

"I spent three weeks there with Colonel Webb's Nineteenth Connecticut right after coming down from Boston in late April," Nate replied.

The Virginian, Nate and Colonel Hamilton bent over the map. The Commander-in-Chief's finger began to stab at it. "Our main body is here," he said, "on the Haarlem Heights. General Putnam has five thousand men down here in the city, but he's going to start pulling them back toward the heights. I figure it'll take him the better part of a week to get his cannon out—he lacks horses, wagons. I loaned Put one of my own riding horses, that's how bad things are. A mare. Hope to God I get her back in one piece."

The Virginian's index finger traced a line along the Brookland coast running up to the western reaches of Long Island Sound. "Howe's regiments are stretched out here, looking down our throats from across the river. No telling when they'll come over or where. I've posted militia units at the likely landing sites—that cove under the Kipp house, below the Murray Hill at Inclenberg, on the flats near the Dover Tavern. But I don't have high hopes of stopping them on the beaches. Our troops are green as grasshoppers—my guess is they'll cut and run as soon as the lobsters bring up some of their line ships and start to cannonade them."

Hamilton caught the expression on Nate's face, "Things aren't as bleak as they appear," he remarked. "As long as the lobsters strike *below* the Haarlem Heights, the general feels confident we can pull most of our troops back to the heights. And the general wins as long as he doesn't lose."

"The heights form a natural defensive line," the Virginian added, talking to himself now, it seemed to Nate; it seems also to me. "After what happened to Howe at Breed's Hill, back in Boston, I don't reckon he'll risk sending his thin red lines straight up the hill at us. We might be able to hold on to the heights for weeks. Months even. Long enough for me to put some starch back into my thirteen armies. Long enough for Congress to vote bonuses so I can enlist new regiments. Long enough to train the ones I already have. With luck the rebellion could have a breathing spell. Unless—"

"Unless?" Nate asked.

"Unless Howe decides to ferry troops up the East River, risk the currents at Hell Gate, and land them in Westchester. From there it's nine miles as the crow flies to the North River and King's Bridge connecting Manhattan to Westchester. If Howe brought up enough troops he could fortify those nine miles, cutting us off on Manhattan. His brother's ships could patrol the two rivers, keeping us pinned here on the heights until we ran out of food. My army—my thirteen armies—would disintegrate. That would be the end of the rebellion and our dream of independence."

Nate couldn't keep from asking, "If that's a possibility, why don't you pull back to Westchester right away instead of fortifying the Haarlem Heights?"

The Virginian slipped the pocket watch into his waistcoat

pocket and lifted one of the cellars. The map snapped back into a roll. "There is nothing more difficult in warfare than organizing the retreat of a defeated army," the Commander-in-Chief said. "I need a victory under my belt—I need to lift morale and hopes—before I can risk a retreat into Westchester. If I attempted it now the armies I have the honor to command would melt away. Inside of a week I would be retreating with Hamilton here and nary a soul in sight."

Someone could be heard galloping up to the house. There were shouts from the portico. The Virginian started for the sliding doors. "What I need to purchase," he called over his shoulder to Nate, "is time. I must know what the lobsters are up to over there in Brookland—I must know if Howe is going to give me time to pull the army together for a retreat."

What transpired after the Virginian left the room I gleaned from reading between the lines of a letter A. Hamilton sent to a Connecticut journalist years later. Hamilton wrote out a *laisser-passer* so that Nate could get across Long Island Sound from one of the Westchester ports. And he gave Nate the name of a patriot in Brookland, the widow of one of the Minutemen killed at Concord, who could put him up while he was scouting the lobster positions. Hamilton even suggested a cover story: If accosted, Nate would claim to be whipping the cat.

"Whipping the cat?" Nate must have asked. (I don't think he would have been familiar with the expression, which came from the Middle States and the South.)

"Whipping the cat," Hamilton would have explained, "is

what itinerant shoemakers call it when they board with a client for as long as it takes to repair his shoes and boots."

Hamilton noted that the lobsters might have occupied New York City by the time Nate reached Long Island; in which case Nate was to nose around the city too and see what he could pick up there. He gave Nate the name of a patriot he could contact in the city, an Israelite recently arrived from Poland, a banker who had loaned sums of money to the rebellion.

It must have occurred to Hamilton (it certainly would have occurred to me) to ask Nate if he had any acquaintances or relatives on Long Island or in New York City who knew he held a captaincy in the Continental Army and might betray him if they spotted him. "There is one such," Nate admitted. He had a cousin, Samuel by name, a lawyer from Providence, nine years older and an ardent Tory. Samuel, who was a Harvard man, had gone over to the enemy in Boston and had sailed away with them when they abandoned the city. Nate had heard on the family grapevine that this same Samuel was serving as Howe's Deputy Commissary of Prisoners in New York.

"I don't need to tell you," Hamilton said, "that you must avoid him at all cost."

"The chances of us running into each other are one in a million," Nate said.

"Which brings us to the matter of codes," Hamilton said.

"I thought I was to bring my report back myself," Nate said.

"You are. But it is prudent to prepare for all eventualities. If you are taken prisoner by the lobsters, the usage and custom of war is such that you will be permitted to write to your family. Your letters will pass through my hands. So I propose we establish code phrases that you can employ in your letters to indicate what you have discovered. Since you are familiar with Addison's *Cato*, and we have a copy at hand, why don't we select phrases from it for you to memorize?"

"No need to memorize," Nate said. "I know most of the play by heart from having read it so often."

"So much the better. You select the phrases." Hamilton handed Nate the Virginian's leather-bound copy.

Nate thumbed through it. "Here is the line that inspired Mr. Patrick Henry's 'Give me liberty or give me death,'" he said. And he passed the book to Hamilton and quoted it from memory. "'Chains, or conquest; liberty, or death.'"

Hamilton copied the phrase into an orderly book. (It was this same orderly book that I discovered four years ago in the Beinecke Library stacks. A handwriting expert has compared the unsigned notations in the orderly book with samples of Hamilton's handwriting and concluded they were written by the same person.) And he told Nate, "Let this phrase stand to mean that the lobsters are going to land behind us, in Westchester, in an effort to trap us on Manhattan island."

Nate flipped through the pages of *Cato* until he came to another patriotic phrase. Again Hamilton copied it off into his orderly book. "Let the second phrase mean the lobsters will give the general the time he needs to prepare the army for retreat," he said.

Hamilton made Nate repeat the phrases and their meanings several times. Then he escorted Nate to the portico of the Morris house. The Virginian was standing with a messenger on the lip of Coogan's Bluff studying the East River through a long glass. In the distance an enemy cutter could be seen tacking from bank to bank as it beat upriver against the wind. A. Hamilton noticed the speck of sail. "It looks as if Howe's testing the currents at Hell Gate," he told Nate. He offered him his hand. "Good luck," he said, "and Godspeed."

19

The bartender, known as Yul because his head was shaven down to his sidewalk-gray scalp, set the whiskey on a paper doily with lacelike edges and slid it across to the man with the toupee, whose name was Howard something or other.

"I'm giving you fair warning," Howard told Huxstep. "I teach mathematics at a junior high school."

"If you don't believe the man," the bartender told Howard, "why don't you put your money where your mouth is?"

Howard ran a finger around the rim of his glass but failed to produce a hum. "There has to be a time limit," he insisted.

Huxstep, sitting two stools away directly across the U-shaped bar from the Admiral, popped some salted peanuts into his mouth and washed them down with a gulp of beer. "Listen, Yul, fifteen seconds is all I need," he said.

The man with the toupee slipped a calfskin wallet from the breast pocket of his blazer, pulled out a crisp fifty-dollar bill and dropped it onto the bar. Huxstep, laughing under his breath, slapped two twenties and a ten on top of it. The mathematics teacher punched some numbers into his wristwatch calculator. "All right, Yul. You count off the fifteen seconds. That way there'll be no discussion." He looked at Huxstep. "Here's the problem. Divide 9876.54 by 4567.89." Yul started to count out loud. "One hundredth. Two hundredths. Three . . ."

Huxstep's eyes strained at the top of their sockets. His lips moved. "The answer's 2.1621667."

Frowning, the mathematics teacher watched Huxstep pocket the money. "I've read about people like you," he told Huxstep. "What's your trick?"

Huxstep laughed. "I'm in love with numbers."

"So am I," Howard gushed. "It's rare to find someone who feels about numbers the way I do." He slipped onto the stool next to Huxstep. "Maybe we could meet for a quiet supper sometime and compare notes. What do you say?"

"What I say," Huxstep said, "is you should fuck off."

Howard smiled smugly. "I like people who play hard to get."

"I'm not playing hard to get," Huxstep informed him. "I am hard to get. Beat it."

Across the bar the Admiral studied his neighbor through lidded, bloodshot eyes. He liked what he saw: the eyebrows plucked into a pencil line, the cheeks lightly rouged, the gold medallion hanging from a delicate gold chain in the *V* of the shirt, the gold studs and the gold cuff links instead of buttons—all the outward signs of a class act. And a body like a Citroën.

So the Admiral talked braininess. "You have a way with

words," he told his neighbor. "May I ask what you wrote your thesis on?"

"Thesis? What thesis?"

"Your PhD thesis."

"PhD! I have never even set foot in college."

"You have to be pulling my leg. Your insights could only come from a systematic investigation of philosophy. More power to you if you are self-taught. You are a bookworm. Own up."

The Admiral's neighbor toyed with a gold-plated lipstick. "I used to read *Reader's Digest* cover to cover."

The Admiral smiled triumphantly. "I could tell there was more to you than looks."

Toothacher's new friend offered a manicured hand. The Admiral seized it eagerly and gave it a conspiratorial squeeze. "My friends call me Pepper," he said.

"If you're Pepper, I'll be Salt."

They both laughed, the Admiral at the prospect of burning another candle at both ends, Salt because what had started out as a dull evening had taken a turn for the better.

The Admiral was about to signal to Yul for refills for himself and his newfound friend when Huxstep came loping over. He nodded toward a booth in the back of the bar, behind the jukebox. "He's here," he mumbled.

The Admiral swiveled on his stool and peered in the direction of the booth. He could make out the figure of a man huddled in its shadows. The figure raised a hand and saluted him with a weak wave.

Toothacher brushed Salt's wrist with his fingertips. "Order yourself a refill on me," he said. "I'll be back in a jiffy." He hiked his lanky body off the stool, ambled across the crowded room and slid into the booth facing the shadowy figure. "Wasn't sure you weren't dead and buried by now."

"I hang in there," chirped E. Everard Linkletter, the Company archivist. "You are looking fit as a fiddle. What lures you up from the Shangri-la for retired naval officers?"

"If I told you would you believe me?"

"Try me."

Toothacher batted both eyes in an innocent wink. "I came up to lobby the Secretary of the Navy for a cost of living increase to my pension."

Linkletter exploded in laughter. "Come on, Pepper. You used to be able to do better than that." The archivist brought a menthol cigarette to his nose and breathed in its aroma. "There was a time when you trusted me with those secrets of yours," he remarked. "Someone's screwed up, hasn't he? The old fox himself, Rear Admiral J. Pepper Toothacher, has been called in to walk back the cat." Linkletter studied Toothacher through dirty eyeglasses. "What are they paying per diem these days, Pepper?"

"Whatever they pay," Toothacher said morosely, "it's not enough." He was thinking of the most recent love letter to Wanamaker, which had arrived that morning, an epistle so tightly held that there was no security rating on the books that pertained, or so Wanamaker had pretended when he flatly refused to let the Admiral see it. *Whoever was writing the love letters,* Wanamaker had ranted in a voice as scruffy as his office, *knew all about Stufftingle and was threatening to expose him if he went through with it.*

"He knows *everything*?" Mildred had asked Wanamaker in alarm.

"Absolutely everything," he had confirmed.

"He knows about the packages we've been smuggling in?" Parker had asked.

Wanamaker had nodded dejectedly.

Webb had shaken his head in disbelief. "He couldn't know *where.* That's simply not possible. Even among ourselves we hardly ever mentioned Kabir."

Wanamaker had flashed a furious look in Webb's direction and the word Kabir had not come up again in the discussion, which had turned around the necessity of canceling Stufftingle. But the Admiral had noted it.

Linkletter raised a finger in an effort to catch Yul's eye. "My doctor told me not to drink, so I switched doctors. What's your pleasure, Pepper?"

"I invited you," Toothacher said. "I'm buying. Are you still presiding over the Company's dusty archives?"

"Here it comes," Linkletter moaned. "It never fails. The day I meet someone who doesn't want to know something outside channels I will give up cigarettes *and* sex."

The Admiral leaned over the table until his head was inches away from Linkletter's. "Does the word *Kabir* ring any bells in that brain of yours?"

Linkletter jerked back in surprise. "I don't believe it," he exclaimed. "I simply refuse to. You're the second person this week to ask me about Kabir."

The Admiral's bulging eyes bored into Linkletter. "Who," he asked, "was the first?"

The Company archivist sighed. "Come on, Pepper. You've known me long enough to know I won't answer a question like that. I don't mind helping out a friend with the odd piece of information he could get by going into the archives himself. But it's not my style to betray compartmentalization."

Toothacher batted his eyes innocently. "And you've known *me* long enough to know I won't let you off the hook easily." The Admiral crooked a forefinger in Linkletter's direction. The archivist leaned cautiously toward Toothacher, who said in an undertone, "People who leave the Company under a cloud would be idiots not to take their private files with them—to make sure the Company didn't change its mind about paying a pension." The Admiral narrowed his eyes to stir his memory. "An excerpt from a police blotter crossed my desk when I worked at counterintelligence. I have a photocopy in Guantánamo. It came from a Tampa, Florida, precinct, I remember. It mentioned lewd behavior. At a playground. Exposing a sexual organ to a minor."

"It wasn't true," Linkletter burst out. "Not a word of it. The minor in question was nineteen years old and a professional. The Director himself decided the evidence was too flimsy, my services too valuable—"

"The Director is dead," Toothacher said in a bored voice. "Long live the Director."

"I retire in two years, three months and nine days," Linkletter whispered plaintively. His eyes watered with emotion. "You wouldn't. . ." He studied Toothacher's weathered features. "You would!"

"Who," the Admiral repeated his question, "was the other person to ask you about Kabir?"

20

In the penumbra of the smoky light filtering through dirty windows, Admiral Toothacher circled the room. His nose twitched of its own accord at the odors—staleness, mildew, stubbed-out cigars, synthetic carpet permeated with dust. He removed the impossibly tacky color photograph of the President from the wall and examined the cobwebs behind it. He ran his fingertips over the joints of the bricked-in chimney. He inspected the once wilting, now dead, plants on top of the safe, lifting them one at a time from their plastic flowerpots. He examined the safe. He tapped a knuckle against the grimy windows, noticed for the first time that there were double panes to prevent lasers from picking off voice vibrations and reproducing what was said in the room.

How could he have done it? he wondered. The paper trail led to dead ends. The people trail also. Which left electronics.

Somehow the author of the love letters had ticked to rods and hair triggers and wedges and Stufftingle and Ides of March, and last but by no stretch of the imagination least, Kabir.

Toothacher circled the conference table as if it were mined. Paper plates, plastic utensils, empty diet cola cans littered the table. On an impulse he swept them with the back of his arm into a large government-issue wastebasket lined with a blue plastic garbage sack. As an afterthought, he jerked off the felt tablecloth scarred with cigarette burns and tossed it into a corner. He watched the particles of dust float up from the felt in the half light and imagined for an instant that he was descending through a cloud of Wanamaker's dandruff.

He warily circled Wanamaker's desk, studying the stains on the glass top. He toyed with the black plastic levers of the squawk box. He slid open a desk drawer. It was filled with hundreds of paper clips bent into distorted shapes. He spun the swivel chair one complete revolution and listened to its squeak. He let his gaze drift to the only other object on the desk—the telephone.

His eyes, which on ordinary days bulged, slowly widened.

"The telephone," he said out loud. A smile of intense satisfaction spread across his sunken cheeks. There was only one truth, and it was knowable—and he had discovered it.

21

The Weeder keyed his computer for the last time before erasing all traces of Stufftingle from the memory bank. He listened to the rotors humming behind the partition. In the morning, he thought, he would put the whole business behind him. Nature would take its course. Wanamaker would have no choice but to cancel Stufftingle. Operations Subgroup Charlie would go back to keeping track of terrorists. And he would lose himself in the dusty stacks of libraries; in history.

Pinpoints of light danced on the screen. Then two words appeared. "The telephone."

It struck the Weeder as odd that someone had come to the office over the weekend, and the only thing he or she had uttered was, "The telephone." What to make of it?

It could be the cleaning lady tidying up. Or part of a longer conversation that the computer had somehow missed.

Whatever it was, it certainly didn't seem important.

22

Huxstep, driving, glanced into the rearview mirror. Wanamaker was staring morosely out a side window, lost in thought. Huxstep shifted his head until he could make out the Admiral. He was cringing against the opposite door, his eyes tightly closed, his lips curled in an expression Huxstep normally associated with motion sickness.

"Is the Admiral carsick?" Huxstep asked solicitously over his shoulder.

Toothacher's hoarse whisper came floating up to the front seat. "The Admiral is sick, but not from the car."

Going around a curve, the Chevrolet's headlights swept a sign indicating they were approaching a crossroad. "Would the Admiral like to tell me where we're going?" Huxstep inquired.

"Would the Admiral maybe like to tell *me* where we're going?" Wanamaker said. He tried to make his voice ooze with irony, but all his own ear picked up was the unmistakable whine of uncertainty.

"Turn right at the crossroad," the Admiral instructed

Huxstep. "Keep going until you come to a small bridge. Then pull up and kill the motor and the lights."

Huxstep found the bridge and did as he was told. The Admiral popped out of his side of the car and ambled onto the one-lane suspension bridge with a sign at each end suggesting that trucks over a certain weight had better find another way of crossing the river. Wanamaker caught up with the Admiral. "Why?" he asked Toothacher.

"Why what?" the Admiral shot back, although he knew what the question would be.

"Why have we come all this way—an hour out of Washington—in the middle of the night? What kind of wild-goose chase are we on?"

Toothacher mumbled something about them needing to talk without being overheard.

"My office has been checked for bugs. If that doesn't satisfy you, we could have gone into the men's room and flushed the toilet while we talked."

In the darkness the Admiral was unable to make out Wanamaker's features, but he could imagine them—his former man Friday would be smirking derisively, he decided. He would be feeling very put upon, very sorry for himself. And he would be wondering what the Admiral knew that he didn't.

"Suppose we start with Operation Stufftingle," Toothacher said.

Wanamaker finally managed to inject some irony into his voice. "Be my guest."

"Stufftingle," Toothacher announced with conviction, "is not a Company operation."

A muscle would be twitching over Wanamaker's right eye about now, the Admiral knew.

Wanamaker asked very quietly, "What makes you think that?"

"I was not born yesterday," the Admiral said. "I figured out that much before I boarded the plane from Guantánamo. If Stufftingle were a Company operation, you would have gotten one of the Company hotshots to walk back the cat for you."

In the darkness of the suspension bridge Wanamaker cleared his throat. It came across as a bad imitation of the river gurgling underfoot. When he started to speak again, his tone of voice told the Admiral that his expression had changed to the one that was expressionless. "You didn't bring me all the way out here to tell me that," is what Wanamaker said.

"Your Operations Subgroup Charlie," the Admiral persisted, "is an iceberg."

Wanamaker's face was suddenly visible as he touched a lighted match to the tip of a Schimmelpenninck. The Admiral confirmed that his expression was totally devoid of expression. "Even outdoors," Toothacher said, "I would prefer it if you didn't smoke."

"Rank," Wanamaker remarked with studied stiffness, "is supposed to have its privileges. Right now I hold the rank of employer."

The Admiral smiled to himself. If he harbored any doubts about Operations Subgroup Charlie being an iceberg, they had been dispelled by Wanamaker's attitude. He was annoyed because Toothacher had stumbled on the truth. Like all petty spirits, his reaction to being annoyed was to annoy back. "The tip of the iceberg visible above the waterline," the Admiral continued, perturbed by the cigar smoke but determined not to give Wanamaker the satisfaction of knowing it, "is a bona fide United States government agency—an Operations Subgroup of SIAWG. You have stationery with letterheads. Embossed. You have written protocols tucked away in your office safe—you're supposed to be keeping track of half a dozen terrorist organizations. You have BIGOT-listed clients in SIAWG and beyond to whom you distribute your product. You have a payroll. You hold meetings. You swipe office supplies. You make personal phone calls on the office phone. You fight for a larger slice of the SIAWG budget. In short, you go through the motions of doing what your charter says you are supposed to be doing."

The end of Wanamaker's Schimmelpenninck glowed brightly in the dark, then became dull again.

"Which brings us to the invisible part of the iceberg, the part underwater," the Admiral continued. "That part of the iceberg is a secret off-the-table operational unit within a known operational unit. My guess is it consists of you, your man Friday, Mildred, plus Parker and Webb. I know from experience how these things are patched together. I used to do roughly the same thing when I ran Naval Intelligence. There are some operations that need to be kept away from the prying eyes of Congressional Oversight. You get the Saudis to funnel their loose change through various and sundry Swiss accounts. You arrange for a cutout or two to muddy the water. If you were a gentleman, I'd be willing to make a gentleman's bet that my per diem, my hotel room with its view of park, all the expenses for the invisible part of your iceberg come from some place other than the United States Treasury Department."

The Admiral thought he heard Wanamaker swallow a yawn. "Am I boring you with things you already know? Only say the word and we will skip ahead."

"Skip. Skip. That way we won't have to stand out here all night."

"No offense intended, but you are certainly not senior enough to have done all this on your own. I assume you were the brainchild of the late, great Director. The Iran-Contra business had his fingerprints all over it. Your Operation Stufftingle does too. It is common knowledge that he liked to cook creatively without having congressional cockroaches scampering around his kitchen. Did he supply you with a specific brief?"

A quarter moon edged out from behind a cloud and the Admiral caught a glimpse of Wanamaker's eyes. There was something about them—a gleam of satisfaction? a pinprick of certitude?—that indicated he was very pleased with himself. At first glance it was hard for Toothacher to see why. At second, too.

Wanamaker shrugged a shoulder. "He gave us a compass heading. We are still marching. Some of us think of our little operation as a memorial to his memory."

"Tch, tch," the Admiral cooed into the night. "How extraordinarily touching." His voice turned singsong; he might have been lecturing on the fundamentals of intelligence methodology at the Farm. "Kabir, of course, is Amir Kabir College in Tehran, which by a curious coincidence happens to have an American five-megawatt nuclear research reactor on campus. And Stufftingle"—the Admiral let the word hang in the cold, moist night air for a long moment—"Stufftingle is the code name of a plot, run by the off-the-shelf unit within Operations Subgroup Charlie, run by you, Wanamaker, to explode an atomic device in Tehran and let the world think the ayatollahs had an accident while trying to fashion a bomb of their own."

The Admiral took Wanamaker's strained silence for assent. He filled his lungs with air until his rib cage ached, then slowly exhaled. "It is an idea whose time had come," he said softly. "Absolutely first-rate. Difficult to see why we didn't do it years ago."

Wanamaker, to the Admiral's intense discomfort, inched closer. "You—approve?" he whispered huskily.

"Perhaps you could see your way clear to extinguishing your cigar now," Toothacher remarked. When Wanamaker sent it spinning into the river, he added, "Of course I approve. An atomic explosion in Tehran will eliminate most of the ayatollahs and discredit the ones who survive. It will leave the secular pragmatist in the driver's seat. Iran will see which side its bread is buttered on and return to the fold. The eastern frontiers of NATO will become secure. Middle East oil will no longer be menaced. The Saudis can go back to worrying how to invest their profits. Stability will return to that part of the world. The Russians will suffer a strategic setback." Here the Admiral employed a gesture he normally reserved for lovers; as uncomfortable as it made him, he forced himself to fling a fatherly arm over Wanamaker's dandruff-flaked shoulders. "The crucial thing is that the explosion must be primitive," he said.

"We thought of that," Wanamaker said proudly. "The technology, the fabrication of the device are straight out of our 1945 atomic manuals."

Wanamaker couldn't see it, but the Admiral was batting both eyes at him in a conspiratorial double wink. "Wedges," Toothacher murmured.

"There was a suggestion," Wanamaker plunged on eagerly, "that we should quietly evacuate American nationals, but I smothered the idea in the crib. Nobody will be able to point a finger at us. The explosion will be a dirty one—plenty of fallout, radioactivity all over the joint, meaning the bomb was primitive, glued together by religious fanatics who didn't know which end was up, who miscalculated the configuration. The ayatollahs fucked up and the thing blew up in their faces."

"Hair triggers," murmured the Admiral.

"We've been smuggling in uranium for a year and a half," Wanamaker confided. "A handful at a time. Hidden in the saddle bags of camels. In the stuffing of pillows. In sacks of fertilizer. The people who were doing the smuggling didn't know they were smuggling, that's how well Parker organized things. It's all sitting there in a sub-basement storage room at a nursing school next to Kabir waiting to blow. When they measure the blast on the Richter scale, they'll trace the center of the explosion to the campus. Kabir's atomic pile went bananas. The chain reaction got out of hand. There was a meltdown, an explosion." Wanamaker was so excited he was stuttering. "B-b-boom. No more K-K-Kabir C-C-College. No more T-T-Tehran."

"Rods," murmured Toothacher. He might have been lulling a baby to sleep.

Wanamaker got a grip on himself. "Teach the bastards to mess around with uranium," he sneered. "You play with fire, what happens is you get burned."

"It's a brilliant scheme," the Admiral said. He removed his arm from Wanamaker's shoulder and turned to stare down at the river, which he could hear but not see. In the distance a train whistle screamed in pain. The Admiral sighed; there was pain in that sound too. "It makes me sick to the stomach to think all that effort is going down the drain because of a handful of love letters."

The comment struck Wanamaker with the force of ice water. "For a minute I forgot about the leak," he said sourly. "If only—"

"If only I'd been able to find out who sent them . . ."

"Yeah. Maybe . . ."

". . . maybe we could have . . ."

"Could have maybe neutralized the threat."

"And gone ahead with Stufftingle."

"Yeah. Gone ahead with Stufftingle," Wanamaker agreed.

The Admiral turned away from the river to face Wanamaker. "It's not too late," he announced.

Wanamaker wasn't sure he had heard correctly. "Not too late for what?"

Toothacher lingered over each word. "Do you happen to know someone named Sibley? Silas Sibley?"

"Yeah," Wanamaker said. "I do know a Silas Sibley. What about him?"

"Does he have a grudge against you? Is there any reason he might be out to get you?"

"It's possible," Wanamaker said carefully.

"How possible?"

"Now that you mention it, very possible. What makes you think Sibley wrote the love letters?"

"He was inquiring about Kabir not too long ago."

"How could he know about Kabir?"

"I spent all day yesterday nosing around the Campus. Came across a lot of fellows I hadn't seen in years. Asked about some of my colleagues. Asked about my students at the Farm. Heard you were running something called Operations Subgroup Charlie over at SIAWG, keeping track of terrorist groups. Heard Sibley ran some kind of computerized operation out of New York. Very hush-hush. No one seemed to know for sure what he was up to. It couldn't be archives because they're here in Washington. Which leaves eavesdropping."

"Huxstep swept the office for bugs," Wanamaker reminded the Admiral. "And the windows have double panes so nobody can pick off voice vibrations."

"Your windows are too dirty to pick anything off them," the Admiral couldn't keep from commenting.

Wanamaker was thinking out loud now. "It couldn't be Parker or Webb or Mildred who tipped him off—none of them would give the time of day to someone like Sibley. The asshole thinks he's some kind of intellectual. All he's got is a good memory."

"Which narrows it down to . . ." The Admiral let the sentence trail off. He could sense Wanamaker leaning toward him in the darkness, holding his breath so as not to risk missing a word.

"Which narrows it down to?" Wanamaker prompted when the Admiral didn't continue.

"The telephone," Toothacher said triumphantly.

Wanamaker laughed out loud. "First thing I had Huxstep do was check the telephone for bugs."

"You don't understand," Toothacher whispered. "There's no bug *in* the telephone. The telephone *is* the bug. Back in the seventies, before I retired, I remember hearing rumors about equipment that could convert weak impulses picked up by ordinary telephones on their own cradles into recognizable speech. Nobody thought there was much of a future in it—the equipment was huge and had to be quite near the target phone, as in the next room. Which ruled out listening to the Russian ambassador talking to his station chief. Which ruled out almost everything except tapping into your occasional hotel room through the telephone."

"What's all this got to do with Sibley?"

"Don't you see it? Computers would have changed all this, and Sibley is a computer freak. He could program a computer to transform incredibly weak impulses into recognizable speech. He could program the computer to sift through the take for whatever nuggets interested him. All he would have needed in order to find out about Stufftingle was your phone number."

From the far end of the bridge came the sound of a car door opening and slamming closed in annoyance. A bored voice called, "In case anyone's interested, it's a quarter to two in the ayem."

Wanamaker let a moist whistle trickle through his teeth. "The *telephone*!" he exclaimed. "That's how he found out about rods and hair triggers and wedges and the Ides of March. Wait till I tell—" Wanamaker caught himself in midsentence. Toothacher thought he heard his mouth snap shut.

The Admiral laughed dryly. "I didn't think the late lamented Director would have turned you loose to operate on your own. It wasn't his style. When he knew he was dying of cancer, he would have passed you along to someone he trusted—someone in the superstructure who massages your ego and tells you what a fine job you're doing when your spirits are low." Toothacher slipped into his father confessor role. "You want to tell me who it is?"

"I can't. He made me swear."

The Admiral acted hurt.

"Honestly," Wanamaker said. "I would if I could, but I can't." When the Admiral didn't say anything, Wanamaker asked, "What do we do now?"

"When's the last time you laid eyes on Sibley?"

Wanamaker told him about the Yale reunion the previous spring. "It all fits. The asshole wanted to know what I was up to."

"What did you tell him?"

"I told him to fuck off."

"That must have been when he decided to zero in on your phone."

"I told him something else," Wanamaker remembered. "I told him if he found out what I was up to, I'd have to get him murdered."

Walking in lockstep, they started back across the bridge toward the car. "During my watch," the Admiral mused quietly, "my collaborators never really understood what made me tick. I didn't get my kicks out of fighting the cold war. I wanted to win it. You know something, Roger—you don't mind if I call you Roger?—it's not too late. If we bring off Stufftingle, it could turn the whole ball game around. It could set off an avalanche of victories." Toothacher brought his arm up again and let it settle across Wanamaker's shoulders; community of interest, in the end, was stronger than physical repugnance. "Now that we're in this thing together," he said, his tone as fatherly as he could push it, “why don’t you concentrate on Stufftingle and let me worry about the author of those love letters.” In the darkness the Admiral’s bulging eyes blinked furiously. “Aside from everything else, I have a personal score to settle with friend Sibley.”

23

The raspy voice of the thickset man filtered through a haze of tobacco smoke. "Be careful," he warned. "There are things I want to know and things I don't want to know. I leave it to your intuition to distinguish between the two."

Wanamaker could barely contain his excitement. Words spilled out. "The Admiral's identified the author of the love letters," he announced. He wondered if the thickset man had had the men's room checked for bugs. As a precaution, he turned on the cold water faucet full blast. It occurred to him that the thickset man might think Wanamaker didn't trust him, so he began to rinse his hands under the running water.

At the next sink the thickset man coughed up a grunt of satisfaction. He studied his image in the mirror as if he hadn't seen it for a long time.

Wanamaker glanced uneasily at the door. "You sure we won't be interrupted?" He pictured the two young men in loose-fitting sport jackets blocking with their bodies the door to the men's room. "What if somebody has to pee very badly?"

"My people won't prevent him from urinating. They will only prevent him from urinating *here*."

Wanamaker opened his mouth to giggle at what he thought was a joke. Then he decided it hadn't been meant as a joke and aborted the laugh. "About the love letters, the guy who sent them's named Silas Sibley. You want to know how he ticked to Stufftingle? Or how the Admiral ticked to him?"

Sucking thoughtfully on his pipe, the thickset man said, "No."

Leaving the faucet running, Wanamaker began drying his hands on a paper towel. "Then all that's left to talk about is what we're going to do to neutralize the leak."

The thickset man pursed his lips and shook his head.

"You don't want to know that either?"

"Definitely not. The only thing that interests me is Stufftingle. All I want to know is that it is back on track. How you get it back on track I leave in your very professional, and I assume very discreet, hands. I don't really give a damn what you people do, so long as you don't do it in the street and frighten old ladies walking their spaniels."

"Yeah, well, there is still the small matter of locating the guy who wrote the love letters in the two weeks and two days left to us before the Ides, but my Admiral friend doesn't foresee any great problem there because the asshole who wrote them doesn't know we know he wrote them."

The thickset man seemed disturbed about something. "We?"

"The Admiral and me."

"The Admiral and you?"

"The Admiral figured out what Stufftingle was on his own—"

The thickset man turned on Wanamaker. "Someone outside your cell is aware of Stufftingle? I thought it was clearly understood—"

"There's nothing to get nervous about because the Admiral's all for it. He thinks it's a first-class idea, something we should have done years ago. You have to understand about the Admiral. The thing that motivates him is nostalgia. He's nostalgic for the days when an agent used a code name and left a sample of his Morse 'fist' on file so the enemy couldn't send phony messages over his call sign. He's nostalgic for when everyone knew who the enemy was and anything you did to weaken or embarrass him or confuse him was legitimate, and you didn't have to go sucking up to the turkeys from Congressional Oversight. Listen, the Admiral's one of us. He's offered to see the business of the leak—" Wanamaker started selecting his words carefully so as not to tell the thickset man something he didn't want to know—"through to its logical conclusion, if you get what I mean without my actually going and spelling it out."

"He's going to plug the leak?"

"Him and Huxstep and Mildred. Right."

"What will happen if they fail?"

"The Admiral's anticipated that contingency. He's cooked up a worst-case cover story. If the leaker goes public, we'll claim he has a history of mental instability. The Admiral has a shrink up his sleeve who's preparing a written diagnosis—schizophrenia, whatever. If we need to, we'll pull that out of the files to protect ourselves." Wanamaker shrugged a shoulder. "It'll be our word against that of a lunatic."

"Does this Admiral friend of yours"—Wanamaker didn't miss the sarcasm here—"know about me?"

"He's no dummy, the Admiral. He could find his way through a labyrinth of half-truths blindfolded. He's figured out I must be reporting to someone in the superstructure, but he doesn't know who. And you can bet he's not going to find out from me."

"That is precisely what I am betting," the thickset man remarked. He flashed a thin smile at his reflection in the mirror and seemed genuinely gratified when his expression smiled back at him. When he spoke, he appeared to be addressing the reflection in the mirror. "Thank you for bringing me up-to-date," he told it, and he reached into his jacket pocket to turn down the hearing aid.

"The pleasure—" Wanamaker started to say, but he saw that the thickset man could no longer hear him, and didn't waste breath finishing the sentence.

24

While Huxstep worked his way through an enormous ring of keys, the Admiral, wearing spit-shined oxfords and a jumpsuit, checked in with Mildred. "Traviata, this is Parsifal. Do you read me?"

Mildred's voice, sounding as if it originated underwater, filtered back over the walkie-talkie. "Parsifal, this is Traviata. I read you five by five, Admiral."

The Admiral winced. "We use code names like Parsifal and Traviata," he lectured the walkie-talkie, "in case anyone is listening in on this channel. That way they won't be able to identify who is speaking."

Mildred clicked on after a long pause. "My tradecraft is rusty, but I'm a fast learner," she said.

"Any activity on the street?" the Admiral asked Mildred.

The walkie-talkie burst into life. "Quiet as a morgue, Parsifal."

At the door of the Weeder's apartment, Huxstep growled, "I think I got it." The key he had slipped into the lock clicked audibly as he turned it. "One more to go and we're inside," he told Toothacher.

The Admiral ambled over to the head of the stairs and looked down five flights to the front door. The three floors directly under the loft where Sibley lived were rented by mail-order houses. The young woman who lived on the bottom floor had a backlog of mail piled up in front of her door. He and Huxstep appeared to have the building to themselves. And there was Mildred, huddled in the Chevrolet outside, to warn them in the unlikely event that Sibley, who seemed to have left town two days before, turned up.

Another of Huxstep's keys fitted perfectly into the top lock and it clicked open. He eased the door back on its hinges with the palm of his large hand and listened. The Admiral, armed with a flashlight, tiptoed up behind him. "Opening locks," Huxstep muttered, "is like taking candy from a baby."

The Admiral, his bulging eyes rimmed with raspberry red, whispered, "I have trouble opening them even when I have the key."

"It's all in the wrist," Huxstep observed in a bored voice.

Toothacher glanced quickly at Huxstep to see if he was playing with words. It would have been out of character, or at least out of the character the Admiral was familiar with. Huxstep's face was not so much innocent as empty. Nothing hidden there, Toothacher decided. He pushed past Huxstep into Sibley's apartment and switched on his flashlight. The beam stabbed into the corners of a long, narrow loft with uneven knotty pine floorboards and brick walls and a boarded-over skylight. The loft smelled (the Admiral noticed instantly) as if it had been aired and cleaned regularly. No hint, not the faintest, of mildew, of dust. And not an ashtray in sight. If it weren't for an old grudge, the Admiral could have almost liked the man the archivist had referred to as "the Weeder." Near the back wall, behind an open kitchen space, Toothacher could make out a neatly made double bed covered with a cashmere shawl. A small black-and-white television set stood on a stool facing the bed. An Eames chair and a footstool and a reading lamp were off to one side. An enormous gilt-edged mirror was leaning against the wall near the Eames chair; the Weeder, the Admiral realized, had positioned the mirror so that he could glance up from his book and *see* himself reading. Which raised the intriguing possibility that Silas Sibley, like so many others, related to an image of himself he invented for the mirror more than an inner self that existed independently of the mirror.

Toothacher's flashlight played over some bookcases built against an entire wall facing the open kitchen. "Start there," he instructed Huxstep. Grunting, Huxstep headed for the back of the loft. The Admiral spotted a long table that obviously served the Weeder as a desk.

Smiling to himself in anticipation, he settled into the wooden desk chair with the high cane back. Every item on the table seemed to be in its place. There was a color photograph, in a silver frame, of a small boy with long blond hair building sand castles on a beach. There was a fish fossil that doubled as a paperweight. There was a cut glass inkwell filled with ink and an old-fashioned pen with a gold nib jutting from a cut glass holder. Next to the inkwell was a lined grade school notebook. Toothacher reached for the notebook and began thumbing through it. There were alternate entries, one written in the flowing hand of someone who prided himself on penmanship, the other printed in rigid block letters crowding onto each line as if space were rationed.

"I assume," read one notation written in rigid letters, "from the amount of tissues in the wastebasket that you have a head cold. Don't say I didn't warn you about bathing in a bathroom with a broken radiator. I'm leaving some homeopathic pills, you dissolve two of them under your tongue four times a day, and some thyme for infusions, drink all you can, eat also, you starve a fever, you feed a cold. And for God's sake get the radiator fixed. Also have you given some thought to what I said last week about aspirins?"

The notation was signed, *Yours sincerely, Mrs. Doolittle.*

"Many thanks," said the next notation written in flowing script, "for the homeopathic pills and the thyme. I admit to feeling better already. As for the aspirin a day, I feel I am too young to worry about heart attacks. But I appreciate your mentioning it. I left a pile of shirts on the bed—if you have time, you can iron them. If not, not."

The entry was signed, "S. Sibley."

Another entry, in rigid printed letters, read: "The vacuum cleaner needs bags. The iron needs distilled water. The kitchen needs paper towels and liquid soap, no matter what the ads say one brand is as good as another so buy whichever's cheapest. I need a vacation but what with one thing or another I can't afford to take it and wouldn't know where to go if I did, but thanks for suggesting it, you are definitely my kind of white liberal, I don't mean that as an insult, just the opposite. Yours sincerely, Mrs. Doolittle."

The Admiral flipped to the last entry in the book, written in Sibley's flowing script. "Tomorrow I'm off and running for three weeks," it said. "With any luck I may be able to fill in some missing links. If you can air the loft and vacuum before I return, I'd appreciate it. S. Sibley." There was a postscript: "Could you check the box downstairs and bring up any mail—I don't want to advertise that nobody's home."

Huxstep called from the back of the loft, "There must be two, three hundred books here. There's a hundred more stacked on the floor of the closet. What you want me to do with them all?"

"Hold each one by the spine and shake it—see if anything falls out."

Huxstep, muttering under his breath about how there had to be better ways of making a living, went back to the bookshelves. The Admiral turned to the wooden filing cabinet next to the table. He pulled open a drawer, saw typing paper, opened another, found envelopes, opened a third, discovered a thick folder tied with a ribbon. He set it on the desk, undid the ribbon, opened the folder. Inside was what appeared to be the carbon copy of a typed manuscript. The first pages contained a quotation:

INSTRUCTIONS for the inliſting of MEN

. . . let our manners diſtinguiſh us

from our enemies, as much as the caufe
are engaged in.
IN PROVINCIAL CONGRESS
at New York June 20th 1775

Intrigued, the Admiral turned to the second page and read, "For starters, I'll do my man Nate: In my mind's eye I see him still dancing leaf in the rebellion's gusts."

The perspiration on Toothacher's palms, the tingling in his scalp told him he had come across something significant. The Admiral leaned eagerly over the manuscript and plunged on. He heard the beat of the kettledrum on the bowling green. He passed "Whose truth? Which truth?" He witnessed the execution of Sergeant Hickey. He came to the part where Nate takes two steps forward. His friends try to talk him out of volunteering. Nate persists. The Commander-in-Chief, not a very sympathetic figure, personally briefs him. "I need to know what the lobsters are up to." Exit the Commander-in-Chief. When last seen, the Weeder's man Nate is selecting patriotic phrases from Addison's *Cato* to use as codes.

The Admiral looked up. E. Everard Linkletter, his archivist friend, had filled him in on Silas Sibley. This Nate he was writing about was a distant relative of his and a lifelong obsession. It struck Toothacher that Sibley was doing to Nate what he, the Admiral, was doing to Sibley, walking back the cat on an operation that had gone wrong. Sibley was taking Nate's mission apart piece by piece to discover why his illustrious ancestor ended up the way he did. "I'm off and running for three weeks," Sibley had written in the notebook to his cleaning lady. "With any luck I may be able to fill in some missing links."

Off and running where? The Ides of March was two weeks away. If he and Huxstep and Mildred could catch up with Sibley and neutralize him before then, Wanamaker could go ahead with Stufftingle. But the Ides of March was the absolute limit. Kabir was being closed down permanently on the fifteenth. The faculty and the atomic facility were being transferred to a remote base in the countryside. It would take Wanamaker years to smuggle enough uranium into the new site and mount the operation again. Faced with this delay, the locals in Tehran, not to mention Wanamaker's contact in the superstructure, would lose their nerve, would scurry back to their holes. A great occasion to make the world more congenial to American interests would have been lost forever.

The Admiral's flashlight played over the desk. Under the fossil paperweight was a pile of unopened envelopes that the cleaning lady, "Yours sincerely, Mrs. Doolittle," must have brought up. Toothacher leafed through them. Most of them were bills, bank statements, advertisements. Two were personal letters. Toothacher held the envelopes up to the flashlight one at a time, but he couldn't make out the writing because the letters inside were folded. He reached into a pocket of his jumpsuit and produced a length of bamboo that had been carefully split not quite to the end. It was a trick of the trade the Admiral had picked up from an agent in Hong Kong. Working the bamboo into the first envelope through a small opening at the corner of the flap, Toothacher pinched the folded letter in the split bamboo. He carefully turned the length of bamboo so that the letter wound itself around it, then pulled both the bamboo and the letter out through the small opening. He unwound the letter, flattened it on the desk and read it. It was from the director of Yale's Beinecke Rare Book and Manuscript Library in New Haven. "This will confirm our phone conversation of yesterday," it said. "Browse till the cows come home, Silas. If you stop by my home Sunday morning, I'll give you the back door keys. You'll have the place to yourself."

Toothacher checked a Master Plan of Leads to Run Down appended to the Nate manuscript. Sure enough there was an entry marked "Beinecke Stacks—A. Hamilton's missing letter to Nate's brother Enoch could be buried in the uncatalogued Hamilton papers."

Using the length of bamboo, the Admiral returned the letter to its envelope and extracted the second letter. Unrolled from the split bamboo and flattened on the desk, it was cryptic to the point of rudeness. "On the phone you were very persuasive," it said. "But I'm having second thoughts. My privacy is more important than your wild-goose chase, at least to me. Forget my yes. Please don't come. Please." There was no signature on the letter, no return address on the envelope. The stamp had been canceled at Concord, Massachusetts. On Sibley's Master Plan of Leads to Run Down, the pot of "gold at the end of the rainbow" entry read: "Molly's diary—Concord descendants?"

The Admiral switched off his flashlight and stared into the darkness for a moment, imagining the loft, the bed with the cashmere quilt, the boarded-over skylight; imagining Huxstep pulling books off the shelves and shaking them by their spines; imagining the Weeder curled up with a good book in his Eames chair watching himself reading in the mirror. Except for two tours of duty on board destroyers, both cut short because of chronic seasickness, Toothacher had spent all of his career in intelligence work. And although he had never admitted it, had never put words to the thought, he had been plagued by a hesitation. It was an article of faith with him that there was one truth and it was knowable—but once you had discovered it, what then? Did knowing an enemy's capabilities really tell you anything about his intentions? Did he have a capability because he intended to use it or because he wanted you to think he might use it? Therein lay the essential flaw of intelligence work; a flaw that left many of its practitioners half-paralyzed with uncertainty. But now the Admiral found himself engaged in another sort of intelligence-related activity—one unequaled for its purity, its primitiveness. Here there was no uncertainty, no hesitation, no self-doubt.

It was called the manhunt. And the Admiral found it very much to his taste. Tracking the Weeder beat the Guantánamo happy hours by a country mile. It even beat burning the candle at both ends.

Toothacher noticed a flashlight weaving toward him in the darkness. Huxstep tossed a handful of papers onto the desk.

"One library card," he said, tucking stray hairs back up into his nostrils, "assorted postcards probably used as bookmarks, two laundry tickets, five theater stubs, three overdue slips from lending libraries, one dated August 12, 1972. If he ever returns the book it'll set him back"—Huxstep let his eyes drift up in their sockets as he made a quick calculation—"5,656 days at twenty-five cents per makes $1,414."

Convinced that the manhunt was off to an auspicious start, the Admiral began putting things back the way he had found them. "Get on the horn to Mildred," he snapped to Huxstep. "Tell her we're on our way out."

Huxstep, who had a child's love of gadgets, fingered the walkie-talkie. "Traviata, this is Parsifal's jackass-of-all-trades," he said. "Are you still alive? We're coming out."

There was a burst of static. Carried along on it, like a buoy riding a ground swell, were the exultant words, "Praise the Lord!"

PART TWO
Whipping the Cat

He liv'd Deſir'd and died Lament'd.
A Friend I sot much by but he is
gone. . .

1

For once, the Weeder thought, I ought to do myself:

In his mind's eye he could see himself, the frayed collar of his once serviceable, now threadbare overcoat turned up against the thick crystals of snow slanting down at him like tracer bullets. His hair, a deep brown, had grown out since his divorce; he was once again wearing it as he had during his college days, which was long enough to indicate he was a marginal member of the establishment, as opposed to being in its mainstream. He was paler than usual, having spent the last eight months indoors installing and programming his computer. Wrapping his fingers around a paper cup full of scalding coffee—he had bought it to warm his hands—he made his way through the burying ground of Coventry, Connecticut, pausing to read the messages to posterity carefully selected by the late lamented before their deaths and fastidiously engraved on the thin gray stones jutting at odd angles from the frozen earth. Where time and wind had worn away the writing, the Weeder ran his fingertips over the engraving, deciphering the messages as if they had been written for the blind.

> Halt paſsenger as you go past
> Remember time it runneth fast

> Skill was his cash

> Where there is Contention there is evil work

> Virtuous Men will Delight in Virtuous Actions

The Weeder had a historian's fascination for cemeteries. Old tombstones, he had long since decided, were the American equivalent of morality plays. Nate, of course, didn't have a tombstone. He had what was properly called a cenotaph—a marker for someone whose body was buried elsewhere. The inscription on it began:

> Durable Stone preserve the monumental record

If only durable stone could preserve the monumental record of Nate, like the Weeder a cranky but ardent patriot, a reluctant spy who thought that reading other people's mail was the lesser evil. Unfortunately durable stone wasn't the solution. The only way to preserve the record—to discover it and illuminate it and preserve it—was through the good offices of the historian. And time was running out on him.

History, like a great mass of snow on a glacier, was piling up; it would one day come spilling down, burying the historian in an avalanche of facts.

The way the Weeder saw it, the outlook for the historian was bleak. The more history that piled up behind him, the less chance he had of coping with it. It was one thing to study the last three or four hundred years. It was altogether another to study three or four hundred thousand years, or three or four million. Imagine trying to specialize in European political history between the years 100,000 and 200,000. Or writing a history of the American presidency when there had been 50,000 presidents. The prospect would be too daunting. Only mad dogs and your occasional Englishman—here the Weeder smiled to himself; history desperately needed a giggle now and then and he couldn't resist supplying it, even in his thoughts—would even try. And they would fail. The human race was destined to lose history. What the Weeder was describing was the end of the world, or at least the end of the world as he knew it. He believed the day would come when there would be too much of a past for historians to make a systematic investigation of it. Which would leave everyone stranded in a present. And stumbling toward a future that they would have to confront without benefit of a sense of where they came from.

The train of thought depressed the Weeder. He saw himself fighting a rearguard action. Slowing down the inevitable. Holding off the hordes from the steppes.

Very dramatic, the Weeder thought. Another intellectual convincing himself that what he did was important.

The coffee, cooling, no longer warmed his hands and he decided to drink it as he headed back toward his beat-up Volkswagen Beetle, which he hoped would one day qualify as a classic car. He had accomplished a good deal in the last two days. Before leaving New York he had purchased an old violin in a pawnshop, hidden the Stufftingle printouts inside it and deposited the violin in another pawnshop. He had slipped the pawn ticket into an envelope and mailed it to himself care of General Delivery, Concord, Massachusetts. That out of the way, he had headed for New Haven and the Beinecke Rare Book and Manuscript Library. He wanted to arrive late Saturday and work in the library Sunday, when nobody would disturb him, which explained the detour to Coventry, Connecticut, to the burying ground with the morality plays on the tombstones and the monumental record on Nate's cenotaph.

Arriving in New Haven late Saturday afternoon, the Weeder checked into a motel on the outskirts of town, confirmed his appointment at the Beinecke with a quick phone call to the head librarian, then on the spur of the moment drove downtown. He left the Volkswagen in a crowded faculty parking lot just off campus and wandered around until dark. Yale evoked a flood of memories in the Weeder; he looked back on his undergraduate and graduate years with much more than nostalgia. It was the scene of his first love—and his first hate.

Was it a comment on him, or the world in which he lived, he wondered, that he could no longer recreate the love, but the hate had the rich, fresh aroma of newly turned earth?

He browsed around the student bookstore to see what texts they were using these days, then installed himself in a booth—his booth, with his initials, and hers, carved into the back of the bench—at the Copper Kitchen and ordered a hamburger, well-done, with french fries and a milk shake. In his day the same meal had cost eighty-five cents. Now it was five dollars. He eavesdropped on the conversation in the next booth—three young men, obviously Yale students, were discussing the pros and cons of registering for the draft. As he waited in line at the cash register to pay his check, the Weeder read the notices tacked up on a bulletin board. Rides were being offered and sought. Apartments also. Used stereo equipment, roller skates, a small refrigerator, an electric guitar, a double bed were for sale. Not much had changed over the years. It was dark out by the time the Weeder paid his bill and started meandering back toward the faculty parking lot.

Tradecraft had never been one of the Weeder's strong suits—at Camp Perry, known in Company circles as the Farm, he had more or less laughed his way through what the new recruits referred to as "Freshman Cops and Robbers." But coming out of the restaurant, the Weeder found himself doing something he hadn't done since the Farm—working the street. He absently tracked the two young men with long hair taking turns pushing each other down High Street in a supermarket shopping cart. He observed the gray-haired professor wearing a thick bathrobe over designer blue jeans, walking a toy poodle fitted with a bright green muzzle; the professor was talking to the dog in Latin. The Weeder saw a bearded man warming his hands in the pockets of a greatcoat as he tried to flag down a taxi with his chin. He took in the courteous drunk—it was the Weeder's feeling that liquor brought out the Renaissance man in some people, the fascist in others—who finally got the taxi with an airy wave of his hand. He watched the fat bag lady rooting through the garbage in a wire trash can, and the thin one, fat with layers of clothing, curled up on a basement grate. He even noticed the rail-thin middle-aged woman wearing high-heeled galoshes and a 1930s scalp-hugging feathered hat with a black veil that fell like a mask over half her face; she appeared to be studying the map at a bus stop. But he never saw her take the tiny walkie-talkie from her carpetbag and talk urgently into it after the Weeder passed. And he never saw the shadowy figure in the doorway farther up the street lazily shift his weight from one foot to the other; he never saw the sudden brightening of a flame, as if a breath expelled from someone's lungs had been momentarily ignited.

The Weeder was just reaching the entrance of the parking lot when he heard footsteps gaining on him. He glanced over his shoulder. A hulking figure of a man wearing a sleeveless fur-lined leather vest and leather trousers was jogging with short mincing steps to catch up to him. His arms were covered with tattoos; the man, passing under a streetlight, was near enough for the Weeder to make out "begun to fight" on his right arm. His hair was cropped short, his head cocked to one side, his pewter-colored eyes fixed with great intensity on the Weeder, his mouth curled up in a crooked smile. Something was obviously tickling him. A transparent jug dangled from a forefinger hooked through its handle. From time to time the man with the patriotic tattoo brought the jug to his lips and threw back his head and gulped some of the contents, then spit it into the gutter. Frightened, the Weeder called out, "What is it you want?"

The wino, which is what the Weeder took him for, stopped a few paces away. "What I want," he replied in a brittle voice, "what I need to have is your money and your life." He took another swig of mouthwash from his jug and spit it out again.

The Weeder, backing away, tried to protect himself with humor. "You mean, 'or.' Your money *or* your life."

The wino didn't laugh. "I mean *and*." He slipped a cigarette lighter from his vest pocket and lit it with a flick of his thumb and adjusted the flame until it was long and thin.

The wino was close enough now for the Weeder to hear the hissing of the gas. "You're crazy," he cried.

"That's one possibility," the wino shot back. "There are others."

"Who are you?" the Weeder whispered in alarm. The wino seemed vaguely familiar. Where had he seen him before?

The Weeder backed up against the hood of a car in the parking lot. He stood, transfixed, as the wino brought the lighter to his lips and bellowed out a burst of flame. The wino had misjudged the distance. The flame only warmed the Weeder's clothes.

Terror flooded through the Weeder's body like a tide as he scurried away between two cars. He looked around in desperation for a sign of life, but there was no one in sight. He scrambled behind a polished Ford and cast a panicky look back. The wino was wading into the parking lot after him, gulping from his jug and gargling and spitting mouthfuls of kerosene onto the pavement. He brought his cigarette lighter to his lips again and exhaled several trial breaths of bluish fire. Then he bellowed out another great breath of flame. The Weeder ducked under it and darted away. Fingering an imaginary hair mole on his neck, he remembered one of Nate's favorite maxims: A long life has a lingering death. And he heard Nate's laughter peeling through his skull—the laughter of a twenty-one-year-old who feared death and longed for it.

The wino breathed fire again and the Weeder felt the heat on the back of his neck as he slipped between two cars. He realized that the peal of laughter trailing after him wasn't Nate's but the wino's as he worked his way between the parked cars toward the Weeder, all the while forcing him back toward the corner of the lot where the high, windowless rear wall of a brick building met the chain link fence with the neat coils of razor wire strung across the top. "What I like, what I do well," the wino shouted between fiery breaths, between bursts of laughter, "is violence."

And then there was only a handful of cars left to hide behind and it filtered through to the Weeder's confused brain that what was happening was unreal. He tried to push it away as if it were a bad dream but it wouldn't go. He looked around wildly. The car he was cowering behind seemed familiar and he thrust his hand into his pocket and found a key and jammed it into the lock of the beat-up Volkswagen and pulled open the door and threw himself in, slamming the door behind him and hammering down with his fist on the button that locked it as the wino tugged viciously at the handle. The wino backed off and swigged more mouthwash and brought the lighter up and bellowed fire at the car, engulfing it for a long moment in flame, singeing the paint, melting the rubber on the windshield wipers. Fumbling with the key the Weeder fitted it into the ignition. He twisted the key and pumped the gas with his foot. The motor resisted, then spurted into life. He threw the car into gear and slammed it into the car ahead, pushing it forward a foot or two as another avalanche of flame buried the Volkswagen. The smell of burnt rubber, of singed paint stung the Weeder's nostrils as he threw the car into reverse and slammed it into the car behind, forcing it back slightly. In the space he had created he maneuvered the Volkswagen out of the line of parked cars and, accelerating through a wall of flame, sped toward the entrance of the parking lot and the safety of the street.

2

Wanamaker was beside himself with anger. "What do you mean 'almost but not quite'?" he raged into the phone. He realized he was talking over an open line and lowered his voice to a near whisper, as if that would solve the problem of security. "What kind of an answer is that?" he demanded.

"Our jackass-of-all-trades has let him get away," the Admiral explained with a calmness that was not human.

There was a moment of silence as Wanamaker digested this. Presently he said, "He'll recognize the jackass-of-all-trades from when he was your driver on the Farm. He'll know we know."

"Not necessarily," the Admiral said. "Our jackass has changed over the years. In my opinion it's not likely our friend will remember him. My guess is he'll take what happened for an ordinary mugging."

"He'll go to the police," Wanamaker warned. "We'll have to trot out the story about him being off his rocker."

The Admiral could be heard snickering over the phone

line. Wanamaker obviously wasn't thinking things through logically. "He'd have to explain who he is," Toothacher said. "He'd have to get into the business of whom he works for. Phone calls would be made. Questions would be asked. Stories would be checked. The whole thing could become very sticky. If I know Sibley, he'll assume it was a coincidence."

"What makes you so sure?" Wanamaker asked. He hoped to God the Admiral knew what he was talking about.

"He'll assume it was a coincidence because he'll desperately want it to be a coincidence. Anything else would put him out of his league, would affect his digestion, his bowels, his ability to get a nightly ration of sleep."

"Where do we go from here?" Wanamaker wanted to know.

"If at first we don't succeed," the Admiral breathed into the mouthpiece, "what is it we do?"

3

Coming off a white night, the Weeder obliged himself to think the thing through again from the beginning. He approached the problem from every conceivable angle, tortured himself with possibilities (which tended, because they existed, to take on the solidity of probabilities), eventually concluded that there was no way the Admiral could have traced the love letters back to him. Which reduced the mugging attempt in the faculty parking lot to an ugly coincidence; an episode best forgotten. Comforted (though not completely convinced; there was still the nagging familiarity of the firebreather to account for), the Weeder picked up the keys to the Beinecke from the head librarian, let himself into the library through a back door, installed himself at a binder's desk in the glass tower within the building where the rare books and manuscripts were stored. He opened the folder containing the A. Hamilton papers, recently unearthed, newly acquired, as yet uncatalogued. His mind wandered to the burly man swigging mouthwash from a transparent green jug, but he forced himself to concentrate on the business at hand.

"I am a bookworm," he had told the new DDI, Rudd. "For play I bury myself in the corners of libraries and read." Which was what he proposed to do now.

He began weeding through the Hamilton papers. There were itemized bills for services rendered, for clothing purchased, for repairs to the roof over the earth closet in the backyard, all dated after the turn of the century, so the Weeder knew he was dealing with the right time span. There were drafts of letters, dictated but unsigned, written—if the Weeder's amateur eye was any judge—by the young Harvard tutor who had served as Hamilton's secretary between 1799 and his death, which was the period when Nate's brother Enoch boasted of having received a letter from Hamilton. Most of the letters were filled with gossip about political figures of the day. The mayor of New York was said to have taken a bribe from a construction firm angling for a contract to build horse-drawn public transportation vehicles, which were to be called "street-cars." A. Burr was said to have lost his new wife's fortune in a land reclamation scheme and was consoling himself in the arms of a black mistress in New Jersey. G. Washington was supposed to have so many wooden teeth in his mouth that he went to a carpenter for repairs rather than a dental surgeon.

Stuck between two pieces of blank paper with watermarks that said "Fool's cap" was an unsigned, undated partial draft of a letter that recalled the "troblous times." "A Remarcable Patriote" had volunteered to spy behind the British lines while pretending to "Whip the Cat." The author of the letter had had the signal honor of "superintending" the mission. There followed a detailed description of how the patriot had crossed Long Island Sound and had made his way across Long Island to the village of Flatbush, to the house of the widow of a Concord martyr. From there, with the help of the young widow, he had scouted the British positions in Brookland and the western reaches of Long Island, had discovered the "opres-ing Britich, freshe from their Victory over the Colonials, Rejoyceing as if Bedlam was broke loose. " According to the widow's diary, which Hamilton claimed to have read, the patriot had gleaned British intentions, had devised a plan to thwart them. A coded report had been sent back that had provided the Commander-in-Chief with vital information. If the war had not been lost then and there, it was safe to say it was due in no small part to the "Martyr in ye glorious Cause of Liberty," whose end had been so "cruel and uncristion" it aroused "Pastion" in all who knew the "True and Reale storie."

There had been periods in the Weeder's life when the discovery of a document that mentioned Nate by name, even one with a cryptic reference to him, would have reduced him to dizzyness. Now, however, a corner of his brain was obsessed with the event of the previous night, with the burly mugger who had tried to incinerate him. The Weeder was unable to shake the queasy feeling that he was missing something important, something that went to the heart of the matter. Had he seen the mugger before? If so, where? For the hundredth time he let snatches of conversation trail through his thoughts, picking at them for clues.

"What is it you want?"

"What I want, what I need to have is your money *and* your life."

The Weeder had given him a chance to correct the slip. "You mean '*or*.'"

"I mean *and*."

"You're crazy."

"That's one possibility. There are others."

Sitting at the binder's table, gazing sightlessly at the stacks of rare books around him in the glass tower, the Weeder once again explored these other possibilities. It could have been a random mugging. Or a case of mistaken identity. Or an attack provoked by drugs. Or the attacker could have been, as the Weeder had suggested to him, stark raving mad. An image of Admiral Toothacher, lecturing back at the Farm on methodology, came to the Weeder; smiling slyly, the Admiral had summed up possibilities at the end of his talk. "Or all of the above," he had said in a singsong voice. "Or none of the above. Or any combination thereof."

And then, suddenly, it came to the Weeder; the vision of the Admiral at the Farm had triggered a memory. Toothacher had arrived in the morning and departed in the evening in a sparkling black limousine with shiny whitewall tires and a small admiral's pennant flying from the right front fender. The door to the limousine had been held open, the car had been driven by a hulking chief petty officer with short cropped hair and eyes the color of pewter. It had been driven by the man who had attacked him in the faculty parking lot, who had demanded his money *and* his life!

Another snatch of conversation, one the Weeder had unconsciously avoided, echoed through his head.

"So what governments are you stabbing in the back these days?" he had asked Wanamaker when they ran into each other at the Yale reunion the previous spring.

"If you were to find out," Wanamaker, smiling smugly, had replied, "I suppose I'd have to get you murdered."

So the attempt on his life had not been a coincidence! The Admiral had walked back the cat, had somehow traced the leak and the love letters to the Weeder. Having found the leak, they were trying to plug it.

Shivering, the Weeder rose to his feet. He felt an icy hand caress his spine. He would race off to the nearest police station, he would tell the sergeant on duty—what? That a mugger had tried to incinerate him the night before because he knew that an agency of the United States government was planning to explode a primitive atomic device in Tehran on the Ides of March? Because he had set out in his bumbling way to stop what he considered an atrocity without bringing the whole world down on the Company? Nobody would believe him. Even worse, someone might—and he would be fitted into a straitjacket and shipped back to the Company in question by the local police who preferred not to get involved in matters of national security.

Whatever he decided to do, he would be a fool for hanging around Yale. They had been waiting for him once, they would be waiting for him again. He tried desperately to remember some of the things he had learned at the Farm about avoiding surveillance. All he could come up with was the story of the OSS agent who had thrown the Gestapo bloodhounds off the scent by urinating on his tracks. He couldn't see that urinating on his tracks would have the slightest effect on the people who were after him. It occurred to him that the best thing would be to abandon his clothing at the motel, abandon his almost classic car. He would rent an automobile in New Haven and disappear into New England. Even if they discovered he had rented a car, they would have no way of knowing in what direction he had headed. If he could manage to stay out of their clutches until the Ides of March . . .

From somewhere below him in the glass core of the Beinecke Library came the thud of a heavy fire door being slammed closed. The sound seemed to skate along the glass walls of the building within a building, to resound through the stacks. At the back of the glass tower, another fire door slammed shut. And a third. The Weeder edged between two stacks and peered down through the glass wall at the main lobby, sandwiched between the inner glass tower and the outer shell of the building, two stories below him. A rail-thin woman wearing a scalp-hugging feathered hat with a black veil masking half her face (was he imagining it or did she look familiar too?) was standing at the main desk, looking up. She spotted the Weeder and wagged a finger at him, as if he had disobeyed a biblical injunction and was being mildly chastised for it. A burly man the Weeder instantly recognized as the fire-breather from the faculty parking lot the night before appeared at the other end of the lobby. He was holding an enormous pistol, fitted with a silencer, at present arms. He saw the woman with the veil pointing and followed her finger until he spotted the Weeder. The burly man formed his left forefinger and thumb into a pistol and sighted over it at the Weeder. He mouthed the words, "Bang, bang! You're dead!"

And then the Weeder saw the Admiral, hunched over like a parenthesis, his mane of chalk-colored hair flying off excitedly in all directions. The Admiral backed up to get a better view of the Weeder, studied him with his bulging eyes for a moment, then turned toward the large red fire box on the wall. He broke the glass with a small hammer hanging next to it, pulled open the door and pushed down the large brass lever to the position labeled Danger—Exhaust.

From the dozen or so grilles installed in the walls of the inner glass tower came an ominous hissing.

The Weeder had worked in the library his junior and senior years and understood instantly what the sound meant. The Beinecke housed some of the rarest books and manuscripts in the world. In the event of fire, there was a system to seal off the glass core where the books were stored by closing hermetic fire doors and then pumping out the air. No air, no fire. There was supposed to be an alarm to warn the people working in the stacks that they had thirty seconds to clear out.

A pulse throbbed in one of the Weeder's ears as he raced for the narrow metal staircase that corkscrewed up to the top floor of the core. Plunging up the steps, already short of breath, he became aware of the gravitational drag of the earth pulling at him through the soles of his shoes. With each step lifting his feet took more effort. His vision started to blur. A rasp stuck like a bone in the back of his throat. His lungs burned. Gasping for air, he clutched the railing and hauled himself up, hand over hand. He reached the top floor and sagged against a whitewashed brick wall and lashed out wildly with his palm, searching for the small glass box that had been installed during his senior year. The throbbing in his ear grew into a roar, drowning out the hissing, and the space around him began to go dark, as if the light were being sucked out of the glass tower along with the air. Suddenly the tips of his fingers struck something smooth. He willed his fingers into a fist and plunged it into the glass, groped through the shards for the mask, fumbled in what had become a nightmare to fit it over his face as his knees ceded to gravity and he sank in the general direction of the center of the earth.

4

Wanamaker kept a tight rein on his emotions, grunting into the telephone every now and then to indicate he was receiving the Admiral loud and clear and not appreciating a word he said. Had he misjudged the Admiral after all? he wondered. Walking back a cat was a cerebral activity perfectly suited to Toothacher's manifold talents; acting on the conclusions may simply not have been his cup of tea. Wanamaker shrugged a shoulder. When he came right down to it, what choice did he have?

"On paper," the Admiral was saying, "the plan looked perfect. Maybe that was the problem . . . the perfect is the enemy of the good. Our jackass-of-all-trades removed the fuse to the alarm system so it wouldn't go off when we closed the fire doors. The air, according to the printed notice on the fire box, was extracted from the inner glass tower in thirty seconds. Are you still there, Wanamaker?"

Wanamaker grunted.

"We waited eleven minutes before pumping the air back in. Eleven minutes should have been enough to suffocate him three times over. Houdini could only hold his breath for four minutes."

Wanamaker, bored with the details of the game when he already knew the final score, grunted again.

"Our jackass and your man Friday went in and searched the stacks from top to bottom. You can imagine our stupefaction when they couldn't find our friend." The Admiral must have sensed that he was losing his audience. "Aren't you curious how he got out?"

Wanamaker grunted. The Admiral decided to interpret this as an expression of interest. "They didn't find our friend, but they did find a glass box built into the side of a wall on the top floor that said, 'Oxygen mask for emergency use only. Break glass with hammer to get mask.' Or words to that effect. The glass, of course, was broken, the oxygen mask missing. Nearby there was a metal ladder spiraling up through the roof of the glass tower to a submarine-like escape hatch. The escape hatch led through a crawl space to the roof of the library. On the back wall of the library building was a fire escape, with the bottom length of ladder lowered to the ground. Are you getting the picture?"

Another grunt crept stealthily over the telephone line, followed closely by a question: "You still think he'll assume it was a coincidence?"

For a moment the Admiral didn't respond. Then, very quietly, he said, "You ought to know that our friend saw me."

"You let him get a look at you!"

The Admiral could hear the note of astonishment in

Wanamaker's voice, could picture him rolling his ungroomed head from side to side in frustration, could imagine the flurry of dandruff flakes, dislodged, drifting past the rumpled shoulders of his unpressed sport jacket into an open container of low-fat cottage cheese. Toothacher screwed up his face in disgust. In his view what was killing the Company was too much HYP—too much Harvard, Yale, Princeton. When he caught up with the Weeder there would be one less.

"He was looking down from the stacks," the Admiral continued. "He saw me depress the handle that set the pumps to work sucking out the air."

"Good God! If he saw you, he recognized you. We both took your course at the Farm." Wanamaker must have been lighting a fresh Schimmelpenninck from the soggy stump of an old one glued to his lower lip, because he didn't say anything for a while. Then, "He'll go to the police."

"What would he tell them?" the Admiral asked. "That the Company he works for is trying to kill him? The detectives would commit him for psychiatric observation. If they believed him, the whole story would come out—Stufftingle, the Ides of March, the Company eaves-dropping through ordinary garden-variety telephones. Think of the headlines in *The New York Times*. Think of the scandal. Congress would castrate the Company. No, no, fortunately for us, our friend has a reputation as a patriot. My guess is he'll run for his life. We should be able to catch up with him in a matter of days. Ha! He'll still be a patriot, but with any luck, he'll be a dead patriot."

5

The Weeder tried the number from a downtown Boston booth, got the recorded message again. "You've reached Snow," a husky voice, vaguely self-conscious, vaguely irritated, snapped. "I don't take calls or return them except on Sundays. And then not always. Don't bother leaving a message."

He left one anyway. "It's me again. Silas Sibley. This is the fourth time I've called in three days. I've come a long way to see you. I'll call back later in the day. Can you do me a favor and turn your machine off and answer your phone? It's important. To me, at least."

To kill time he drove over to Charlestown and climbed Breed's Hill and roamed around the battlefield for several hours. Listening to the wind whistling past his ear, the Weeder felt the pull of history and slipped over the line into an incarnation. The whistle of fifes was carried to him on the wind—the lobster lines, decimated in two previous assaults, were forming up for the third attack. He could see the hundred or so militiamen behind the rail fence on the flank of Breed's Hill fitting new flints in their muskets so the guns wouldn't misfire. Cocking his head, he thought he heard the moans of the British wounded crawling away from the rebels. He caught the distant sound of shouted commands. It was the British general Howe ordering his men to remove their heavy backpacks so they could advance more rapidly. The Weeder saw Howe taking up position at the head of the light infantry and grenadiers heading for the rail fence. Colonel Knowlton, in command of the militiamen at the rail fence, yelled for his men to hold their fire. Howe shouted an order. The front rank knelt, the lobster line aimed and dispatched a volley at the rebels. Most of the shots flew high; the lobsters, the Weeder knew, tended to overshoot because they used too much powder for the weight of lead in their cartridges.

Howe drew his saber. The Red Coats leveled their bayonets and broke into a trot. When the lobster line reached the stakes that the rebels had hammered into the ground forty yards from the rail fence, the militiamen fired. The Weeder could see the young officers around Howe crumpling to the ground. The lobster line itself cracked like an eggshell. Howe could be heard bellowing urgent commands. The Red Coats closed ranks and continued on. The Weeder could see Colonel Knowlton waving an arm wildly; could see the militiamen, out of powder, lacking bayonets, scurrying away. The Red Coats fired a last volley at the fleeing rebels. Smoke obscured the rail fence, then slowly drifted away. The Weeder spotted Howe staring back across the fields at the scores of Red Coats sprawled in the grotesque positions that dead men assume. Howe's face was a mask of shock, of dismay. The thin throaty cheers of the surviving lobsters reached the Weeder.

And then, as if a needle had been plucked from a phonograph record, the cheering stopped and the Weeder found himself listening again to the wind whistling past his ear. The sound lured him back against his will into the present. His face corkscrewed into a sheepish grin as he realized what had happened: running for his life across a Colonial landscape, he had taken momentary refuge in history.

It wasn't the first time that history had provided this service; had given him a place to go when he didn't like where he was.

His lifelong obsession with Nate had been part escape, of course. But there had been more to it than that. Much more. The Weeder had always attributed his fascination with Nate to an emotion he presumed he shared with his illustrious ancestor, namely an abiding commitment to a delicate tangle of lovers and relatives and friends; to an extended family which, when you pushed it out far enough, constituted the entity known as country. In a deep sense, Nate and the Weeder subscribed to the same social contract: With all its faults there was something here, some ideal, albeit unachieved, worth fighting for.

Running, and running scared, looking over his shoulder to make sure the Admiral wasn't one jump behind him, the Weeder felt closer to Nate than he ever had before. Nate too had been running scared; had been looking over a shoulder; had (the Weeder supposed) failed to see whatever it was that finally caught up with him in time to avoid it; had gone to meet his fate fortified, as far as the Weeder could figure out, only by a cranky patriotism, a vision that derived its power from a knowledge of how things were and how they could be. Nate, in short, had had high hopes. The Weeder, following Nate's star, shared them.

The sun was hovering over the rooftops of Charlestown when the Weeder squeezed into a telephone booth, fed some coins into the slots and dialed the Concord number again. It rang four times. A female voice came on the line.

"Yes."

"It's Silas Sibley. We spoke on the phone three weeks ago. You said I could come up and talk to you about a project I'm working on."

"Didn't you get my letter?"

"Your letter? No. I left New York last week. I was doing some research in New Haven."

"I wrote you that I'd changed my mind." The voice on the other end of the line hesitated. "Can I ask you a question?"

The Weeder said, "Please."

The voice changed pitch slightly. It was interested instead of defensive. "What sign were you born under?"

"I'm a Capricorn."

"What's your ascendant?"

"To tell you the truth I don't know what you're talking about."

"What's your birth date?"

"I was born the same day as Elvis Presley, January eighth."

The response seemed to alter the chemistry of the conversation. "Ah," said the voice on the other end of the line. Then, reluctantly, "Come if you must." She gave him directions. Did he know the road that ran past the North Bridge? Seven and a half miles after the bridge he was to turn right. There was a mailbox. Painted bright red. The road was unpaved. Eventually it forked. He was to stay left. The road ended at a house. The voice on the phone suggested a time. The Weeder eagerly agreed. He started to mumble his thanks but the line went dead.

Back in his car, the Weeder's thoughts drifted to the Admiral. He would have discovered the scorched Volkswagen parked on a side street near Yale by now. He would have guessed that the Weeder had switched to a rented car and started asking around. He might have gotten a description of the Hertz car the Weeder was driving; might have asked the state police, on a pretext, to look out for it. Searching his memory, the Weeder recalled a lecture at the Farm about avoiding surveillance. "Change cars, change trains, change buses, change hotels," a one-time station chief had advised. "Change clothing, change routines, change habits, change anything you can possibly change."

"How about wives?" the Weeder, always ready with a quip, had asked innocently.

The class had laughed. The instructor had said, "If you can change wives it wouldn't hurt, but it's probably easier to change cars."

With three hours to wile away before the rendezvous, the

Weeder decided to cover his tracks. He drove through rush hour traffic to Logan Airport and abandoned his Hertz Toyota in the long-term parking area. He hopped an airport shuttle to the terminal, waited in line for a taxi and asked the driver to take him to an Avis office in downtown Boston. The taxi driver studied his passenger in the rearview mirror. "You can get a bus over to the Avis place here at the airport," he said.

The Weeder shook his head. "I'm superstitious about renting cars at airports."

Muttering something about different folks having different strokes, the driver swung his car into traffic.

At the Avis counter the Weeder made a point of asking directions to Cape Cod and even had the agent trace the route on a map for him. Then he headed out the Massachusetts Turnpike toward Concord. He got to the post office just as it was closing and retrieved the pawn ticket he had put in an envelope and addressed to himself care of General Delivery, Concord. He stopped for a hamburger and french fries at a diner, lingered over two cups of coffee to make time pass, finally started toward the house where the woman who called herself Snow lived.

He turned off the main road at the red mailbox and bounced along the unpaved road full of potholes, his headlights playing on snowbanks from a storm the previous week, on fallen trees, on what was left of an old fence. Around a curve the headlights picked out the weathered planks of a one-story house set in a clearing. Light from several candles flickered in a window. The Weeder killed his headlights and walked up to the door.

It opened before he could knock. A woman wearing corduroy jeans and a loose-fitting flannel shirt stood in the doorway. She held a candle in a holder with a reflector that directed the light onto the Weeder. Her own face was lost in shadows.

"I'm Silas Sibley," the Weeder announced.

"You don't look like a Capricorn," the woman observed.

"What do Capricorns look like?"

"Generally speaking, they don't look frightened. They're more open, more seductive. You really didn't get my letter?"

He shook his head. "I must have left New York before it arrived."

The woman said, "What's done is done. You might as well come on in. My friends call me Snow. If you become one you can too. Until then you can call me Matilda."

The Weeder closed the door behind him, stamped his feet on the mat, threw his overcoat across the back of a wooden chair and installed himself in front of a fire crackling in the chimney that formed the center of the house. He held his hands toward the flames and rubbed his fingers together.

The woman named Snow set her candle down on a small table. She glanced in annoyance at the Weeder's overcoat, decided she didn't like where he had thrown it and hung it from a peg on the back of the door next to a mackinaw. Watching her, the Weeder thought: What she cares about she is fanatic about.

Snow appeared with a glass and offered it to the Weeder. "Prune cider," she announced. "Homemade, it goes without saying. When's the last time you saw prune cider in a supermarket? Drink it—it's good for the digestion, ingrown toenails, warts."

The Weeder took his first good look at Snow. She was younger than he had expected. She had incredibly pale skin and dark straight hair cut short and parted in the middle, with wisps curling off negligently from her sideburns. There was a pencil-line scar over her right brow. Her fingers, curled around the glass she offered him, were long and thin, her nails bitten to the quick. She seemed more tangible, more down to earth, than he had imagined she would be the two times he had spoken to her on the phone. It came as a relief to him that he would not have to invent her.

Taking the prune cider from her, the Weeder looked around the cabin, or what he could see of it in the flickering light of the chimney and half a dozen candles. It seemed to be an echo of her: spare where she was gaunt, solid, no-nonsense furniture to match her solid, no-nonsense clothes. An assortment of cameras and lenses and tripods was heaped on a long scrubbed oak table in a corner. A high, narrow framed black-and-white photograph of a nude hung on one wall. The woman in the photo, seen through a partly open door, masked her face with her fingers and peered through them at the camera. Her eyes conveyed shyness or sadness—or all of the above. The photograph was illuminated by a candle set on the floor. In the photo the nude was illuminated by a candle set on the floor at her bare feet.

The house smelled of freshly baked cookies, which the Weeder spotted cooling in a tray on a window ledge above a wood-burning stove. It also smelled of camphor.

"The camphor," Snow said, reading his mind, "comes from the mackinaw over there. I found it yesterday in a trunk filled with camphor balls." Walking with a limp so slight it seemed more like a hesitation, she crossed the room and sat down in a rocking chair. She rocked back and forth, toying with a gold wedding band as she sized up her invited, then uninvited, then reinvited guest. The Weeder seemed mesmerized by the photograph of the nude. "You are wondering whether the woman in the photograph is me, but you are too conventional to ask," Snow guessed. "The answer is yes. Kundera has a character somewhere who talks about a girl's face lighted by the nudity of her body. That's the effect I was trying for." She twisted in the chair to look at the photograph, studied it for a moment. "In the end, clothes are a form of mask," she observed, thinking out loud. Turning back to the Weeder, she waved a hand toward his clothes. His trousers were rumpled, his sport jacket frayed at the sleeves, his shoes scuffed. There was a suggestion of irony in her voice as she asked, "Is this how you normally go calling?"

The Weeder grinned sheepishly. "Thoreau, who came from this neck of the woods, said you should distrust any enterprise that required new clothes."

Snow flashed a strained smile that the Weeder immediately recognized; it was the smile people used when they wanted to keep from crying. He had seen it on his mother's face at the funeral of his father; had seen it in the mirror the day he came home from work to find his wife had taken his son and left for good.

"What is it you want from me?" Snow asked.

"What I want," the Weeder told her, "is polite intercourse."

"That's a strange way of putting it."

"Why did you change your mind about seeing me after I phoned from New York?"

"I figured I had enough to worry about without adding your problems to my list."

The Weeder thought of the nails bitten to the quick, the strained smile thrown up like a barrier against tears. He realized that she had been ambushed—though by what, he couldn't say. "What do you worry about?" he asked her now.

"I worry about urethane in the wine, about acid in the rain, about parasites in the sushi, about radon in the potato cellar under the house. I worry about too much ozone in the air damaging my lungs. I worry about the earth overheating. I worry about a new ice age. Only yesterday I read that our galaxy is heading for a collision with the Andromeda galaxy."

"That won't happen for billions of years," the Weeder said. "The sun will have burned out by then."

Snow nibbled absently at a cuticle. "I worry about that too. Just because the sun sets at night is no guarantee it will rise in the morning." She leaned back tiredly in her rocking chair. The Weeder, remembering Nate, thought: People who are afraid are more interesting than those who aren't. Snow must have been reading his thoughts because she snapped, "I don't worry to be interesting. I worry because I'm lucid."

"Lucidity," the Weeder remarked, "is the enemy of passion. You're always aware of yourself being aware of yourself."

Snow regarded the Weeder as if she were seeing him for the first time. After a moment she said, "Aside from polite intercourse, what do you really want from me?"

"Snowden's your married name, isn't it, Matilda? Your maiden name was Davis. Your father was one of the Acton Davises, a direct descendant of Isaac Davis, who was killed leading the Acton Company against the British at the North Bridge in Concord in 1775."

The Weeder put his glass down on the edge of the chimney and settled into a high-backed wooden chair facing Snow. "Isaac Davis was married to a second cousin he met on Long Island. Her name was Molly. In those days a girl's father picked her husband for her—it had to do with uniting families and farms, not love. When Isaac fell in love with Molly, he asked her father for her hand in marriage and was flatly refused. So Molly got herself pregnant by Isaac to force her father's hand—he could risk a scandal or let them marry and hush things up. A great many girls did this in those days. It was the only way they could have a say in whom they married. Her father gave his consent and the young couple married and moved to Acton. The baby died a few days after it was born and the death was recorded in the Acton town ledger. Isaac was killed at the North Bridge. Molly was given her widow's third, which consisted of a slave named John Jack, who was valued at a hundred and twenty pounds sterling, a horse and a cart and some cash—and sent packing by her husband's family, who had enough mouths to feed. She returned to Long Island and wound up keeping house for a great-aunt living on a small farm in the village of Flatbush. Her child, your ancestor, was born on that farm."

"I don't see where all this is leading," Snow said. "I don't see what you want of me."

"I'm coming to that. Molly's maiden name was Fitzgerald. She detested the British with a passion. There wasn't anything she wouldn't do to get at them. She became an ardent, outspoken patriot, championing the rebel cause at town meetings, which—if you read the minutes of the meetings—rubbed some of the town elders the wrong way, since women in the Colonies weren't supposed to meddle in politics. Isaac, on the other hand, seems to have been very proud of her. When the British threatened to march on Concord, Molly organized the women into groups that made cartridges and rolled bandages. After she was widowed and exiled to Long Island, she wrote an acquaintance of her late husband attached to the Commander-in-Chief's staff offering her services to the rebel cause. Two days ago I discovered an unpublished letter from this acquaintance, whose name was A. Hamilton, indicating he took her up on the offer. A spy sent out behind the British lines made his way across Long Island to Molly Davis's farmhouse in Flatbush. She helped him scout the British positions in Brooklyn."

The Weeder, drained, settled back in his chair.

Snow rocked forward in hers. "And then what happened?"

"That's just it. I don't know. The trail ends with Molly Davis. A week later the spy was caught by the British and hanged at an artillery park in Manhattan on what's now the corner of Third Avenue and Sixty-Third Street. What happened during the missing week is a mystery."

"How can I help you solve it?"

"There's a hint in a letter Hamilton wrote to the spy's brother that Molly Davis kept a diary. The answers to my mystery must be in its pages." The Weeder studied Snow's face. "The answer to your mystery too."

Snow didn't understand. "What mystery is *my* mystery?"

"The baby conceived out of wedlock by Molly and Isaac died soon after birth. Isaac was killed at Concord in April 1775. Molly's baby—the great-grandfather of your great-grandfather—was born in Flatbush in 1777. Which means Isaac Davis wasn't his father."

"I've always heard that Molly was pregnant when Isaac was killed, that whoever recorded the birth made a mistake when he copied off the date in the ledger."

"Maybe."

"What does 'Maybe' mean?"

"It means maybe. And it implies 'Maybe not.'"

Snow let the rocking chair glide back again. "My grandfather sometimes went on for hours about the Revolution and Isaac and Molly. He could talk a streak once he started. To me it was all spilled milk, though I admit I used to wonder what she was like."

"She was strong-willed," the Weeder said. "You could see that from the way she got herself pregnant so she could marry the man she loved. She was supposed to have been a great beauty. At least that's what Isaac Davis said, but he may have been prejudiced. I came across two references to her in diaries written by other Acton women. That's how I know about her. Even in the puritanical Colonial times, girls tended to pretty themselves up to attract men. But Molly seems to have toned herself down. Her hands were rough and blistered from working on the farm; she is said to have worked the fields like a man. Her hair, for practical reasons, was cropped short. She favored loosefitting clothes . . ." The Weeder's voice trailed off as he realized he could have been describing the woman sitting across from him in the rocking chair. "I'm guessing," he continued carefully, "but behind her bold gaze must have lurked a shyness, a sadness. She'd been ambushed by grief. She'd lost a baby at birth, a husband. That kind of thing leaves its mark on the eyes."

The Weeder's story, his ardor in recounting it, seemed to weigh on Snow. "If you've come to me for the diary, I don't have it," she said. She noticed the disappointment in his face and added, "Maybe you'll have better luck at the local historical museum—they have a collection of Revolutionary diaries."

"I've been in touch with the museum. I've been in touch with the library. You're my last hope. Are you sure there isn't an old trunk somewhere? That's where you find this kind of document."

Snow shook her head.

"I suppose your grandfather must be dead?"

"Long dead and long buried." A thought occurred to her. "He used to show me photographs in an album."

The Weeder said, "Photographs won't help me—"

"I remember," Snow said, "that he kept the album in an old wooden sailor's chest with an enormous padlock on the outside. I always suspected there were other things in the trunk beside the photo album."

"Where is the chest now?"

Snow thought a moment. "I suppose everything Granddad had went to his wife, who was younger than he was. When she died, she was living with my grandfather's sister, Esther, who's my great-aunt. Esther's still alive. She sold the house and moved to Boston a few years ago."

"Will you give me her address?"

"It won't help you any. Esther's become a recluse. Since she lost all her hair she won't let anyone she doesn't know come calling."

The Weeder asked in a low voice, "Will she see me if you're with me?"

"She might."

He smiled at her. "How about it, Matilda? Will you help me solve our mystery?"

Snow ran the ball of her thumb across the scar over her eyebrow. "I'll make you a deal," she said suddenly. "I don't drive anymore and I need a ride into Boston tomorrow. You drive me in and hang around while I do a couple of errands, and I'll take you over to meet my great-aunt Esther."

6

Wanamaker missed the beginning of the call because of a burst of static. "Say again," he demanded once the line had cleared.

Huxstep, who had shoehorned his bulky body into a public telephone booth in Concord, said, "You-know-who told me to call you."

"Why doesn't you-know-who call me himself?" Wanamaker demanded.

Huxstep had the good sense to ignore the question. "You want I should give you the good news or the bad news first?"

Wanamaker groaned something about having enough static in his life already. "Start with the good," he said.

"The good news is we traced the Hertz car to the long-term parking lot at Logan Airport. The airport cops spotted it there about five hours ago."

To Wanamaker that sounded like bad news. "We've got ten days left before the Ides of March and you're telling me he took a plane somewhere?"

"He took a taxi somewhere," Huxstep said. "The somewhere

was an Avis office in Boston. He thought he was muddying the water. But it was amateur hour, you see what I mean?"

"So you got a fix on the car he's driving," Wanamaker said, trying to coax Huxstep through the narrative.

Huxstep would not be hurried. "He made a big point of asking directions to Cape Cod, so we knew right off he wasn't going there."

"Did you, or did you not, locate him?" Wanamaker wanted to know.

"Since this part of the story comes under the heading of good news, you ought to be able to figure out the answer."

Wanamaker was tempted to remind Huxstep that he was a utility infielder talking to the man who managed the team, but he decided this would only divert the conversation unnecessarily. So he waited for Huxstep to continue.

Huxstep cleared his throat with so much enthusiasm that Wanamaker thought he was being disconnected. Huxstep went on. "You-know-who, meanwhile, remembered something from our visit to the subject's loft in New York. The subject was looking for a pot of gold at the end of the rainbow, which said pot of gold was supposed to be in Concord, Massachusetts."

"What pot of gold?" Wanamaker asked, thoroughly confused. If this was the good news he hated to hear the bad.

"So we staked out the three roads into Concord," continued Huxstep, determined to tell the story in his own way, "me on one, your man Friday on another, you-know-who on the third. And guess what your man Friday saw one hour into the stakeout?"

"The Avis rental car," Wanamaker said tiredly.

"The Avis rental car," Huxstep agreed. "So after that all we had to do was some elementary road work and we knew where he was sleeping and who he was visiting."

"You mind if I ask you a question?" Wanamaker said, his voice oozing irony.

"It's your nickel."

"When is you-know-who going to terminate the operation?"

"Your question brings me to the bad news part."

"I was hoping you might have forgotten."

"The bad news part is the subject has been in contact with the pot of gold at the end of the rainbow, and you-know-who is worried that he might have told her the story of his life."

"That is definitely bad news," Wanamaker agreed.

"So unless you object, you-know-who is thinking of"—here Huxstep read off, word for word, what the Admiral had printed out for him on the back of an envelope—"killing two birds with one stone. But to do that he has to wait until the birds of a feather flock together."

Wanamaker exploded. "Unless I object! You tell you-know-who that I'm sitting here in Washington and he's out there in the goddamn catbird seat and it's up to him to figure out what to do, and not me, and once he figures out what to do, he should go and do it. You tell him that rank has its privileges, and one of them is operating independently without trying to lay off the blame on someone else if things go wrong by getting that someone else to authorize something at a distance. You tell him—" Wanamaker ran out of steam. "You tell him," he said in a tight voice, "to plug the leak. How he does it is his business."

"I will pass on your instructions," Huxstep said with unaccustomed dignity. "Plug the leak. How he does it is his business."

7

The Weeder was squirming at an execution taking place in his imagination. He tossed on his hammock of a bed listening to the dull hum of traffic on the highway beyond the motel. A toilet flushed somewhere on the floor above him and the water spilled through pipes in the wall near his head. He heard the sound of the tires of a slow-moving car crunching on gravel in the motel driveway. His heart missed a beat. He leapt from the bed and checked the door to make sure it was double-locked, then parted the curtains the width of a finger. The Weeder expected to see the Admiral pointing at the door of his room. He expected to see the burly man with the enormous handgun held at present arms, and the woman with the veil start toward it. But the only thing he saw was a dozen parked cars. He watched for a long while but there was no sign of life in any of them. Had he imagined the wheels crunching on the gravel? Had he imagined the Admiral, the burly man, the rail-thin woman? Had he imagined the attempts on his life?

If only he had. But he could still feel the heat of the flame from the fire-breather on the back of his neck. He could still see the burly man sighting over his finger and mouthing the words "Bang, Bang! You're dead!"

Feeling not the slightest bit sleepy, the Weeder slipped back into the hammock of a bed. He closed his eyes and tried to empty his head of thought. He had a vision of himself skating between thoughts, avoiding them as if they were patches of thin ice. The patches were marked by warning posts planted in the ice. One said Rods. One said Hair triggers. One said Wedges. He skated safely past the posts toward images vaguely visible on the horizon. In his mind's eye he could see one of them—it was Nate jumping barefoot from a longboat into the shallow water off a North Shore beach, wading ashore in the darkness and sitting on a rock to put on his stockings and the shoes with the silver buckles. He thought he could make out Molly, her dark hair cut short, walking toward Nate with an imperceptible limp, her eyes wary of a new ambush—only it wasn't Molly he was seeing, it was the woman named Snow, washed by currents of melancholy, too lucid to be passionate, always aware of herself being aware of herself.

8

Wearing washed-out jeans tucked into ankle-length leather boots and the mackinaw that smelled of camphor, carrying a leather knapsack filled with cameras and lenses slung over one shoulder, Snow strode with the peculiar gait that was less than a limp and more than a hesitation toward the Weeder's car. "Morning," she said, climbing in on the passenger's side. "Sleep well?"

"Not really," the Weeder said. He detected the odor of camphor and realized that in the space of one day he had come to associate the smell with her. "I had that weird kind of insomnia where you keep dreaming you're awake." He shifted into drive and started down the dirt road toward the main road.

"What you need to do," Snow explained, setting her knapsack on the floor of the car between her legs, "is brew yourself up some herb tea last thing before going to bed. Besides making you sleep like a baby, it's good for memory, broken nails and your sex life."

The Weeder glanced sideways at her to see if he was being teased, but she seemed deadly serious.

"I'm glad to get a ride into Boston," Snow announced. "When I'm on my own I never seem to get to where I started out for, at least not on time."

"You get distracted," the Weeder guessed. He turned onto the main road heading toward Concord and studied the rear-view mirror.

Snow noticed him peering into the mirror but didn't think anything of it. "It's not a matter of distractions," she said. "It's a matter of me. Before he died, my husband"—she flashed the smile that kept the tears at bay—"used to say I reminded him of late roses. What he meant was that I had an addiction to lingering."

The Weeder asked quietly, "How long have you been a widow?"

"Forever. At least it seems like that sometimes."

"I didn't mean to pry."

"My husband was killed in a car accident four years ago this spring. I was driving at the time."

"I think I see," the Weeder said.

She turned to him almost eagerly. "What do you think you see?"

"I think I see what ambushed you," he told her.

"I never thought of it as an ambush," Snow said. She brought a fingernail to her teeth and began nibbling on it. "When I could help it I never thought about it at all."

"That may be one of your problems," the Weeder suggested.

"Dime store psychology," Snow snapped.

They rode in silence for a long while, Snow absorbed in avoiding her thoughts, the Weeder absorbed in his driving and the rearview mirror. He turned onto the ring road that led to the Turnpike and downtown Boston. Remembering another trick from his countersurveillance course on the Farm, he slowed down and drove in the right lane. Through the rearview mirror he thought he saw another car slow down and pull into the right lane half a mile behind him—or was he imagining it? He speeded up, switched to the middle and then the left lane and passed several dozen automobiles before settling back into the right lane again. He studied the rearview mirror but didn't see anything out of the ordinary.

"You have a curious way of driving," Snow commented.

"Where are we going?" the Weeder asked.

"First stop is a gallery near the docks in downtown Boston. I'm having a show of some of my 'Invasion' photos. It's my last chance to check the lighting."

"What are 'Invasion' photos?"

"I did a series I call Invasions of Privacy. You saw one on my wall last night. Nudes, mostly, seen through doors that are open just a crack, through slightly parted curtains or Venetian blinds. What I'm getting at, in my way, is that we live in a world of invasions—countries invade other countries, governments invade our bedrooms, men invade women, television invades our homes, punk rock invades our culture. And so on. It's a long list. We spend our days listening to the details of the latest invasion and wait our turn. What's changed is that in the old days we knew when we were being invaded and could make a stand. Nowadays the invasions are more subtle—sometimes we don't even know they're taking place."

Snow's photographs, in thin silver frames hanging on whitewashed walls, made the Weeder squirm. They were invasions of privacy, and more. At the heart of each photograph was an intimacy, a wound. There was a series of three photos of old women, naked, seen through bathroom doors ajar a few inches. One was powdering her body. The second was shaving with a safety razor. The third had caught a glimpse of her reflection in a full-length mirror and was studying herself with a sad, unbelieving expression on her wrinkled face. There were several photographs of a slender young woman or, more properly, vertical slivers of her glimpsed through a partly open door; the third in the series, hanging directly opposite the photograph of the old woman who had caught a glimpse of herself in the mirror, showed the young woman with her head cocked, studying with a critical eye her naked body. It was clear from her expression that she liked what she saw. There was another series, taken through parted venetian blinds, of a naked middle-aged man with a cigarette dangling from his lips, watching television. In one photo he stared at the screen as if he had heard a joke but didn't get it.

"So?" Snow asked. They were back in his car, heading along the Fitzgerald Expressway toward the North End, where Snow planned to photograph squatters in an abandoned building earmarked for demolition. "What did you think of my Invasions?"

"Some of them embarrassed me."

"They were supposed to. Anything that's really good—that cuts deep—is embarrassing. Sometimes I think that all art involves an invasion of privacy—in the case of a novel, I suppose the author more often than not is invading his own privacy. Listening to Callas is an invasion of her privacy in the sense that she permits you into parts of herself so private you are embarrassed to be there."

"I always thought she let me into parts of *myself* I'd never been to before."

"That too," Snow said. She studied the Weeder with interest. "What is it you do for a living? Are you one of the invaders of privacy or an invadee?"

"I work for the government," the Weeder said vaguely.

Snow said, with obvious irritation, "That puts you on the side of the invaders."

"I guess it does."

"If you are one of the invaders," Snow asked, "why do you keep staring into your rearview mirror?"

"I like to keep track of the cars behind me."

"You're not very convincing when you lie. Take a left here. Park next to the fence. We'll walk the rest of the way. I don't want the squatters to see the car and get frightened off."

The building that loomed ahead, six stories, stood alone in the middle of a pile of rubble from surrounding buildings that had already been demolished. Except for two enormous cranes with teardrop-shaped wrecking balls dangling from their raised arms, the lot was deserted. A hand-lettered sign over the entrance to the building read: NO ENTRY—TRESPASSERS WILL BE PROSECUTED.

Snow took a Leica from her knapsack and fitted a telephoto lens onto it. "There was an article a few days ago about squatters occupying the building and refusing to move unless the city provided them with cheap housing," she explained.

The Weeder studied the building. "If there are people around, they're keeping a low profile."

Snow stopped to stare at the gaping holes where the windows had been. "I once saw a beehive with one wall made of glass. You could watch the bees making honey. Imagine if one wall of an apartment house was made of glass."

"Another invasion of privacy," the Weeder said.

"Another invasion of privacy," Snow agreed. "We're all fascinated by the things we fear." She started for the door. "Wait here if you like."

The Weeder caught up with her. They exchanged looks. He raised an eyebrow in a shrug. She smiled the first real smile he had seen on her face since he met her and ducked through the door into the shell of the building. The Weeder took a careful look around the lot. Satisfied that it was deserted, he followed her.

With Snow leading the way they climbed a staircase littered with trash and debris. At each floor Snow put her head into the hallway and listened for a moment. On the sixth floor she began to explore the apartments. Some of the walls had already been demolished, sinks and bathtubs pried loose, toilets shattered with sledgehammers—probably, Snow noted, by the demolition people to prevent squatters from using them. The windows had been ripped out and an icy wind cut through the gaps. Snow kicked in frustration at a heap of empty sardine tins; there had been squatters here after all but they appeared to have left. The tins went clattering across the naked planks of a kitchen floor where the linoleum had been pried up. "I guess I brought you out of your way for nothing," she said.

From outside came the sound of tires crunching on debris. The Weeder edged over to a gaping hole in a wall. A light snow had begun to fall and the crystals slanted in through the hole into his face. Squinting into the snowflakes, he looked down.

Six floors below a dark-colored four-door sedan crept to a stop in the middle of the lot. Three of the four doors opened. The Admiral, the rail-thin woman with the veil masking her eyes and the burly man with the handgun held at present arms emerged. The woman and the burly man trotted off and disappeared from view. The Admiral, his back arched into a parenthesis, looked up at the building, saw the Weeder and waved cheerily. He might have been coming to take tea.

Snow started toward the hole in the wall but the Weeder pushed her roughly back into the room. "We've got to get out of here," he announced in a voice so laced with fear that Snow instantly understood that their privacy was about to be invaded—and brutally.

The Weeder started for the stairwell. From the lot came the pulsating scream of a hand-cranked siren, then the muffled backfires of two crane motors spurting into life. At the staircase the Weeder leaned over the railing and looked down.

"Why are we running?" Snow asked in a frightened whisper.

"There are people outside who want my money *and* my life," the Weeder replied.

At that moment one of the teardrop-shaped wrecking balls exploded through a wall into the building one story below them. An instant later the second ball burst through another wall, pulverizing everything in its path. The floorboards on which they were standing vibrated violently. A cloud of debris and dust drifted up in the stairwell, obscuring the Weeder's vision, making it difficult to breathe. Snow, thoroughly terrorized, pulled a bandanna from her pocket and held it over her mouth and nose. The Weeder covered his face with a handkerchief and, pulling Snow along with him, backed away.

"What are you doing?" Snow cried through her bandanna. She tried to slip out of his grasp. "We've got to get down the stairs."

"There's no staircase to go down," the Weeder told her. "That's what the noise was—they've demolished the staircase between floors."

"You mean we're trapped up here?"

The Weeder dragged her back into a room and pushed her into a corner. Below, the motors of the cranes raced. And then a teardrop-shaped wrecking ball bit cleanly through the wall directly across the room from them and arced up to the ceiling before falling back through the wall and disappearing. The second wrecking ball exploded through the wall into the room behind them. The air turned opaque with dust. Snow screamed. The Weeder, his eyes tearing, located her from the scream and got a grip on her mackinaw and pulled her through a doorway into a hallway. They stumbled down the hallway into another room as one wrecking ball, and then the other, burst through outer walls behind them.

"They're trying to bury us alive," Snow cried.

"They're going to destroy the floor above the break in the staircase," the Weeder said. He looked around wildly. "We've got to get to a lower floor."

Outside, the two wrecking balls pummeled the building, exploding into it in brutal one-two punches every fifteen or twenty seconds. Each pair of explosions seemed louder and nearer than the previous ones as the giant teardrops worked closer and closer to where the Weeder and Snow were huddled.

Snow sank to her knees and pressed her palms to her ears to ward off the explosions. "Do you know the people who are doing this to us?" she sobbed.

The Weeder settled down beside her and put an arm over her shoulder. "I know them," he admitted bitterly. "I'm an idiot for getting you involved."

One of the wrecking balls reached the room next to them with a terrible smashing sound, followed by the peal of plaster raining down. The wall against which Snow had her back trembled. Snow was trembling too and the Weeder's description of Nate flashed into his head: like Nate, she was dancing leaf to gusts. There was another explosion in the next room, more violent than the previous one. The Weeder knew time was running out on them. He tried to move but his feet felt leaden. In his heart he knew there was no hope now, and no way out. Their crushed bodies would be discovered by a bulldozer driver clearing away the mountain of rubble. With a great effort the Weeder tried to pull Snow to him. She resisted. Angrily. She pounded on the floor with the palm of her hand. The pencil line scar over her eye turned livid. Tears streamed down her cheeks, leaving tracks on her dust-stained skin. The Weeder brought his mouth close to her ear and shouted out something he had just discovered. "I would have liked to love you."

Snow said something to him but it was lost in the explosion of a wrecking ball smashing into the building.

"What?" the Weeder yelled.

She brought her lips near his ear. "Tell me who you are," she yelled in a voice choking with terror.

He shook his head. The question made no sense. You can't tell someone who you are by telling them who you are, he thought. Then he realized he had said it out loud.

She pressed her lips violently against his ear. "Then show me who you are," she screamed.

Her words seemed to loosen the knot of fear in the Weeder's chest. He willed one foot to move, then the other. The wrecking ball reached the wall behind Snow; one instant the wall was there, swaying, cracking, the next it had disintegrated and he could see, through the swirling dust, the teardrop-shaped thing swinging back into the sky. It reached the limit of its arc and hung there and started back toward them. He jerked Snow to her feet and, moving backward, drew her through a door as the wrecking ball smashed into the corner where they had been huddling.

Grasping her mackinaw, the Weeder pulled her along a hallway. The mere act of putting distance between himself and the teardrops gave him strength. He spotted a small room filled with sinks and pipe joints and pulled her into it. On one wall was a small incinerator door, and right next to it a larger door.

The Weeder wedged Snow into a corner and opened the larger door. He discovered a shaft with two thick ropes running down through it. He reached out and pulled on one rope to see if it was attached to anything at the top of the shaft; it gave way immediately, but as he pulled it down hand over hand the other rope started up. From the shaft came the grinding, squeaking sound of something mounting. Outside the room the two wrecking balls smashed into the walls of the hallway. The Weeder tugged frantically on the rope. A shelf came into view. He pulled it up until it was level with the bottom of the door. He turned toward Snow, who was staring with vacant eyes at the ceiling quivering over their heads. Plaster rained down. He reached out and gripped the front of her mackinaw and drew her to him, then positioned her so that she was sitting on the edge of the door and slowly folded her onto the shelf.

One of the teardrops crashed into the wall of the hallway outside the small room. Overhead, a large piece of ceiling broke off and came splintering down behind the Weeder. He started to pull frantically on the rope, sending the shelf and the girl down the shaft. Darts of cold stung the back of his neck and his cheeks. Still pulling on the rope, he looked up. Flakes of snow were slanting in through the hole in the ceiling. There was another explosion outside in the hallway as a teardrop catapulted into a wall. The small room rose and fell under the Weeder's feet as if it were riding a ground swell. For a second or two he thought the floor would buckle and disintegrate, but it held. The Weeder jerked on the rope but couldn't make it descend any more. He thought it was stuck—that the girl was trapped in the shaft. Then it dawned on him that the shelf must have reached the basement. He hefted himself onto the lip of the door and swung his legs into the shaft. Grabbing the rope and twining his ankles around it, he started to slide down. The palms of his hands burned, but the sound of the teardrops crashing into the walls above him kept him from breaking his descent. He landed on Snow, who cried out in pain. Above their heads a teardrop crashed into the shaft. The rope jerked up out of the Weeder's hands and came sliding down on top of him and Snow. The shaft filled with plaster dust. Snow sucked in air in great heaving gasps; she sounded as if she were drowning. In the darkness the Weeder kicked savagely at the walls of the shaft. One of them suddenly gave way. A door opened. Snow spilled through the door and collapsed onto the cement floor of the basement.

Groping toward the dim light, the Weeder followed her and slammed the shaft door behind them.

Far above their heads the thunderclaps, duller, more distant, reverberated as the teardrops continued to hammer away at the building.

9

The Admiral was ecstatic. "It is not the kind of thing you believe when it is described to you," he whispered fiercely into the mouthpiece of the public telephone. "You'd have to see it with your own eyes to fully appreciate it. Your man Friday worked the levers like a man. First, we destroyed the stairwell between the fifth and sixth floors." The Admiral filled his cheeks with air and mimicked the dry burst of an explosion. "One second it was there, the next it was gone. There was no way they could get down. After that it was only a matter of systematically demolishing the upper story of the building. The walls disintegrated in clouds of dust. I've never witnessed anything like it in my life. It was"—he racked his brain for the appropriate word—"teratogenic."

"Tera what?"

The Admiral tore the word into its component parts, savoring each morsel. "The prefix, *terato*, is from the Greek. It means 'monster.' The suffix, *genic*, means 'producing.' Monster producing! You see what I'm reaching for?"

Wanamaker managed to get another word in edgewise.

"You are one hundred percent sure our little problem has been solved?"

"One hundred and fifty percent! Two hundred even! The workmen will discover their mangled bodies in the rubble when the rest of the building is demolished. They will surely be impossible to identify. If you want my opinion, the police will not know one was a man and one was a woman. Rag dolls. Broken bodies. Limbs, heads, sexual organs all over the place." The Admiral let out a cackle of high-pitched laughter. "They may not be able to identify the corpses as human. They may think some animals got trapped up there."

Wanamaker said, very gently, "Can I have a word with the jackass-of-all-trades?"

Toothacher was taken aback. "You want to speak to the jackass?"

"If you don't mind."

"I've already told you everything there is to tell."

"I need to talk to him about some housekeeping chores."

"Housekeeping chores?"

"If you don't mind."

Wanamaker could hear the Admiral cough several times in confusion. Then he heard Toothacher's voice, pitched high, almost hysterical in fact, call, "Huxstep, front and center."

There was the dull thud of the phone banging against metal. Huxstep came on the line.

"Yeah?"

"Can you talk?"

There was a pause. Wanamaker, his ear glued to his phone, heard the door of the booth slamming.

"Yeah, I can talk."

"What the fuck is going on with you-know-who? He sounds like he flipped his lid."

"He's on a high, is all. It happens when you're not used to it."

Wanamaker thought Huxstep was referring to a drug the Admiral had taken. "Not used to what?"

Huxstep cleared his throat in embarrassment. "Violence."

"Oh."

"He was real calm while it was going on. Directing traffic, you might say. More to the left. More to the right. But he got sort of carried away when it hit him what had happened. You got to understand, all his wars have been fought out in his head up to now."

"Will he be all right?" Wanamaker asked anxiously. The last thing he needed was a crazy retired admiral on his hands.

"It'll pass," Huxstep said. "It almost always does. I'm gonna give him a night on the town to sort of celebrate. Take his mind off it, focus on pleasures of the flesh, like they say."

"If there is any chance of him having a breakdown," Wanamaker warned, "I want him under lock and key."

A note of affection crept into Huxstep's voice. "Don't go worrying your head about it. I'll babysit him till his pulse is beating normal. Then I'll bring him in." Huxstep seemed to be talking to himself now. "A man like him you come across once in a century of Thursdays. Underneath the spit and shine he's genuine leather. Leave him to me," he added gruffly. "You-know-who is the keeper of the flame. I'm the keeper of you-know-who."

10

The Weeder sat on the edge of the tub in the upstairs bathroom, holding out his hands, palms up. He turned his head away as Snow, wrapped in a terrycloth robe, dabbed antiseptic on the wounds. She unscrewed the cap from a tube of homeopathic cream and squeezed a gob of it onto each palm. Soaking in a hot bath had calmed her down, though from time to time her lips trembled, her voice cracked, as if she were suddenly remembering, suddenly reliving. "You can start by rubbing your palms together," she instructed him. "And by telling me what's going on. Who were those people? And why did they want your money *and* your life?"

The Weeder rubbed his hands together and inspected them. A raw burn mark slanted diagonally across each palm.

"You haven't answered my question," Snow reminded him.

He raised his eyes and looked directly into hers. She turned away and walked across the bathroom—her limp was more pronounced now, probably because she was exhausted—and leaned tiredly against a tiled wall. The white of her bathrobe blended with the white of the tiles, so that all that seemed left of her was her deathly pale hands and face. "If you're right about what you said before," she ventured, "they tried to kill me along with you because they assumed you had already told me what you won't tell me now." She could see he was wavering. "Just before Virginia Woolf filled her pockets with stones and drowned herself in a river, she wrote something about having gone too far to come back again. Me too"—Snow's voice faltered—"I've gone too far. If you are offended by invasions of privacy, think of those balls crashing through the walls of that building."

He had thought about little else—while they were cringing in the pitch darkness of a windowless basement laundry room listening to the teardrops eating away at the sixth floor; when they tunneled out of the building at nightfall, Snow shaking like a leaf, and cleared the snow off the window of his rented car; when they drove through the silent streets without exchanging a word, the outside sounds muffled, Snow's teeth chattering from fear, the Weeder's eyes glued to his rearview mirror.

Snow emitted a nervous laugh. "In view of what we've been through, I invite you to call me what everyone else calls me, which is Snow."

The Weeder said, "You're not going to believe what I tell you. You'll think I'm making it all up."

She smiled one of those smiles she used to hold back the tears. "Try me."

And so he told her: about the organization in the government he actually worked for; about Wanamaker and

Operations Subgroup Charlie and Stufftingle; about Kabir College and vicious circles of uranium imploding, forming a critical mass, starting an uncontrolled chain reaction, otherwise known as an atomic explosion; about how he had stumbled across it all while trying to settle an old score with Wanamaker; about how he had tried to head off the atrocity by threatening to expose it; how Wanamaker had called in a retired admiral named Toothacher to walk back the cat and plug the leak. Once the Weeder started talking he found it difficult to stop. The emotional strain of the last few days put pressure on the language he used to describe his experiences. Words, phrases spilled from his lips. He sidetracked, backtracked, skipped ahead, drew conclusions and provided the evidence in bits and pieces afterward. "Wanamaker was responsible for her death. If he had shown the slightest remorse, given the faintest indication he was *sorry.* But he didn't, did he? And I had to wipe the smug smile off his face. So I invaded his space, his privacy, and found out about Stufftingle. And now he's trying to invade mine."

"Ours."

He nodded. "Life is arranged in vicious circles too," he plunged on. "I knew Wanamaker was on to me, was trying to eliminate me, because I recognized the burly guy in the parking lot, the one who tried to incinerate me—he used to be the Admiral's driver. I remembered him from when the Admiral came down to lecture at the Farm. His name was something like Hukstep. That's it. Huxstep, with an *x.* He used to do arithmetic tricks—he could multiply numbers in his head faster than you could work out the problem on paper. I remember we were all taking a course, it was called Tradecraft, Introduction to. It was a requirement, even for historians, even for future weeders of trivia. They would blindfold us and drop us off at night in a cornfield in the middle of nowhere and tell us to find our way back to the Farm before dawn. I was brought in by state troopers thirty-six hours later. They told us to sneak into a factory producing jet fighter planes and steal anything we could get our hands on. I was arrested by the security people as soon as I put a foot in the door. One thing I did right, though. They told us to follow someone—anyone—who worked on the Farm and report back on where he went, what he did. To this day I don't know why I picked the Admiral. I followed him two nights running. Two nights running Huxstep drove him to a roadside bar out in the boondocks. It was a pretty seedy place. The Admiral was burning the candle at both ends, so to speak. So I wrote it all up in my report and handed it in to my instructor. The next day the director of the school called me down to the front office. He was reading my report when I walked in. It was two pages long. Succinct. The punctuation was correct. I am very interested in punctuation, which tells you how things are related. 'You're not to talk about this report to anyone,' the director said. 'Ever. The Company doesn't make a habit of washing its dirty linen in public,' the director said. The Admiral's retirement was announced in the newspapers a week later."

The Weeder rambled on, chopping the air with his rope-burned hands, talking about how the Company had lost its moral compass; had adopted the tactics of the enemy; had become the enemy. Historians were painfully familiar with the precedents, he said. This was what had happened to the Bolsheviks after their revolution: to fight White terror they invented Red terror. And when Red terror triumphed it became institutionalized. It was no longer a matter of persuading people who disagreed with the Bolshevik point of view but of terrorizing them. Wanamaker's Operation Stufftingle had to be seen as Company terror, institutionalized. My man Nate, the Weeder said, would turn over in his unmarked grave if he knew about this. It was not what he had put his life on the line for. Was Snow—without thinking he used her name for the first time—was she familiar with the instructions issued by the Provincial Congress for raising an army? No? The Weeder happened to know the passage by heart, had even used it as an epigraph to his dossier on Nate. And he lifted his eyes and recited: "Let our manners distinguish us from our enemies, as much as the cause we are engaged in." Manners, of course, was to be understood in the old sense of the word, that is, as a reference to the moral aspects of conduct. Socrates, who had a tendency to reduce all philosophy to manners, argued that the greatest wisdom, the best manners, allowed you to differentiate between good and evil. In our day, in our society, manners refer to the way you hold your fork, and the Company, through the good offices of its obedient servant Wanamaker, was able to convince itself that our national interests would be advanced by the seemingly accidental explosion of an atomic bomb in the heart of Tehran.

The Weeder would have continued if Snow's great-aunt hadn't called upstairs, in a voice musical with age, that the soup was as hot as it was going to get. Snow ducked into a bedroom and threw on some clothes and came back to take the Weeder down. "The good part about what happened," she told him, "is that they must think we're buried in the rubble of that building, which means we're safe for a while. It could be weeks before they find out otherwise."

"The Ides of March is a week from Tuesday," the Weeder noted.

"What has that got to do with anything?" Snow asked.

"That's when the bomb is supposed to explode in Tehran."

Snow understood what he was driving at. "Unless—"

"Unless they know I'm alive and will blow the whistle on them if the bomb goes off."

"You're not—"

The Weeder said, "I don't see that I have much choice." And he added with a twisted, abashed smile, "I have my man Nate to think about."

11

Snow's great-aunt Esther was ninety-two years old, so she claimed when she was invited to give her age. Clicking dental bridges with the tip of her tongue, she held court from the head of the kitchen table, a thick knitted shawl draped over her shoulders to hide her fragility, a brightly colored scarf draped over her head to cover her baldness. "Don't be so polite—help yourself to more," she instructed the Weeder, pushing a serving dish in his general direction. She hiccupped once, brought her arthritic fingers up to her mouth and held her breath for a moment. Then she edged her hand away and waited with wide eyes to see if she would hiccup again. When she didn't a sly smile illuminated her face. "If there's one thing that doesn't impress me it's politeness. You know what they say? They say politeness doesn't put butter on parsnips. I don't have the faintest idea why anyone would say that but they do." She lost her trend of thought, turned sharply to Snow and demanded, "Where was I?"

"You were talking about politeness. You were saying it didn't put butter on parsnips."

Esther seemed surprised. "I said *that*? I must be mad as a hatter." She turned back to the Weeder. "Some folks think I am, you know. Mad as a hatter I mean. The way I see it life is a loop. You start off stark raving sane, moving yourself around like a piece on one of those racetrack board games that were the rage back in the twenties. You get to the point where folks begin to suspect you're a bit weird, you keep on moving round, you come to the part where they think you're off your rocker, and further along they're whispering about whether to commit you or not, that's how crazy you are, and you keep going on round till you reach the place where you're certified mad as a hatter, and then whoops, you're over the starting line and back into sanity country, 'cause in your madness you see things more clearly than the folks who are reckoned to be sane. Which is where I'm at now, young man, and what I see"—Esther fixed the Weeder with her unblinking mischievous eyes—"is you're running from something. Own up, young man. I saw you peeking through the blinds when you got here, you did it again when you came down to supper, but that wasn't what tipped me off. What tipped me off was your eyes. They're brimming with fear. It's nothing to be ashamed of, being afraid. In my experience, which is considerable, folks who are afraid lead fuller lives. Personally I understand fear; fear runs through my body the way sap runs through a tree. I live in fear that each day will be my last on God's earth. Well, I can't, knock wood, complain. I've lived more than most. And loved more than most. And been loved more than most." She glanced tenderly at the ancient fox terrier snoring away at her feet. The dog had lost all its hair because of a skin disease and was as pink-skinned as a newborn pig. "I like to try and imagine what visions are flashing through her head," Esther said, watching the dog's legs and tail twitch. "I expect she's remembering some juicy rabbit that gave her a run for her money." She hiccupped again but disregarded it. "I hope to God I twitch in my sleep," she said with sudden vehemence. "I hope to God I'm remembering some of the juicy rabbits I've chased in my time." She shrank tiredly back into her chair, smiling, clicking a bridge. "I hope to God I've got a chase or two left in me." A faraway look came into Esther's eyes. She let her tongue toy with the bridge for a while, then turned absently toward Snow. "Where was I, dear?"

"You were saying that Silas here is running from something."

"I'm right, aren't I?" Esther insisted.

Snow nodded.

"You know who he's running from?"

Snow nodded again. "It's someone named Nate. The thing you have to understand about Silas"—Snow looked across the table at the Weeder, discovering a truth as she heard herself say it—"is that he's running slowly enough to make sure he gets caught."

Esther hiccupped in exasperation. "That sounds like something fraught with meanings. I don't know as I have the stamina to poke under the surface of things anymore. I've got another question for the both of you." She looked slyly from one to the other. "Are you two sleeping together or apart?"

Snow blushed and said "Apart" just as the Weeder, without thinking, said "Together."

Once again Esther fixed him with her unblinking eyes. "She's got the rights of it and you're just hoping the wish will become parent to the act. Fact is you're not intimate enough to sleep together. The way I figure it, you can be intimate without being sexual but the vice versa is a natural disaster for everyone concerned. Course the young folks today don't see things quite like that, but when they've put as many years under their belts as I've put under mine they will. Good Lord, I do go on, don't I? If folks are destined to be lovers time is the one thing they have going for them—they don't have to *rush.* They can afford to let nature take its course, which is one of the great luxuries of life that has been more or less discarded. Clocks have been speeded up. Everyone's in a mad rush, though they don't have any idea where they're going. Folks are so busy getting nowhere fast they don't bother to communicate anymore."

Esther's tongue pried a bridge loose in her gums and snapped it back into place. "In my experience," she said, scraping back her chair, pushing on its arms to raise herself into a standing position, "the more intimate folks are, the more they have a tendency to communicate in codes. Are you interested in codes, Mr. Sibley?"

The Weeder stood up. "As a matter of fact I am."

Esther indicated with a jerk of her head that she expected the Weeder to follow her into the living room. "Tell me about it," she ordered. She brushed him away when he tried to take her arm and, swaying slightly, started toward the door. The Weeder turned back to help Snow clear the table but she waved him away too. "This is what you came for," she said.

"Where was I?" Esther asked as the Weeder settled onto the couch next to her.

"You asked me about my interest in codes."

"Did I? I don't remember that. But that's as good a place as any to pick up a conversation. Truth is I don't sleep when I go to sleep." Here she cackled at a memory. "My father, may he rest in peace, used to say old age was a shipwreck but it's only in the last twenty years that I understood what he was getting at. Since sleep is out of the question I like to keep the conversation going as long as possible. So, young man, I invite you to tell me about your interest in codes."

"I'm interested in one code in particular," the Weeder said. And he told Esther how his man Nate had arranged with A. Hamilton to send back information using coded phrases taken from Addison's play, *Cato.*

"My father was something of a Revolutionary War buff," Esther remarked. "He would have loved to hear your stories about Nate. He was mighty proud of the fact that his great-grandfather was one of the first killed by the British—he was shot dead leading his men against the North Bridge at Concord. My father's grandfather was born during the Revolution. I remember my father boasting about how his great-grandmother once helped an agent of General Washington's . . ."

"His great-grandmother would have been Molly Davis," the Weeder said excitedly.

Esther clicked a bridge into place in surprise. "Now how would you know about Molly Davis?"

"And the agent she helped was my man Nate."

"Your man Nate, who you're running away from but slow enough for him to catch up with you?"

The Weeder smiled, nodded. "Did your father ever mention Nate's name in connection with Molly Davis?"

Esther thought a bit. "Don't remember him ever talking about Nate, to tell the truth. But I remember him describing the arrival of General Washington's agent in Flatbush. Molly, I'm embarrassed to admit it, had a slave—"

"John Jack."

"That's the one. John Jack. He happened on someone spying on her through the window. He rammed a gun into the small of the man's back and marched him around to the front door." Esther leered lecherously. "Your man Nate, if he and the agent were one and the same, was a *voyeur*, young man!"

"How did your father know so much about Molly Davis?" the Weeder asked.

"I suppose he learned some of it from his father and grandfather, and some of it from Molly's penny notebook."

The skin on the Weeder's face tingled. "What became of this penny notebook?"

Esther said, "Why, I imagine it's still tucked away in that old sailor's chest of his in the attic. Do you want to take a look at it?"

Speaking very quietly, the Weeder said, "I'd jump at the chance."

12

Here, at last, is the part where my man Nate meets Molly Davis:

I see him as distinctly as if I were walking alongside him as he made his way down the spine of a dirt lane that cut under the heights of The New Lots to the village of Flatbush. The night would have been as bright as a night with a sliver of a moon can get. A warm, damp breeze was probably blowing in from the Atlantic, making the planets appear swollen and near enough to touch. A shower of meteorites blazed high overhead, leaving long-fading fingers trailing across the heavens. On either side of the lane, fireflies filled the dark fields with thousands of pinpricks of light as they flashed urgent coded messages to each other. So Nate would have imagined then; so I imagine now.

Nate, dressed in coarse breeches and an old coat with deep pockets, carrying his wooden shoemaker's kit strapped to his back, was roughly halfway between The New Lots and Flatbush when his ears caught the drumbeat of hoofs. He scurried into the underbrush in time to avoid a lobster patrol, Grenadiers, judging from their high bearskin hats silhouetted against the stars. They passed close enough for Nate to hear the brass matchboxes fastened to their chests tapping against the brass buttons of their tunics.

Several miles down the lane he found the farmhouse that A. Hamilton had described—it was on the outreaches of Flatbush, the second house down from the communal barn with the date "1747" carved over the double doors. As a matter of prudence, Nate decided to scout the house before announcing his presence. He could hear the notes of a pianoforte coming from a front room, but he couldn't make out who was playing because the shutters had been fastened for the night. Weaving between the fireflies, Nate circled around to the back of the house. Nearby a dog howled and several other dogs farther down the lane took up the cry. The barking ceased as suddenly as it had started. Nate spotted a faint light where a back shutter had been left ajar. He climbed over a fence and crossed the yard to the shutter. All the panes of the mullioned window behind the shutter but one had been replaced with animal skins stretched and oiled. Nate pressed closer to the single pane that remained. He found himself looking into a small bedroom. Against one wall was a narrow truckle bed covered with an indigo-blue quilt. In the middle of the room was a naked woman. She was standing in a low tin tub filled with water, her profile toward Nate, her nose and mouth covered with a bandanna soaked in camphor, the pungent odor of which reached Nate outside the window. A whale oil lamp with a floating wick was set on the floor next to the tub and its flame projected flickering shadows of the woman as she sponged herself in the tin tub.

Staring at her shadow dancing on the wall and ceiling, Nate surely caught his breath and leaned forward. The skin on his face must have tingled. He would have followed each movement she made, oblivious to everything else in the world. I can see her in my mind's eye reaching for a towel folded over the back of a settle chair. I imagine her about thirty years old, with incredibly pale skin and (over the bandanna) eyes that conveyed shyness or sadness. Or all of the above. Her dark hair would have been cut short and parted in the middle, with wisps curling off negligently from her sideburns. Her shoulders would have been bony and narrow, her breasts small and jutting, her stomach flat, her pubic hair a tangle of damp curls. Throwing the towel over a shoulder, she stepped from the tub and walked with a slight limp (her leg had been broken in a fall from a horse and badly set) to a mirror hanging on the inside of a door.

Watching the woman as she studied her reflection in the mirror, taking in the lean line of her back, her buttocks, her muscular thighs and calves (it turned out that she covered the equivalent of twenty miles a day spinning on her "walking wheel"), taking in her bare ankles and her bare feet, Nate surely lusted after her as he had never lusted after anyone or anything in his life.

Contrary to published reports, my man Nate was no archangel. The fact of the matter is he had never set eyes on a naked woman before. He had imagined one often enough;

had peeked with his classmates at sketches of the female body in medical texts at Yale; had once sweet-talked a girl into taking off her stockings and slippers and wading in the Connecticut River with him; had been mesmerized by the memory of her bare ankles and her bare feet for months afterward. But the vision that confronted him now transported him to a different level of existence. He felt lightheaded. He heard his heart pounding. He sensed an erection forming and instinctively thrust it into the side of the house. (I know you are out there, Nate, lurking in the crevices of your myth, squirming as I approach. I'm getting uncomfortably close, aren't I, Nate?)

He would have been content to stand with his nose pressed to the pane of glass and his erection pressed against the wall, watching the naked woman for the rest of his natural life if he hadn't felt the business end of a blunderbuss stabbing into the small of his back under his shoemaker's kit. In the darkness behind Nate someone chuckled quietly. "Figured as how them dogs wasn't howlin' for nothin'. Ol' equalizer's loaded with buck 'n' ball," a Negro voice announced. "Jus' move a muscle, ol' John Jack, he gonna cut you into two peepers 'stead-a one. Now go'n lift them hands a yours straight up."

Nate raised his hands over his head and froze.

"Now you gonna start yerself walkin' real slowlike 'round to the front door, which is where a gentleman, which is what you sure as hell ain't, would-a come to in the first place."

Nate risked a glance over his shoulder, made out the tall Negro holding the blunderbuss and did as he was bid. He reached the front door of the farmhouse, pushed it open with the toe of his shoe and stepped into the room. A woman bent with age, wearing a thick knitted shawl draped over her fragile shoulders, sat on a stool in front of the pianoforte, nodding and singing as she played what Nate recognized as an old English nursery rhyme. An old dog twitched in his sleep at her feet.

Here is her song:

If buttercups buzz [she sang, off-key] after the bee;
If boats were on land, churches on sea;
If ponies rode men, and grass ate the cow;
If cats should be chased into holes by the mouse;
If mommas sold their babies to gypsies for half a crown;
If summer were spring and the other way round
Then all the world would be upside down.

And thumping on the keys with her arthritic fingers, the old woman started to repeat the refrain:

Then all the world would—

Suddenly she caught a glimpse of the Negro pointing his blunderbuss at a stranger. Her eyes widened. Her mouth worked, but no sound emerged. Then she found her vocal cords and screeched, "Molly! Come quick! John Jack's gone and caught himself a rebel!"

A door flew open. The woman who had been sponging

herself in the tub stood under the lintel, one hand raised and touching it. She was wearing a man's flannel dressing gown buttoned up to her neck. Her feet, visible beneath the hem, were still bare. The bandanna that had been over her mouth and nose was gone, but she still reeked of camphor.

"Found 'im peepin' thru the winda," John Jack reported. He prodded Nate in the back. "Who went, an' said anythin' 'bout you lowerin' them hands'a yours down?"

Nate's hands shot up again. He addressed the young woman. "You must be Molly Davis."

"What do you want from me?" she asked from the door.

"What I want," Nate told her, "is polite intercourse."

The woman measured Nate with her sad eyes for a long moment. Presently she asked, "What is your name?"

Nate told her. She hesitated, then indicated with a jerk of her head that she expected him to follow her into the bedroom. John Jack and the ancient woman exchanged looks. John Jack shrugged and lowered his blunderbuss. Nate let his hands sink of their own weight to his sides, thrust them into the deep pockets of his waistcoat and plunged past Molly into the bedroom, into the odor of camphor. She followed him and closed the door. He turned to face her. The tin tub half-filled with water stood like a lake between them.

Once again he saw her standing naked in the tub, saw the curve of her breast as she reached for the towel, and he had trouble collecting his thoughts. "I have a letter," he finally managed. "For you. From A. Hamilton."

Slipping the wooden shoemaker's kit from his shoulders,

Nate sat down on the settle chair, took off his right shoe and removed a folded letter from its hiding place between the inner and outer soles. Stepping around the lake Molly accepted the letter, scooped up the whale oil lamp from the floor and walked with an almost imperceptible limp to the bed. She placed the lamp on a night stool, sat down on the edge of the mattress and slit open the seal with the edge of a fingernail. Moving her lips, sounding out each word, she read the letter. "We must burn this," she said, looking up at Nate. "I will help you in every way I can." Her eyes avoided his. "Is it true you were spying on me through the window?"

Nate reddened. "I wanted to be sure I had the right house." He nodded toward the bandanna soaked with camphor, neatly folded on a side table and, hoping to change the subject, asked, "Why do you breathe in camphor?"

Molly said, "A woman in the village told me that a handkerchief soaked in camphor and held to the nose five minutes each day will prevent the yellow fever, beside purging the nasal passages and the lungs. You smile at things you don't understand. It does you no credit. Back in Ireland they have a saying—what butter and whiskey won't cure there's no cure for. But I don't hold with that. I believe in herb plasters and quince juice and lily roots and a salve made of opium and honey. It is well known that arsenic taken in small doses cures indigestion. The resin of a dragon tree calms the swelling that comes from gout." Molly became aware of Nate's eyes riveted on her. "Why do you stare at me? Because you saw me without clothing? You must be very innocent.

Are you tongue-tied? Say something." Molly's eyebrows glided toward each other, her mouth stretched into a suggestion of a smile, though it seemed to Nate to be the kind of smile that was an alternative to tears. "To start with, tell me where you are from."

"Connecticut."

"Where in Connecticut?"

"Coventry."

"Are Connecticut folks still hot for the war?"

"Lukewarm would be more like it," Nate told her. "In some townships they were obliged to pick names from a hat to fill the quota of recruits for the summer campaign. Some whose names were picked paid substitutes to take their place. I heard of one man who sent his black slave in his place."

"A good victory will change all that," Molly said confidently. "Do you know about the lobsters landing at Kipp's Cove on Manhattan Island?" When Nate shook his head in surprise she added, "John Jack came in from the Brookland Heights with the news this afternoon. Seems like the lobsters went across in barges from the New Town Creek on the fifteenth. The Continentals holding the beach cut and ran as soon as the lobsters turned up. They say General Washington was almost taken as he tried to rally his troops."

"What happened to General Putnam and the men holding New York City?"

"They're supposed to be working their way along the Broad Way toward the Haarlem Heights and Washington's main body. If the lobsters haven't already occupied the city, they soon will."

Nate allowed as how the military situation looked bleak. Molly agreed. Nate explained why Washington had dispatched him behind the British lines. "He figures he's got to hold out on the Heights for a good month or two if he's going to pull his regiments together for a retreat. He sent me to find out if Howe plans to give him the time he needs."

Molly stood up. Once again her shadow danced on a wall behind her. "I know the western reaches of the Long Island like the palm of my hand," she said. "I used to picnic with Isaac at the New Town Creek. We will start off first thing in the morning."

"We? Who said anything about you coming along?"

"The roads are crawling with lobster patrols and Tory roadblocks," Molly said. "You'll be less conspicuous if you're with a woman. I can say I'm taking you back home to whip the cat. The lobsters will wink at each other and whisper snide comments, but the chances are good they'll let us go on." Before Nate could disagree she started for the door. "Be careful what you say in front of my great-aunt," Molly instructed him before she opened it. "She's a diehard Tory and always mentions Farmer George in her prayers. So do I—I damn his soul to burn in purgatory till the end of time."

Molly prepared a glass of warm milk laced with honey for Nate, found him a spare blanket and installed him on a pallet on the dirt floor of the larder. Returning to her bedroom, she pulled a document box out of her dowry trunk, unlocked it with a key she kept hidden in a crack between two floorboards, pushed aside some legal papers (her marriage certificate, the deed to John Jack) and removed the diary she had been keeping in a penny notebook since her marriage. She flipped to the entry recording the death of her husband, Isaac. "Ambuſh'd by greeſ," she had noted on a page stained by tears. "Life seems not worth living." She turned to the last blank page, dipped a goose quill into a jar of ink and carefully printed out the following:

"Septembre the twenty second, 1776. An Agent from General Waſhington by name Nate Hale, a remarcable man with out corruption albeit stil a yuth, sent out to scout ye Enemy lines, ariv'd this night at ye farm in Flatbuſh. Being nak'd and at my Toilet I spied him loytring at my window but giveing way to pastions long thout ded I made no outward sign and tarry'd the more to be seen. I aſk myſelf if it be sinful & contrary to nacher to deſire to be deſir'd." Molly looked up from the diary to reflect on the moral aspects of the problem, then bent her head and wrote: "And I reply: NO!"

I'm up to Nate and Molly scouting the British dispositions:

At first light next morning Molly—still smelling vaguely of camphor—roused Nate, who was sleeping like a baby on the floor of the larder. She handed him a steaming cup of mocha coffee as he stepped into the common room. Through the open front door Nate could see John Jack attaching the traces of a buck cart to a gray mare. Molly drew on a dust cape over her dress and, walking with a limp so slight it seemed more like a hesitation, went outside. Nate hefted his wooden shoe repair kit onto one shoulder, swallowed the last of his mocha and followed her. Down the lane the first cocks were crowing into the morning. Hiking her skirt (knowing Nate he would not have missed the flash of her ankle), Molly climbed nimbly onto the seat of the cart. Nate deposited his kit in the back and took his place alongside her. John Jack handed up the reins to Molly. "See that Great-aunt wears her shawl," Molly instructed the Negro. "If she complains of swelling in her joints, mix a thimbleful of resin from the earthenware jar with her tea. We'll be back in two days, God willing." With a cluck of her tongue and a snap of the reins she set the horse into an easy trot.

Smoke spiraled up from the chimneys as Nate and Molly made their way through the deserted lanes of the village and headed through Flatbush Pass toward Brookland and the British positions in the marshlands north of the town. They encountered a Tory roadblock on the northern end of the pass, but the two guards who were awake were content to check Nate's wooden shoe repair kit and hand him a recruiting leaflet, which he read out loud to Molly as they continued on their way.

"It's addressed to 'All Intrepid Able-bodied Heroes,'" he told her. "Listen to this garbage. 'Spirited fellows who are willing to engage will be rewarded at the end of the war, besides their laurels, with fifty acres of land.' At least on our side most of the men who engage do so out of patriotism."

"And what is patriotism?" Molly inquired.

"Why, nothing more or less than the feeling you have for a country, for its people; nothing more or less than the conviction that their manners distinguish them from their enemy; that they are capable of boundless energy and boundless generosity and boundless justice."

"You harbor no uncertainty about this rebellion of ours?"

"About the rebellion I am not at all in doubt. About what comes afterward I am less sure."

Molly asked for instances. Nate gave some. John Adams claimed that by balancing the legislative, executive and judicial branches of a government against one another, the tendency in human nature toward tyranny could be checked, but Nate wasn't convinced. Nor was this the only problem he foresaw. In victory would the standing army that Washington was so desperate to raise subvert the liberties it was created to protect? Would Washington become king of the Colonies? Would the larger states in an eventual union devour the smaller ones? Would the slave states, by exploiting cheap labor, oblige the antislave states to adopt their ways in order to compete economically?

"Would you then impose your antislavery point of view on the states that favor slavery as a condition of joining the union?" Molly wanted to know.

Nate agreed he would if he had his way. "I don't see how we can complain about being slaves to the British on the one hand, and keep a sixth of our citizens in a state of perpetual slavery to us on the other hand. There is no logic in this, not to mention justice."

Molly plucked the whip from its sheath and beat in annoyance at the flank of the mare, which quickened her pace. "You surely consider it inconsistent of me to be a rebel against the King and a slave owner at the same time."

"I meant no criticism of you—"

"Your meaning was clear. John Jack came to me as a part of my widow's third when my husband was killed. He was valued at a hundred and twenty pounds sterling. I got him and the mare and the buck cart and my dowry trunk and fifty pounds sterling and a fistful of Continentals not worth a plug of tobacco and some pewter plates and my walking wheel and the clothes on my back, and was packed off to play nursemaid to my great-aunt, who had a spare bedroom and needed looking after. Without John Jack I'd have to pay someone to plow and sow and reap, and that would be the end of us." The mare, running now, was foaming at the corners of her mouth and droplets of foam were spraying back onto Nate and Molly, but she didn't appear to notice. "You're so hot under the collar about Negro rights, but a married woman has less rights than a slave. A slave can sue a white man or a Negro but a married woman doesn't exist as far as the courts are concerned. She can't vote or sue or put her name to a contract. She can't even draw up a will. A slave can keep what wages he earns, some have even saved up enough to buy their freedom, but a wife's wages belong by law to her husband." Molly became aware of the horse foaming and drew back on the reins, slowing her to a walk. She looked sideways at Nate and said bitterly, "When have you ever heard of a wife saving up enough to buy her freedom?"

"Was marriage so bad to you then?" Nate asked.

"Isaac was a gentle man and good at lovemaking and I dearly miss his company," Molly said. She added passionately, "But that doesn't change one thing I have said about a married woman being more of a slave than a slave."

Molly fell silent and Nate decided it was the better part of wisdom to let the issue rest. A company of Royal Artillerymen in blue and red tunics overtook the buck cart, coming from Graves End. Nate counted fourteen six-pounders and five wagons covered with tarred canvas and probably filled with powder and shot. The artillerymen astride the horses pulling the cannon bantered with Molly as they rode past. "What a lass like you needs is a King's man," shouted a trooper with a gray beard.

"Do you think you can get it up, what with you being this far from home?" Molly shouted back gaily.

"If I can get it out I can get it up," the trooper retorted to the amusement of his comrades.

"Watch you don't anger them," Nate whispered, but by then Molly was laughing at every remark and giving back as good as she got. She pulled up to rest the mare and let the dust raised by the artillerymen settle, and started off again. The cluster of houses that formed Brookland came into view as they climbed the heights and followed its crest. At the edge of town a half dozen Light Dragoons with dirty red plumes jutting from their brass helmets stopped the buck cart and questioned them. Molly explained that she had been visiting a great-aunt in Flatbush and was returning home to Brookland with a shoe repairman she had picked up on the road. The lobsters exchanged knowing looks, checked Nate's wooden kit and let them pass.

They stopped for wedges of meat-and-vegetable pie and tankards of cider at The Sign of the Black Kettle on the waterfront of Brookland. The main room of the inn was crowded with merchants and traders and they had to squeeze in on a bench across from two coopers who were nibbling raw garlic cloves with their meal. Farther down the table half a dozen young officers from a Tory regiment were drinking Madeira. One of them could be overheard boasting about Washington's days being numbered. A Tory with a sickle-shaped whisker on each cheek asked how far it was from Frog's Neck to King's Bridge. Eight, maybe nine miles as the crow flies, someone guessed. The Tory with the whiskers said something that Nate didn't catch. The others laughed boisterously. Nate and Molly avoided each other's eyes.

After lunch they walked the length of the waterfront, examining the cargo ships and men-of-war tied up or anchored out waiting their turn for a pier. Nate noted the names of the men-of-war and counted their guns, and ducked behind a toolshed to scribble in his notebook Latin words, which, when sounded out, read:

HMS *Roebuck*, forty guns
HMS *Orpheus*, thirty-two guns
HMS *Carysfort*, twenty-eight guns
HMS *Rose*, thirty-two guns
HMS *Phoenix*, forty guns

"Did you notice anything curious about the British warships?" Nate asked Molly as they climbed back into the buck cart.

"Only the Union Jack, the sight of which brings bile to my throat," she replied.

"Ships of the line have four to six longboats each. But there were none in the davits, and none alongside, and none at the piers."

"Maybe they are all off to Manhattan, provisioning."

"Maybe," Nate said thoughtfully.

"Which implies 'Maybe not,'" Molly noted.

The highway outside of Brookland was crawling with lobsters going in both directions. Molly talked her way past two roadblocks, one manned by Tories, one by Northumberland Fusiliers in bearskin hats, and put the mare into a fast trot as they headed up the highway that skirted the New Town Creek and led to the New Town and, beyond, the village of Flushing. Off to the left a gently rolling series of slopes hid the low-lying marshes that surrounded the creek. "It's from there the lobsters launched their boats against Kipp's Cove," Molly explained, waving a hand.

"We ought to take a gander at it," Nate suggested.

Molly drove the buck cart off the highway and hid it and the mare behind a thick tangle of wild blueberry bushes. Leaving her dust cape in the cart, popping blueberries into her mouth, she trailed after Nate across the fields toward a rise. As he neared the top he crouched low and crawled the last few yards. Molly, her lips dyed blue, crawled up beside him and together they looked out through the tall grass at the New Town Creek, with the East River and Manhattan Island beyond. The afternoon was stifling hot and filled with the dry ticking of crickets. Kipp's farmhouse and, farther north, Turtle Bay and the Beekman mansion overlooking it were all visible across the river. The creek itself, angling off toward Nate's right, was crammed with longboats moored in rows a dozen abreast—Nate counted nine rows—and buzzing with activity. Scores of tents had been set up parallel to the creek line, and hundreds of men could be seen stacking kegs of powder and cartons of shot on the shore near the boats, cleaning cannon or muskets, caulking boats that had been beached and turned upside down. Beyond the tents, in a field, a sergeant major was putting half a hundred highlanders in kilts through their paces; on a shouted order that Nate could just hear, the men knelt and made as if to fire, then gave way to a second rank that knelt and made as if to fire in turn. Nate whistled under his breath and put a palm on Molly's back, which was soaked through with sweat. "The ones in blue coats are Hessian Grenadiers, the ones in green, Jaegers. They say the Jaegers were recruited from hunters and game wardens in Germany and are all sharpshooters. The yellow uniforms over there must be the 29th Worcestershires; we took one of them prisoner outside Boston. The purple are the 59th East Lancashires. See the white leggings and scarlet coats? Those must be the famous 5th and 52nd Grenadiers—the ones Howe led against my Colonel Knowlton at the rail fence beneath Breed's Hill. If I had to guess,

I'd say there were three thousand men out there if there was one."

Molly asked, "How many men can one of those longboats hold?"

Nate was recording what he saw, in Latin, in his notebook. "I should think fifty or sixty."

"Nine rows of boats with twelve to a row makes a hundred eight boats, plus the three being caulked makes a hundred and eleven, multiplied by, say, fifty, makes"—she scratched some numbers in the dirt with a fingertip—"Five thousand five hundred fifty." Staring out at the British soldiers, Molly's eyes narrowed. "When I see lobsters the Irish in me smothers the woman in me," she said in a bitter undertone.

"How old were you when you came across to the Colonies?"

"I was going on seven."

"Do you remember Ireland at all?"

"I remember the humiliation of living in an occupied country. I remember the violence of the occupiers—the people baitings, the bear baitings, the public hangings. Once the lobsters strung up a fourteen-year-old girl for stealing a lace handkerchief. Till the day I die I'll hear her screams as they carted her through the streets with a sign around her neck. I remember the sound of the sea and the swell of the sea that took me away from all that, or so I thought. And here they are again. You and your like fight because you are patriots. I fight because I'm doing what the Irish anywhere in the world get the most pleasure out of—killing lobsters."

Nate finished scribbling notes to himself in the notebook. He remembered the Tory officer at the Black Kettle mentioning King's Bridge and Frog's Neck. "Where exactly is Frog's Neck?" he asked Molly.

"If you follow the East River up a few miles past Hell Gate and the Two Brothers, where the river empties into the sound there's a spit of land sticking out of the north shore that looks like a frog's neck."

Nate remarked, "I heard the rapids at Hell Gate were treacherous."

"Depends on the season," Molly said. "Depends on who's piloting the boat. The locals sail through all the time to fish in the sound."

In the distance the sergeant major, drawing out his words, could be heard crying, "Fix . . . bayonets." Nate, preoccupied, mumbled, "Folks in my neck of Connecticut have a saying: You can't plow a field by turning it over in your head. We've seen all we need to. Let's go."

Here's where Nate figures out what the lobsters are hatching and devises a scheme to thwart them:

Nate and Molly doubled back toward Brookland, taking their sweet time so as not to arrive before the Tories guarding the roadblocks had been relieved by the afternoon shift. They left the buck cart behind a shed near the waterfront and the mare in a fenced-in field, tipped a teenage boy to keep an eye on both and crowded onto the flat ferry to

New York City, arriving as the sun was setting behind the Jersey ridges. A silken breeze blew in from the Narrows, ruffling curtains in open windows. The wide city streets were filled with mounds of uncollected garbage that crawled with rats as large as rabbits. Several children with homemade bows and arrows stalked the rats, but they scurried away into the garbage before the hunters could get a shot at them. The barricades that the colonials had thrown up on the approaches to the river had been demolished by the lobsters and piled in heaps against the sides of buildings. Nate spotted a ROOMS TO LET sign on a sprawling clapboard house a block up from the ferry landing and knocked on the door. He started to turn away when the landlady, fixing her shrewd eyes on him, announced that there was only one room and one bed available, but turned back when he felt Molly's elbow jabbing into his spine. He paid for the room and scrawled an invented name on the ledger in the hallway, caught Molly's eyebrows arched suggestively and hastily added "and wife" after his signature. Nate hefted his wooden kit onto his shoulder and he and Molly followed the landlady up two flights to a small back room with a window with leaded panes looking out on a vegetable garden. There was a high narrow bed against one wall, a ceramic basin under a hand pump against the other wall. For decoration there was a broken banjo clock and a line portrait of George III that had been torn from a magazine and framed.

"The candles," the landlady announced, nodding toward

the two tapers in pewter holders on the table, "are extra. You can settle up when you leave."

As soon as the landlady had departed Molly turned on Nate. "How can you be sure?" she demanded, picking up the argument where it had been left off.

"There are two things we know about the lobster General Howe," Nate insisted. "He's an expert on amphibious operations—he's already proven that twice, once in shifting fifteen thousand troops to Graves End to attack Long Island, the second time in the landing at Kipp's Cove to attack Manhattan."

"Just because—" Molly started to say, but Nate plunged on.

"The second thing we know about Howe is that he was badly shaken by the losses the lobsters suffered assaulting Breed's Hill. He shies from frontal assaults against fixed positions the way a horse shies from a stone fence. He showed this when he forced our boys on Long Island to retreat behind the Brookland Heights fortifications, and then failed to assault the heights, giving General Washington time to slip his entire force across the river to Manhattan."

"I still don't see—"

"Let me finish my reasoning. Howe has installed his forces on Manhattan facing the colonials on the Haarlem Heights. The way I see it, he has two choices. He can launch a frontal attack on the heights and risk running into the kind of fire he faced at Breed's Hill, risk suffering the same kind of losses—and don't forget, when Howe loses a man, killed or wounded, he has to look to England for a replacement. Or he can mount another amphibious operation—ferry a mess of soldiers past the Hell Gate rapids, land them at Frog's Neck and set up a blocking line between Frog's Neck and King's Bridge. With the British warships patrolling the East River and the North River, and lobsters in front and behind, Washington would be trapped on the Haarlem Heights. Morale, already low, would deteriorate even more. Desertions would increase. Food supplies would dwindle. Congress would blame Washington, Washington would blame Congress. If Howe were patient enough there is every chance the Colonial army would wither on the vine without a shot being fired. The rebellion would be over."

Molly walked to the window and stared out at the weather cocks on the roofs opposite. "I am obliged to admit your reasoning is persuasive," she finally said.

"I am obliged to agree," Nate said gloomily. "At least it explains the presence of the hundred and eleven longboats, and the five thousand five hundred fifty lobsters, hidden in the Newtown Creek. If Howe was only going to ferry them across to Manhattan to reinforce his bridgehead at Kipp's Cove, he could accomplish that from the Brookland ferry landing."

Molly turned to face Nate. Her smile was a hedge against tears. "If you are right everything is lost."

"Perhaps not," he said thoughtfully. And he outlined for her the scheme that he had been concocting: What if he were to compose a report, in Latin, giving details of Howe's dispositions, and most especially a description of what he had seen at the Newtown Creek? What if he were to draw the conclusion, supported by snatches of overheard conversation, that the lobsters planned to land a force at Frog's Neck with the intention of cutting off Washington in Manhattan? What if he were to append a notation to the report saying it was a duplicate, that the original had already been dispatched to Washington? Molly could write out in her hand a second letter purporting to come from A. Hamilton. Let them come, it could say. Breed's Hill will look like a picnic in comparison. Or words to that effect.

A. Hamilton could hint in his letter that Washington had already taken precautions against Howe's forces—had hidden cannon on the Two Brothers to rake the lobster longboats as they passed Hell Gate, had fortified Frog's Neck and every likely landing place within twenty miles. Nate could hide the rough notes from his notebook, along with these two documents, between the inner and outer soles of his shoes, and allow himself to be captured. The papers would fall into Howe's hands. The British would be convinced that Washington was aware of their plans and was waiting for them, and would call off the amphibious operation. Washington would have time to reinforce the army on the Haarlem Heights, train recruits, organize an orderly retreat through Westchester. Howe would lose by not winning; Washington would win by not losing.

Molly shivered. "They'd hang you as a spy."

"There is as much chance of my being exchanged as hanged," Nate insisted. "In either eventuality, it is the custom to let prisoners send letters back. Your friend Captain Hamilton fixed up some coded phrases for me to use. If I saw that Howe had fallen for my story, I could signal Washington by employing one of the codes in a letter."

In the fading light Nate caught the expression of horror on Molly's face. "Put yourself in my place and say honestly whether you would not act as I propose to act," he pleaded.

"It is too high a price to pay," Molly declared passionately.

"Where I come from they have another saying," Nate told her. "What we obtain too cheaply we esteem too lightly."

Molly saw there would be no talking him out of his scheme. Perhaps she could discourage him by picking on details. "How do you propose to get yourself captured?" she demanded. "By walking up to the first lobster you see and turning yourself in? They will smell a rat."

"I've thought of that," Nate said. "I have a cousin from Portsmouth, one Samuel by name, a through and through Tory, who holds the post as Deputy Commissary of Prisoners here in New York. He knows me for a rebel and an officer in the Continental Army. If he caught sight of me he would surely turn me in."

Molly breathed a sigh of relief. "There must be ten or fifteen thousand souls in New York. It could take weeks before you discovered your cousin's whereabouts. By then, if your reasoning is correct, the lobsters will be manning the line between Frog's Neck and King's Bridge and the rebellion will be all but over."

Nate looked preoccupied. "Hamilton gave me the name of

someone in New York to turn to in an emergency. He ought to be able to find my cousin Samuel for me."

Here, now, is Molly contributing to the rebellion:

Molly watched from the shadows of an alleyway across the street as Nate strode up to number 22 Wall Street and boldly knocked on the front door. A flickering light appeared in a window, the door opened and Nate disappeared inside. He emerged twenty minutes later. Checking to be sure there were no patrols in sight, he crossed to the alley, took Molly by the arm and started back toward the rooming house. After a while Molly asked, "Now will you deign to tell me who you saw in there?"

"A Jew broker named Haym Salomon."

Molly seemed surprised. "I have never yet met a Jew. What is he like?"

"He seems civil enough. He read my letter of introduction and agreed to help me. By good fortune he is personally acquainted with my cousin's superior in the Commissary of Prisoners, a man named Loring. Salomon said if I returned at sunrise he'd tell me where I could find cousin Samuel."

"Oh," Molly said. She had been praying Nate would run into a dead end.

Back in their room Nate lit the two candles and set out paper, ink and a quill on the table. Molly's lower lip trembled. Tears threatened to overpower a sad smile as she observed him from the window. He was really going through with it.

Nate's quill scratched across the paper as he wrote out, in Latin: "*Exemplum linerarum missarum ad ducem Washington.*" "That should turn the trick," he said. "'Copy of original report sent to Washington.'" He looked up and collected his thoughts and continued writing, in Latin: "Howe preparing amphibious operation designed land large body at Frog's Neck and trap you on Manhattan Island. I personally saw 111 longboats hidden in the New Town Creek along with large number of troops and provisions."

Putting the paper aside to let the ink dry, Nate prepared another sheet. "It's you who will write out this one," he told Molly, and seating her in his place, pacing behind her, peeking occasionally over her shoulder, he spelled out the Latin words as she wrote them: "For the eyes of Captain Hale," he began. "Hmmm. What would Captain Hamilton say in such a letter? Something about my report being extremely valuable. And a hint that Washington had fortified the Two Brothers and Frog's Neck." Concentrating on his Latin, Nate started dictating.

When Molly had finished and the ink was dry Nate carefully folded both letters, along with two pages of his raw notes, between the soles of his shoes. "All that's left," he said, "is to organize things so that the letters fall into Howe's hands."

Taking a deep breath, Molly announced in a hoarse whisper, "If you are absolutely set on going through with this mad scheme of yours, I propose that we marry ourselves."

Nate's eyes widened. "Marry ourselves? Are such things done?"

"The world," Molly reminded him, "*is* upside down." She smiled at his discomfort. "You are clearly a virgin," she added. "The least I can do is make sure you don't die one. Consider it my contribution to our common cause. But before I can bed you we must exchange vows."

Nate, insulted, said, "What makes you so sure I am a virgin?"

Molly limped over to him and put a hand on one of his shoulders. "The way you looked at me through the window when I was at my toilet makes me think it."

"You saw me looking and did nothing?"

"You must understand: Before I was ambushed by grief I grew accustomed to living the life of a married woman . . . there are things you miss when fate deprives you of a husband." She added anxiously, "Contrary to what is generally supposed, women have appetites too."

Nate reached impulsively for her hand. "The moment I saw you I knew I would have liked to love you. What vows would you have us say to each other?"

"I would have us pledge to govern our house, in the unlikely event the Lord ever gives us one, according to God's word."

"I pledge it," Nate declared eagerly.

"I too pledge it. I would have us renounce all pride, ostentation and vanity in apparel and behavior. I would have us promise to give honest attention to friendly rebuke and admonition."

"I pledge it."

"I too pledge it. Finally I would have you pledge to love

and honor me. And I would pledge in return to obey you in so far as obeyance does not trespass on principles dearly held."

"I do pledge it and with all my heart," Nate said urgently.

"I too pledge it with all my heart," Molly whispered.

She studied his face and said, "If the spirit moves you, you may kiss me now."

Still holding her hand, he leaned forward and touched his lips to hers.

Molly turned away so he wouldn't see the tears brimming in her eyes. She crossed the room and removed the framed line drawing of George III and set it down facing the wall. Then she blew out both candles.

Nate said with panic in his voice, "I must have light."

Molly lighted one of the candles and placed it on the floor next to the ceramic basin. Shadows danced on the walls. Nate said something about how he loved shadows, about how you needed light to have them. Molly worked the hand pump until she had half-filled the basin with water. That done, she began to remove her clothing—first came her pointed pumps, then her sand-colored thigh-length stockings. She undid the tiny buttons down the front of her dress and slipped out of it. She reached down and grabbed the hem of her shirt and straightening, drew it over her head. Bare-chested, wearing only homespun knickers, she looked across at Nate, standing in the middle of the small room, his mouth agape, his head angled as he stared at her shadow dancing on the wall and on the ceiling.

"I have never before seen anything so beautiful—"

"It is unnecessary, even undesirable, to speak at moments such as this."

She turned away from him and undid the ribboned waistband of her knickers, and let them fall to the floor and kicked them away. Then she stepped into the ceramic tub and, bending to wet a sponge, she began to wash herself. Her voice drifted back over her bare shoulder. "You may undress now, Nathan, and turn down the bed."

She heard his shoes, his clothing falling to the floor. She felt his trembling hands on her shoulders turning her around. She smiled to hold back the flood of tears but it was no use. She pressed her wet skin to his dry skin, she fitted her body into the curves of his, she burrowed under his chin with her face, she pressed her lips to the hair mole on his neck, she sobbed as she had sobbed only twice before in her life.

13

To the Admiral's bulging eyes, Wanamaker's outer office wasteland looked as if it had been hit by a tidal wave. Desks, coffee tables, swivel chairs, filing cabinets, magazine racks, the telephone switchboard, the two standing lamps, the government-issue metal coat tree (duly stamped MARK something or other, MOD. something or other) had all washed up in the middle of the room. The pile was covered with white paint-stained canvas drapes. Two men in white paint-stained overalls, with paint-stained cigarettes glued to their lower lips, were wielding rollers, methodically covering the grimy walls with a fresh coat of cerulean blue. Admiral Toothacher paused in front of the miniskirted receptionist, who was sitting on the only uncovered chair in the room painting her fingernails a shade of metallic gray best described as pewter. She looked up, suppressed a smile at the sight of the chalky hair flying off in all directions, asked, "So what do you think, Admiral?"

"What do I think about what?" the Admiral inquired starchily. He was a bit put off at being addressed so directly, and so familiarly, by a *secretary*.

"The color, natch."

Toothacher glanced at the walls, found the color unremarkable, admitted as much.

"I'm not talking about the walls. I'm talking about my finger nails." And the secretary waved one drying hand, fingers spread-eagled, in his startled face.

"I have seen worse, I just don't remember where," the Admiral commented with premeditated gracelessness. (It was one of the quirks of his personality that the happier he felt the ruder he became.) "Can I interrupt your *work*"—he emphasized the word insultingly—"long enough to inform me if R for Roger Wanamaker has arrived yet?"

The secretary regarded the Admiral with undisguised disdain, shook the stiff locks of her home permanent to indicate that the promotion policies of her government were an unfathomable mystery to her, cast a devastatingly bored look at the door leading to the inner sanctum to suggest that the early bird was digging for worms somewhere behind it. The Admiral directed his bulging eyes on the door with such intensity that the secretary suspected him of having X-ray vision. By the time she realized how ridiculous the idea was he had disappeared into the room and slammed the door emphatically behind him.

Inside, one look at Wanamaker's sidewalk-drab two-day stubble was enough to convince the Admiral that something was amiss.

"You look as if you are carrying the weight of the world on your shoulders," he commented as he dusted the lopsided armchair facing Wanamaker's desk with his handkerchief and gingerly fitted his body into it.

"I'm having a bad day with gravity," Wanamaker conceded.

The Admiral decided he would be generous and break the ice. "Aren't you going to offer me a choice of coffee, tea or something with a kick to it?" he asked. He flashed what his wife had once laughingly described as his smile of complicity.

Wanamaker thrust a Schimmelpenninck between his teeth and lit up. A perfect halo of smoke wafted into the Admiral's face as Wanamaker pushed a telegram across the desk. Toothacher ducked under the smoke ring, leaned forward, angled his head and read the telegram out loud. "'I'm alive and well. Stuff*b*ingle is not. The Weeder.'"

"Bingle, of course, should be tingle, as in Stuff*tingle*," Wanamaker noted glumly. "The *t* got replaced by a *b* somewhere between here and Boston, which is where the telegram came from."

"Someone is pulling your leg," Admiral Toothacher ventured with a sinking heart.

Another halo of smoke emerged from Wanamaker's puffy lips. Some words leapt like trained circus dogs through it. "There-is-no-corpus-delicti!"

"No corpus delicti?"

"In the rubble. In Boston. I checked."

"That is simply out of the realm of possibility."

Wanamaker pried open a paper clip with his thick, squared-off fingernails and began twisting it into various shapes. He worked the metal back and forth until it snapped and discarded the halves in a desk drawer. "You have let me down badly," he told the Admiral. Wanamaker's expression was totally expressionless, but his voice had slipped into a range normally associated with eulogies. "I used to idolize you," he said. "You were an icon for me, a father figure. I thought you were the only thing standing between us and the Bolshevik hordes." Wanamaker shrugged a shoulder to indicate that times had changed. "Now you can't even arrange things so I can explode a relatively small atomic device in the city of my choice."

Trying to avoid Wanamaker's eye, Toothacher let his gaze drift across the room. It settled on the tacky photograph of the President, the Admiral batted both his eyes to bring it into focus, then caught his breath in surprise—the President appeared to be *blinking back* at him. Toothacher plucked a large handkerchief from a pocket of his blazer and wiped away the perspiration that had accumulated on his brow. He bitterly regretted this visit to Wanamaker's office. He should have taken the first plane back to Guantánamo and retreated into the boredom of its happy hours without saying good-bye to his former man Friday. Now his clothes, his hair, would smell of fresh paint, of tobacco. His clothes could be dry-cleaned, his hair washed with soap and water. But the stain on his reputation—that was another matter. Watching Wanamaker suck on his cigar, the Admiral was suddenly overwhelmed by the sensation that he had been wasting his time; wasting his life. How he longed for the halcyon days when everyone used code names—his, he remembered, had been Parsifal—and was required to give a sample of his Morse "fist" so that no one could send messages in his place. In those days an espionage agent had to be something of a metaphysician, shoring up, against his ruin, seemingly unrelated fragments to get a handle on the ultimate nature of reality, of existence. It had all been very pure, very beautiful even. But the world had moved on.

The Admiral sighed inwardly. If he could wind up this last assignment on a positive note, he vowed never to allow himself to be lured out of retirement again.

"What day are we today?" the Admiral asked Wanamaker.

"The seventh."

"That still leaves eight days to the Ides," Toothacher noted without much enthusiasm.

14

Biting on a cuticle, Snow flipped to the next page in the Weeder's manuscript. She was up to the part that described Molly and Nate exchanging vows. Her eyes became moist. She pulled a handkerchief from her jeans pocket, noisily blew her nose, continued reading.

The Weeder noticed Snow's shoulders trembling. "Where are you?" he asked quietly.

"I'm in the boardinghouse," Snow replied. "Molly has just asked Nate to renounce all pride, ostentation and vanity in apparel and behavior." She bent back to the page, gasped softly, turned impatiently to the next page, read it, lifted her head, closed her eyes, breathed through her nostrils. When she felt calmer she read the entry a second time. "Oh," she murmured. "It's an incredible story. And the way you tell it—what's amazing is she doesn't try to hide. She makes me feel as if—"

The Weeder finished the thought for her. "As if you were invading her privacy. As if you were photographing her naked through a slightly open door."

Snow nodded carefully. “I’ve always thought of my photographs as wounds, and the language you would use to describe the photographs to a blind person as a kind of bandage over those wounds. Molly was ambushed by grief—that’s her wound. And she is treating the wound with language. Describing a wound is one way of treating it. When she tells Nate she has appetites, she’s talking about more than sexual appetites, I think. She’s talking about an appetite for life in general; she’s talking about the absolute necessity to relate to people, which is incredibly difficult to do once you’ve been ambushed by grief.”

The Weeder said, “You’re speaking from experience, obviously.”

Snow nodded slowly. “I was driving the car when my husband . . . when Jeb was killed. If I had been more alert . . . if I had been quicker.” She shrugged tiredly. “If, if, if, if.” The smile that kept the tears at arm’s length installed itself on her lips as she turned back to finish reading what the Weeder had written.

Across the room he watched her devour the manuscript. The unrelated fragments he had collected over the years were falling neatly into place: General Howe’s cryptic reference, in a note to his brother, about how the Colonial spy being an officer in Colonel Knowlton’s regiment made all the difference; Montresor’s account, in a letter to his wife, of being summoned to translate some Latin documents into the King’s English; the story, contained in a diary, of Provost Marshal Cunningham’s refusal to let a condemned man write last letters or give him access to a clergyman; A. Hamilton’s story of having worked out coded sentences with Nate; the description of an execution in John Jack's oral history.

Snow finished reading the manuscript, looked up at the Weeder. "My great-aunt Esther told you all these things?" she asked.

"She let me have a look at Molly's diary. I filled in the gaps."

"How do you know so much about Nate?"

The Weeder grinned sheepishly. "It's me, Nate."

Snow studied his face, not sure how to take this piece of information. "You're Nate?"

He could see the idea startled her and backed off. "In a manner of speaking."

The Weeder walked over to stare out the window. The night was filled with the low hum of traffic from the turnpike, which cut through the neighborhood two blocks away. Across the alley way, in a boxlike apartment building, a young woman in jeans could be seen through a first-floor window with its shade half-drawn. She was leaning with her back against a wall, talking into a telephone. At one point she held the phone at arm's length and stared at it, as if she couldn't believe what she was hearing, then brought it back to her ear and resumed the conversation. Snow came up behind the Weeder—he could feel her breath on his neck—and looked at the woman. The Weeder shook his head. "I've lost my appetite for invasions," he muttered. "One way or another I'm getting out of that line of work."

"For me," Snow said, "invasions can still be instructive." She studied the Weeder's reflection in the window, noticed that he looked preoccupied. "Where are you?" she asked.

"I was thinking about my man Nate. I was thinking about how he got the lobsters to change their plans. Howe never did land at Throg's Neck and strap Washington in Manhattan." The Weeder's eyes appeared to lose their ability to focus. Thinking out loud, he said, "In the end Nate's scheme was brilliantly simple. He set out to convince Howe that his enemy knew what he was up to. If I could convince Wanamaker that *his* enemy knows what he's up to . . . His voice trailed off.

Snow asked, "Who is Wanamaker's enemy?"

"It's the Russians who are Wanamaker's enemy. It's Savinkov who is"—the Weeder spun around; his eyes focused on Snow—"Wanamaker's enemy."

"Savinkov?"

"He's the KGB station chief in Washington. One of the things I did for the Company was eavesdrop on Savinkov. If I could somehow convince Wanamaker that the Russians know about the bomb, that Savinkov is only waiting for it to explode to leak the story to the world, the Company will have to abandon Stufftingle the way Howe had to abandon the amphibious operation against Throg's Neck."

Snow wasn't sure she followed him. "How could this Savinkov know about the bomb unless he had a spy in Wanamaker's office?"

"That's just it," the Weeder said. "What if I were Savinkov's spy? What if I had been spying for him all along?"

"But you're not. You weren't."

"I could pretend. It shouldn't be too difficult to drop a clue in the right place." Suddenly the Weeder's eyes widened in discovery. "I could use the dead drop in Boston!"

"Now you're losing me," Snow admitted. "What's a dead drop?"

The Weeder grasped her wrists. "It could work! A dead drop is an out-of-the-way hiding place agents use to pass messages and money and film back and forth with their handlers. When I was eavesdropping on Savinkov I found out he knows that the FBI is servicing his dead drop behind the radiator in the men's room of a museum here in Boston. Which means that if I were to deposit something in this particular drop Savinkov wouldn't get it, but the FBI would."

"What could you put in the drop?"

The Weeder beamed. "What Nate put between the soles of his shoe—evidence. I could start with the pawn ticket, which would lead the FBI to the printouts on Stufftingle. The FBI wouldn't know what they were and would turn to the Company for help. The Company would never tell the FBI what it meant—but my bosses would draw the appropriate conclusion. Stufftingle had been compromised. I could add a personal note to Savinkov—in Latin, why not? because he speaks Latin, and how would I know that unless I worked for him? I could say here's the final batch of printout on Stufftingle. I could inquire about something personal—something that only someone who knew Savinkov intimately would be familiar with. His hemorrhoids! I could ask him if the medicine I recommended for his hemorrhoids had helped him!"

Snow took the Weeder's hands in hers and turned them so that his palms were facing up. She touched the scabs that had formed over the rope burns. "Your life lines have been erased," she noted worriedly.

The Weeder pulled his hands free and turned to stare out the window. He went over the whole thing again in his mind looking for flaws, but couldn't find any. "The beauty of it," he said, "is that they won't be able to reschedule another Stufftingle after the Ides of March deadline passes. Once they think the Russians know about it they'll have to cancel Stufftingle permanently."

Snow asked, "What will they do to you if they think you're a Russian spy?"

The Weeder shrugged; the answer seemed evident. "They can't very well put me on trial. I know too much. About Operations Subgroup Charlie of the Special Interagency Antiterrorist Working Group. About Stufftingle."

Snow let this sink in for a moment. "Did you ever think of bypassing the CIA? Of going to the Justice Department, for instance? Or the President?"

"What do I do? Waltz into the Oval Office and say, 'Mr. President, there are things going on out there you should know about.' Consider the possibility that he already knows about it, that he may have authorized Stufftingle. The President and the CIA's late lamented director were thick as thieves. It would have been entirely in character for the director to mention, in an offhand way, that he was going to explode an atomic device in Tehran unless the President had a coughing fit in the next ten seconds. And when the President didn't cough, to set the wheels in motion."

"You're paranoid," Snow said. "There are people in the White House or the Justice Department who would be appalled if they discovered what was going on. It's not only the business of the bomb—what's it called?—Stufftingle. It's also the attempt to kill the one person who is trying to stop this insanity."

"You're forgetting about the world being upside down," the Weeder told her. He added impatiently, "I know what I'm talking about. I know how these things work. And being naive doesn't increase anyone's chance of survival."

"I'm not naive," Snow said flatly. "And I'm not convinced you're right."

"My problem isn't to convince you I'm right," the Weeder remarked moodily. He produced the pawn ticket from the billfold of his wallet. "It just might work," he said.

15

Waiting his turn in line, the Weeder couldn't help overhearing two teenage girls giggling away behind him. "I know a better one," the girl with the nasal voice informed her friend. "My botany teacher told us about this insect, see, that's got no vagina."

"Like how does it do it, then?" her friend asked in awe.

"Well, the male of the species punches a hole in the female of the species with his, you know, thing, is how. He punches the hole and then he screws it. You're supposed to be able to tell how many times she's done it by the number of holes she's got in her."

The second teenage girl said seriously, "Wow! I guess we're lucky we come equipped. That way the parents can't keep track of our sex lives."

Both girls burst into peals of laughter.

Snow's great-aunt Esther, whom the Weeder had talked into coming with him so he would be less conspicuous, observed his expression out of the corner of her eye. A sly smile played on her lips as she said in an undertone, "When

I was their age we talked clean but thought dirty. It seems to me what they're doing is a lot more wholesome, not to mention more fun." She snapped a bridge back into her gums for emphasis.

The Weeder said, "I'm beginning to wonder if there is anything that can shock you."

"I've seen it all," Esther agreed, "and imagined the rest."

"Me too," the Weeder remarked, "I've imagined the rest."

When their turn came the Weeder bought two tickets and ushered Esther past the guard into the Isabelle Stewart Gardner Museum. Built to resemble a Venetian palace, it had been commissioned by the rich and seductive Mrs. Gardner, who had wanted to transplant a piece of Venice to Boston. "Beats where I live by a mile," Esther observed, squeezing the Weeder's arm as they surveyed the central patio overrun with plants and trees, and the delicate Gothic facades rising off it. "There's a Sargent portrait of Mrs. G. somewhere. Let's find it."

"I'll catch up with you," the Weeder said, gently detaching his arm from hers.

"Where are you off to?"

"The men's room, if you must know."

"Why don't you come right out and say you need to pee instead of beating around the bush. It's a natural bodily function and nothing to be ashamed of." Snapping her bridges, Esther tottered off to find the Sargent portrait.

The Weeder drifted around the patio toward the toilets, lingered to study the vines coiling up the columns as he tried to spot the FBI stakeout team that would surely be posted near Savinkov's dead drop. The likeliest candidate he could find was a clean-cut young man in blue jeans and basketball sneakers taking pictures with a telephoto lens directly across the patio from him. What gave him away were his lightly tinted aviator sunglasses. Behind the Weeder a middle-aged man reading the museum's guidebook emerged from the men's room and started up the steps toward the first floor. The Weeder glanced across the patio in time to see the FBI agent aim his camera and take a photograph of the man with the guidebook. It occurred to the Weeder that he had witnessed another in an endless series of invasions of privacy. Maybe Snow was on to something after all, he thought. Maybe invading each other's privacy was the basic way people related to each other these days.

The Weeder pushed through the door into the men's room. From behind the locked door of a stall came the sound of a hacking cough. He took the envelope he had meticulously prepared the previous night out of his pocket and slipped it behind the radiator. Then he washed his hands and dried them under the hot air blower and headed for the exit.

To make the letter to Savinkov more believable he had purposely left it unsigned. But the FBI would have his fingerprints on the envelope and the photograph of him coming out of the men's room. It wouldn't take them long to put two and two together, to sound the alarm. The computer printouts in the pawnshop would be retrieved. Wanamaker would be brought in to authenticate them.

Those whose job it was to leap to conclusions would announce that Stufftingle had been permanently compromised and must be scrapped.

That was the up side. The down side was that the hunt for the Weeder's scalp would begin in earnest.

16

Snow profited from the Weeder's absence to use the phone. She had to call a friend in Providence to get the phone number of Michael Fargo's parents. Mrs. Fargo remembered Snow very well from her son's wedding and gladly passed on Michael's home phone number in Georgetown. Snow pressed Mark's wife, Sally, for Michael's private number at the Justice Department.

Snow stared down at the slip of paper with the telephone number scrawled on it. She was sure Silas was dead wrong. There were people in high places whose moral compass still pointed true north. And Michael Fargo was one of them. Snow had known him since his law school days; Michael had been Jeb's closest friend, and best man at their wedding. If there was one person in the world she would trust with her life it was Michael. She would sound him out, feel her way. Silas would see she had been right.

Snow reached for the phone and dialed the Washington number. A telephone rang. A man, all business, came on the line.

"Fargo."

"Michael?"

There was a crisp "Who's this?"

"It's me, Snow."

"Snow! My God. A voice from the grave!" Michael Fargo faltered. "I'm sorry I said that. I wasn't thinking. It's been three years, hasn't it? Since we buried Jeb. I'm glad you called."

"Michael—"

Snow hesitated. Fargo heard the hesitation. "Is something the matter, Snow?"

Tears flowed. Between them Snow managed to get out, "I need help, Michael."

17

Fargo pushed the menu across the table to Snow. "Order something," he said.

"I don't think I can eat," Snow said.

"There's a shrimp curry most folks find tasty, dear," the waitress suggested helpfully.

"She'll take the shrimp curry," Fargo told the waitress. "I'll take number seventeen, with french fries and broccoli."

The waitress, who wore a large button on her smock identifying her as Minnie, tore off a copy of the order, tucked it under a salt cellar, smiled and left. Fargo raised his Bloody Mary to Snow and started sipping it.

Snow said, "It was real nice of you to come up so quickly."

Fargo said, "Jeb was my best friend. Which makes you my best friend-in-law. Tell me how I can help you."

"What exactly do you do at the Justice Department?" Snow asked.

"You want to know what I do at work?" Fargo repeated. He took another sip of his drink, studying Snow over the rim of the glass. She had lost weight, grown gaunt even, since he had seen her at Jeb's funeral. The scar over her eye had been livid then; now it was a barely noticeable pencil line. "I'm the assistant head of the department's Criminal Division, if that means anything to you," he finally said.

"I know this sounds dramatic, but could you get an appointment with the President?"

"Which president?" It dawned on him what she was asking. "You mean *the* President?"

Snow flashed a pained smile, nodded.

Fargo's eyebrows arched. "I guess you do need help if you're asking me about my access to the Oval Office."

"Answer the question."

Fargo shrugged. "I've been in the Oval Office half a dozen times but I've always been riding on the Attorney General's coattails. He brings me along to answer questions. It's the kind of situation where I don't speak unless I'm spoken to."

Snow's face screwed up in disappointment. "I was hoping you were senior enough to get in to see the President if you wanted to."

"Look, I'm not sure where this conversation is going, but if it would help move things along, I am senior enough to see the Attorney General any time I need to. And the Attorney General has unlimited access to the Oval Office."

Snow brought a cuticle up to her teeth and began gnawing on it. Fargo asked, "What's this about, Snow?" And he added very gently, "Jeb trusted me. You can too."

Snow seemed to gather herself, like a runner before the start of a race. "Okay," she blurted out. "Let's see what happens." And in long run-on sentences that broke off only when she came up for air, she proceeded to tell him about the atrocity an agent named Wanamaker was going to commit; how someone she knew had stumbled across details of the operation, which was code-named Stufftingle, while running a top secret Agency eavesdropping program; how he had attempted to head off the atrocity by threatening to leak evidence indicating the CIA was responsible if Wanamaker went through with it; how the Agency had attempted, on three occasions, to eliminate him; how she was desperately afraid they would succeed the next time they tried.

"How are you using the word *eliminate*?" Fargo asked.

Snow said, "Eliminate as in murder." And she described the three attempts on Sibley's life.

"Your friend told you about the fire-breather cornering him in the parking lot? About the air being pumped out of the library?"

Snow nodded miserably.

"He told you about the wrecking ball?"

Snow caught the note of doubt in Fargo's voice. Looking squarely into his eyes, she said with quiet intensity, "He didn't have to tell me. I was there. It was my head the building came down on."

Fargo's attitude changed instantly. "You were there with him? You saw it?"

Snow said, "Maybe now you'll believe me."

"Why didn't you go to the police?"

"I wanted to but my friend said it was out of the question.

He said they would check his story with Washington. He said the Agency would claim he was crazy and come and get him."

"Tell me again about this atrocity he says the Agency is planning to commit. What proof does he have?"

"He's hidden some computer printouts of conversations in which the atrocity is discussed."

"Why doesn't he take his printouts to the newspapers? Splash it across the front pages? The Agency couldn't very well eliminate him once he exposed the plot."

"You don't understand," insisted Snow. She felt she was reaching the limits of her patience, of her strength. She decided she would make one last effort to convince him. "My friend is a patriot. He wants to head off the atrocity without dragging the Central Intelligence Agency through the mud, and the United States along with it."

"Who else besides you and your friend know about this?"

"As far as I know, no one."

The waitress turned up carrying a tray filled with food. She set the shrimp curry down in front of Fargo and the number seventeen in front of Snow. "Enjoy," she said.

Snow and Fargo didn't bother exchanging plates; neither felt like eating now. Fargo pursed his lips, considering the problem for a long while, finally asked, "Is your friend aware you phoned me?"

Snow closed her eyes for a moment. "When I suggested trying to go over the head of the Agency he got annoyed. He thinks . . ."

"What does he think?" Fargo encouraged her.

"He thinks the President may have authorized the whole thing." She leaned forward. "Will you help us, Michael?"

Fargo nodded. "I'll nose around the shop and see what I can come up with. How do I get in touch with you?"

Snow sat back. "I'll get in touch with you," she said quickly. She watched him carefully to see how he would take this.

Fargo just smiled faintly. "Do you think your friend would agree to meet me?"

"Depending on what you come up with, I could try and convince him."

Fargo watched Snow raise a cuticle to her teeth. She badly needed reassuring, he saw. He reached for her hand. "You can count on me," he told her.

"That's what I seem to be doing," she noted uncertainly.

18

The Attorney General heard Fargo out without interrupting him. "You did the right thing to come to me," he announced in the famous raspy voice that came across during television interviews as honest combativeness. "I take it your lady friend didn't tell you the name of the man in question."

Fargo shook his head. "That's understandable. She's frightened."

The Attorney General removed a tiny hearing aid from his ear and massaged the area that had been irritated by the device, then replaced it. "What did you say?" he asked.

"I didn't say anything," Fargo said.

"Oh, I thought you said something. About your lady friend: She has good reason to be frightened, but from what you've told me I don't think she understands where the real danger lies. Her friend's name is Silas Sibley. I have a file as thick as your fist on him. Until he failed to show up for work about ten days ago he was a member of a Central Intelligence Agency Techint team collecting serial numbers of Russian tanks in East Europe, Syria, Egypt, even the ones captured over the years by the Israelis. The object of the study was to come up with a definitive estimate of Soviet tank production capacity. This Sibley fellow was supposed to be an ace with computers. He matched the serial numbers against other information, ran the whole thing through his computer and circulated a minority report claiming that the Soviets had doctored their serial numbers to throw just such a study off track. Sibley made a case that their actual tank production was considerably less than we thought." The Attorney General produced a gold and silver cigarette lighter, angled the flame into the bowl of his pipe and sucked it into life. "Since our antitank production line is geared to their tank production, his report stirred up quite a storm. His conclusions were double-checked by an interagency group of specialists. They decided that it was Sibley, not the Russians, who had doctored the numbers."

The Attorney General puffed thoughtfully on his pipe, exhaled. A haze of vile-smelling smoke obscured his head. "The specialists raised the possibility that Sibley was working for the Russians. His access to documents was restricted while our people looked into this. Sibley panicked. He fired off bitter letters complaining he was being hounded for not telling the military establishment what it wanted to hear. He flatly refused to take a lie detector test on the grounds that it was notoriously inaccurate. We did manage to slip a psychiatrist onto the committee that heard him out. The result," the Attorney General said, "was a psychiatric profile that indicated the man was stark raving mad." The Attorney General lifted the phone and said very quietly, "Bring me the psychiatrist's report on that Sibley fellow, will you?" He regarded Fargo through a haze of tobacco smoke. "I don't pretend to understand all the technical jargon," he said, "but you can get the general drift reading it yourself. Functional paranoia, delusions of persecution, delusions of grandeur, all jumbled up with a healthy death wish symbolized by an obsession with Nathan Hale. Sibley had been going around telling people he was a direct descendant of Hale's. He said he was reconstructing the Hale story from references buried in letters and diaries, but in fact he seems to have made the whole thing up. He was inventing everything. The Hale story, plots within the government. Everywhere he turned he saw enemies. People trying to kill him. That sort of thing."

A male secretary holding a sheet of paper came across the carpeted office. The Attorney General nodded toward Fargo. The secretary handed him the report and left. "Sibley," the Attorney General went on, "has a particular grudge against a college roommate who wound up, like him, working for the Central Intelligence Agency. Sibley apparently thinks this roommate was responsible for the death of a girlfriend at college. I forget the roommate's name."

Fargo, scanning the report, said, "Wanamaker."

"That sounds right. Wanamaker."

Fargo looked up from the report. "Have you ever heard of an operation code-named 'Stufftingle'?"

The Attorney General nodded slowly. "'Stufftingle' is the

name of Wanamaker's shoestring operation. He analyzes Soviet telephone directories to try and figure out the pecking order in the various Soviet ministries."

"My lady friend," Fargo said, "says that her friend claimed that the word *Stufftingle* came from a joke circulated at the Los Alamos atomic project during World War Two."

The Attorney General shrugged. "You know as well as I do how these code names are chosen. They're picked from lists compiled by computer, which joins together random syllables to form unintelligible words. I suppose it's always possible that a given two- or three-syllable word has some historical significance, but if this is the case with Stufftingle it is pure coincidence." The Attorney General pointed at the psychiatrist's report with his pipe. "Read the next to last paragraph."

Fargo's eyes went back to the report. "It is imperative," the psychiatrist had written, "that Sibley undergo extended psychiatric treatment by highly skilled professionals. Until then it must be remembered, in dealing with him, that it is vitally important to *never challenge his delusions.* When he is pinned down the delusions seem to multiply; he invents new stories to justify the old ones he told. If he is backed into a corner there is a strong possibility he could become violent."

The Attorney General said, "If he had turned up for work on schedule the psychiatrist's suggestion would have been acted on. Sibley would have been packed off to some quiet private hospital the Agency keeps for these purposes, and treated."

Fargo laid the report on the desk. "You're forgetting one thing," he said. "My lady friend was with him during the third attempt on his life."

The Attorney General sucked on his pipe without answering, and Fargo wondered if he had turned down his hearing aid. He had seen him tune out of conversations before. Raising his voice, Fargo said, "My lady friend was with him during the third attempt on his life. She witnessed it."

"I heard you the first time," the Attorney General snapped. "I was thinking. Assuming your lady friend got the story straight, we only have Sibley's word for the first two attempts on his life—and you have to admit they seem like scenes out of a James Bond movie. As for the third attempt, as I understand it, your lady friend went to an abandoned building earmarked for destruction to photograph squatters. Sibley accompanied her. It was lunch hour. They parked their car in the street so as not to frighten off the squatters and went inside. They climbed the steps to the top floor. Still no squatters. Suddenly two wrecking balls began demolishing the building." The Attorney General sucked on his pipe and exhaled again. "The demolition people came back from their lunch break, assumed the building was deserted and started working. Like most paranoiacs, Sibley fitted a piece of reality neatly into his delusions. He told your lady friend they were trying to kill him. She believed it."

"So did I," Fargo admitted.

"If you want to help your friend you'd better make sure Sibley gets professional assistance, and quickly. Remember what the psychiatrist said about the possibility of him becoming violent. Let's hope your lady friend doesn't back him into a corner."

"Let's hope," Fargo agreed worriedly.

"Do you think you could talk her into setting up a meeting between you and Sibley?"

"I can try," Fargo said.

"Be careful not to let on you have doubts about him," the Attorney General warned.

"I'll say I checked his story and want to help."

"You need to meet him face to face."

"To work out a way to stop the atrocity. To punish those responsible."

"That's the ticket," the Attorney General said.

19

The Weeder took the news badly. The color drained from his face. His eyes narrowed. A lid twitched. He peered distractedly at the street between two slats of the Venetian blind.

"I swear to you," Snow said from across the room, "I didn't tell him where you were."

"He could have followed you."

"I saw him hail a cab. I saw him leave. I lost myself in a crowd at Copley Square. I changed buses twice."

"He could have traced the call when you phoned him back."

"I dialed from a downtown booth."

The Weeder watched an automobile cruise slowly past Esther's house. When it disappeared from view he turned to stare at Snow. "I don't understand how you could do something that dumb," he said impatiently. His eyes darted around the room, settled on a pewter candlestick with a cream-colored candle in it. He went over and hefted it, absently measuring its weight. "I know those people in Washington—they're all alike. What else did you tell him?"

Snow looked at the candlestick, then at the Weeder. "That's all. I give you my word."

"You didn't tell him about my pretending to be a Soviet spy?"

"I didn't say a word about that part."

"You said I was trying to prevent an atrocity. That's all?"

"I told him about the attempts to kill you."

"Three attempts. Did you tell him there were three attempts?"

Snow nodded. "I described the first two—the man with the tattoos who tried to incinerate you, the business in the library when they pumped out all the air."

"Did he believe you?"

Snow smiled nervously. "Silas, you're frightening me," she whispered.

"I have to know if he believed you," the Weeder insisted. "Everything . . . *everything* . . . depends on it."

"I don't think he really believed me until I told him about the third time they tried to kill you—until I told him I was there and witnessed the whole thing."

Some of the tension seemed to seep from the Weeder's face muscles. To Snow it looked like a tide receding. A thin attempt at a sheepish grin spread across his lips. "Tell me again what he said this morning," he ordered.

"I told you twice already."

"Tell me a third time."

"He said he had nosed around. Those were his exact words. He said he was convinced you had stumbled onto something important. He said that you and he had to put your heads together."

"I could go downtown and call him," the Weeder remarked.

"He won't talk to you over the phone. He thinks it's too dangerous. He says he absolutely has to meet with you." Snow reached out to rest her fingers on the Weeder's knuckles. "I know Michael Fargo, Silas. I'd trust him with my life."

"You're trusting him with *my* life," the Weeder pointed out.

Snow said very quietly, very convincingly, "If it comes down to it, I'd trust him with your life too."

"That's easy for you to say—"

Snow retorted angrily, "It's not easy for me to say at all. This is the first time since Jeb's—" She took a breath, started over again. "You mean a great deal to me."

The Weeder asked reluctantly, "Where does he want to meet me?"

"In a fish restaurant near the wharfs. Tomorrow. At noon."

"Do you have to confirm it?"

"He said not to call him back—the less we used the phone, the better, he said. He'll be there. He's counting on me to talk you into coming."

"I don't know," muttered the Weeder.

The room was growing dark. He walked over to the blind and parted the slats with a finger and looked out again. The street was deserted. The yellowish lights the city had recently installed made everything in sight look unreal, invented. He noticed a sliver of a moon hanging over the roof of the house across from them. That, at least, looked genuine enough.

"There was a sliver of a moon the night my man Nate made his way across Long Island to Flatbush and Molly," he remembered.

Snow sensed he was slipping into a role, into an incarnation, but she refused to follow him; refused to recite lines someone else had spoken; refused to live a life that had already been lived.

The Weeder set the candlestick down on a floorboard. He found a match and, cupping a palm around the flame, lit the wick. Instantly, shadows danced across the wall. His eyes brightened and he looked around as if he had suddenly been transported to a magic lantern theater. "I love shadows," he whispered. He stared at the candle, spellbound by the thinness, the blueness, the stillness of the flame leaping from it.

Snow limped over to him and drew him to his feet and put her arms around his neck. She shivered, got control of herself, kissed him on the lips. And smiling a smile that held back a torrent of tears, she started to undo the tiny buttons down the front of her shirt.

20

"What are you doing?" she asked as the Weeder started to walk through the shopping mall, diagonally across from the fish restaurant, for the fifth time.

"I'm practicing something I'm not very good at," the Weeder said. He made no effort to suppress his bitterness. "Where I used to work, it was called tradecraft." He plunged his gloveless hands deeper into his overcoat pockets and studied the window of a record store, using it as if it were a mirror, looking in it for remarkable things—lean young men wearing belted raincoats and lightly tinted aviator sunglasses, window-shopping for things they were unlikely to buy. "The last time I tried this particular trick of the trade I wound up being cornered in a parking lot by a wino breathing fire." On the spur of the moment he pulled Snow into a store that sold clothing and made her try on a pleated skirt while he surveyed the passing crowds through the window. Snow played the game. "How do you like me in lilac?" she asked, pirouetting to make the skirt flare around her feet.

The Weeder caught a glimpse of her ankles, remembered

his man Nate noticing Molly's ankle as she climbed into the buck cart. "Try the one in black," he suggested, and turned back to the window.

The sun came out from behind a cloud as they left the store. Snow glanced worriedly at her wristwatch. "He said we should be there at noon. It's twenty after."

And still the Weeder hesitated. As far as he could see everything was in order, but given his lack of professionalism that didn't mean much. "How did he react when you described the third attempt on my life?" he asked Snow again. She understood he needed reassurance and supplied a generous dose of it. "When he realized he wasn't getting the story secondhand—when he realized I had almost been killed too—he believed every word. He's on your side, Silas."

Snow smiled encouragingly and gestured with her head toward the fish restaurant, which was in the middle of a street that had been closed to traffic. His breathing became shallower. "All right," he said reluctantly. "Let's go and talk with this friend of yours."

They crossed the street and turned down the block past a heavy man wearing gloves with the fingertips cut off selling roasted chestnuts from a pushcart. They passed a band of black teenagers dressed in identical jackets with "Bom to Love" splashed across their backs—the boys were gathered around a ghetto blaster set on an orange crate. The fish restaurant loomed ahead. An elderly couple emerged from the doorway into the sunlight, winding long colorful scarves around their necks, laughing. Snow was looking at a dwarf selling Japanese hand puppets in another doorway when she heard the screech of brakes. The sound registered first, then the thought that it was out of place on a street where cars were prohibited. She spun back and reached for the Weeder but he wasn't there—through the crowd she could see his arms flailing as he was hustled by four men in dark suits into the back of a car. The door was slammed behind him. Pushing through the crowd, Snow screamed "Silas!" Her cry was drowned in a squeal of tires as the car lurched away from the curb. Nodding in time to the music, the teenagers with the ghettobuster watched Snow lunge after the car disappearing down the street. The elderly man with the colorful scarf around his neck called uncertainly, "Shouldn't somebody notify the police?" The heavy man who had been selling chestnuts held up a plastic identification card in the flap of a wallet. "The show's over, folks," he called. "Move along. Kindly go on about your business. The show's over."

Staring after the car, Snow felt a hand grip her elbow. She tried to pry it loose, discovered there was no strength left in her fingers, looked up into Fargo's ashen face. "You bastard," she whispered hoarsely. Then she screamed, "Bastard! Bastard! Bastard!" as he steered her toward another car that had pulled up to the curb. The heavy man wearing gloves without fingertips opened the back door and Fargo tried to force Snow inside, but she twisted around and swung weakly at his face. Fargo ducked under the blow and caught her wrists and pinned them against the open door of the car. "He's mentally ill," he told her. "He made it all up."

"You're the one who's mentally ill," Snow cried. "You used me."

"I have the proof," Fargo pleaded with her.

Snow wrenched a wrist free and spun around and struck her head sharply against the side of the car. Her body shook with sobs. "They're going to kill him—"

The heavy man grabbed Snow's head to prevent her from hurting herself. Behind Fargo the teenagers lined the sidewalk, watching, nodding in time to the music. Fargo told Snow, "Nobody's going to hurt him. He's sick. He needs professional help. We're going to see he gets it."

The two men maneuvered Snow onto the backseat of the car. Fargo climbed in alongside her and waved a hand at the driver.

"Where are we going?" Snow mumbled as the car rounded the corner and moved out into traffic. It was clear she didn't give a damn.

"To an office," Fargo said. "As soon as you've calmed down I'm going to prove to you he's mentally disturbed."

The sun disappeared behind a cloud and thick flakes of snow began to drift down; the crystals were directed by the air flowing around the car past the side window. It occurred to Snow that the flakes were falling in the wrong direction, that the world *was* upside down. She let the lids close over her eyes of their own weight and sank back into her seat. She had been ambushed again . . .

The driver turned off Commonwealth Avenue into a side street, then turned off the side street and pulled up at a deserted loading ramp. Fargo got out and came around and opened the door and offered Snow his hand. Ignoring him, she swung her legs out. She imagined the lilac skirt swirling around her feet, felt the Weeder's eyes flicker to her ankles as she started up the steps. She was too feeble to protest when Fargo slipped his arm through hers and steered her into a padded freight elevator. She leaned back against the padding, felt her weight rush to her feet as the elevator soared. Her weight redistributed itself when the elevator coasted to a stop. The doors opened. Fargo looked at her. Her face a mask of anguish, she heaved herself off the wall and stepped into the corridor. A young woman in a striped business suit with padded shoulders was waiting next to an open door. She took a firm grip on Snow's arm and led her down the hall to the ladies' room. "Splash some cold water on your face," she told Snow. "It will help you."

The young woman escorted Snow back down the corridor into an office, then through a door into a sparsely furnished inner office. She pulled a chair up to a coffee table. Snow sank into it. "Can I get you anything?" the young woman asked. "Warm milk? A stiff drink?"

Snow didn't respond. The young woman glanced at Fargo. He nodded toward the door. The woman left. Fargo drew up a second chair so that it was facing Snow and sat down. The coffee table separated them. It was made of glass. Snow could see Fargo's shoes through it. They appeared to be brand-new. Distrust any enterprise, Silas—quoting Thoreau—had said, that required new clothes.

"This isn't going to be easy for you," Fargo began. "But you might as well face up to it now as later." He held out a piece of paper. Snow looked at it without seeing it. Fargo said, "What you don't know *can* hurt you." He let the paper drop onto the coffee table in front of her.

Snow's eyes drifted to the paper. "What will that change?" she asked. "Anyone who can type can put things on a paper." She smiled, but the tears flowed anyhow. "He warned me being naive wouldn't increase his chances of survival."

"Read the paper," Fargo said softly.

"Someone once said it's dangerous to be right when the government is wrong. I guess it is."

"Read it."

"What kind of game are we playing?" Snow demanded with sudden vehemence. "If I read it I'm going to have to act as if I believe it because I'm afraid you'll kill me too if I don't swallow it—if I believe he was stark raving sane and put his life on the line to prevent an atrocity."

"When you read it," Fargo said, "you'll believe it because it rings true—because you will think back on things he did and said and it will fit in with what you're reading."

Snow reached out and edged the paper along the table top. Her eyes were swimming in tears and she had to wipe them away with the back of her sleeve in order to focus. She read the title: Psychiatrist's Preliminary Report on Silas N. Sibley—Top Secret. "I didn't know he had a middle initial," she murmured.

Fargo said, "The *N* stands for Nathan, of course. The

initial is not on his birth certificate. Nor is it on his official Agency service record. He started using the *N* about two and a half years ago."

"What does that prove?" Snow demanded. "He's a descendant of Nathan's. It's natural that he would want to add the *N*."

"Read on. He's not a descendant of Nathan's. He comes from English stock that emigrated to this country in the middle of the last century."

Snow began reading the first sentence of the psychiatrist's report. It was all invented, of course. They were trying to discredit him so that nobody would believe his story about the atrocity.

"He didn't live and work in New York," Fargo said. He droned on like a voice-over to a documentary film. "He lived and worked in Washington, DC. He wasn't involved in a program to eavesdrop on people through their phones—I checked that out personally. He was analyzing the serial numbers of Soviet tanks. I've seen his report, the one where he says the Soviets cooked the numbers. I've held it in my hand, Snow."

Snow forced herself to read on. The clinical detachment of the tone, the certainty with which the psychiatrist trotted out his arguments and put them through their paces, rubbed her the wrong way.

"There is an Operation Stufftingle," Fargo was saying. "There is a Wanamaker, and he was a roommate of Sibley's at Yale—though there seems to be no evidence of a grudge between them, no record of a girl's death. Sibley was doing what all paranoids do—he was constructing a make-believe world using bits and pieces of the real world. Stufftingle is the code name for Wanamaker's program that analyzes the structure of Soviet ministries from their phone books—from how many extensions someone has, from the order of the numbers."

Snow was reaching the end of the report now. "The seeds of his disorder—probably traceable to a chemical imbalance—were lurking inside him, waiting to burst into life," the psychiatrist had written. "There is good reason to believe that Sibley has been walking a very fine line between sanity and insanity for years. Whenever the 'present' became too oppressive for him he took refuge in a 'past' that he invented—he pulled the past over his head the way a child afraid of the dark pulls a blanket over his head in bed. For a time this technique seems to have supplied him with the relief he needed. More recently, however, he began inventing a 'present' as well as a 'past.' F. Scott Fitzgerald has a sentence in *The Last Tycoon* about how we live in the present, and when there is no present (that is, when there is no present that is congenial to us), we invent one. Fitzgerald might have been describing Sibley. At this point in time it is difficult to say exactly what pushed him over the line. It could have been his divorce. It could have been the trauma of his separation from a child he adored. The years of meticulous and painstaking work in the back rooms of the CIA must have been extremely frustrating for someone who saw himself as a hero and a patriot. The shock of having the CIA not only question the results of his study on Soviet tank production but seriously consider the possibility that he was a Soviet agent surely contributed to the breakdown.

"To sum up: I think we are dealing with an all-too-classic case of someone whose mental health was fragile to begin with; who was subjected to insupportable personal and professional pressures; who then cracked like a piece of old crockery when the results of his work were questioned and his security clearance was withdrawn. For a great many of its employees the Central Intelligence Agency is family, and Agency disapproval or outright rejection can result in the disintegration of the facade the employee's psyche has been barricaded behind. We have seen this kind of phenomenon before. We will unfortunately see it again. It is an occupational hazard that goes with the terrain. Formulating a specific diagnosis for Sibley under the present circumstances is extremely difficult. I am fairly certain, however, that an eventual diagnosis, made under clinical conditions, will mention functional paranoia with delusions of persecution, delusions of grandeur and a vigorous death wish. I suspect schizophrenia from the fact that Sibley appears to be able to meander in and out of the role of Nathan Hale at will."

Snow handed the psychiatrist's report back to Fargo. He looked at it, shook his head reflectively, tucked the report into a manila folder marked EYES ONLY. "Admit," he said, "that you're beginning to wonder."

Snow remembered asking Silas how he knew so much about his man Nate. It's me, Nate, he had replied. Even then she hadn't been sure how to take that piece of information.

"What about the third attempt on his life?" she asked Fargo now. "I suppose you can explain that away too."

Fargo pulled three sheets of paper from the folder and offered them to Snow. She read them quickly, handed them back. Fargo said, "I took those depositions myself. The foreman, the two men who worked the cranes, swear on a stack of Bibles that they searched the building when they came back from their lunch break. Of course they didn't do anything of the kind, but they're not about to admit it and lose their jobs. They sounded a warning blast on the hand-cranked siren—you said you heard a siren, remember?—and waited to see if anyone stuck his head out of a window. When nobody did, they started in with their wrecking balls. Did you or Sibley go to a window and scream at any point to attract attention?"

"He saw the Admiral drive up. The man with the tattoos who tried to incinerate him in the parking lot, the woman, were with him."

Fargo asked very gently, "Did *you* see them?"

A whimper of frustration escaped Snow's lips.

Fargo stood up. "I want to show you something." He steered her into a waiting elevator, pushed the basement button. They rode down staring wordlessly at the padded door. It parted. Fargo led the way through a brightly lit, spotlessly clean garage. Half a dozen automobiles were parked in it. Some of them had been taken apart, piece by piece, in a search for hidden drugs. Two agents in coveralls had jacked up a Mercedes 190SL and were removing the tires. They looked at Fargo and the woman, nodded and went back to work.

Fargo guided Snow to a tow truck parked in a corner of the garage. A beat-up brown Volkswagen Beetle was still attached to its crane. The car's front wheels were off the ground. "What kind of car did Sibley drive?" Fargo asked.

She remembered him mentioning something about a VW Beetle.

Fargo opened the driver's door of the Volkswagen and reached for an envelope attached to the inside of the sun visor with rubber bands. He removed a registration certificate from the envelope and offered it to Snow. "This particular Volkswagen belongs to Silas Sibley. You'll notice there is no middle initial, but the certificate was issued before he started using the *N*. After the two attempts on his life in New Haven he abandoned the car near Yale. Do you notice anything curious about the car?"

When Snow shook her head Fargo said, "He told you, and you told me, that the first attempt on his life took place when he returned to the faculty parking lot to get his car. He escaped by locking himself inside the Volkswagen, banging into the car ahead and then the one behind to give himself room to maneuver, and driving off while the Admiral's driver, the man named Huxstep, breathed fire on the car. That's what he said, right? Huxstep breathed fire on the car and Sibley could smell the singed paint and burning rubber. Take a good look at this Volkswagen, Snow. Does it look as if it has been subjected to fire and heat? Look at the bumpers. They're rusted, but they don't look as if they've been used to push cars around."

Snow ran her fingers over a fender. Paint flaked off in her hand. She could see patches of rust coming through the paint in places. She turned to Fargo and asked, "How long have you had the car down here?"

"Jesus, Snow, we didn't repaint the damn thing and put on new bumpers."

"You could have."

Fargo slipped his arm through hers and steered her back toward the elevator. "There is one proof that will convince you," he told her. "It's that nobody is going to kill Sibley. There is no reason to—there is no scheme to commit an atrocity that has to be protected. He'll have to be isolated for a while, naturally. He had access to Agency secrets. He can identify Agency employees. But he's going to be helped back onto his feet. When he's well again the Agency will retire him with pay. They'll find him a job, give him a new life." He smiled worriedly. "If you decide to, you can share that life with him."

Snow studied Fargo's face; he clearly believed what he was telling her. If there was a plot, he wasn't part of it. But somebody might have set out to fool Fargo . . .

"I'm telling you the truth," Fargo said with emotion. "Trust me."

Snow could hear Silas's peal of laughter echoing through her skull. "Whose truth?" he seemed to say. "Which truth?" She tossed her shoulders tiredly, brought a cuticle to her lips. "I don't know whose truth to trust," she admitted.

21

The Weeder came up slowly, carefully, pausing every twenty or so yards until he became accustomed to the depth. At one marker he started to hear voices but they were too far above his head to make out what they were saying. Two markers farther up he got a whiff of ether. The odor provoked a memory: One of the two men in the back of the car had pinned his wrists while the other had clamped a thick wad of gauze over his mouth and nose. Before consciousness had slipped through his fingers he remembered screaming Snow's name into the ether-soaked gauze. He wondered now why he had done that. After all, she was on their side. He floated up to the last marker, the one directly beneath the surface. Rays of dappled bluish light tickled his body. The sounds coming from above became more distinct. "He's all yours," someone was saying. A woman said, "Thanks for the favor. The Company owes you one." Several people laughed pleasantly. They might have been taking tea. Car doors slammed. A motor spurted into life. A machine whined, cranking open something big. Diffused light poured in. A car drove away. The machine whined, closing whatever it was that had opened. The light became dappled, bluish again. "He's coming out of it," the woman's voice, close to his ear, called out. "Check the handcuffs," a man called back from outside the room. "And make sure he don't yell."

The Weeder's eyes batted open as the strip of cloth was pulled across his mouth He could feel someone knotting it at the back of his head. He bit down on the cloth and gagged, and gagged again, and started to suck air wildly through his nostrils.

"He'll croak before we can question him," Mildred called in panic. Pushing her chest into his face, she reached behind him and undid the gag, then sat back on her haunches. She dangled the gag in his face. "Promise me you'll be a good boy and not dazzle us with witticisms," she said breathlessly, "and I won't put it on again."

The Weeder managed to nod. He looked around. He was in some sort of cabin, sitting on the floor with his back to one wall. His wrists were handcuffed behind his back and the handcuffs were attached to something metallic embedded in the wall that stabbed into his spine. He shifted his position, rolling onto a haunch, to ease the pain. There were double doors at one end of the cabin and a little round window at the other end. Mildred, wearing the 1930s feathered hat with the veil that masked half her face, settled onto a bunk bed built into the wall opposite him, her legs spread, her skirt hiked, revealing garter belts with clasps attached to the folds of dark transparent stockings. Huxstep's face appeared in the round window. He pushed it open on its hinge and aimed an enormous pistol with a silencer fitted on the barrel at the Weeder.

The Weeder gasped. Mildred whined, "What about the interrogation?" as if she were afraid of being cheated.

Smiling cruelly, Huxstep thumbed back the hammer. "We'll invent it," he said, and he pulled the trigger. The sharp click of the firing mechanism struck the Weeder with the force of a bullet. He sank back into the piece of embedded metal and cried out in pain.

Huxstep laughed under his breath. "It was a joke," he growled at Mildred.

Sparks of admiration kindled in her eyes. "You could have fooled me."

"History," the Weeder remarked weakly, "needs a giggle now and then."

"Uh-uh," warned Mildred, leaning forward to wiggle a finger in the Weeder's face. "Remember what I told you about dazzling us with witticisms."

Huxstep closed the porthole. The Weeder could see his back—he seemed to be manipulating controls. A motor started up with a roar. The floorboards under the Weeder vibrated. Diesel fumes invaded the cabin. Mildred produced a handkerchief and held it over her nose. Huxstep shifted into gear and accelerated. Rolling gently from side to side, the cabin started to move. The sound of water washing up against its sides reached the Weeder.

"We're on a boat!" he exclaimed.

"The Admiral said you were a bright boy," Mildred commented through her handkerchief.

"Where are you taking me?" the Weeder asked.

Mildred stared at him with the unblinking eyes of a turtledove. "To see the sea."

The Weeder shifted onto a haunch again and tried to ride the gentle rise and fall of the floorboards under him. The diesel fumes gradually disappeared. He could hear over the motor the bark of sea gulls, the tinkle of a buoy passing close aboard, the distant moan of a foghorn. Presently the sounds faded and there was only the drone of the motor and the lapping of water against the hull, and the snoring of Mildred, who had been lulled to sleep by the motion of the boat. The Weeder grew stiff, shifted his weight onto his other haunch. In her sleep Mildred rolled onto her side, continued snoring. After what seemed to the Weeder to be an eternity the pitch of the motor changed. It was being throttled back, left to idle. Mildred stirred, looked at her wristwatch, sat up so abruptly she banged her head against the side of the bunk. "Fuck," she exclaimed. Rubbing her head, she opened one of the double doors and called out, "Are we there?"

"I think I hear it," Huxstep called back excitedly.

Mildred cocked an ear, flashed a toothy smile as she caught the put-put-put of rotors. The whine of a motor grew louder. To the Weeder it sounded as if a giant eggbeater was hovering directly over the boat. Someone landed with a thud on the roof of the cabin. The put-put-put of the rotors receded, then faded altogether. The Weeder could hear shoes scuffing the planks over his head. Someone was working his way aft. Mildred threw open the second door and stood aside.

Dressed in a Navy windbreaker with a blue baseball cap set on his mane of chalk-white hair, Admiral Toothacher appeared at the doors. He stooped and ducked into the cabin. "Well, well," he exclaimed, rubbing his hands together in anticipation, "what do we have here?"

"What we have here," Mildred said, "is trouble."

Still looking at the Weeder, the Admiral told Mildred, "Be so kind as to close the doors on your way out."

Mildred's feelings were obviously hurt. "Aye, aye, sir," she said with a scowl. She slipped out of the cabin, banging the doors shut behind her.

Hunched over like a parenthesis to avoid hitting his head, Toothacher settled onto the bunk facing the Weeder and unzipped his windbreaker. He ran a forefinger under the turtleneck of the black skintight sweater he was wearing to alleviate the chafing. "I trust you won't object to Mildred's absence," the Admiral remarked. "I myself prefer the company of men to that of women. Don't get me wrong. Women can be good company, but only when they are reasonably sure of their ability to seduce. Mildred, you will have concluded from her readiness, her eagerness even, to expose a length of thigh, to rub a breast against your elbow, is not at all sure of her ability to seduce. But then only the very beautiful or the very rich or the very ugly are. So, Silas—I hope you will not be offended if I call you by your given name—on top of everything else you've been doing, you have been spying for our Russian friends."

The Weeder tried to register surprise, innocence. The letter he had planted behind the museum radiator had fallen into the right hands after all. "What makes you think that?" he asked.

From the inside pocket of his windbreaker the Admiral pulled a wad of photocopies. "My Latin is not what it once was," he told the Weeder, "but with the aid of a dictionary it was child's play to translate. '*Haemorrhoidane tibi etiam molesta est?*' That means, 'Are your hemorrhoids still bothering you?' How did you know Savinkov had hemorrhoids, Silas?"

The Weeder glanced around in desperation.

"There is no way out," Toothacher said coldly. "Attempt to be rational. For your own good, for your peace of mind, answer my question."

"What's going to happen to me?"

"What will happen to you happens to everyone eventually. You will die. The question is whether you will die painlessly and with dignity, or . . ." He let the sentence trail off suggestively.

An image of Snow came to the Weeder—he remembered the photograph of her, nude, seen through a partly open door, a candle next to her bare feet. She had invaded her own space, then she had invaded the Weeder's space; she had not believed him, had betrayed him. He would have to steel himself to pay the price of that betrayal. He hoped he had the courage. He would take his cue from Nate. . . . "I am ready to die," he told the Admiral.

Toothacher snorted. "You only regret that you have but one life, et cetera, et cetera. The fact is that nobody is ever ready to die, although everyone is actually in the process of dying—Mildred with her ridiculous hat, the young girls with their obscenely thin skirts clinging to their obscenely thin thighs, the hookers Huxstep unearths, God knows where he finds them, with their insolent smiles. What is there to smile about? The only people who smile are those who don't know enough, who don't know they're dying." The Admiral realized he had been carried away, smirked in embarrassment, repeated his question. "Savinkov? Hemorrhoids? If you please?"

"During one of our meetings I noticed he was sitting on an inflated rubber tube. I assumed he had hemorrhoids. I remembered an advertisement about a medicine and brought him some the next time I saw him."

"We all seem to be good at diagnosing other people's symptoms," the Admiral remarked. "How long have you been working for Savinkov?"

"I don't work for him. I collaborate. Two, two and a half years."

"How did you first get in touch with him?"

"He got in touch with me. He struck up a conversation while we were waiting in line for a movie. We had a drink together afterward. He told me he was a Hungarian refugee. We met occasionally for lunch or dinner. We became friendly. One day he came right out and told me who he was and what he wanted."

"And what exactly did he want?"

"He wanted information that would help him, help the Russians, rein in the Agency's global schemes of domination. Savinkov understood I was a patriot, that I would only give him information when I believed my side had lost its moral compass—trying to overthrow elected governments because they were socialist, organizing the assassination of officials who were anti-American, that kind of thing."

The Admiral unfolded a photocopy of the computer printouts that had been retrieved from the pawn shop. "When you found out about Stufftingle you naturally passed this information on to him."

"Not in the beginning. I tried to head off the operation by letting Wanamaker think there had been a leak. When I realized that you had been called in to walk back the cat, that Wanamaker still seemed to be going ahead with Stufftingle, I began to feed some of the printouts into dead drops. In the back of my head I suppose I hoped that the Agency would get wind that Savinkov knew about Stufftingle and call it off."

The Weeder, Toothacher realized, still considered Stuff tingle to be an Agency operation. It had never occurred to him that Wanamaker was freelancing.

"How often did you meet with Savinkov?"

"Once he started running me we met only occasionally. When I wanted to pass something to him I usually put it in a dead drop. I'd alert him by dialing a number he gave me and letting the phone ring three times before hanging up."

"How did Savinkov pay you?"

The Weeder feigned outrage. "I never took a penny from

him. I told you, I had the interests of my country at heart. I am a patriot, even if you don't see it that way."

The Weeder shifted positions again. Whichever way he turned now, sharp pains stabbed through his back. Toothacher, comfortably installed on the bunk, was indefatigable. He doubled back over the ground he had covered, probing for contradictions, inconsistencies, outright lies. "How many times do I have to tell you I wasn't in it for the money!" the Weeder burst out at one point. "Savinkov offered me cash payments—he said if I didn't want cash he could open a secret account in Switzerland—but I flatly refused."

"You are following in the footsteps of your illustrious ancestor, if I read you correctly," the Admiral said.

"I hope to God I am," the Weeder replied with emotion.

The interrogation dragged on as the Admiral tried to tie up loose ends. "I don't remember the telephone number," the Weeder said, carefully steering clear of details that the Admiral could check. "Behind a toilet in the Smithsonian, under one of those wire wastepaper baskets behind the Lincoln Memorial—there were so many dead drops I can't remember them all."

"Of course I told him about my eavesdropping program," the Weeder admitted in reply to still another question. "I had an assistant who worked with me. I had to be sure Savinkov never referred to me, never mentioned his penetration of the Agency near a phone."

By midafternoon even the Admiral was beginning to tire. "There is one last item I'd like to take up with you," he told the Weeder. "Some years back I was invited down to the Farm to lecture to a class of new recruits. While I was there you spent two nights following me, then wrote up a report on my . . . activities. The report, signed by you, was shown to me when I was obliged to take early retirement—"

"Oh, God, you're not going to dredge up something that happened fifteen years ago. We were instructed to follow someone as part of a course on surveillance. I picked you at random. There was nothing personal."

"You ended my career at random," the Admiral said, barely moving his lips as he spoke. "You ruined my life at random." He collected his papers and zippered up his windbreaker. It occurred to him that waiting all those years was what made it so sweet. Revenge was a meal that tasted best cold.

The Weeder started to ask, "When . . . how long . . ."

Toothacher understood the question, waved a comforting hand. "That bridge won't be crossed for two or three days yet," he said. "What are we today? Ides minus three. I will have to report back to Washington before the final decision can be taken on you, on Stufftingle. The worst case must be examined. Alternatives must be explored. But I will tell you, in all honesty, that there is little doubt what your fate must be, given the situation we all find ourselves in. There can be no question of your being brought to trial. Surely someone with your intelligence can empathize with this point of view even if you are not inclined to agree with it."

"I am in great pain," the Weeder said as the Admiral got up to leave. "There is a piece of metal digging into my back."

The Admiral looked down at the Weeder, took in the awkwardness of his position, clucked his tongue in sympathy. He ducked out of the cabin, returned soon afterward trailed by Huxstep, who was struggling with a large block of cement, the kind used to weigh down temporary traffic signs. The stump of a metal pole, with a hole drilled neatly through it, protruded from the cement. Seeing the block of cement the Weeder's heart started beating wildly. Huxstep wrestled the block to the cabin floor, reached behind the Weeder and unlocked one of the handcuffs, freeing the Weeder from the piece of metal sticking out of the bulkhead. Then Huxstep locked the open cuff through the hole in the metal pole jutting from the cement block, attaching the Weeder to the block by one wrist.

"In case you was wondering," Huxstep said, "that's to make sure you sink to the bottom so nobody finds your corpse."

The Weeder turned on the Admiral, who was watching behind Huxstep. His words became gasps for air. "You promised . . . you gave your word . . the end would be painless . . . dignified."

The Admiral looked offended. "What do you take us for? Throwing someone to the sharks while he is still alive is the kind of thing our adversaries would do. In liberal circles it is popular to suggest that two enemies warring for any length of time tend to resemble each other, but this is not at all true. At least not in our case. Our manners distinguish us from our enemies. Huxstep here has strict instructions to shoot you *before* throwing you overboard."

The Weeder sat up, massaged the welts on the wrist that had been freed. He caught Huxstep sizing him up with eyes the color, the coldness of pewter. He had seen toughness before but Huxstep represented a different order of things. He had a toughness that was more than skin deep, that was indistinguishable from viciousness. It had to do with the way he looked out at the world and obviously didn't give a damn about it. "I hope he remembers," the Weeder remarked morbidly.

Mildred stuck her head through the double doors. "I think I hear the helicopter," she announced in a grating voice that somehow always managed to get on the Admiral's nerves.

"I don't think it is likely that we will meet again," Toothacher told the Weeder, "but I want you to know I won't soon forget you. You will be another secret that will go to the grave with me." He raised his baseball cap in salute and threaded his bony fingers through his tangle of hair. "You will be another of my white hairs."

22

And here, finally, is Nate's reunion with his Tory cousin, Samuel:

At first light Nate escorted Molly to the Manhattan island ferry point. She was loath to leave him but he reminded her of her vow to obey. "I am not violating principles you hold dearly but acting on them," he insisted.

The ferryman called for those who were crossing to Brookland to come on board. Several merchants carrying haversacks filled with wares walked onto the ferry. Molly clung to Nate's coat. "Your patriotism is as strong as my hate," she whispered, "but I will not let you go."

Nate gently pried loose her fingers. "I am not asking you for permission."

He stepped back. Molly raised her eyes to the heavens, as if there were something there that could change the course of history. Her gaze fell on a sliver of a moon pale with first light. "How the moon requires night," she said absently. Then she added urgently, "Me also, I require night." And she backed onto the flat ferry and stood with her eyes riveted to Nate's as it eased away from the dock. She stared at him until he was lost in darkness.

Carrying his wooden kit slung over one shoulder, Nate quickly made his way to Wall Street, to the alleyway across from Haym Salomon's house. In the street in front of the house an orderly was holding the reins of half a dozen horses. There was a commotion at the front door. Two cavalrymen dragged Salomon down the steps into the street. His wife stood on the top step stifling her tears in an apron. A cavalryman tied Salomon's hands in front of him, then passed the end of the cord up to another cavalryman who had mounted his horse. Taking a good grip on the cord, he dug his spurs into the flanks of his mount. The horse started forward at a brisk pace. Salomon, a man in his middle thirties, was almost jerked off his feet as he stumbled after the cavalryman holding the leash. Laughing, the other cavalrymen swung into their saddles and followed. They turned a corner and disappeared from view.

Nate sprinted across the street and up the steps. Salomon's wife was still standing at the open door staring at the empty street, at the dust from the cavalrymen's horses settling back onto it.

"What happened?" Nate asked breathlessly.

"They had a warrant accusing him of being a colonial spy," Salomon's wife said miserably. She added, "Haym scribbled a note for you when he heard them coming." She reached into an apron pocket and handed Nate a folded slip of paper. "God keep you, young man," she said hastily, and retreated into the house.

Nate unfolded the note. On it Salomon had scrawled: "Your cousin breaks fast daily around the hour of nine at Fraunces' Tavern."

A housewright delivering sidings to a building site directed Nate to Fraunces' Tavern, the old De Lancey mansion at the corner of Pearl and Broad. The sun was up by the time he got there, the street in front of the tavern crowded with wagons and horses being held by stable boys provided by "Black Sam" Fraunces, the enterprising proprietor. Nate turned around the tavern several times, then decided he might as well break fast himself while he was waiting. The tavern was crowded and noisy. He eventually found a place at a corner table next to a beefy constable who eyed him and his wooden kit with curiosity when he sat down. A waitress with her bosom swelling over the top of her bodice brought a steaming cup of mocha coffee, half a loaf of bread and a small wooden tub of butter. The constable finished his meal, leaned back, lit a cigar and dispatched a dense cloud of vile-smelling smoke into the air. Coughing, Nate waved a hand to clear it away—and found himself staring straight into the eyes of his cousin Samuel, standing with his back to the bar not three yards away.

Samuel, who had just turned thirty, smiled caustically. "Of all people," he called.

"Small world," Nate agreed.

The constable slipped one large hand under the wide leather belt that ran from his left shoulder to his right hip and looked from one man to the other.

Leaning confidently back against the bar, Samuel toyed with Nate the way a cat toys with a field mouse. "What brings you to New York, cousin?"

"I am repairing shoes nowadays."

A guttural laugh seeped through Samuel's lips. "I always wondered what skills they taught at Yale."

"Times are difficult," Nate remarked.

"Isn't that the god-awful truth." Samuel cocked his head. "Odd no one in my family mentioned anything about you repairing shoes. Last I heard you had quit teaching Latin and taken a commission in the rebel army."

At the adjacent tables all conversation abruptly ceased. The beefy constable turned slowly to study Nate. "What's this about you being a rebel officer?"

Nate had a sudden loss of nerve, a sudden urge to run for it. He imagined himself (I imagine him too) peering through the single glass pane, watching Molly at her toilet; imagined her cry of surprise, of sheer pleasure, when she caught sight of him. He shook his head as if he were dismissing a persuasive image and replied evenly to the constable, "I don't guess there's any point in me denying it."

Here is the interrogation of my man Nate:

After his arrest at Fraunces' Tavern by the beefy constable, Nate was handed over to a squadron of Light Dragoons, who bound his wrists and ankles in irons, hustled him into a stagecoach and started out for General Howe's headquarters at the Beekman Mansion overlooking Turtle Bay. The stagecoach, with two brass-helmeted dragoons inside and a dozen others riding ahead and behind, headed up the Eastern Post Road that ran from New York City to King's Bridge. Because the day was scorching hot there was a brief pause at the spring-fed Sunfish Pond to water the horses then the coach and its escort started up the flat-topped rise that some called Inclenberg Hill and others called Murray's Hill, sped past the driveway leading to Robert Murray's country house and continued on toward Turtle Bay and the Beekman Mansion.

Arriving in midafternoon, Nate was delivered into the custody of Howe's Irish Provost Marshal, William Cunningham, a hulking man with short-cropped hair and patriotic tattoos (FOR GOD AND GEORGE III, BRITANNIA RULES) on his arms. Hobbling because of the ankle chains, Nate was hustled into a toolshed next to the greenhouse. His wrists were secured behind his back, with the chain laced through a jagged piece of metal embedded in one of the wall planks. Nate squirmed as the metal dug into the small of his back, tried to find a comfortable position, failed. "I am in great pain," he told Cunningham.

"Are you, now?" Cunningham asked with a sneer. "The poor fellow's suffering great pain," he told the guards. Several of them smiled knowingly. Before they closed the door, leaving the prisoner in total darkness, Nate caught Cunningham sizing him up with eyes that had the color, the coldness of pewter. He had seen toughness before but Cunningham represented a different order of things. He had a toughness that was more than skin deep, that was indistinguishable from viciousness. It had to do with the way he looked out at the world and obviously didn't give a damn about it.

With the sun beating down the temperature inside the toolshed became stifling. Nate lost all track of time. He tried changing his position but whichever way he turned, sharp pains stabbed through his back. In order not to dwell on the pain he summoned up an image of Molly, seen through the window of her room, nude, a candle next to her bare feet. He remembered the feel of her wet skin as she pressed her body against his. He heard her voice saying, "If you are absolutely set on going through with this mad scheme of yours, I propose that we marry ourselves." It had been an indelible encounter, beyond the polite intercourse he had experienced before, beyond even his wildest flights of fantasy.

Outside the toolshed the guards were being changed. Nate was brought back to the present—brought back to the metal stabbing into his back—by the grunts of relief coming from the Northumberland fusilier being replaced. He heard orders shouted from the Beekman Mansion. A crisp "Aye" came from the fusilier at the door. A key turned in the padlock and the door was pulled open. I can imagine Nate squinting as the sunlight stabbed into the interior of the toolshed. Two fusiliers, sweating profusely under their brass helmets, burst in, leaned their rifles against a broken plow and set about undoing the chain that held him pinned to the metal embedded in the wall. His wrists were freed and manacled in front of him. Jerked roughly to his feet, Nate hobbled between the guards out of the shed, across the well-tended garden alive with late snow-white roses, toward the back entrance of the mansion.

As he reached the wooden steps leading to the kitchen, the door ahead was thrown open and a tall fusilier emerged. He held a rifle in one hand and a chain leash attached to the manacled wrists of Haym Salomon in the other. Nate looked at him in horror. The Jew was almost unrecognizable—his face was full of purple bruises. One eye was swollen shut. His nose was twisted to one side and caked with dried blood. Salomon shook his head imperceptibly and tried to whisper something, but his lips were too swollen to form words.

"Bring the spy along smartly now," Cunningham bellowed from the kitchen, and Nate was sent flying through the doorway by the flat of a hand on his back. Cunningham, wearing breeches held up by braces and a sweat-and-blood-stained shirt, smiled at him as if he were greeting a long-lost friend. He nodded at the fusilier, who produced a ring of keys and unlocked the manacles from Nate's wrists and ankles. Massaging the welts on his wrists, Nate heard Cunningham bark, "Strip." He looked at Cunningham, then at the dozen or so fusiliers lounging against walls and tables. "If you won't undress yourself," Cunningham snarled, pronouncing each syllable of each word carefully, "my boys here will be doing it for you."

Moving stiffly, trying to maintain what dignity he could, Nate pulled his shirt over his head, then kicked off his shoes. He removed his stockings and breeches. "Strip," Cunningham said, pointing to Nate's drawers, "means down to the bone."

Nate hesitated. Several of the fusiliers pushed themselves off the wall. Nate quickly removed his drawers and stood naked in the middle of the kitchen. He was vaguely ashamed of the whiteness of his body, of appearing naked before his enemies. Cunningham nodded at the clothes. A fusilier spread the garments on the kitchen table. Scratching absently at the inside of a nostril, Cunningham turned to inspect them. He searched methodically, running his fingers along every inch of every seam, feeling the hems to see if anything had been sewn within, examining stitching to see if it showed signs of having been redone. As he finished each garment he discarded it on the floor. Finally only Nate's shoes were left. Cunningham picked one up and turned it in his large hand, looking at it from various angles, poking at the sole to see if he could pull it loose. He reached inside and dug his fingernails under the inner sole and pried it up. Nate heard his snort of delight when he caught sight of the folded letters. Cunningham tucked the stray hairs that had appeared back up into his nostrils with delicate clockwise thrusts of his thick pinky. He found the pages from Nate's notebook folded under the inner sole of the other shoe. Flinging the shoes at Nate's feet, he collected the documents, struggled into a tight uniform jacket and rushed from the room.

"Can I put my clothes on, then?" Nate asked.

One of the fusiliers said, "What do you take us for? Hanging you while you are stark naked is the kind of thing the rebels would do. We are not like our enemies." The other fusiliers laughed.

Nate pulled on his clothes and waited. He could hear flies buzzing in the kitchen, voices droning in the heart of the house, a pulse throbbing in one of his ears. It came to him as a revelation that he was desperately afraid of being afraid; that it was this deeper fear that kept the normal fear for life and limb at arm's length.

Someone shouted an order out of a window. Minutes later a horse galloped up to the kitchen door and a captain with engineer's insignias on the sleeves of his uniform came running in. He glanced at Nate and disappeared into the hallway. A quarter of an hour went by. Cunningham returned to the kitchen, beckoned Nate with a jerk of his head and pushed him down a corridor. An orderly stood before the sliding double doors of the drawing room. He opened them and stepped aside. Cunningham put a hammerlock on Nate and marched him into the room.

The Commander-in-Chief of His Britannic Majesty's Expeditionary Forces in the Americas, Major General William Howe, sat on a high-backed settle chair, peering through a magnifying glass at the documents Cunningham had discovered in Nate's shoes. To Nate's eye, the General had the lean, hungry look that comes from presiding over a military campaign from which little glory was to be derived; it was common knowledge that Howe complained bitterly that His Majesty's ministers had such a low opinion of the American fighting potential that any setback, not to mention a defeat, could put an end to the General's career. (It was surely not lost on Howe that the debacle at Breed's Hill in

Boston had put an end to his predecessor's career.) With his sloping shoulders, his sunken cheeks, his pasty complexion, his chalk-colored hair, Howe looked to Nate like a *fin de race* nobleman who knew not only where the various bodies were buried, but what they had died of—and who had profited from their deaths and could be accused of murder if the need arose.

Captain John Montresor, the engineering officer who had arrived in such haste earlier, was leaning over the General's shoulder, translating the Latin into the King's English. "'*Litterae tuae maxime prosunt. Cum flumiuem experti erint, qui e Duobus Fratribus supererunt, numguam litus propter te praeteribunt.*' That could be taken to mean, 'Your report was extremely valuable. When they take to the river, those who . . . survive, yes, survive is right . . . those who survive the Two Brothers will never get past the landing beach, thanks to you.'"

Montresor straightened. "Does the expression 'Two Brothers' mean anything to the General?" he inquired.

Howe looked up at Nate, standing in the middle of the room. The General reached out and caressed the ivory grip of a pistol that served as a paperweight on his desk. "Perhaps we should put the question to the spy," he suggested.

Nate said, "I have been chained like a dog in the toolshed for hours. Can I have a glass of water?"

Captain Montresor, a tall man with an open, honest face, went to the sideboard, filled a glass from a pitcher and offered it to the prisoner. Nate grabbed the glass in both hands, drank off the water in one swallow, dabbed at his lips with the sleeve of his shirt.

"About Two Brothers," Howe said. "Can you tell us what it refers to?"

Nate shook his head. Cunningham grabbed Nate's wrist and started to twist it behind his back. Howe waved him off with an impatient finger. "That will not be necessary, Provost Marshal. Two Brothers is the name of two small islands in the East River immediately beyond Hell Gate. Forewarned by this spy, Washington has obviously fortified the islands, as well as the landing beaches at Frog's Neck. It is good fortune the spy fell into our hands, along with these documents." Howe addressed Nate directly. "In the end you have not done your cause a service. My amphibious operation would have speeded the resolution of this foolish war. Less blood would have flowed on both sides. Reconciliation would have been easier. Now things will drag on. But the *denouement* is inevitable. Enlistments will expire. Your militiamen will return to their homes. That so-called Congress of yours will never raise a second army. The rebellion will peter out. The Colonies will return to the royal fold."

Nate shook free from Cunningham's grip and stepped forward. "The real rebellion is in our hearts—it is the loss of affection and respect for your king and your country. Nothing can alter that."

Howe sniffed the air delicately. "Your own Ben Franklin has said, 'Passion governs, and she never governs wisely.' You prove his point. However, the passions of the several millions of your countrymen will eventually be cooled by military and economic realities. As for me," he continued, addressing Montresor and two staff officers, "I am committed to Marshal Saxe's dictum that the best commander is the one who achieves his ends by maneuver rather than engagement. Since Washington is forewarned about this maneuver, we will bestir ourselves and invent another."

"What of the landing barges in the New Town Creek?" asked one of the staff officers.

"Give the order for them to return to their respective ships," Howe said. "And bring the assembled troops across the river to reinforce our army facing the Haarlem Heights."

From behind Nate Cunningham growled, "What is the General's pleasure with the prisoner? Will it be the inglorious tree, as befits a spy?"

Nate brought a hand up to the hair mole on his neck.

Howe scraped back his seat and came around the desk to take a closer look at Nate. "What is your name?"

"Nathan Hale."

"Your rank?"

"Captain."

"What is it you do in civil life?"

"I hold a diploma from Yale Academy for the instruction of Latin, the classics and penmanship."

"You are sensible you risked being hanged when you put aside your uniform?"

For answer Nate shot back, "Was the General sensible he

risked being shot when he led his Grenadiers against the rail fence at Breed's Hill?"

"He should be flogged for insolence before being hanged," declared one of the staff officers.

"My question," Howe said, "is in effect well answered. I respect courage, the more so when it is exhibited for a lost cause. I am inclined to charity, Captain Hale." He spoke past Nate to Provost Marshal Cunningham. "Incarcerate him in a prison ship for the duration of hostilities." Howe started toward his seat, then turned back. "I neglected to ask what unit you served in. I am a keen student of the colonial order of battle."

Nate elevated his chin with pride. "I served with Colonel Webb's Nineteenth Connecticut Volunteers until I was given a captaincy in Knowlton's Rangers."

General Howe's face froze. The two staff officers avoided looking at each other. A cruel smile crept onto Cunningham's lips. Speaking barely louder than a whisper, Howe asked, "Do I understand you to be referring to Lieutenant Colonel Thomas Knowlton?"

"The same," Nate acknowledged. A pulse started pounding in his ear again.

General Howe could be heard breathing loudly through his nostrils. With each breath his face became redder, his eyes more inflamed. "Knowlton is an assassin, a criminal!" he burst out. "The marksmen he commanded at the rail fence were under orders to pick off my officers. Aiming at officers is against all the established rules of warfare. Every single member of my staff was killed or wounded. The ensign, Hendricks by name, carrying my wine flask was shot through the eye. And you dare to mention Knowlton to me as if he was a civilized officer! His militiamen crammed rusty nails, pieces of glass into their muskets. The wounds they inflicted were terrible. Terrible! I shall not forget until the day I die the carts loaded with wounded making their way back down Breed's damned hill. The surgeons sawed off limbs as if they were cutting kindling for the winter."

Howe strode around the desk and sat down abruptly in the settle. "I am inclined to charity," he said, "when charity is merited." He addressed Cunningham directly. "The spy is to be hanged by the neck until dead, and left hanging three days as an example to others who would follow his lead. Said sentence to be executed no later than tomorrow morning. Dismissed."

So here it is at last (Henry James's dying words), the Distinguished Thing (another nervous clearing of a dry throat; the author still squirms at executions that take place in the imagination):

For Nate it wasn't a matter of sleeping or not sleeping; the word no longer had any meaning, any relevance. It was a question of sorting through a maze of emotions, of dealing with the overlapping waves of panic that surged against his heart, interrupting its beat, threatening at any instant to choke off what little breath he had. Execution by hanging, as an imminent event, didn't frighten him as much as the idea that he would forever cease to exist. He believed in an Almighty Creator but not in an afterlife; the concept seemed too convenient to be true. What was left was a yawning void into which he would leap with dignity if only he could remain master of his body, of his brain. He worked through a tangle of thoughts to his mother and father, his brothers and sisters; he imagined their horror, their shame, at the news that he had been hanged as a spy. He thought too about Molly; he imagined her face contorted in grief. He thought about his mission; he would go to the inglorious tree more peacefully if he could know that the cause he served, in which he deeply believed, had profited from his death. But for it to profit he would have to get word back to General Washington.

That would be his last preoccupation, one that would keep the overlapping waves of panic at bay . . .

At midnight Nate called for the duty officer and asked for a taper and writing materials, which were duly brought by a tall fusilier with a waxed mustache. The fusilier unlocked the prisoner's wrist manacles so he could pen the traditional last letters. Nate addressed the first one to his brother Enoch, carefully burying the code sentences from Addison's *Cato* that he and A. Hamilton had agreed upon in the heart of the letter—the sentences that would indicate to General Washington that the British were not going to try and trap him in Manhattan; that he would have time to organize an orderly retreat into Westchester. The second letter, with the coded sentences again embedded in its heart, was addressed to his father, and ended:

> I send my most filial duty to my Mother
> and sincere love to my Sisters and am as I ever
> hope to be, in this World and in the Next,
> Your dutiful son
> Nathan

At dawn the fusiliers led Nate out behind the toolshed to attend to his toilet. A low morning mist covered the ground like a cushion of snow. It reminded Nate that he would never experience winter again, never throw snowballs at his sisters in the fields behind the house in Coventry, never warm his hands before a flaming hearth. He waded through the ankle-deep mist to the rain barrel and splashed water onto his face. The bath had a calming effect on him. Provost Marshal Cunningham turned up soon after. "Who is it gave orders for the condemned spy to be allowed to write letters?" he ranted when one of the fusiliers handed him the two envelopes.

"It is customary—" the fusilier with the waxed mustache started to explain.

Cunningham cut him off with a sneer. "Nothing is customary save I make it so." So saying he tore the letters into halves and into halves again and threw the scraps onto a heap of garbage waiting to be burned.

The overlapping waves of panic surged against Nate's heart. "Let me at least have the comfort of a minister," he said.

"There will be no letters and no minister," Cunningham told Nate. He barked at the fusiliers, "We will hang him and be done with it."

An army supply wagon drawn by two horses was brought around and Nate, chained hand and foot and guarded by a dozen fusiliers, set off for the Royal Artillery Park opposite the Dove Tavern, about a mile farther along the Post Road. Cunningham, accompanying them on horseback, rode ahead when the Artillery Park came into view to see whether his instructions had been carried out regarding the preparations for a hanging. He was furious when he discovered the artillerymen had only just begun constructing the gibbet. When the supply wagon drew up Cunningham started to issue orders for the condemned man to be chained to a wagon wheel while they waited. At that moment Captain Montresor emerged from the chief engineer's marquee nearby. He took in what was happening, walked up to Cunningham and offered the spy the protection of his tent. Several artillery officers who had strolled over to take a look at the condemned man were watching. Feeling it would have been awkward to refuse, Cunningham reluctantly consented.

Montresor helped Nate down from the wagon and led him into his tent. He pulled over a camp chair and gestured for him to sit on it. "Can I offer you a brandy?" Montresor asked.

Nate, bewildered by the officer's hospitality, nodded. Montresor poured a stiff brandy and handed Nate the tumbler. With his wrists chained, Nate took it in both hands and tilting his head, downed it in one gulp. Relishing the burning sensation in his throat, he handed the tumbler back to Montresor. "I am beholden to your consideration," he said.

A professional soldier who had a secret sympathy for the Colonialists' cause, Montresor was greatly impressed by the dignity and grace of the young man awaiting execution. "How old are you?" he inquired of Nate.

"I am twenty-one."

Montresor, who was almost twice Nate's age, shook his head in pity. "You have not yet tasted of life," he remarked.

Nate managed a crooked smile. "I have tasted liberty, which is more to be valued than life."

From outside the tent came the sounds of the carpenters sawing, hammering. Nate glanced at the open tent flap with a distant look in his eyes. Montresor asked if he wanted another glass of brandy. Nate didn't respond. Montresor walked over to the flap and looked out. The carpenters were raising the gibbet into place. He turned back to Nate. "I would ease your pain if I could," he said softly.

Nate said, "There is something—"

Montresor approached the camp chair. "If it is within the realm of possibility I would most willingly do it."

Nate told how Cunningham had destroyed the letters he had written to his father and his brother. "I am devastated by the dishonor I will bring on my parents when it is discovered their son was hanged as a spy. If I speak a patriot's speech before they—before my execution, will you convey my words to my countrymen so that it can be said I died a patriot's death?"

"I give you my word as a gentleman," Montresor vowed. "I am due to cross the lines this very evening under a flag of truce to negotiate an exchange of prisoners. I will recount your last words then."

Nate felt a pang of conscience at the way he was using the Englishman. But he comforted himself it was in a noble cause. And every truth had many sides. He was showing the Englishman one side, telling him a truth. He said to Montresor, "I thank you with all my heart for this service."

"I will do it gladly," Montresor assured him. "Go meet your fate with peace of mind on this score at least."

From somewhere outside an order was bellowed. Scores of soldiers could be heard falling in on parade. A kettledrum struck up an ominous rhythm. Cunningham appeared at the tent flap. "You have run out of time just as I was running out of patience," he informed the condemned man.

Nate pushed himself up from the chair. He looked Montresor in the eye for a moment. "I thank you again for the hospitality of your tent. I would take it as a favor if you would bear witness to my execution."

"I will," Montresor agreed in a subdued voice. "God rest your soul."

Nate almost smiled. "I think there is a good chance He will. I count on it."

With that Nate, walking with as firm a step as the chains attached to his ankles permitted, left the tent. The sun was high and incandescent. Squinting, Nate looked at it not as if he would never see it again but as if he had never seen it before. Its warmth on his skin felt painfully delicious. A hundred or so artillerymen were drawn up in two formations on either side of the gibbet. Several dozen civilians stood behind the artillerymen. Others, attracted by the sound of the kettledrum, were wandering over from The Sign of the Dove; some still held tankards of ale in their hands. Cunningham prodded the condemned man in the back with his fingertips. Nate took several deep breaths and started toward the gibbet, toward the noose dangling from it.

Nate well remembered the execution he had witnessed on the bowling green, remembered the spittle dribbling from the quivering lower lip of the condemned man, remembered thinking, If it ever comes to that, I swear to God I will never lose control of myself. And he raised his chin, raised his head high, straightened his shoulders and continued on as if he had no reluctance to get where he was going.

A dray had been parked directly under the gibbet. The fusilier with the waxed mustache took hold of Nate's elbow. "God bless you, boy," he whispered under his breath as he helped him up onto the dray.

Nate obliged himself to look around. He saw the noose dangling inches from his head, felt an icy hand lightly caress his spine. He raised his eyes to a pewter sky, to a pewter God. A moment more, he told himself, and it will be over. Only give me the dose of courage I need to get through it with dignity. He struggled to keep his limbs from trembling, his heart from sinking under the weight of pure fear. He let his eyes drift back to the crowd. He spotted Molly's slave, John Jack, off to one side. His face was a mask of agony. Seeing he had caught Nate's eye, John Jack nodded vigorously and then brought a hand up to his face to wipe away the tears. Nate nodded back once, turned his head, was relieved to see Captain Montresor standing stiffly next to a rank of artillerymen. He nodded at Montresor. The captain lifted his cap in salute.

The crowd grew deathly quiet. Cunningham climbed onto the dray, fitted the noose over Nate's head and tightened it around his neck. Nate tried to speak. His mouth worked but no words emerged. Dear God in heaven, he thought. Help me. The code passage from Addison's play was on his tongue, the lines Cato recites when he sees the body of his son Marcus, and Nate opened his mouth and flung them into the deathly still midmoming air. "How beautiful is death when earned by virtue! What pity is it that we can die but once to serve our country!"

The beat of the kettledrum quickened. Cunningham jumped off the dray and motioned to the two fusiliers holding the traces. They started forward, pulling the dray with them. Nate tiptoed along the floorboards to keep his footing, then ran out of dray and dangled from the noose. A muted sigh, an exhaling of many breaths, came from the crowd as Nate danced at the end of the cord, which was slowly strangling him. The fusilier with the waxed mustache started to wrap his arms around the jerking knees of the hanging man but Cunningham, smiling cruelly, waved him off.

Here is a post scriptum:

John Jack came back from Manhattan barely able to speak. Gradually Molly pried the details out of him. He had seen the shadows of birds racin' cross the ground, had looked up, but there wasn't no birds, he told her, there was jus' Mister Nathan dancin' at the bitter end of a rope. After a god-awful long while the dancing stopped. Poor Mister Nathan was left to twist gently in the breezes coming in off the river.

For a while Molly, who had dreamed the night before that life was stirring in her womb, tried to sob; but a voice in her warned that if she started she might never be able to stop. Later, beyond tears, numbness set in. She dipped her quill into the inkwell and wrote on a blank page of her diary:

> Septembre the 22nd
> Ambuſh'd, again, by greef. Nate hang'd
> in Artillery Park. He liv'd Deſir'd and
> died Lament'd. A Friend I sot much by
> but he is Gone . . .

23

Fargo telephoned Snow from Washington every day. All he ever reached was her answering machine. "The doctors are quite pleased with the way things are proceeding," he recorded one day. "Your friend is eating well. He's even put on some weight. I have to tell you, Snow, that they've diagnosed schizophrenia, but there have been breakthroughs in the treatment of schizophrenia. He's in very professional hands. There is no reason under the sun to be pessimistic about the outcome of therapy."

"He's getting along just fine, Snow," Fargo reported to the machine another time. "All things considered, he's in good spirits and eager to get started with his analysis. Everyone is extremely hopeful."

A third message from Fargo said, "He's under sedation, naturally, but the doctors think they can gradually decrease the dose as therapy proceeds."

The next time Fargo phoned he found a message addressed specifically to him on the answering machine. "If this is Fargo," Snow's recorded voice challenged, "tell me this: Have you seen him with your own eyes?"

When Snow played back the tape she could hear Fargo exhaling in frustration. "The answer is no, I haven't seen him with my own eyes. But I've talked to people who have—his assistant, Marvin Wesker, for one. That buddy of his from his college days, Roger Wanamaker, went out to visit him. The Attorney General has taken a personal interest in the case. He's spoken on the phone with the doctor in charge. If everyone is lying about Sibley, then our government is a lie, our whole system is a lie." Fargo hesitated. Snow could visualize him shaking his head in annoyance. Finally he spoke again. "I hope this convinces you."

It didn't. Snow felt trapped between two persuasive truths. She needed to know which truth was invented and which was real. The next day she took a bus into Cambridge and went directly to the Widener Library. She still had a valid library card from the time, a year before, when she had audited a course on the history of photography. She decided to begin with the word *Kabir*.

There was nothing under Kabir in *The New York Times Index*. On a hunch she checked a recent guidebook on Iran. The index listed "Amir Kabir College, formerly the Polytechnic College of Tehran University." Snow went back to *The New York Times Index*, found a listing for the Polytechnic College. There had been an article on it in the *Times* in January 1982, and another in March 1984. Snow noted the dates and the page numbers, signed out the microfilms and threaded the first one through the viewing machine. She flipped through the newspaper until she came to the article. It described nervousness in the American intelligence community over rumors circulating in the Middle East that the Polytechnic College had been transformed into a nuclear research center. The second article was more specific. It cited informed sources as saying that the college's five-megawatt research reactor was believed to be operating twenty-four hours a day. The sources speculated that the reactor's fuel load of five kilograms of enriched uranium might one day be diverted to nuclear weapon production.

Kabir, at least, was not a figment of Silas's imagination.

Tracking down *Stufftingle* proved more difficult. The librarian shrugged bony shoulders, shook spring-shaped locks of hair, decided that all she could suggest was for Snow to go through the indexes of books on the subject. She hoped Snow wasn't pressed for time because there would be hundreds. She gave Snow the appropriate Dewey decimal number off the top of her head. Snow installed herself at a table in the stacks, carried over an armful of books on atomic energy, nuclear fission, the Los Alamos project, and related material, and began checking the indexes for the word *Stufftingle.* She kept at it all morning and half the afternoon. She was beginning to have difficulty focusing when she opened a thin book entitled *Secret,* by Wesley W. Stout. She almost didn't believe it when she came across a reference to Stufftingle in the index. She thumbed excitedly through the book to page thirty-nine. The words *Oak Ridge* and *burlesque secret document* jumped out at her. She read on:

> They are taking plumscrate, raw plumscrate mind you, and putting it into ballisportle tanks . . . Next, this is taken to the sarraputing room . . . At this point, of course, is when they add thungborium, the ingredient which causes the entire masterfuge to Knoxify . . . At 12:20 on the third Tuesday night of each month, 800 men known as shizzlefrinks, because their brains have been siphoned from their heads, are lined up in single file, each given two ingots of ousten-stufftingle (name of the finished product) and away they march . . .

Not only was there a Kabir College. There was a Stufftingle too!

Snow caught an evening plane to Washington, installed herself in a hotel at the airport and checked the telephone directory. There was no one in it named Toothacher, either in Washington proper or the surrounding countryside. She tried to remember the name of Silas's assistant but it wouldn't come to her. Snow's mother had claimed that the best way to remember something was to think about something else. Following her mother's advice, Snow lay down on the double bed and closed her eyes and concentrated on Silas. She was able to duplicate his voice in her head, the way it lingered over syllables at the end of a sentence when he wasn't sure of himself, the way the words came in a rush when he felt he had something to prove. She remembered the cord burns on his palms, remembered telling him, "Your life lines have been erased."

Snow sat up abruptly. "Marvin Wesker," she murmured. "That's his name." She grabbed the telephone directory and leafed through to the *W*'s. Sure enough there was a listing under *Wesker, M.* She scratched the address on a notepad next to the phone and bolted from the room.

Three quarters of an hour later she found herself ringing the doorbell of a fourth-floor apartment near the Buffalo Bridge at Q Street. The sound of loud music came from behind the door. The volume was turned down. The door opened the width of the safety chain. A young man with a thin, humorless face and enormous ears with wire spectacles hooked over them said, "Yeah?"

"You don't know me," Snow began. "My name is Matilda Snowden. I'm a friend—a good friend, actually—of Silas's."

Wesker let his gaze drift from her head to her feet and then work its way back up to her head again. He clearly liked what he saw because he cracked a smile and announced, "Any friend of Silas, et cetera, et cetera. Come on in."

He motioned her to a sofa, asked if she could do with a drink, and when she said no thank you, settled into a chair facing her. "Do you recognize the music?" Wesker asked, nodding toward a tape deck in a bookcase. "It's a golden oldie, 'California Dreamin'.' The Mamas and the Papas. If I can't get you something to drink, what *can* I do for you?"

"I was told that you'd been to see Silas."

"Who gave you that tidbit of information?"

"A friend of mine who works in the Justice Department. His name is Fargo. He said he'd talked to you on the phone."

"I may have talked to a guy from the Justice Department," Wesker said carefully. "But I never told him I'd seen Silas. I told him I'd been out to the, eh, hospital."

"You went out to the hospital and you didn't see Silas?"

"Hey, I don't want to get you into trouble or anything, but I'm going to have to report that you came around asking about Silas like it is."

"Report me if you have to. It won't change anything. How come you didn't see Silas?"

"He'd had a bad night. He was under sedation. The doctor said it wasn't such a good idea to visit him right then."

"Did the doctor tell you what's wrong with Silas, Mr. Wesker?"

"Only that he was sick."

"Sick?"

Wesker fidgeted uncomfortably in his chair. "Sick in the head," he said. "Listen, why don't you go and see him yourself?"

Snow said, "They won't tell me where he is."

"Hey, if you're really a friend of his you know who he works for, huh? And who he works for, its board of directors so to speak, they get very jumpy when one of their employees has a more or less nervous breakdown. It's no state secret that the Company has state secrets which it has got to protect, huh? If it will make you feel any better I can tell you the hospital is as modern as they come. I'm thinking of going out again the weekend after next weekend. I'm on the list of people who are allowed to visit. That's because there's nothing Silas can say that I'm not cleared to hear. You want me to give him a message?"

"Tell him—" Snow had a sudden thought. "Have you worked with Silas a long time?"

"I can't talk about work."

"Can you say whether you worked here in Washington or in New York? Surely that's not a state secret."

Wesker blinked rapidly but didn't reply.

Snow tried a different approach. "Silas told me what you and he did."

Wesker shook his head. "He oughtn't to have done that. The Company gets all hot under the collar if we talk about what we do with anyone who's not cleared to listen."

Snow insisted, "I have to know if he was telling the truth."

Wesker arched his eyebrows as if to say he was genuinely sorry he couldn't help her.

"Look, I'll tell you what he told me," Snow said, "and you keep looking at me if you can confirm it."

"I can't do that—"

Snow decided to use Fargo's version of the truth. "Silas said he worked with computers," she began.

Wesker continued to look into her eyes.

"Something about doing a computer study of the serial numbers of a certain kind of equipment."

Wesker looked at her, blinking uncomfortably.

"Of tanks." When Wesker didn't look away she ventured, "Of Russian tanks, actually."

Wesker shifted his gaze to one side. Snow said, "Oh!"

"Hey, don't take my looking away for anything. You made the rules of your little game, but I didn't say I would play. I can't divulge information on what we do. No way."

Snow smiled in appreciation. "I understand."

Wesker caught her smile. "I don't think you do." He laughed nervously. "For all I know you could be a Russian spy. So don't go away thinking you know more than when you came. I just listened politely."

"Right," Snow agreed. "And thanks."

"Oh, Jesus. Don't for Christ's sake thank me. I didn't do anything."

At the door Snow turned to ask a question. "Did Silas ever mention an Admiral Toothacher to you?"

Wesker shook his head stubbornly. "Wild horses couldn't get me to answer any more of your questions."

Snow lay awake in her bed that night sorting through possibilities. Kabir College existed. So did Stufftingle. Wesker seemed to say that the story about Silas studying serial numbers of Soviet tanks was phony, which meant that the story Silas told about running an eavesdropping operation was true. And someone did try to kill Silas by bringing down a building on his head; Snow had been there, had seen it with her own eyes, even if she hadn't seen the Admiral and his two colleagues. Which meant that Silas had been telling the truth all along. She had been a fool to get in touch with Fargo, to believe the story they had cooked up about Silas being mentally disturbed; she would never forgive herself for delivering him into their hands. Silas was probably in a "hospital" all right, but it was no accident that Wesker hadn't been allowed to see him. Silas had probably had a bad night—being quizzed by Company interrogators working in relays. A terrible thought occurred to Snow. They would have gotten their hands on the material Silas left in the dead drop, would be convinced he was a Russian spy. The Company's board of directors, as Wesker called it, couldn't afford to accuse Silas publicly and let him come to trial; couldn't take the risk of Silas talking about Stufftingle in open court.

Oh God, she thought, Silas would never be allowed to leave the hospital alive!

What if she were to go to the newspapers and tell the whole story? No, that wouldn't work. The Company would trot out evidence that Silas Sibley was stark raving mad or better still, that no one with that name worked for it; would talk the newspapers out of running the story; would even arrange things so that Snow herself wound up in that little "private" hospital of theirs. And that would be that.

On the other hand, if she could get someone who knew about Stufftingle, who knew about the attempts on Silas's life, to help her, she could try and strike a deal with the Company. If the board of directors could find it in their hearts to let Sibley go free, Silas and she would forget Stufftingle ever existed, would disappear.

But who could help her? And why would he help her?

A name came to her lips. She pronounced it out loud. "Admiral Toothacher!"

Silas had once followed the Admiral, had discovered him

burning the candle at both ends, after which the Company had preferred to quietly retire Toothacher rather than wash its dirty linen in public. If she could follow the Admiral and catch him burning that candle, it would give her the leverage she needed to talk Toothacher into helping her, into helping Silas.

But before she could follow him she had to find him.

She tried the Department of the Navy, Personnel Office, first thing in the morning, but was informed that it dealt only with people on active duty. The chief petty officer Snow spoke to suggested she try the Veterans Administration. A civilian time server there sent her around to the Office of Naval Reserve. "Sorry," a woman wearing lieutenant junior grade stripes on the sleeves of her uniform informed Snow. "We don't give out addresses."

"I don't want to see the Admiral," Snow explained earnestly. "I want to send him something. My husband admired Admiral Toothacher enormously. He served under him when the Admiral was captain of a destroyer. My husband died in an automobile accident"—it dawned on Snow that she was doing what the psychiatrist claimed Silas did, constructing a make-believe world using bits and pieces of the real world—"I was driving . . . that's how I got this." With her fingertips she traced the thin scar over her eye. The tears that brimmed in her eyes were real enough even if the story she told was part fiction.

"I'm sorry about your husband—"

Snow could see the woman was wavering. "Anyhow, he

built this scale model of the destroyer, you see. In his will he left it to Admiral Toothacher. That's why I'm trying to get his address—so I can send him the model of the destroyer."

The lieutenant screwed up her mouth, weighed the pros and cons, finally said, "Wait here a minute." She went over to a computer terminal and punched in a name. A dossier flashed onto the screen. The lieutenant copied off an address on a slip of paper and handed it to Snow. "Your admiral retired to Guantánamo, Cuba, but he seems to have returned to Washington at some point."

Snow thanked her profusely.

"Rules," the lieutenant said, "are made to be bent."

The address the woman gave Snow turned out to be a seedy apartment hotel on lower Wisconsin. Snow bought a tiny Minox in a camera store, loaded it with very fast black-and-white film and installed herself in an all-night drugstore that had one long window on the street and another separating the store from the hotel lobby. Sipping coffee at the counter, Snow had a good view of the hotel's giant revolving door and main desk. Night fell. Streetlights came on. Dozens of men came and went but none of them fit the description Silas had given her of the Admiral. One elderly man with snow-white hair sauntered out of the elevator around 9 P.M. holding two white poodles on leashes, but he was too short and too fat to be called lanky. Snow ordered another cup of coffee, her fifth, slipped two dollar bills onto the counter and told the waitress to keep the change. Outside a heavy rain began to fall. The tired black woman behind the counter leaned across to Snow.

"If you're looking to turn a trick," she said, "you probably came to the wrong hotel."

"I'm not looking to turn a trick," Snow said. "I'm looking for a friend."

The waitress obviously didn't believe her. "No skin off my nose whatever you're doing," she said.

The hour hand on the clock in the lobby was just clicking onto 10 P.M. when the elevator doors opened and a tall, lanky man emerged. Snow recognized him immediately. He was in his late fifties, with a mane of chalk-white hair, a slight stoop, pasty complexion. The Admiral ambled past the drugstore window less than three yards from where Snow was sitting, and she saw the aviator glasses and, behind them, the bulging eyes that seemed to take in absolutely everything. Snow noticed that his sunken cheeks had a dab of rouge on them. A hulking man with close-cropped pewter hair and ramrod-straight posture came forward to meet the Admiral. They exchanged a few words. The Admiral nodded, slipped a raincoat over his shoulders as if it were a cape, and followed the hulking man through the revolving door to the street.

Snow grabbed her coat and darted out of the drugstore into the street. Outside the revolving door the hulking man had opened a large black umbrella and was holding it over the head of the Admiral as he hustled him into the back seat of a blue Dodge parked at the curb. Snow went over to the taxi stand to her left, jumped into the first cab on the line. "You see the car pulling away from the hotel?" she asked the driver.

"Sure I see the car pulling away from the hotel," he replied with a laugh. "If I didn't see it I'd be blind. If I was blind I couldn't get a hack license."

"Can you follow it?"

The driver, whose name according to the framed identification plaque was Ernest E. Rosencrantz, perked up. "You want that I should actually follow that car?"

"Please."

The Dodge with the Admiral in it joined the flow of traffic. Ernest E. Rosencrantz worked his windshield wipers and pulled out behind it. "This ain't for some kind of candid camera program?" he asked.

"It's my husband," Snow explained. "He told me he was going to play duplicate bridge. I don't believe him."

Colored lights ricocheted off the glistening pavement as the blue Dodge, weaving through traffic, drifted down "The Strip" in Georgetown, then turned off M Street onto a side street, then onto another and pulled up in front of a door with a neon sign sizzling over it that said CH CK's. The taxi pulled up several car lengths behind. Ernest E. Rosencrantz pursed his lips. "The *U* is missing. Been missing for months. Chuck's is what it should say."

The burly man came around to the sidewalk side of the Dodge, opened the umbrella and held it over the Admiral's head as he got out of the car and walked to the door. He pushed a button. A small window in the door opened, a face appeared in it. The Admiral muttered something. The window closed, the door opened and the Admiral disappeared inside.

"Is that the bridge player?" Rosencrantz inquired.

Snow nodded.

"If you don't mind my saying so, he looks a little on the old side for you."

The burly man returned to the car and slowly cruised the street, hunting for a parking space. He found one near the corner, walked back and disappeared in turn into Chuck's.

Snow started to pay the driver. "Say, you look like an all right lady," Rosencrantz said. "Maybe you should think twice about going in there." He smiled in a fatherly way. "Duplicate bridge is definitely not what they play at Chuck's."

"I need to see for myself," Snow said.

Rosencrantz shook his head philosophically. "I think you're in for a surprise."

Snow held out some bills. "Life is made up of wounds and scar tissue, Mr. Rosencrantz." She flashed the smile that held back tears. "I've passed the wound stage. I'm working desperately on the scar tissue."

Rosencrantz pushed her money away. "Pay me when you get back to the hotel," he told Snow.

"You mean you'll wait for me?"

The driver waved a hand in embarrassment. "Wounds. Scar tissue. I'll be here when you come out."

"You're one in a million, Mr. Rosencrantz."

"That's not what the wife says," Rosencrantz noted dryly. "I should get you to write me a testimonial."

Snow ducked from the taxi and ran through the rain to the door with the neon sign sizzling over it. She pushed the buzzer. The small window opened. A man with a pinched face peered out. He took in Snow and said, "You sure you know where you're at?"

"I'm meeting a friend," Snow told him.

The window closed, the door opened and she slipped in. The man with the pinched face took her raincoat and handed her a red chip with a number on it. "There's a twenty-five-dollar minimum per," he informed her.

Snow pushed through a curtain of beads into the nightclub and looked around. A dozen or so couples—men with men, women with women—were dancing to slow canned music on a mirrorlike surface in the middle of the room. Strobe lights flickering from a large diamond over their heads made it seem as if the tent-shaped roof was in motion. There were booths along two walls filled with flickering candles and dark figures, and a long mahogany bar off to Snow's right with candles spaced along it every yard. The Admiral was sitting on a stool near the middle of the bar, engrossed in conversation with an elegantly dressed gentleman on the next stool. The hulking man who had held the umbrella for the Admiral was sitting farther down the bar nursing a drink, toying with the melting wax of a candle, passing a forefinger with excruciating slowness through the flame.

Snow strolled past him. "This taken?" she asked him, nodding at the next stool.

"It is. By you," he replied without looking up from the candle he was playing with.

Snow hefted herself onto the stool. The bartender hovered. "What do you recommend?" she asked.

"Here they usually ask me who I recommend," he said with a suggestive smirk.

The hulking man laughed under his breath. The bartender said, "Nobody complains about my daiquiris."

"A daiquiri, then."

"Lime or lemon?"

"Lime."

The bartender filled a large glass with crushed ice, rum, lime juice, tossed in several spoonfuls of sugar, capped it with a metal cover and began shaking it to a cha-cha rhythm. He iced a glass and strained the liquid into it, popped in a straw and set the drink down in front of Snow. Wiping the surface of the bar with a wet rag, he asked the hulking man, "Can I top you off?"

"Later."

"Tell me again," the bartender asked the hulking man, "what makes a perfect number perfect."

"A perfect number is perfect," the hulking man explained wearily—he had obviously been over it before—"if it's the sum of its divisors other than itself. Take the number six. It can be divided by one or two or three, and it's the sum of one and two and three. Or twenty-eight. It can be divided by one or two or four or seven or fourteen, and it's the sum of one and two and four and seven and fourteen. It's perfect."

"Huxstep here," the bartender confided to Snow, "has a thing about numbers. Go ahead, try him."

Snow studied the profile of the customer sitting on the stool next to her. So this was the man who had tried to incinerate Silas in the parking lot, who had worked one of the wrecking balls that had almost killed her. Another piece of the puzzle was falling into place. Huxstep wasn't a figment of Silas's imagination either. She remembered Silas mentioning that Huxstep could solve complicated mathematical problems in his head. Snow decided to put him to the test to make sure he was the same man Silas had talked about.

"Do you have a pocket calculator handy?" she asked the bartender.

He took one from the drawer of the cash register and gave it to Snow. She punched in some numbers, looked at the result, said to Huxstep, "Can you divide eight sevens by 368.7?"

Huxstep's face screwed up, his eyes narrowed, his lips moved. Presently he said, "21095138."

"Where does the decimal point fall?" Snow demanded.

"After the fifty-one."

Snow said, "That's amazing."

"Don't say I didn't tell you," the bartender said, beaming.

A short woman with gold-rimmed sunglasses drifted over and sat down next to Snow. She popped a filter-tipped cigarette between her lips, angled her head toward Snow and asked, "Do you have fire, honey?"

The bartender held out a book of matches. The woman looked at him in annoyance. "Did I ask you for fire, Charlie, or did I ask the lady here for fire?"

Charlie backed away.

"How 'bout it, honey?"

Snow said she didn't smoke.

The woman said with a laugh, "No vices?"

"I drink," Snow admitted. She sipped her daiquiri.

"I'm relieved to hear it," the woman said. She looked at the bartender. "Whatever she's drinking, Charlie, bring two more. And I'll take your fire now."

Around the curve of the bar the elegantly dressed gentleman sitting next to the Admiral left his stool and walked off toward the booths. The Admiral leaned forward to catch Huxstep's eye, batted both his lids in a conspiratorial double wink; Snow had the impression that he was pleading for something. Huxstep slid off his stool and made his way to the edge of the dance floor. He tapped a thin young man with shoulder-length bleached blond hair and a face that looked half-Indian, drew him off the dance floor. He spoke to him for a moment, indicated the Admiral with his eyes, peeled off some bills from a thick wad and gave them to the young man, who folded the money away in the rear pocket of his skintight leather jeans.

At the bar Snow fumbled for something in her pocketbook.

"Funny I never seen you here before," said the woman who had bought Snow a drink.

"That's because I've never been here before."

"Uh-huh," the woman said.

Huxstep, his eyes glued to the Admiral, returned to his seat. The young man who looked half-Indian eased himself onto the empty stool next to the Admiral and began talking animatedly with him. Toothacher leaned over and whispered something in his ear. The young man rewarded him with a high-pitched laugh. His shrill voice could be heard over the music. "I'll bet you say that to all the boys," he exclaimed.

"No, really," the Admiral could be heard protesting. "I knew the instant I saw you there was more to you than looks."

The young man eased an arm over the Admiral's stooped shoulders. The Admiral, beaming, leaned across the bar to catch Huxstep's eye and nodded once. Huxstep went back to his drink. "I think I'll take that refill now," he told the bartender.

"You earned it," Charlie remarked.

"He's a grand old man," Huxstep muttered. "Salt of the earth."

"He's lucky to have you," the woman next to Snow ventured.

"It's me who's the lucky one," Huxstep insisted.

"Lost something in your pocketbook?" Charlie asked Snow.

"Not anymore," she said, and she came out with her wallet and asked for a check.

"You only just arrived," the woman next to Snow said in a hurt voice. "You haven't drunk the daiquiri I bought you."

"The real action doesn't start for another hour or so," Charlie added.

"I've got to go," Snow told the woman.

The bartender, the woman and Huxstep watched Snow disappear through the beads of the curtain. Charlie delivered his verdict with a shrug. "Wants to go for a dip but afraid of getting wet."

The woman shook her head in disgust. "Story of my life."

24

Snow was keeping an eye on the hotel lobby through the window behind the drugstore counter late the next morning when the elevator doors opened and the Admiral, suppressing a yawn, stepped out. His face was full of blotches, his hair disheveled. He wore backless bedroom slippers on his large bare feet and had an enormous terrycloth bathrobe wrapped around his lanky body. He threaded his fingers through his chalk-white hair as he shuffled across the lobby to the mail desk. The elderly man with two white poodles on leashes stopped to have a word with the Admiral. Snow left her seat at the counter and went to the phone booth at the back of the drugstore. She pushed a coin into the slot and dialed the hotel. Through the booth, through the drugstore window, she could see the desk clerk checking the Admiral's cubbyhole and handing him a newspaper and his mail. The desk clerk turned his back on the Admiral and reached for the phone.

"Please, I want to speak to Admiral Toothacher."

"Hang on."

Snow could see the clerk calling the Admiral back to the desk.

The Admiral's voice, hoarse, cranky, came over the line. "That you, Huxstep? Don't you think it's a bit early to be making plans for the night? You could at least wait until I have had my morning bath."

Snow covered the mouthpiece with a hand. "This isn't Huxstep."

The Admiral, puzzled, asked, "Who is this?"

"Open the manila envelope you got in the mail this morning."

"I beg your pardon."

"Open it."

Over the telephone Snow could hear the Admiral slitting open the envelope. Through the drugstore window she could see him start as he caught sight of the photographs. Taken with the Minox through a hole in her pocketbook, developed early that morning at the store where she bought the camera, one showed Toothacher whispering into the ear of the young man who looked half-Indian. Another showed the young man with an arm over the Admiral's shoulder. The Admiral, visible over the boy's shoulder, was flushed with excitement. In the lobby the Admiral shoved the photographs back into the envelope and looked around in panic. He came back on the line.

"Who are you?" he whispered harshly. "If you want money you're barking up the wrong tree. All I have is my retirement checks and they barely cover my bar bill."

"I don't want money," Snow said.

There was a long pause. "What do you want?"

"I want Silas Sibley set free. If he isn't released, and soon, those photographs are going to wind up on every city desk in the country. I don't think the Company would appreciate that. A former head of Naval Intelligence, a former CIA big shot spilling secrets in a gay bar."

When Toothacher finally replied, Snow detected a note of pathos in his voice. "Whoever you are you're making a terrible mistake. I don't know any Silas Sibley. My God, I haven't been associated with anyone or anything official in Washington for years."

"I'm not bluffing," Snow warned.

She could hear the Admiral breathing heavily into his end of the telephone connection. "Dear kind lady, if you have an ounce of charity in your heart I ask you, I beg you, don't do this to me. Even if I wanted to help you I couldn't. You're blackmailing the wrong person. I don't have the vaguest idea who this Silas Sibley is. I'm an old man. You can't drag me through the mud like this. You'll ruin me. Dear God in heaven, you absolutely have to believe me. I'm telling you the truth."

Snow whispered, "Whose truth? Which truth?" And then she severed the connection.

25

The wind off Nantucket had picked up, the seas too. On top of everything else the Weeder was seasick. He had vomited twice already (into a wastepaper basket, supplied in haste by Mildred) and had not been able to hold down any food for the past twenty-four hours. Although she hadn't thrown up Mildred was faring no better. She kept her eyes tightly closed most of the time, claiming the motion of the boat made her dizzy when she opened them.

Of the three only Huxstep was operational. He reacted to the Weeder and Mildred the way people who aren't seasick usually react to those who are—it made him feel very superior and more cruel than usual. He described meals he had eaten and threatened to light a cigar until Mildred moaned something about shooting him if he did.

Around midafternoon the radiotelephone crackled into life. Huxstep switched from the loudspeaker to the handphone, listened for a long moment to someone issuing instructions, snapped "Right as rain, Admiral," and hung up. He knelt on the deck next to the Weeder. "Listen up. It seems like you're getting a phone call in five or ten minutes. It's your lady friend from Concord. She's being plugged through from a hookup in the Justice Department. Here's the story. She's been told you are tucked into a bed with starched sheets and hospital corners in a private Company asylum. Without being specific you confirm that. You do a lot of listening, a little talking. Got it?"

"What makes you think I'll do as you ask?" the Weeder demanded.

Huxstep sneered. "If you screw up I'll light a cigar and blow smoke in your face."

Mildred, lying on the bunk with her eyes closed, said, "You don't want your lady friend becoming suspicious, do you? The Admiral might decide she was better off dead than red, you see what I mean?"

The radiotelephone came alive a few minutes later. Huxstep adjusted the toggle switch so that both the loudspeaker and the hand phone would work, and put the phone into the Weeder's free hand. He kept a finger on the toggle switch in case he had to cut off the conversation.

The Weeder heard an operator's voice patching through the call. "I have your party," she said. There was a burst of static, which cleared. A man's voice asked, "Is Sibley on the line?"

The Weeder said, "I'm here."

The line clicked several times. Snow's voice, slightly breathless, said, "Thanks, Michael. Silas, is that you?"

"Snow?"

"Oh, Silas. Thank God. How are you? Where are you?"

The Weeder regarded Huxstep. He kept one hand on the toggle switch. With the other he fingered a cigar. "I'm in a hospital," the Weeder replied. "I'm getting on great. Really. How are you?"

There was a surge of static on the line. When it cleared Snow could be heard calling, "Are you still there, Silas? What's causing all this static?"

Snow's voice seemed to come from far away, from another world. The Weeder made an effort to project himself into her world, to imagine it. But there was an unbridgeable abyss between her world and his. Huxstep was gesturing for him to reply. He keyed the telephone and said, "The Company doesn't use regular telephone lines for obvious reasons."

"Silas, you're not furious with me, are you?"

"No. You did the right thing."

"Oh God, if you only knew how relieved I am to hear you say that."

"Tell me what you're up to," the Weeder asked. He was desperate to keep the conversation going. It was the last one he would ever have with her. "Have you been taking any photographs? Are you invading anyone's privacy?"

"Actually, yes. Remember the time you were vacationing at a farm and followed someone you shouldn't have?"

For a moment the Weeder didn't know what she was talking about. Then it came to him. He hadn't been vacationing at a farm; he had been going through basic training at *the* Farm. And the person he had followed had been Admiral

Toothacher. Show was trying to tell him something. He flashed a sheepish grin in Huxstep's direction. "I remember," he told Snow.

"Well, it gave me an idea and I did the same thing. Only I took pictures."

The Weeder felt a rush of excitement. So she believed him after all! "Are you going to publish them?" he asked.

"That depends. You can't just go and publish photos of someone—you have to get him to give you a release."

"Sounds like you're on to something good," the Weeder said. "I hope you can pull it off."

"Take care of yourself, Silas. You have to, you know, because when you get out of there I'll be waiting for you."

"I promise to be a good boy," the Weeder said.

"I need to tell you something, Silas." Another burst of static drowned her out. ". . . to exchange vows when you are. Hang in there, okay?"

"Concentrate on your photography project—that way you'll have less time to worry about me."

"I will, Silas. Well, good-bye for now."

"Good-bye."

Huxstep flipped the toggle switch. "I think you did all right," he said.

"I think so too," the Weeder agreed.

For the first time in days the emotion he was suppressing wasn't fear but hope.

26

The meeting took place on the Ides of March in the elevator on the minus-four level of a downtown Washington office building. The Attorney General was clearly depressed; it looked as if an operation far more imaginative than the Iran-Contra affair had come to a dead end. Sucking on the stem of a dead pipe, he turned up his hearing aid and said, "We can thank our lucky star the FBI came to me with the letter he wrote to Savinkov. I hate to think of the consequences if they had gone directly to the Company."

Wanamaker asked worriedly, "Won't they come around asking questions when nobody gets back to them?"

"I told them they had stumbled on an ongoing operation," the Attorney General said. "I talked national security. As far as the FBI's concerned the matter ends there."

Wanamaker shook his head in irritation. "Who would have thought the asshole was working for Savinkov? I suppose that means we have to dismantle Stufftingle."

The Attorney General shifted his gaze to the third man in the elevator. The Admiral's eyes were rimmed with red and clouded with worry. For him the worst case was still the most likely, the most interesting, the most stimulating. But for once in his life it wasn't the most congenial. So he argued the best case. "I went out to the boat to interrogate him," he told the Attorney General. "He tried to convince me he was a Russian mole, but I don't believe it. There are a dozen holes in his story."

"Don't make the mistake of trying to tell me what you think I want to hear," warned the Attorney General.

The Admiral bridled. "I grant you the great problem with the intelligence community is it inevitably caters to its clients. That was never my style when I ran Naval Intelligence. It is not my style now. I operate on the principle that, whether it is convenient or not, there is only one truth."

The Attorney General seemed unimpressed. "How do you explain someone admitting to be a Soviet agent when he isn't? It's a bit farfetched, if you ask me. Kind of thing that happens in one of those le Carré books but not in real life."

"Why did he post a love letter to Savinkov in a dead drop?" Wanamaker chimed in. "Why did he leave the pawn ticket? Explain that?"

The Admiral ignored Wanamaker and addressed the Attorney General directly. "Savinkov's an old pro—he probably realized the FBI was on to that particular drop. If Savinkov knew, then the Weeder knew; don't forget he was targeting Savinkov on his eavesdropping program. Which means when the Weeder planted the letter and the pawn ticket behind the radiator, he *intended* them to fall into the hands of the FBI and eventually the Company. Remember, he thought the Company was behind Stufftingle. He was a patriot—he wanted to head off what he considered an atrocity. He calculated that if the Company thought Savinkov had been tipped off about Stufftingle, the operation would have to be permanently canceled."

The Attorney General digested this while he lit his pipe. He filled the elevator with a cloud of vile-smelling smoke. "When you come right down to it," he finally said, "it really doesn't matter whether we can prove he is a Soviet agent. The possibility clearly exists that he may be, which means the possibility also exists that our Russian friends know about Stufftingle and will expose us if we go ahead with it." He issued his orders to Wanamaker. "Dismantle Stufftingle. Destroy the uranium. Pull out the people who know about it. Burn your records. Cover your tracks."

"What do I do with the Weeder?" Wanamaker asked.

The Admiral spoke up before the Attorney General could answer. "There is no reason to do anything with the Weeder. All he wanted was to head off Stufftingle. Now that it's canceled he'll play ball."

Both the Attorney General and Wanamaker stared at the Admiral. "There's no way we can turn him loose on the streets as if nothing happened," Wanamaker said. "The Weeder's a walking bomb, not to mention a Russian agent."

"I agree," the Attorney General announced flatly. He nodded curtly at Wanamaker. "I leave the matter in your competent hands." And he reached inside his jacket pocket and turned down his hearing aid to indicate the discussion was over.

The Admiral, in desperation, grabbed the Attorney General's elbow. "You're making a mistake," he said urgently. "Terminating the Weeder could be dangerous." He cast around wildly for arguments, came up instead with disjointed sentences. ". . . left footprints . . . letters . . . implicate Wanamaker and Subgroup Charlie . . . people in the wrong places could ask the right questions . . ." He stared into the Attorney General's blank eyes and realized he hadn't heard a word. The Admiral released his elbow, backed slowly out of the elevator to join Wanamaker. The two young men in loose-fitting sport jackets backed into the elevator. The doors slid closed.

"Do you want to take care of the matter or should I?" Wanamaker asked his former icon, his ex-father figure.

In a daze the Admiral mumbled, "I'll break the news to Huxstep."

27

The wind, the seas, had calmed down. The Weeder too. He clung to the buoy of hope Snow had thrown him from her world. The cliche—where there's life there's hope—had it backwards. Where there was hope there was life.

As soon as Mildred was able to open her eyes her spirits picked up and she began flirting with Huxstep. "I have an almost uncontrollable weakness for tattoos," she confessed, pushing her breast into his wrist as she rolled back his right sleeve. She ran her fingers over the faded blue pennant tattooed on his biceps, tracing the words GIVE ME LIBERTY OR GIVE ME DEATH. "It must have hurt when they did that," she said with respect.

Huxstep grunted. "Suffering pain is not something I remember." He looked over at the Weeder, sitting on the deck with his right wrist handcuffed to the cement block. "Inflicting pain is another story."

Mildred arched invisible eyebrows. "Let me see what you have on that other arm of yours," she said huskily.

On the shelf above Huxstep's head the radiotelephone

speaker emitted a burst of static. The Admiral's voice, more nasal than usual, could be heard over the static. ". . . you there? For God's sake, answer."

Huxstep flicked a switch onto broadcast and growled into the handphone. "Where else would I be?"

The Weeder, watching from the deck, braced himself for the verdict.

". . . make the nearest landfall and put him ashore."

Huxstep's eyes narrowed imperceptibly in disappointment. He repeated the order to be sure he had gotten it right. "You want for me to make the nearest landfall and put him ashore?"

"Affirmative. I repeat. Affirmative."

Mildred grabbed the phone out of Huxstep's hand. "I want to speak to Mr. Wanamaker," she shouted.

The Admiral's voice crackled over the circuit. "I'm acting for Wanamaker. Today was the Ides of March. The ball game is terminated. In this business there are no extra innings. Put Huxstep back on."

Huxstep took the phone. "I'm here."

The Admiral pleaded, "If you love me, for God's sake turn him loose."

Huxstep winced at the word "love," tried to swallow the emotion that welled up, failed. He muttered "Wilco" into the phone, clicked the toggle switch to Receive. The loudspeaker fell silent.

Mildred, her face contorted, her eyes reduced to slits, produced a minuscule handgun from under her skirt. "If you won't do what has to be done, I will," she whispered.

Huxstep appeared to hesitate. "The Admiral seemed pretty sure of himself."

"The Admiral's not running this show," Mildred argued. "Mr. Wanamaker is. And I'm the one who's Mr. Wanamaker's man Friday, not you. You're the jackass-of-all trades, like you said. For all we know someone may have been holding a gun to the Admiral's head when he talked to you. For all we know it wasn't even him but someone imitating him."

"That's a possibility," Huxstep agreed. He seemed confused. Mildred hammered home her points. "It doesn't make any sense to release him. He knows too much. Even if they've called off Stufftingle he knows it existed. He knows about Mr. Wanamaker and Subgroup Charlie. He knows you tried to kill him in the parking lot. He knows we tried to kill him in the library, in that abandoned building. You're crazy if you think he's going to let bygones be bygones after all this spilled milk."

Huxstep regarded the Weeder and nodded. "You got to be right. The Admiral must have been off his feed this morning." He removed his Smith & Wesson .357 Magnum from a drawer and carefully fitted the silencer onto the barrel.

Mildred's eyes ignited with desire. Her chest heaved as she whispered, "Only wound him, Huxstep. That way we can see his eyes when we throw him overboard."

Huxstep looked at her with new interest. "I don't think I gave you enough credit. You're bursting with ideas."

"I've got others," Mildred noted suggestively.

"I guess you have," Huxstep said.

In his mind's eye the Weeder could hear the beat of the kettledrum quicken. A moment more, he told himself, and it would all be over. He shut his eyes and struggled to keep his limbs from trembling, his heart from sinking under the weight of pure fear. His head began spinning, as if he had reached a height without adequate oxygen. The last thing he heard before he blacked out was the hiss of Huxstep's Magnum spitting out the bullet that punched a hole the size of a fist in anything it hit.

28

The Admiral made no effort to hide his irritation. "You're supposed to put your foot down on the brake, not the gas pedal, when the light turns orange," he said dryly. "Jesus, where did you learn to drive?"

Huxstep took a quick look at his watch and concentrated on the road.

Toothacher wrinkled up his incredibly Roman nose in displeasure. "For a couple of quarters there are places where you can vacuum a car," he remarked. "You wouldn't be out of pocket. You could pass it off as an extra toll and get reimbursed. Wanamaker would never know the difference."

Huxstep turned onto the unmarked road that ran parallel to the airport's perimeter. "Another thing," the Admiral said. "The story you gave Wanamaker about the Weeder bashing Mildred with a wrench seemed pretty farfetched. Couldn't you have thought up something slightly more"—he racked his brain for the right word—"plausible?"

That was too much for Huxstep. "I would like to respectfully point out that the Admiral has been in the car forty-five fucking minutes and he has so far managed to complain about everything under the sun including my driving and my vacuuming and the story I made up to explain to the dumbest fucking agent in the entire United States of America intelligence establishment why one of his lady employees won't be showing the half of her face you could see under that veil at the office no more."

"One thing I've noticed," the Admiral said sweetly, "is that your sentence structure doesn't improve with time."

Huxstep snorted, tucked the stray hairs that appeared back up into his nostrils with delicate clockwise thrusts of his thick pinky.

The Admiral closed his eyes in pain.

Huxstep turned off the road at the gate in the chain link fence guarded by a squad of Marines in full battle dress. An officer checked his laminated pass and saluted. The enlisted men dragged open the gate and waved the car through. The shuttle to Guantánamo stood at the bitter end of a runway, its engines revving. Huxstep pulled up near the portable steps. A seaman deuce wrestled the Admiral's two Vuitton suitcases up the steps and into the plane. Huxstep came around and opened the door for the Admiral.

Stepping out onto the tarmac, Toothacher feigned surprise. "Well, that's a new arrow in your quiver," he yelled over the whine of the jet engines. "I'm not accustomed to you holding open doors."

Huxstep yelled back, "Fuck the Admiral."

"Tch, tch," cooed Toothacher. He caught Huxstep's eye

and batted both of his lids at him in a conspiratorial double wink.

Huxstep melted. "It won't be the same around here without the Admiral," he shouted awkwardly.

"Me too," Toothacher agreed. "The idea of happy hours at Guantánamo without you to run interference doesn't thrill me."

Huxstep angled his head away so the Admiral wouldn't see the mist in his eyes. "You can't say I didn't go and prove it," he yelled.

"Prove what?"

"That I"—Huxstep took a deep breath to work up his nerve and screamed—"love the Admiral more than numbers."

Toothacher nodded emphatically. "You did," he shouted. "You do—I know it."

Huxstep buried the Admiral's hand between both of his and squeezed it, then turned quickly and fled back to the safety of his car. Toothacher organized the various limbs of his lanky body so that they would function more or less harmoniously and ambled up the portable steps toward the stunning-looking petty officer with the handlebar mustache smiling invitingly from the plane's door.

29

Sucking on the wedge of a lemon, Snow rewound the tape on her answering machine and played it back. Fargo's voice, tripping over words as if they were obstacles to conveying information, came across loud and clear. "Snow, it's me, Michael. Your friend Sibley has slipped away from the hospital. It happened two days ago. I only just found out about it. I'm coming up on the next plane." Fargo left a telephone number in Boston for her to call if Sibley showed up before the FBI agents arrived. If she forgot the number she could call the local police and ask them to get in touch with Fargo at the Justice Department's Boston office. "Be careful, Snow," he added. "I don't think he's dangerous but you never know. If you hear from him, humor him. Play along with whatever story he tells you."

Snow smiled to herself. He must take her for a complete idiot. She wasn't going to fall into that trap again. Silas hadn't slipped away from any hospital. The Admiral, to save his own skin, had arranged for him to be set free. She hoped Silas was smart enough to realize she would be watched and stay away from her. She hoped he wouldn't stay away forever.

Snow could tell from the blinking light that there was another message on her tape. It began with the sound of a dental bridge clicking into place in a gum. "Guess who came to dinner?" a musical voice asked.

The words came equipped with the mocking laughter of someone who twitched in her sleep remembering the juicy rabbits she'd chased in her time.

30

Great-Aunt Esther opened the front door and pulled Snow inside and locked and bolted the door behind her. "He's upstairs," she whispered excitedly.

Snow peeled off her mackinaw, stamped her boots to get the snow off and followed Esther into the house. "How is he?" she asked her great-aunt, who was bareheaded and bald and wore an enormous cashmere shawl wound around her frail body.

"He's sleeping like a baby," Esther told her. "He didn't admit it in so many words, but he's had a bad time of it. Whoever he was running from must have caught up with him. It's written on his face. It's written in his eyes."

With Snow limping after her, Esther tiptoed around the hairless dog stretched out on the carpet and went upstairs. She eased open the door to a bedroom at the end of the hallway. The flame from a single candle dispatched flickering shadows across the walls of the room. Fully dressed except for his shoes, with a needlework bedspread thrown over him, Silas was curled up in a fetal position in the middle of a four-poster.

"He wouldn't go to sleep until I lit the candle," Esther whispered. "I think he's afraid of the dark."

Esther drew Snow out of the room. "Let him sleep it off," she whispered.

"He doesn't have a hangover," Snow protested.

"I wasn't suggesting he had," Esther said. "I was suggesting he could use a rest." Esther regarded her grandniece. "You are a little bit jumpy yourself, if you want to hear the truth."

Snow smiled sadly. "It took me a while but I know the truth."

Esther snapped a bridge into place. "That's more than most can say."

Snow sank into a rocking chair next to the four-poster, pulled a blanket up under her armpits and mounted guard over the figure sleeping on the bed. When the candle burned down she lit a new one from the sputtering flame of the old one and embedded it in the holder. She dozed off toward midnight but came awake when Silas started moaning. A moment more, he seemed to mutter under his breath, and it will all be over. He shifted position on the bed, arching his spine as if something was jabbing into it, then settled back onto the mattress. The sight of him curled up on the bed aroused emotions in Snow she had considered dead. She had been ambushed by grief. Then, like a hostage who becomes emotionally involved with her captor, she had become attached to her grief; it had been her habit. Now she was being ambushed once more—this time by love.

She must have dozed again around first light but woke

with a start to find Silas sitting on the edge of the bed staring at her. "Did I say anything in my sleep?" he wanted to know.

Esther had been right about his face, his eyes, Snow realized. "You were asking for a moment more. You were saying it would all be over."

The Weeder stood up and Snow came off the rocking chair into his arms. They clung to each other. After a while Snow took his hand and examined it. The scab had fallen off. His life line was visible again. The sight of it seemed to reassure her. She returned to her chair and began rocking back and forth on it. The Weeder settled onto the floor at her feet. "Tell me what happened," she urged him.

Hesitantly at first, gathering momentum as he went along, the Weeder described his ordeal: how he had been anesthetized by the men who picked him off the Boston street; how he had come to on a boat, manacled to a piece of metal jutting from a bulkhead; how the Admiral had promised he would be shot before being thrown overboard; how, thanks to Snow, Toothacher had phoned up and instructed Huxstep to release him; how Mildred and Huxstep had argued after the Admiral's phone call—

Snow kept the chair rocking in the same rhythm. "All this happened—when?"

"The Admiral phoned Huxstep a few hours after you phoned me. It was the Ides of March. Huxstep put me ashore late that night."

"Was Huxstep with you on the boat the day before the Ides of March?"

The Weeder nodded. "He was there the whole time I was there."

Snow said, "Huxstep's the one who does tricks with numbers."

"That's right."

"Go on with the story," Snow ordered. She smiled encouragingly.

The Weeder described Mildred pulling out a minuscule pistol. She had been ready to shoot him herself if Huxstep wouldn't do it. Huxstep had looked as if she had convinced him. He had fitted a silencer to his gun. It had been a terrible moment—the Weeder had been certain Huxstep was going to shoot him. His head had started spinning, his heart had started sinking under the weight of pure fear. He remembered hearing the beat of a kettledrum, the hiss of a gun going off as he fainted. When he had regained consciousness the boat had been heading toward Nantucket, the lights of which were visible on the horizon.

"What happened to Mildred?" Snow asked.

The Weeder shrugged. "She was gone. So was the block of cement. So were the handcuffs."

Snow rocked forward and cradled his head against her thighs. "You put your life on the line to stop an atrocity," she said. "You're every inch the patriot Nate was."

"You really think that?" the Weeder asked.

"Anyone who knew the nightmare you'd been through would think that," she assured him.

The Weeder's head burrowed into her lap. When he spoke again his words were muffled. "Knowing you believe in me changes the way I look at the world," he said.

31

It was Great-Aunt Esther who talked them into going to the concert at a neighborhood hall. Because of her hair, more exactly because of the lack of it, she preferred not to let herself be seen in public any longer. But there was no reason for them to hang around the house like two caged birds. Spread your wings, she urged with the leer of someone who longed to follow her own advice. Go for test flights.

The auditorium, usually used for town meetings and slide lectures, was on the small side. The members of the orchestra were tuning up as Snow and the Weeder found their places in the middle of the fourth row and read the mimeographed program notes. A group of Harvard music students was going to play Haydn's Symphony no. 45 in F-sharp Minor, known as the *Farewell* Symphony, as it had been performed, with Haydn himself conducting, before Count Esterházy in 1772. A lighted candle was set into a holder attached to each music stand. The houselights dimmed. The stage flickered with candlelight. The conductor appeared from the wings. The audience applauded.

Great-Aunt Esther had been right about a concert being just what the doctor ordered. Snow had her arm linked through the Weeder's and could feel the tension slipping from his body as soon as the orchestra started playing. At one point he whispered, "To think my man Nate was at Yale when this was first performed." A few minutes later he grinned sheepishly at her and it was almost possible for her to believe that the world was right side up.

It wasn't, of course. Not that Silas had lied to her; the reality was more subtle. He had invented a truth—his truth, the truth he badly needed. He had concocted the story about Huxstep being on the boat; the night before the Ides of March Huxstep had been sitting next to her in the bar in Washington. If Silas had imagined Huxstep on the boat, it meant he had imagined the boat too. Fitting in bits and pieces of reality, he had imagined everything—his eavesdropping operation, the scheme to explode an atomic bomb in Tehran, the love letters he had sent to Wanamaker to head off the plot. He had invented the story about the old Admiral being summoned from retirement to trace the leak. He had imagined the attempts on his life in New Haven. Even Nathan's story had been a figment of Silas's imagination. He had invented Nate's life and superimposed it over his own life, as if the whole thing were a double exposure. Great-Aunt Esther had given Snow a look at the "diary" she had shown to Silas. It was an old penny notebook filled with recipes and herb remedies that Molly Davis had collected over the years. There was no mention in it of Nate or a British plan to trap

Washington on Manhattan or the Revolution; no suggestion that Nate was the father of Molly's child. Nate may have "Liv'd, desir'd and died lament'd," but not by Molly.

Haydn had scored his symphony so that the various instruments finished playing at different times. As each musician's role came to an end he blew out his candle and left the stage. When the Weeder realized what was happening the tension flowed back into his limbs. There were still four candles burning on the stage. A cellist blew out his and left. The music became thinner as the auditorium grew darker. An oboe player extinguished his candle. The Weeder shivered. The violinist, playing alone now, reached the end of the score. The conductor summoned the last note out of the instrument with his fingertips and let it trail off. Then he and the violinist blew out the two remaining candles and quit the stage.

The auditorium was as dark and as still as a pit. The Weeder, trembling, buried his face in Snow's shoulder. He asked very quietly, "Can you get someone to light a candle?"

The house lights slowly came up. The Weeder kept his head on Snow's old cardigan, which Esther had found for her in an attic trunk. It still smelled from camphor balls. The Weeder noticed the odor for the first time. It tripped a memory. He felt the pull of history and slipped over the line into an incarnation. "Molly smelled of camphor the night I met her," he told Snow.

On either side of them people were filing up the aisles. This time Snow didn't hesitate; desperate not to lose him, she plunged after the Weeder into his incarnation. "I propose we marry ourselves," she said urgently. She knew time was running out; another ambush lurked ahead for both of them.

The Weeder smiled Nate's smile. "Are such things done?"

Snow looked over her shoulder, spotted Fargo and two men waiting at the auditorium doors. So the police had relayed her message after all. "You need to understand," she told the Weeder. She was reciting lines but her voice had a real sob buried in it. "Before I was ambushed by grief I grew accustomed to living the life of a married woman."

She faltered. The Weeder cued her. "Contrary to what is generally supposed—"

"Yes," Snow said. "That's it." She was in Molly's role now and playing it with all her heart. "Contrary to what is generally supposed, women have appetites too."

The Weeder grasped her hand in his. "What vows would you have us say to each other?" he demanded. He peered into her eyes, aching for an answer.

The auditorium was almost empty now. Snow could see Fargo and the others starting down the aisles toward them. She threw her arms around the Weeder and hugged him to her. Tears spilled from her eyes, her voice choked up. "I would have us pledge unconditional trust in each other," she said softly. "This is the only thing that counts between two people."

The Weeder whispered, "I pledge it with all my heart."

"I too pledge it," said Snow.

32

Wanamaker lurked in the shadow of the balcony, watching with a smug smile as the two young men in loose-fitting sport jackets put a hammerlock on the Weeder and steered him up the aisle. Huxstep, peering from a wing of the stage, formed his left forefinger and thumb into a pistol and sighted over it at the Weeder's back. The Attorney General, standing next to Wanamaker, noticed Huxstep mouthing the words, "Bang, bang! You're dead!" "What you do with him," he mumbled, angling the flame of his lighter into the bowl of his pipe, sucking the tobacco into life, "is clearly not something I need to know."

Wanamaker started to giggle at what he thought was a joke; Huxstep's gesture had left little room for doubt about the fate that awaited the Weeder.

Wanamaker's attitude irritated the Attorney General. He released a cloud of vile-smelling smoke into his face. "I don't see what there is to laugh about," he snapped. "You plugged the leak, but not before the Russians found out what you were up to."

"It could take a while," Wanamaker ventured, batting feebly at the smoke screen, "but we can get Stufftingle back on track."

The Attorney General appeared interested. "What do you have in mind?"

"With any luck," Wanamaker said, "we ought to be able to find out where the Iranians have set up their germ warfare shop. We ought to be able to smuggle in enough contaminated microbes in a year, a year and a half on the outside, to set off an uncontrolled biological reaction, otherwise known as a plague."

"Frame a proposal," the Attorney General suggested, "but be careful not to leave a paper trail." He caught sight of Fargo escorting Snow toward the emergency exit. "What about the girl?" he asked.

"She's no threat to us," Wanamaker replied. "She's convinced the asshole is a raving lunatic—she's convinced he invented us."

The idea that he might be a figment of someone's imagination seemed to amuse the Attorney General. "Wouldn't it be funny if she were right?" he said, and reaching into his pocket, he began to turn down the hearing aid.

Continue reading for a sample of

THE DEFECTION OF A.J. LEWINTER

1

There was a curtain of silence between the end of the play and the first ripple of applause. Distracted by the silence, Chapin let his attention drift from the balding American in the aisle seat.

It was his first lapse of the day.

Chapin was a fat man and he envied grace and poise the way a cripple admires athletic agility. He sat on the hard wooden chair breathing heavily, a massive form in the midst of the diminutive Japanese, and watched with almost sensual pleasure as the masked actors of the Kanze Noh Company glided soundlessly across the *hashigakari* bridge to the wings. Without understanding all its subtleties, Chapin was drawn to the Noh drama. He had never admitted that to anyone, for he recognized it as a strange obsession—especially for someone in his line of work. He wondered vaguely what had brought the American to the theater.

The American!

When Chapin glanced back at the aisle seat it was empty and his man was sprinting up the carpet toward the exit. Still caught up in the mood of the Noh, Chapin was reluctant to break the cobweb threads of imagination that bound him to the stage. Wearily, he pulled his bulky body over the legs of four Japanese and headed up the now jammed aisle toward the lobby. For a man of his size and age, he moved rapidly. But by the time he reached the front steps of the theater, the American had disappeared into the river of people flowing through the streets of downtown Tokyo.

Chapin stood on the steps and threaded his fingers through his thinning hair. It was his first "fadeout" in years and his professional pride was bruised. Control would be furious. As he turned to search for a telephone, something caught his eye: the familiar profile of a man, framed in a window of a taxi pulling away from the curb.

Chapin squeezed into another taxi and told the driver: "*Ano kuruma o otékure.*" In Japanese, Chapin thought, the phrase didn't sound quite as ridiculous as it did in English.

The two taxis, 100 yards apart, swung past Toronomon and the black wrought-iron gates of the American Embassy and struggled up a steep hill, caught in a jagged mob of cars and buses and trucks noisily converging on Roppongi. The early evening breeze blew through the open window against Chapin's face, and with it came the reddish dust from a torn-up stretch of road where a new subway line was being built. Chapin saw that his driver was enjoying the chase; with his forehead almost touching the steering wheel, he cut in front of a dump truck and put the car onto the rough bedding of the trolley tracks near the crest of the hill. Using only his left, white-gloved hand, he spun the wheel full left and broke into the small intersection of Roppongi Crossing. By now he was directly behind the other taxi. Chapin leaned forward and tapped the driver on the shoulder. "*Kimi Wa, beteran no untenshu da né*—That's nice driving."

At the far end of the crossing workmen wearing thick ocher-colored waistbands and bandannas on their foreheads strained against a stalled dump truck. Drivers leaned on their horns as the traffic piled up. In the taxi ahead of Chapin, the impatient passenger stepped out, paid the driver, and edged between the two cabs toward the curb. As his face came into full view, Chapin realized that he had been following an American—but the wrong one.

Chapin paid his driver and hurried to the telephone booth in front of the Kinokuniya Supermarket. Before dialing, he unwrapped a piece of dietary chewing gum, popped it into his mouth, and rolled the tin foil into a ball, which he toyed with throughout the conversation.

The number rang twice. A man's voice said in Japanese: "Four-nine-nine-six-five-two-nine."

Chapin read off his own number in English and hung up. Fifteen seconds later the phone rang.

"Hey, George, this is me," Chapin said, wheezing nervously.

"Where the hell've you and Honeybucket been?" George said.

"In Marunouchi," Chapin answered. He tried to make the rest sound like an afterthought. "Everything's fine. Our friend just treated me to five and a half hours of Noh. Now we're in Roppongi. Honeybucket's across the street in an antique shop. I'll stick with him through dinner and tuck him in at the hotel."

2

Lewinter had lived through the moment a hundred times in his imagination, but it had never occurred to him that the guard wouldn't speak English. He looked across the glass-topped table at the obstinate, Slavic face and had to fight back the frustration and fear welling up inside him.

"Listen," Lewinter said again, this time more patiently, more respectfully, "I've got to speak to the *ambassador*." And he repeated the word three times, as if the mere repetition would make the guard understand. "I'm an American-ski," he added.

The two Japanese cleaning ladies scrubbing the marble floor of the embassy lobby looked up, curious. The guard, new to his job and still unsure of himself, hesitated. Finally, with a shrug, he picked up the telephone and summoned the duty officer.

Watching him dial, Lewinter felt some of the tension drain away. At last he was getting somewhere. For the first time, he took in the surroundings: the Japanese women, by now hard at work; the uniformed guard concentrating on a Russian newspaper; the small portrait of Lenin in a too elaborate gilt frame; the cracks in the marble floor; the chandelier with its dusty black electric wire coiling up to the flaking ceiling. It was not what he had expected. Not at all.

Tiptoeing over the still-wet marble, the duty officer, a small, brooding Armenian with thick eyebrows, came over and planted himself directly in front of Lewinter.

"Yes," the Armenian said, smiling and pointing at his watch, "since fifteen minutes, we are completed for the day."

"I must speak to your ambassador," Lewinter said, wondering how much English the Armenian understood. "I want to go to the Soviet Union."

"It is misfortunate," the Armenian said, "but the visa department completes at five. Retry tomorrow after nine."

"You don't understand me," Lewinter said. "I'm an American. I want to go to the Soviet Union permanently—to live there."

"Permanently?" the Armenian repeated, and searched for the meaning of the word. He found it, and understood it. He thought of a friend of his who once passed up an opportunity to buy some documents in Istanbul—and wound up franking stamps in Tbilisi. With a jerk of his head, the Armenian motioned to the American to follow him down the hall.

Left alone in a large, mildewy room jammed with overstuffed furniture, Lewinter settled into an easy chair with a broken spring and waited. In the last half-hour he had taken the most crucial step of his life, and yet the whole thing seemed ludicrous. He had planned the defection for months with his usual relish for detail—the trip to Japan, the pills, the shampoo, the X-rays, the last-minute postcard to Maureen, even the book to read on the plane to Moscow. But somehow he had ended up on the set of a Hitchcock film—in a shabby embassy, in an antique room, in the midst of people who did not speak his language. He could almost see himself sitting there looking faintly uncomfortable, faintly ridiculous, staring at the high ceiling, crossing and uncrossing his legs, and wondering if he was being watched by someone other than himself.

Lewinter emerged from his thoughts and realized that he had been listening to the sound of men's voices. The door opened. The man who entered looked as if he had strolled off an American college campus. He had everything except the pipe between his teeth; thin and stoop-shouldered, he wore a bow tie, a beige button-down shirt, an open Harris tweed sports jacket with suede elbow patches, rumpled slacks, and a pair of loafers. His kinky hair was long and bunched at the sides and back; that and his high forehead made him look like an intellectual. His eyes were khaki-colored and there was something about them that projected the man's ironic cast of mind.

He smiled warmly and pulled up a chair next to Lewinter. "What high school did you go to?" he said in perfect English.

"What do you mean what high school did I go to?" Lewinter said, edging back his chair. He had a reflex suspicion of people who tried to strike up instant friendships. "First you keep me waiting half an hour, then you walk in with a question like that. Do you have the vaguest idea why I'm here?"

"Look, calm down," the Russian said. "It's only been twenty minutes. They had to get me back to the embassy. Anyhow, my question about the high school has a point. You can tell a lot about an American from the high school he went to. Take me, for instance. I went to Horace Mann. All the guys there were upper middle-class bourgeoisie—not exactly the kind of person you expect to see in a Soviet embassy after closing hours asking for political asylum. You see," he said, tapping his forehead and laughing, "I *do* know why you're here—and I'm always thinking. Watch out!"

Lewinter couldn't help but warm to the Russian. "What were you doing at Horace Mann?" he asked.

"My father, good Communist that he was, worked his way up the Soviet Foreign Service to Riverdale," he said. "He was attached to the UN Secretariat for six years. What high school *did* you go to?"

"Bronx High School of Science," Lewinter said, surprised to find that he wanted to answer the question.

"Aha!" the Russian said, slapping Lewinter's knee. He pointed a finger at him in mock accusation. "Petit bourgeois, intellectual, I.Q. of at least one thirty-five, not very good at sports, didn't have sexual intercourse until you were in college—if then. I'd say you were Jewish, except you don't look Jewish. How did I do?"

"Fine except for the sexual intercourse part," Lewinter lied. He turned serious: "We could argue the merits of Bronx Science over Horace Mann all night—*but I haven't got all night.* I've figured out my chances very carefully. Either I get out of

Japan on your eight o'clock plane or I'm probably not going to get out at all." He pulled out his pocket watch and clicked it open. "I've got two and a quarter hours left. I've got to speak to your ambassador."

"I suspect that my ambassador is the last person you want to see," the Russian said. A smile spread across his face. "He's great at cutting ribbons, but he passes on his serious problems to me. If you're a serious problem"—and here he put the palms of his hands flat against his chest—"I'm your man."

Lewinter believed him.

The Russian took a small green notebook from his breast pocket and uncapped a felt-tipped pen. "Now that I've broken down your defenses with my spontaneous charm, it's time, for the real Yefgeny Mikhailovich Pogodin—that's my name—it's time for me to reveal myself. Sitting before you is a man who is one-quarter Marxist, one-quarter humanist, and one-half bureaucrat." His pen hovered over the notebook. "Your name?"

Lewinter felt as if he was in the hands of a painless dentist. "A. J. Lewinter. Initial *A*, initial *J*, capital *L*, small *W*."

"What does the *A* stand for?" Pogodin asked.

"Augustus. The *J*'s for Jerome. But I only use the initials."

"Well, Mr. initial A initial J Lewinter, age?"

"Thirty-nine."

"Address?"

"Cambridge, Massachusetts."

Pogodin looked up. "What do you do in Cambridge?"

"I'm an associate professor at MIT and a specialist in

ceramic engineering. For the last four years I've been working on ceramic nose cones for the MIRV Program."

The Russian jotted down Lewinter's answer in his notebook, then lingered over the page, rereading what he had written. Without looking up he asked: "What brought you to Japan, Mr. Lewinter?"

"The ecological symposium at Waseda University. I delivered a paper there yesterday. When I'm not working on nose cones, I'm a bug on ecology. A couple of years ago I developed a scheme for a national solid-waste-disposal system. Its potentials are fantastic. It involves collecting solid waste in regional centers for processing and recycling. Would you believe, with our problems in America, I couldn't get a rise out of Washington—even though I proved on paper that the entire system would amortize itself in thirty-five years." Lewinter paused. "Am I going too fast for you?"

But Pogodin had stopped writing.

"Why do you want to go to the Soviet Union?"

"How can I even begin to answer that question?" Lewinter said. "I could tell you about the deterioration of the American dream—the pollution, the crime, the political corruption, the isolation of intellectuals, the drugs, the repression of dissent. But there's another reason. I'm part of that famous military-industrial complex. I've lived inside it. I know what I'm talking about. My country is in the process of constructing a first-strike nuclear arsenal. And as sure as we're sitting here some general in Washington is going to suggest we use it. I want to give you parity so that they won't be tempted. I want to give you MIRV."

It suddenly occurred to Pogodin that he was dealing with an insane man. In Pogodin's world, intelligence operations were long, tedious affairs in which hundreds of people labored over scraps of information, constructing a single piece of a jigsaw puzzle that might—perhaps—fit into some larger picture. Strangers didn't walk in off the street and offer you the pot of gold at the end of the rainbow. And yet. . .

"Let me tell you what's going through my mind," Pogodin said. Having interrogated hundreds of people, he had long ago discovered that candor was a powerful weapon—more so because it was the last thing in the world people in Lewinter's position expected. "If you have what you say you have, it would be an important break for us. And you would naturally find us very grateful. But people don't walk in off the street with this grade of information. So I am obliged to consider the other possibilities. You may honestly believe that you have this information; but you may believe it because other people want you to believe it. Knowingly or unknowingly, you could be a plant, someone sent to make us swallow false information. Or you could be a class-A nut. There are other permutations, but they're too complex to go into. So I put it to you: If you were in my shoes, what would you do?"

"If I were in your shoes," Lewinter said, playing the game, "I wouldn't pass up the possibility that I'm at least as important as I say I am—and maybe more so."

"Yes, you could," Pogodin said. "You don't know the rules of this game."

"What are they?"

"At this point in our relationship, you have to provide us with a token of your sincerity," Pogodin said. "Defection"—the Russian stressed the word—"is a delicate matter. You have to give us something to chew on."

The invitation dangled before Lewinter. He considered his laminated ID card, his MIT. faculty card, his passport. But he knew that none of these would get him on the eight o'clock plane to Moscow.

"Look," he said, "I could give you the formula for the trajectory of one of the decoys in a MIRV. You can cable it to Moscow. Surely there must be someone there who can vouch for its value."

Without a flicker of expression, Pogodin offered the green notebook to Lewinter.

"Do you need a pen?" he asked politely.

"No, thank you, I have my own," Lewinter said, and he began to write in a precise hand.